I'll Always Be with You

I'll Always Be with You

✑ Violetta Armour

iUniverse®

I'LL ALWAYS BE WITH YOU

iUniverse books may be ordered through booksellers or by contacting:

iUniverse
1663 Liberty Drive
Bloomington, IN 47403
www.iuniverse.com
1-800-Authors (1-800-288-4677)

Because of the dynamic nature of the Internet, any web addresses or links contained in this book may have changed since publication and may no longer be valid. The views expressed in this work are solely those of the author and do not necessarily reflect the views of the publisher, and the publisher hereby disclaims any responsibility for them.

Any people depicted in stock imagery provided by Thinkstock are models, and such images are being used for illustrative purposes only. Certain stock imagery © Thinkstock.

ISBN: 978-1-4917-6830-3 (sc)
ISBN: 978-1-4917-6832-7 (hc)
ISBN: 978-1-4917-6831-0 (e)

Library of Congress Control Number: 2015909426

Print information available on the last page.

iUniverse rev. date: 10/2/2015

༄༅ ༄༅

"If ever there is a tomorrow when we're not together, there is something you must always remember. You are braver than you believe, stronger than you seem and smarter than you think. But the most important thing is, even if we are apart, I'll always be with you."

*—Christopher Robin to Winnie the
Pooh in Pooh's Grand Adventure:
The Search for Christopher Robin*

༄༅ ༄༅

＊＊＊

"There is no pain so great as the memory of joy in present grief."

—*Aeschylus*

＊＊＊

To the memory of my brother Vladimir,
whose stories kept me spellbound at an early age.

Part One

Teddy

Arizona
May
1999

I never meant to kill my dad.

Everyone tries to console me. They say things like: "Not your fault, Teddy." "Damn drunk driver, that's who killed your dad, not you." "You're not to blame."

But how do I stop blaming myself? *I* was the one driving. *I* walk away without a scratch on the outside, but inside the cut is deep. A gaping hole. Don't know how to close it.

You might say it was a driving lesson gone bad. My grief counselor says sarcasm is my defense mechanism. Whatever. Seems a little late for defense now.

Mary

I had the dream again last night.

I'm standing at the kitchen island, chopping tomatoes when Teddy and Stan leave to pick up the pizza. As they go out the door, I hear Teddy say, "Can I drive, Dad?" Teddy, so eager to drive anywhere with the ink barely dry on his permit.

The doorbell rings. A pizza delivery boy stands there smiling, holding the black square pack that keeps the pizza piping hot. "Mrs. Kostoff?"

"Oh dear," I say. "Must be a mistake. We said 'pick up,' not 'delivery.'"

"I'm delivering because no one picked it up. Sorry I'm late, but there's a terrible accident down the street. Once the pizza is ordered, we have to collect payment. You will pay for this pizza, won't you, Mrs. Kostoff?"

At that point I startle awake. My nightgown is soaked with perspiration, my pillow is soaked with tears, and I am reminded again of how dearly I am paying for that pizza.

In real life, the doorbell did ring while I was chopping tomatoes, but instead of a pizza guy, it was a police officer standing there.

The words he delivered cut deeper than the serrated tomato knife I was still holding in my hand.

Teddy

My final assignment in Sophomore Honors English is: Write an essay describing who you *really* are. Be creative. For example, if you were a part of speech, what would you be and why.

Three weeks ago I could have told you who I was. Now? I don't have a clue.

It's like my life has two phases: B.C. and A.D. Not in the religious sense 'cuz I know now there is no God. More like *Before Crash* and *After Dad*. Or *After Death*. All the same.

B.C. Teddy was a normal teen, maybe tall for my age, six feet two inches, kinda clumsy. Best thing was making the varsity basketball team. Not bragging, but Coach said not many sophomores make a 5-A varsity team.

Used to be the class clown. Made my best friend Wally and the guys laugh. Now? Nothing funny.

Had my first kiss with Liz. Might have gotten a second one if her mom hadn't turned on the porch light. Startled me so much I almost fell backwards off the top step. Nothing scares me anymore. What could be scarier than what's already happened?

In my sleep I hear the crash, over and over. The screeching of tires, the crunching of steel. Then the dreaded silence. The crash sounds never wake me, but the silence does.

When I'm with friends who are talking and laughing their voices echo through a tunnel. It's like I'm hovering above them in an out-of-body experience.

Oh yeah, there's the other thing. I think in headlines now. My grief counselor says the headline in our paper traumatized me. DAD IS KILLED IN SON'S DRIVING LESSON. Mom tried to hide it but I saw it anyway.

And the least little thing makes me cry, which I don't want Mom to see. Isn't she hurting enough already? So I wear sunglasses all the time. Even in the house. Mom never mentions them. Like it's perfectly normal. Phoenix is a sunny place, but come on —shades at breakfast?

How strange to wear sunglasses *now*, after the accident. I should have been wearing them that day. The setting sun was blinding. I never saw the other car until it was too late. I wish I'd never seen it. I wouldn't have swerved at the last minute. It wouldn't have hit on the passenger side where Dad was. It would have hit us head-on and then I'd be dead too. It might have hurt for a minute but now the pain is endless.

The first time I wore the sunglasses in the house, my seven-year-old sister, Ruby, said, "Teddy, do you want to look like a famous movie star?"

"Yeah, do you want my autograph?"

She gave me a toothless grin. "Yes!" Then she scrunched up her nose. "What's an autograph?" Her giggle gave me a sliver of hope that someday I'll feel good about myself again. If I can make Ruby laugh, maybe I'm not a totally bad person.

My other little sister Cathy, only four, has no clue what I did. When she hugs me it's not out of sympathy. She loves me for who I am. Or who I was. B.C. Teddy.

So I stare at the blank computer screen trying to write my essay. I'm the A.D. Teddy going through the motions of my B.C. life. Part of speech? I used to be an active verb: running, laughing, shooting a three-pointer.

Today? I'm an adjective. Sad.

Mary

I never knew kindness could hurt so much. Delicious casseroles left on our doorstep, neighbors fixing our sprinkler system, offers to babysit the girls. All meant to comfort but instead are sad and constant reminders of our loss.

I'm grateful. Really. But just once I'd like to squeeze a cantaloupe in the produce aisle without a voice over my shoulder, "Mary, how is Teddy doing? How are *you* doing?" I know they mean well, but how do they *think* we're doing?

One good look at me would give them their answer. Although I rarely wear make-up besides mascara, I could really use some now to conceal the dark circles under my eyes. The size eight shorts I wore last summer look like hand-me-downs that I haven't grown into yet. I feel shrunken and diminished, especially next to Teddy who has taken another growth spurt. Some days a shower is too much effort. For what? For who? My blonde hair that shines when clean now looks like the before picture in a shampoo commercial. Of course, that's the day I run into someone I know. Doesn't matter, as I answer them.

"It's hard, but we'll get through this." What I want to say is, it sucks. It sucks. You know it sucks. Why are you asking? Why don't you say something that would let me sympathize with you? Like you just gained five pounds or you locked your keys in the car or the relatives from Hell are coming and never leaving.

Then my self-pity turns to guilt when I think of the Columbine parents. The whole country is still reeling from the shootings last month. Somehow their loss seems greater than mine. I haven't lost a child through a senseless act of violence. Not that a car accident makes any sense.

The last time two people stopped me in one shopping trip, I left the entire cart of groceries in the baking aisle, hoisting Cathy out of the cart so quickly her shoe came off.

"But Mommy, we didn't pay for our groceries," Ruby squealed with a seven-year old's conscience, tugging at my shorts. "That's stealing isn't it?"

"No honey, we're not taking the groceries. I just remembered I left something in the oven." *My heart. Burned to a crisp.*

Back home my escape felt childish. The thought of those abandoned groceries and frozen foods thawing made me sad. I called the store, told customer service I had an emergency and left a cart in the bakery aisle. I went back to the store alone for groceries. The kids still had to eat. And just the day before, I thought I was getting a grip on the roller coaster of emotions. Up. Down. Good day. Bad day.

Someone asked me why I don't hate the drunk driver more than I do. I think of what the grief counselor said, "Resentment is like drinking poison and hoping the other person will die."

It's futile. I need all my energy for Teddy and the girls now.

Rosetta

Indiana
May
1999

I awake to the smell of maple bacon frying and I hear James stirring in the kitchen. After working double shifts I bask for a moment in the realization that it's a lazy Sunday morning. I don't have to jump into scrubs the minute my feet hit the ground running. Instead, I reach for my soft pink robe, faded and worn, but too comfy to discard.

In the kitchen I sneak up behind James who is cracking eggs into a bowl and wrap my arms around his hefty waist.

"Hey, good morning, Sunshine," he says as drops the egg shell in the disposal and turns to wrap his big arms around me.

"Hey, yourself. Smells wonderful. Do I have time for a cup of coffee on the patio?"

"No timetables this morning."

I take a cup of hot coffee with my guilty pleasure of two scoops of hazelnut creamer to the east patio and the morning sun. Our deep purple lilac bushes are blooming and their fragrance in the slight morning breeze offers a promise of new beginnings.

I leaf through the Sunday paper James has left helter-skelter on the patio table and browse leisurely through sections I rarely have time for during the week. When I see Stan's name in the obituary column I catch my breath. *No, it can't be. Stan is too young. My age. What happened?*

I scan the notice quickly and then again slowly. *Stanley Kostoff, age 48, a 1969 graduate of Middleburg High School, died May 3, as a result of an auto accident. The accident occurred in Phoenix, Arizona, where he resided for the past 24 years. His wife, Mary, and their three children, Theodore, Ruby, and Catherine, survive him. His mother, Dora Kostoff, resides in Middleburg, as does his brother Daniel Kostoff, (Joyce) and two nieces. Funeral arrangements are pending.*

I fold the paper carefully, so as not to crease the article, and set it on the patio table. I take a sip of coffee, which now tastes bitter. The day, so full of promise a few minutes ago, has become a melancholy morning with a sadness long forgotten.

I know from nurse's training why scents instantly trigger vivid memories — the olfactory nerve so near the hippocampus where memories are stored. My head knows *why* it happens. My heart *feels* it happening.

So it's no wonder, as the morning breeze wafts the scent of lilacs past me, I am immediately transported to another May, 30 years ago. A deserted country lane near the lake, a full moon, a white graduation dress, the balmy evening air filled with a scent as sweet as the kisses a white boy and black girl shared.

Mary

⦿

June

As soon as we leave the grief counselor's office from our weekly session, Teddy puts his sunglasses back on. Frankly, I'm relieved not to see his doleful eyes. Then I notice how much sadness a mouth can convey. Or a posture. Like he's carrying a sack of bricks — enough for a New York high rise — on his slumped over shoulders.

"Do you think these sessions are helping?" I ask as we drive home.

"How do I know? I'm sad when we walk in and sad when I walk out." Teddy stares straight ahead out the windshield.

"It does give me a chance to tell you again that I don't blame you, Teddy. Not in any way. If Dad had been driving the same thing could have happened."

"Great, Mom. You don't blame me but how do I stop blaming myself?"

My turn to stare ahead. I don't have an answer for that.

I try once again to squeeze more mileage out of the session. Today we talked about stage three of grief, bargaining. The *what if* stage.

I say, "I guess we're normal when we keep asking, 'what if?' That everyone who has a loss asks the question. *What if* we had dinner at home instead of take-out pizza? *What if* we had the pizza delivered?"

"*What if* we just stop talking about it now, Mom? It's bad enough in there. We don't have to drag it out."

I suspect he'll soon wear earplugs as well as sunglasses.

Teddy

Who watches daytime TV reruns? People like us who have no life.

The summer sun in Phoenix is blinding, yet our days are dark. We close the wood shutters on the windows to cool the house and in these dark rooms we sit transfixed like zombies, staring at the flickering images on the screen, which provides the only light in the room. I guess that shows how desperate we are.

Mom takes Ruby to a day camp so she has a reason to get dressed and out the door. I stay with Cathy and am now an authority on *Sesame Street*. I know my brain cells are dying because I actually like hanging out with Big Bird and Miss Piggy. And with Cathy as she gets caught up in their adventures. She excitedly repeats a lot of what they say to me as if I'm not watching. If she's still sleepy she sits on my lap, twirls my wavy hair around her finger and sucks the thumb on her other hand. I like to hold her close and smell the apple shampoo in her blonde curls.

Mom watches the *Golden Girls* reruns, and one day her laugh surprises me. It has been so long since I heard it. When *I Love Lucy* runs the candy assembly line episode and Lucy and Ethel were gobbling chocolates as fast as they could, Mom and I both laugh out loud. Then we give each other a quick guilty glance like we shouldn't be having any fun without Dad.

I watch *Star Trek* reruns. I imagine I'm free floating in space landing on a planet where people wear protective suits that prevent any pain from touching them — inside or out. For now my best protection is my sunglasses. Behind them I practice a technique that helps when the tears start — blink, blink, squint.

When Ruby gets home she wants me to play make believe. Her favorite is dollhouse. "Teddy, you be the daddy." What can I say? It's the least I can do since it's my fault her real daddy will never show up.

Mom keeps encouraging me to get out with my friends. But they act kinda weird around me, like they don't know what to say or do. I used to be the funny one. I know they don't expect me to be the jokester now, but I haven't figured out how I fit in anymore.

I feel most safe with Mom. No need to talk. We can sit around being sad with no explanation or pressure to make other people comfortable. I got an extra big dose of sadness the other night. I woke up in the middle of the night and went downstairs for junk food. It puts me in a food coma and sleep comes for a few hours. As I'm reaching for some Twinkies, I hear Dad's voice and the hairs on my arms rise. I'm afraid to look, but like a magnet, his voice lures me to the dark room lit only by the TV screen. It was probably the last home movie we made in the backyard.

Ruby has a big bubble wand and is running in circles with a long bubble trailing her. Cathy is chasing her, hands outstretched, shrieking, "Me! Me!" Mom turns the camera on Dad, who's grilling burgers and he makes a goofy face. She zooms in closer, closer. The closer she gets the wider his silly grim and then he crosses his eyes. They look more green than brown. Mom calls them hazel. She says she can tell his mood by what shade they were.

In the movie, Mom starts laughing and the camera slips a little. We see the rock garden and Dad's knees. Then I grab the camera and raise it just in time to capture the kiss. Not that Mom and Dad never argued, but I think they also kissed a lot for old married people. "Hey," my voice says on camera. "Cut the mush you two. This is a G-rated movie. And the burgers are burning."

They both start laughing and Dad says to Mom, "Is that *your* smart-mouth kid talking to us?"

Mom's face fakes surprise. "I never saw him before. Must be the paparazzi. 'Cause you're soooo famous. Cameras follow you every-where." We all laugh. Then Cathy falls down and cries, "Boo-boo." I point the camera at her scraped knee.

Mom stops the VCR. Even in the dim light I can see her cheeks glistening with tears. Now our boo-boo is so big a bandage can't cover it.

Teddy

July

Grief catches you off-guard when least expect it. Like a punch in the gut from a stranger casually passing you on the street.

Mom and I take the girls to the Fourth of July parade, a family tradition. When the color guard marches by with the American flag, I take off my cap and put it on my heart like I watched Dad do since I was a toddler.

Dad. So patriotic. So proud to be a first-generation American.

My sunglasses hide the hot tears that spill out. The grief counselor told us the first holidays would be the hardest without Dad.

I was thinking Christmas. Didn't think Fourth of July would throw me under the bus.

Mary

It's July but the big wall calendar in our kitchen where we record all the family activities is still on May. Like our lives stopped that day. I peel off the May and June pages. The only thing written on July is the week we have blocked off for our annual beach trip to California. It's in two weeks and I totally forgot about it. Probably too late to get our deposit back although we've gone to the same beach house for years. Surely, they would understand.

Then I think, why not go? Heaven knows we could use a change of scenery. Get out of this dark house, out of these scorching tempera-tures. But to go without Stan? It doesn't seem right. It won't be right. But then again, nothing will ever be right again ... home or away.

"I'm not going," Teddy says. "It will be too sad without him."

"You can take a friend. Why not ask Wally?"

"I don't think Wally wants to spend a week watching us cry about Dad. You know we will. Some fun that will be."

I tend to agree with him but still feel we should get away.

"Think of your little sisters, Teddy. They love the beach, making sand castles. We can go Legoland, Sea World. Maybe Disneyland for a day."

Teddy scoffs. "Ha, they'll take one look at us and deny admission. Disneyland is supposed to be the happiest place on earth. We won't qualify."

For the first time since the accident, I am so angry at Teddy. I clench my fists as I resist the urge to slap him. Before I do something I'll regret I escape quickly to my bedroom. I lock the door and hide in the shower where I go whenever I have to cry so Teddy won't see me. I have tried to spare him my tears, which only cause him more guilt and anguish, but at this moment I resent that I can't even grieve for my husband without causing Teddy further damage. I hold tight to the shower curtain which I feel like ripping off the rack.

Teddy pounds on the bedroom door.

"Mom, please let me in. I'm sorry, Mom. Please, please open the door."

I rush to the door and the sight of this broken boy sobbing like a baby erases all my anger. How could I, for even a minute, ever think of hurting him? Although he's a foot taller than me, I take him in my arms and try to soothe him.

"It's okay, Teddy. It's okay."

"It's not okay, Mom," he says through his sobs. "It's so selfish of me. I want the girls to make sand castles. Honest I do."

A little laugh of relief comes through my own tears, so relieved that his heart has not turned totally to stone.

Rosetta

Indiana
July

I think of Stan daily now. Thirty years of faded memories surface like oil drops on water. I'm sure grief is causing this, but how can you grieve for something you never quite had? Did I hope that someday we would meet again? That he might come to a class reunion, even though I never attended any for fear I would see him. Now I regret my cowardice. I will never have that chance again.

I watched for the funeral arrangements in the paper and saw that he was buried in the Middleburg cemetery with a graveside service. I didn't have the courage to attend. I never met his family. They never met me. Too awkward to meet now. I was not going to stand alone in the shadows under the branches of a distant tree like they do on television dramas.

Afterwards, I go to the cemetery alone, thinking perhaps that might help put it behind me. The caretaker helps me find the site, which has no stone yet, but many wreaths and flowers. I can't believe he's here, back in Middleburg. Back here, but no longer here. Less than five miles from where we first met.

I expected some sort of resolution, but I walk away feeling empty and worse than when I arrived.

Mary

❧

August

At the bagel shop, Kate and I find a table on the north patio in the morning shade. At 9 a.m. the temperature is already 95 degrees. In August it's no longer a dry heat with monsoon moisture building each day.

"Mary, you've pushed your hair behind your ears three times since we sat down a minute ago. What is it you don't want to tell me?" Kate knows me better than anyone.

They call out our order, which Kate gets.

When she returns, I say, "I do want to tell you, but it's hard." I catch myself pushing my hair again. "I'm thinking of moving to Indiana. Where Stan grew up."

I look at my thumb gripping the cup. I've started biting my cuticles like I did as a teen. Without looking at Kate, I say, "I don't know what's driving me to do this but I am getting signs — sort of."

"You're not basing this decision on that stupid fortune cookie from last week's Chinese take-out are you? What was it? *Make new home for better life.*"

I smile at how preposterous it would be to take a fortune cookie seriously. I picture the little fortune paper swaying from the rearview mirror like a graduation tassel, guiding me into the future. Then the tears start, knowing how much I would miss Kate who, even in my grief, can make me laugh.

I start to tell Kate about the dream, but who moves across the country based on one dream? Not the pizza delivery dream — the other one. It felt so real. Stan was packing the new silver SUV we got after the accident. He made sure the girls were buckled in. Then he kissed them and said good-bye to all of us. *You're not going?* I asked him, totally surprised. *No, but you and the kids need to go home,* he said. *It's where you all belong.*

Kate waves her hand in front of my face. "Hello, earth calling Mary."

I try to explain. "For starters, I hate that intersection. We have to cross it each day just to get out of our subdivision. And Teddy never leaves the house. His friends call. He makes lame excuses. He feels everyone is judging him for what happened. It might be good for him to start over where no one knows." Kate nods but doesn't say anything. I plead my case further. "And there's his Uncle Dan, Stan's older brother. Teddy likes him and he could sure use a male figure in his life now."

"I don't know Mary. It seems rather drastic — a move across the country. I understand you're doing this for Teddy but how about you? Your friends here? To start all over?"

I look at my bagel and wonder why I ordered yet another thing that I won't eat. "It's not just for Teddy. I want to be near Stan's family too. Did I ever tell you about the first time he took me home to meet them?"

"You told me you met in college."

"Yes." I smile at the memory of that day. "You would have loved Papa, Stan's dad. A little five-foot guy." I shake my head. "I don't know how his sons got so tall. As soon as I stepped into their house, Papa stretches his arms wide and says in his Bulgarian accent. 'Velcum to my home.' A little sprig of fresh mint from the garden behind his ear. Within five minutes he offers me his homemade wine. I wish Stan had warned me it was like 150 proof. Knocked my socks off. Then after one of Baba's to-die-for dinners, like a mere ten courses, Papa played the mandolin and sang Bulgarian folk songs."

"Sounds like you were on the movie set for *Zorba the Greek*."

"Really. And Stan's mother. Oh my gosh. Think Aunt Bea on Mayberry, apron and all. Well, maybe a Mediterranean Aunt Bea with her olive skin. I had just lost my own mother and when she hugged me

I wanted to stay pressed in her soft bosom forever. Papa's gone, but the other day when I told Baba what I was thinking, she cried and said in her best English, 'Come, Mary. You come to my home.'"

Kate suggests, "Maybe you should visit before school starts. I would keep the girls if you and Teddy want to fly there alone. You know, a look-see?"

I sigh and say, "Yeah, maybe that would be good. There's not much to see though. It's more a sense. Like comfort food — like mac 'n cheese, chicken pot pie."

"Well, there's no doubt you could use a few good meals. I always envied your petite figure, but really Mary, you could be the poster child for third-world children." Kate covers one of my hands with hers. She eyeballs my bagel. "Are you going to eat that?"

I push it toward her.

She tears off a piece, chews, and says, "I wish we had a crystal ball. As much as I'd miss you, maybe a change would help. You could always come back if it's not right."

"No Kate, if we do it, we have to be committed to make it work. I can't jerk Teddy around like a yo-yo."

"What does your grief counselor say?"

I roll my eyes and mock my counselor's rote command. *"Don't make any changes the first year.* But, Kate, if I wait, then Teddy's a senior. No way I'm going to take him away for his last year." Then I sheepishly admit, "She also pointed out that death of a spouse and relocation are number two and three on the stress chart. I guess I'm crazy to impose more stress than I already have."

"So what's number one?" Kate polishes off my bagel with one last bite.

I give a little chuckle. "I asked her the same thing. Speaking before groups."

Kate laughs. "Why don't you give a speech at town hall tonight and go for the trifecta?"

I start to laugh and the tears gush unexpectedly. "I would miss you so much, Kate." I take the napkin from under my coffee cup and blow my nose, louder than I mean to. The man at the adjoining table gives a disapproving look.

Kate stares him down with a nod toward me. She mouths, "P-M-S." He blushes and gives us a sorry half-smile, like he wishes he could disappear.

Kate asks, "So what would you do there? Go back to teaching? Find a home or stay with Stan's mom?"

"I was thinking about staying with Stan's mom to start. She's alone in that big old house. See if my Arizona teaching certificate is valid in Indiana. Maybe I'll need a class or two. Baba could help with the girls till we settle in. I think she would love feeling needed."

When we walk to our cars, Kate says, "If it's what you decide, I'll help you pack. You know garage sales are my specialty. I'll get top dollar for all your crap that doesn't make the cut." Kate hugs me.

After she gets in her car, she rolls down the window and says, "And stay away from those fortune cookies — Confucius too confusing!"

I laugh as the tears well up again at the thought of leaving her. How many things am I going to lose? My husband, my best friend? My mind? I must be nuts.

Teddy

⌒

There's a fierce monsoon brewing. The wind comes up quickly, and in minutes a wall of brown dust blocks my backyard view of the mountaintop with the red blinking signal towers. I stand on the patio to experience the full dramatic effect of it. When I return to the kitchen, Mom drops a bombshell as loud as the crack of thunder outside.

"Mom, you can't be serious. Indiana? What are you thinking? Obviously, not about me." I rip off my sunglasses to see if it's a total stranger speaking to me.

"Teddy, you've hardly left the house all summer. A new start might be good for all of us. A fresh start with not so many memories." Her eyes plead and she bites her lower lip but I'm not buying into it with any sympathy for her.

"How can moving to Dad's old house, probably sleeping in his old room, be *fresh*? Oh sure, no reminders of him there."

"But those are positive things. About his life. It's hard to avoid the negatives here. Like that intersection."

"It's not exactly my favorite hangout these days either, Mom. But we don't have to move two thousand miles from it." I don't mention that I rode a mile out of my way recently to avoid it. On my bike of course. Who knows how old I'll be when I have the courage to drive again. Headline: SENIOR CITIZEN LOGS MILLION MILES ON BIKE.

Like he knows it's a crisis, our sausage dog, Winnie, starts whimpering. I point to him. "How about Winnie who sits at the back door whining, waiting for Dad to come home each day at six? Are you going to get rid of him too?" I blurt this out and then wish I could take it back as soon as I say it when I see the hurt in her eyes.

Then it's like she never heard me and she goes into organized-Mom mode. The cost of living. It's cheaper in Indiana. Need to save the insurance money for college. Blah, blah, blah. Like a degree from that Podunk high school would get me in a decent college. I don't want to hear it. I put both hands over my ears. Mom stops justifying her reasons, covers her eyes, and starts crying. I can't watch, so I walk away.

I killed my dad and now my mom is killing me.

Mary

ⵣ

The talk with Teddy didn't go well. Gross understatement. But I push on.

First, I call a property manager to rent our home, in case we come back. Then I decide to put it on the market. If we do return, it will be to a different house. Far from the fatal intersection. I make three lists to sort our possessions: 1. Indiana; 2. Storage; 3. Sell. Stay busy, stay focused. It's good to have something to do.

Before bedtime I want to talk to the girls about our move. Maybe it will also help Ruby, who has reverted to sucking her thumb again after having quit two years ago. When I don't see her in bed, Cathy points to the closet. I find Ruby hiding under all her hanging clothes, her face wet with tears.

"Ruby, you don't have to hide to cry. It's okay to cry about Daddy. We're all crying."

"But, but," she sobs, "I heard you say to someone on the phone that you don't cry in front of Teddy. It makes him feel bad."

"Oh, honey, honey. You're such a good sister to think of Teddy." I pull her out gently and hug her. Cathy closes in for a hug too. I sit them down in front of me. All three of us sit cross-legged in a little circle. "Teddy's going to be fine. We all are. Because even though we don't have Daddy now, we have each other. And ... and that's why... why I've decided we are going to move. To Baba's house. To be with more family...they'll help us not miss Daddy so much."

"Will we stop missing him when we get there?" Ruby asks wide-eyed.

I realize that was the wrong thing to say. "No, honey, we'll always miss him, but sometimes a different place and more people around us ..." I'm floundering now. Then I give her an encouraging smile. "Do you know what your cousin Sophie said when I told her you were coming?"

"What?"

"She has a big box of dolls she's too old to play with. They were her favorites and she wants you and Cathy to have them. Isn't that nice?"

Ruby smiles and Cathy claps her little hands.

"But can I still take Amelia?" Ruby asks desperately. Amelia is her favorite cabbage patch doll.

"Of course Amelia is coming," I say. "And I haven't told you the best part yet." They both look at me in anticipation. "At Baba's house you and Cathy can still sleep in the same room but it's much bigger. You'll each have your own bed and you can pick out whatever decorations you want for your side of the room. Won't that be fun?"

I try to make it sound like an exciting adventure. I'm also hoping it will help Ruby stay in her bed. She's been wandering to my bed in the middle of the night for most of the summer.

"I want Little Mermaid," Cathy says. "No, Cinderella. No. Maybe Snow White."

I laugh and cup her sweet face in my hands. "You don't have to decide now. We'll go shopping after we get there."

Ruby looks a little skeptical and puts her thumb in her mouth.

At 2 a.m. I feel her warm body snuggle up to mine, her sleepy breath on the back of my neck.

I have to believe it's going to work out for the best. I wish Stan were here so I could ask him what I should do. I catch myself wishing this a lot and then the painful reminder kicks in. If Stan were here, I wouldn't need to do any of this.

I push on.

Teddy

Enroute
August

If you look at a map of the U.S. and draw a line from Phoenix, Arizona, to Middleburg, Indiana, you can see how far it is. What you can't see is how far it *really* is —- from everything I've ever known. From city to country. From friends to not knowing a soul. Except my cousin Sophie, but cousins don't really count. It's not Middle*burg*. It's middle of *nowhere*.

How could Mom take me away from everything that might have helped me forget? Like Wally and playing varsity ball. Now I have to go through try-outs for some hayseed team I don't even want to play for.

How about Liz? Good-bye romance. I'll be spending my Saturday nights holding a PlayStation like some 12-year-old.

And then Mom had the nerve to say, the night before we left, which happened to be my 16th birthday, "Don't forget to make a wish when you blow out your candles." Right, like what I wish for can ever come true now.

Mary

Enroute

Driving two thousand miles across the country can be tedious under the best conditions. When your passenger is not speaking to you, it can seem endless. Too many hours to ask myself, *This was a good idea because ...?*

Somewhere in Colorado, I reach out again to Teddy. His slumped posture puts another fracture in my already cracked heart. In desperation I say something that even surprises me, "Teddy, I'll make a deal with you. Give it a year. One year where you really try to make it work. If it's awful, I promise you, we'll come back. You can have your senior year at Southwest Canyon." Teddy turns toward me but the sunglasses shade his eyes. "You know I keep my promises," I say with a coaxing smile.

"Well, Mom, I don't really have a choice, do I?"

"You do, Teddy. I'm saying you do. You have a choice at the end of the year."

"I mean right now. Right now we go no matter what. I mean we're on the way."

"Yes, now we're going, but it doesn't have to be forever."

"Okay, Mom," is what he says. What I hear is, "Stop talking about it, okay?"

I pat his knee and wonder what in the world I have committed to. To possibly move again in a year? I must be insane. I'm going to have to define what *really trying* means. Will we revert to charts with gold stars like we did in grade school?

Teddy fiddles with the radio station, which I've let him be in charge of for the entire trip as a cheap token of consolation. We continue to point the car east to the voices of The Backstreet Boys and Arizona becomes a more distant back street with each passing mile.

Teddy

Enroute

"Illinois," Ruby shouts, pointing to a license plate of the car that just passed us. She pronounces the *S* like a *Z*. Someone told me you don't pronounce the *S* at all. I'm wondering what other things I don't know about the Midwest that will make me sound or look stupid.

"Teddy, you promised. You're not even looking," Ruby folds her arms across her chest and puts on her pouty face. I agree to play the license plate game so she stops the silly songs she makes up and repeats endlessly like, "We're driving through Kansas, the corn is very tall." She has boundless energy and, in spite of a booster seat, has bounced and wiggled her way across five states.

Cathy smiles and chatters from her car seat as if we're headed to Disneyland. She squeals over each toy in Happy Meals and bouncy ball playgrounds. How I wish they could work their magic for me again. Too old for playgrounds, too young to be on my own. Like I'm on a bungee cord, suspended between everything in my life. And every once in a while someone yanks at the cord, just to remind me that I'm not in control.

"Phew-yew," says Ruby. "Teddy, Winnie's farting again."

"And you're telling me because ..."

"He's your dog."

"What do you want me to do? Change his diaper?"

Ruby forgets she's mad at me and starts to giggle.

Way to go Winnie. My best true friend, a rusty little wiener dog

Dad got for my fifth birthday but he liked Dad best of all. I couldn't say wiener and he's been Winnie ever since. I look at him curled up and snoring. Headline: DOG GASSES FAMILY ON CROSS- COUNTRY TRIP.

Ruby starts singing again, Cathy nods off to the monotonous chant, and Mom keeps pushing her hair off her forehead like she does when she gets tired. It's been hard to sit beside her when I'm so mad at her, but looking at her right now, trying so hard to be strong and brave, I am so sorry for her and what I've done to her life. My tears are starting. How can you love and hate someone so much at the same time? I blink and stare straight ahead at the long wavy heat lines on the highway.

My life feels the same. Wavy.

Mary

Enroute

What would have been a two or three day trip with both Stan and I driving is stretched into five days. In spite of the countless Starbucks consumed I cannot keep my concentration on the road after six or seven hours. The good news is that we stop early enough each day so that the kids can swim before and after dinner at the motels.

We get rooms with two double beds and both the girls want Teddy to sleep with them, so he takes turns. Two nights with Ruby, two nights with Cathy.

I am relieved that I don't have to sleep with him — afraid that in the middle of the night, in a sleepy longing, I would reach for him, mistaking his long body for Stan.

Teddy

Indiana
September

"We're here! We're here," Ruby shouts as we finally pull into Baba's long driveway flanked by tall leafy green trees. Not a palm tree in sight. I roll down the window. More humid than the steam room at the gym.

"And people say the desert is hot? What do you call this?" I say to no one in particular.

"Teddy, why is your hair so curly? You look like my Cabbage Patch doll," Ruby points to my hair with a weird look on her face.

I look in the rearview mirror, horrified to see my normally wavy dark brown hair in tight ringlets.

"Oh man, what's happening?" I forgot what Midwest humidity does to hair. *Great.*

While Ruby's bouncing up and down to get out, I sit frozen in the front seat, making no effort to move. I know I'm acting like a jerk but once I open that door, it's the first step into a life I don't want. Headline: BOY SPENDS JUNIOR YEAR IN CAR.

Mom turns off the car and takes a sideways glance at me. "I know this isn't easy, Teddy, and I'm not sure it's the right thing. But I can count on you to try, can't I?"

"I am trying Mom." I could remind her that I didn't jump out of the car to join the hitchhikers I saw heading west. I didn't hold up a sign, saying *Help Me, Abduction to NoWhereVille.* That hostage scam had a chance. Mom and the girls are fair-skinned and blonde. I got Dad's Bulgarian genes. Olive skin, dark hair, and those hazel eyes. Dad called me swarthy. "That's what girls like," he told me with a conspirator's wink. Is the missing him ever going to stop?

Mom hits the button to unlock the doors and Ruby flies out of the car to Baba's open arms. Mom looks up quickly, not wanting Baba to see her hesitation. She puts on the be-strong smile she's practiced all summer and waves through the windshield.

Winnie chases after Ruby, but comes to a sudden halt. He meets Buster, Baba's fat yellow tabby cat. A gigantic hiss and arched back send his short legs scrambling, looking back to see if the fat feline is following. In my B.C. life, that might have been funny. Now I'm thinking it's yet another reason not to be here — unfriendly territory.

While Mom gets Cathy out of the car seat, Baba comes to the car, brushing tears aside and wiping her hands on her apron. "Mary, Mary, you make it. So far you drive by yourself. *Mila Muneeko.*" Her English is usually spiced with Bulgarian words. Through the years, we've come to understand what she means in the phonetic jumble. *Mila Mun-ee-ko* translates as something like *little darling.*

"Teddy Bear. Look how big you got. *Golum machan. Tall man.*

When I bend down to hug her round soft body, I get a whiff of what we're having for dinner. Wally said once his grandmother smells like mothballs. Baba smells like whatever she's cooking. I think I have the better deal. So what if I'm the only kid who salivates when he hears the word Grandma, or in my case, Baba. I like that she still calls me Teddy Bear but hope she doesn't do it in front of any friends. Oh, but not to worry. I have no friends here.

Mary

⌧

If someone looked up the word *retro*, they might find a picture of Baba's living room. A step back in time. The furniture is the same as when I first met Stan yet doesn't look old and shabby but preserved and cared for. The end tables have a high polish with crocheted doilies. The coffee table has a turquoise lazy Susan on it, the four sections now empty, but an instant memory of a Christmas visit flashes when each section was filled with nuts — walnuts, hazelnuts, Brazil nuts. Stan teaching a young Teddy how to use a nutcracker.

Was Teddy right? Would there be too many memories of Stan here? Instantly I decide there could never be too many. Baba, her old-fashioned décor and the memory are all comforting to me now. Like a knitted afghan across my lap on a rainy day.

I realize I am looking forward to the change of seasons too. Although we relished basking in the Arizona sun when the rest of the country was frigid, I know now that life itself has seasons and maybe too much sunshine isn't good for the soul.

Baba looks as well preserved as her home for a lady in her mid-70s. Surprisingly few grey hairs in the dark curly hair that both Stan and Teddy inherited. Does she color her hair? Would she tell me if she did? I smile to myself, knowing she would. She's honest, to a fault. She speaks her mind bluntly, often to our amusement. Never seems to consider how her remarks might offend even if she means no offense. What do they say? No filter? The hazel eyes are the same as Stan's, although hers are darker, more brown with just little flecks of green. She has the olive complexion like so many people from Eastern Europe and now some age spots as well.

My friends used to share mother-in-law horror stories. When I didn't have much to contribute, I realized how lucky I was. Baba embraced me from the day we met. I never knew if it was simply to appease Stan or because I had recently lost my own mother.

I suspected, once I got to know her, that her first choice for a daughter-in-law might have been a plump Bulgarian girl who knew the language and the customs. Then I appreciated her acceptance of me even more.

Me, a wispy, frail and fair-skinned blonde with no specific heritage. Like a stray puppy, I was the mutt Stan had brought home, and she took me in.

Teddy

I'm not exactly an interior decorator, but I think Baba's house is the same as the setting of *Happy Days*. Headline: TEEN TIME TRAVELS.

"Come, come. All day I wait. The table is ready." Baba walks quickly into the kitchen.

I suspect there will be enough food to feed an army. Dad always said Baba should have been an Army cook. For the enemy. No one can move after one of her meals. Baba bustles and instantly the table is spread with large platters of food that smell wonderful.

"You went to too much trouble," Mom says, as she fills her plate with an enthusiasm I haven't seen recently. After the accident, I'd find Mom, who used to whip around the kitchen like a TV chef, just sitting at the table, staring at nothing. Sometimes food would be defrosting on the counter as if she had planned to start cooking but forgot to finish.

One time Ruby asked, "Why don't we order a pizza?" Mom and I looked at each other as if Ruby had said, "Why don't we eat nails?"

We haven't had a pizza since that night. It's now on the forbidden food list. Tonight we're inhaling stuffed peppers, crispy roasted potatoes, feta cheese, and hot bread that Baba has torn into generous chunks.

"Eat, darlinks, eat." She cheers us on like an Olympic coach in a marathon eating event.

"Baba, what's this yellow stuff?" Ruby pokes at her chunk of bread.

"Garlic, Ruby. Very good for you. In Bulgaria, we wear the garlic around our neck. It keep the bad spirits away."

I dig into the food keeping my face lowered so no one sees me blinking the tears back. I can't help but wish Dad had been wearing a big chunk of it around his Bulgarian neck four months ago.

"Teddy, your cousin Sophie. She take you tonight to play that game. What they call it? Meeni golf? You like it?"

"Miniature golf? I do, but not tonight Baba." I come up with the lame excuse that I have to unpack the car.

I know Mom would rather I go out, but I'm sure Sophie doesn't want a kid cousin tagging along. Uncle Dan probably made her ask. That's one of the hardest things since Dad's gone. Everyone trying to be too nice. No one riding me the way they used to. Sometimes I just want to scream, "Hey, it's me, Teddy." Maybe a new start will be good where no one knows what happened. Unless Sophie has blabbed to the whole school.

"*I* like miniature golf," Ruby says, still squinting at the yellow chunks in her bread.

I see Baba look at me longingly. None of this is her fault and how could I forget how much she must be hurting too. I can't let her know I don't want to be here.

"Baba, this tastes so good," I say with all the enthusiasm I can muster.

Baba beams. Mom smiles. As if moving here was absolutely the right thing to do, based on a plate of Bulgarian stuffed peppers.

Mary

After dinner I offer to help clean the kitchen but Baba shoos me away.

"Go Mary, you have many things to put away from car. You are tired. You drive all day. There will be many days to help," she takes the dishcloth from my hand.

I don't insist or argue. "I'll go tonight, but only this time. If we live here, I want to help, especially in the kitchen. I know you love to cook, so I'll do the clean-up. Deal?" I ask her. I put my hand out as if to shake.

She laughs and shakes my hand firmly, like a man. "For family, this is better than handshake." She hugs me tightly and I'm glad I am looking over her shoulder so she won't see the tears her hug brings on. When we separate I notice her wringing her hands.

"Are you alright?" I ask.

"The arthritis. Some days good, some days not so good. I'm supposed to do exercises like this." She opens and closes her hands with the fingers outstretched. She rolls her eyes like a teenager, as if the exercise is silly.

"The girls will help you. I think they know a song using their hands like that. Do you take anything for it?" I ask.

"The doctor said Bufferin is best. It's in my *dupa* too. This side." She pats her right buttock. "Maybe you will notice now that you live here, I walk like a drunk sometime. When I first wake up my joints are stiff. Not because I am drinking in the night." She smiles. "But one good thing. I am like perfect weatherman. I can tell you day ahead when it will rain. My joints, they tell me."

"You should have come to Arizona more often. The dry climate would have been good for you." I say this wondering why we never invited her to stay longer on her visits than she did. Or did we? Seems a blur now, like so many things.

"Stan ask me many times to stay. He was good son, but you know, Mary, the older you get, the better it is to be in your own home. Even if it is too big for one old lady. I am happy to have you and the children here. To give it life again."

I walk to the car to get a load of clothes and think to myself, *yes, that's what we want too.* A life again.

Teddy

❧

After I unload the car, I remember that Dad's old backboard has a bright spotlight for night play. That shouldn't be a surprise after watching the movie *Hoosiers* three times with him. Didn't every kid in Indiana play basketball night and day as soon as they could walk?

Wally teased me about not being good enough to make a Hoosier team, but I told him any coach would be happy to have a 5A player. Wally wasn't so sure. "You better work on that jump shot," he said the last time we played.

"Hey, I could make that jump shot all night — in the dark, in the park."

"Oh sure, Dr. Seuss. You'll probably be eating those green eggs and ham on the bench."

"Very funny." I threw the basketball hard, catching him off guard. Wally caught it and doubled over laughing. I knew we were both trying to cover up our real feelings. The sad ones, knowing this would be our last one-on-one. I knew too that I would miss him more than I could ever tell him. More than green eggs and ham.

I shoot baskets until I see the lights going on upstairs and hear Cathy and Ruby giggling through the open windows. At least I have my own room. Mom promised to call the internet company as soon as we got here. I can't wait to set up my computer and e-mail. My lifeline to Wally and Liz.

Thinking of the new laptop Mom got me for my birthday makes me ashamed that I've been so mean to her. I know it was a consolation prize. Like a parting gift on the game shows for the loser. Move to Indiana. Get a laptop. But still, it was pretty nice of her.

Sitting on Baba's picnic table I am surrounded by trees and dense bushes, with no view of the sky. So different than home. I picture our backyard in Arizona. The palm trees swaying in the sunset, the mountains a hazy purple outline. I see our swimming pool with Cathy's little pink raft floating in circles and Ruby's orange noodle poking out one end of the pool. The patio table is set with a red -checkered tablecloth and a big bowl of chips. I can hear Mom's Willie Nelson CD crooning, "You Were Always on my Mind." I can almost smell the hamburgers Dad's grilling.

There's only one thing wrong with this picture. None of us are in it anymore.

Rosetta

The cemetery draws me back. Why am I doing this? What do I hope to accomplish? On my next trip there is a stone in place. Although it's September, summer is hanging on and I realize that I have few summer memories of Stan. Our time together was September through May. Looking back, it seems an extremely short percentage of my life to yield such a long-lasting result.

Someone has planted petunias and geraniums close to the headstone. I wish I had thought to bring something. I leave and go to a grocery floral department where a bouquet of red roses calls out to me. A memory surfaces and I add a pink one in the center. I return to the cemetery and set the vase at the foot of the stone.

I recall the euphoria I felt the day I received an identical bouquet from Stan. Our love was at its height. Before our world came crashing down and before I knew that I could never see him again.

I say, "Rest in peace, my handsome, thoughtful boy."

In my mind he will always be the sweet and optimistic 17-year-old boy I loved. He naively thought our love could survive the turbulent 60's Civil Rights movement.

The flower gesture has brought me some comfort. Hopefully closure. I walk away fearing, however, that like those rosebuds, my heart is starting to peel open again.

Teddy

⌒

Before bedtime, Baba asks me to put some boxes in the attic. With a black marker she has written in large awkward letters that also seem to have an accent, STANLEY. It's hard to believe she left this stuff in his room some, what — 30 years? I think of his life reduced to two boxes and tears spring to my eyes. No wonder I wear sunglasses all day.

I climb the narrow stairs to the top floor. The creaking attic door reminds me of the ghost stories I would tell Ruby on our summer visits. I convinced her that the attic was haunted so she couldn't find me when we played hide and seek. I was so convincing that sometimes I even scared myself.

It's hot and musty and I can barely stand up without hitting my head on the rafters, but I love poking through this old stuff. I pull a long piece of rope that turns on a dim light bulb. There's the wooden sled with a faded Radio Flyer logo, a drum with a music stand that's about to collapse, and worn out brown hockey skates. I've never ice skated in my life and wonder if all the kids here are whizzes on ice. Do I need to skate to fit in? Headline: HOT DESERT BOY MELTS ICE.

I find an empty spot for the boxes next to an old steamer trunk. Dad told me once the trunk contained all the possessions his father brought from the "old country." I lift the dusty lid with a creaking sound. I see what looks like tablecloths and pillowcases with fancy designs.

I pick up faded brown and white photographs with curly edges but don't recognize anyone. If the fire department has a most wanted list, Baba's on it. This place is a firetrap.

I close the lid and turn when my toe bumps another box and I hear music. It startles me at first but then I think it's the tinkling sound of a music box. I shuffle a few boxes and the music starts again. Very softly, a few notes play before it stops. I open the lid of one box and see old shirts. I open another box and there's a faded yellowed newspaper clipping with the headline, "Kostoff Brothers Lead Holiday Tourney Points." It's a photo of someone who looks just like me taking a shot. I can't tell if it's Dad or Uncle Dan. Boy, they wore short shorts then.

There's a faded green letter sweater with a big white *M* on it and a small tattered book bound on the side with a piece of leather, like a shoestring. I open it and see that weird foreign alphabet. A piece of yellowed paper sticks out of it. It says, in English, *Book of Life.* Inside are more foreign words and translations underneath them. Doesn't look like anything that fits *my* life.

I dig a little deeper and discover the music box. It's a globe with a winter scene of a horse-drawn carriage with a man and woman inside. I turn it over and see the key on the bottom. I wind it up and it plays a tune I've heard before, somewhere, but I don't know the name. I should take it downstairs for Ruby and Cathy, but I better ask Baba first. I wind it up again and it's still playing softly as I leave the attic full of relics.

Mary

❧

I'm up in the middle of the night. I was hoping the night wanderings might stop when we left Phoenix, but it's only our first night. I look in on the girls, sleeping soundly in their twin beds, Ruby sprawled out like a snow angel and Cathy curled into a ball, still clutching her stuffed kitten.

Then Teddy, who looks innocent and peaceful in his sleep. My heart aches for him having to start over in a new school. I'm taken back to the first days of kindergarten, watching him bravely take that steep step onto a yellow bus that looked way too big for a little guy. I stood at the curb waving to the little face in the window, saying the universal mother's prayer. That all would go well for him. To make friends. To like school. The same longings return to me now.

I'm not sure I did the right thing but now we're here. Teddy is still unresponsive to me. I don't know how long he'll stay angry. At least he's kind to Baba and the girls.

I look upward, "Stan, give me a sign. Tell me somehow I did the right thing."

Teddy

When I wake up the next morning, my dream is still vivid. In it, the music box was playing. Winnie and Buster, looking like a clever pet store commercial, were doing some fancy footwork in time to the music. The music kept getting louder so I ran to the attic to make it stop.

I'm thinking this weird dream is probably the result of raiding the refrigerator after I tossed and turned. Then I roll over and see the tattered book from the attic on my bedside table. Did I bring it here in the middle of the night? Am I going to add sleepwalking to my nighttime rituals, along with junk food raids?

The book is laid open to a page with Bulgarian words and below them is the penciled translation. *The past cannot be changed but the future is in your hands.*

Mary

I want to visit the cemetery as soon as possible. Alone. I need to talk to Stan. Not like he's going to give me any answers, but I have to talk it out. I am hoping the stone we ordered is here.

Not only is the stone in place but I am surprised to see fresh flowers. Perhaps from Dan? I thought he said he felt bad that he hadn't brought Baba here for several weeks. At any rate, they are lovely. Red roses with one pink rose. An interesting arrangement, I think, but nice nonetheless.

With my finger I trace his name carved into the granite. Seeing the dates brings a stark reality. He is gone. The tears come and I let them flow freely, not having to worry about Teddy seeing me and adding to his guilt. When I am emptied of tears, I blow my nose loudly and actually smile a little.

"Kinda like the rainy day we met, huh?" I say to the stone. "Me all soaked, you so strong."

I touch the top of the stone. "You've been like this granite stone in my life, Stan. Steady, strong. Like a rock. I'm not going to let you down now. I'm going to be strong for the kids. I promise you that." I see an older couple walking close by and I lower my voice.

"But I'm worried about Teddy. I think being with your brother Dan can be a good thing. Maybe that's what you were trying to tell me in my dreams. I'll be back soon. I'll bring Baba and the kids. I love you Stan. I miss you so much. By the way, nice flowers. Just like you to have friends everywhere."

Teddy

I knew the first day of school would be weird and it is. Sophie pulls into the driveway in Blue Bug, a powder blue Volkswagen Uncle Dan restored for her. I hop into the seat beside her and she pats my knee. "I'm glad you're here Teddy."

She's being way too nice. Treating me like I have a terminal disease. I wish she'd call me weird names, like she used to. We pick up three more senior girls. I jump out and they pile into the back seat. All of them are talking at once. It's like I'm not even in the car. Headline: INVISIBLE BOY STARTS SCHOOL.

I have my schedule folded up in my pocket. I pull it out and try to get my bearings. Sophie points me in the right direction. It strikes me funny that although this school is 2,000 miles from Southwest Canyon High, it smells the same. Maybe all school hallways smell like baloney sandwiches, girls' perfume, and dirty socks.

I find my locker with someone else's stuff in it. I can't believe I have to share a locker. In what medieval century was this school built? Based on the size of the lunch bag I see, I assume my partner is a guy. A big guy. I hope he's a jock.

Then out of nowhere a short girl appears at my elbow. She has red curly hair that goes in corkscrew directions and she's pushing purple-rimmed glasses up on the ridge of her nose. She grabs a notebook out of the locker and grins at me. Turquoise braces sparkle. She looks like a character on a Lucky Charms box.

"You must be Teddy. I'm Mindy. Gotta run." She disappears into the crowded hallway. All I can see is her florescent yellow backpack bobbing up and down.

Great. A gremlin for a locker partner. A girl gremlin.

First hour, Honors English, Room 202. Before I go in, I take a deep breath, trying to appear nonchalant. Groups of kids bunched at desks, talking, laughing. A few are in their seats with notebooks open. I look at the empty desks and suddenly the simplest decision, like where to sit, is monumental. Baba's pancakes have solidified like rocks in my stomach.

A youngish man wearing Dockers, a Levi shirt, and a Mickey Mouse tie walks in.

"Ladies and gentlemen, take your seats and start your engines."

Oh, no. Was this lingo going to be part of fitting in? Talking like Mario Andretti or whoever that race car driver is. Great. I don't ever want to be reminded of driving and we move to the home of the Indy 500.

I take the last seat in the row by the door, as if escape were an option. I'm behind a bouncy blonde ponytail. She's frantically writing a note that she passes to the girl on her left who opens the note and turns to look at me. She turns away, embarrassed that I've seen her look, but not before I notice her pretty green eyes. I'm sure I have an expression like a deer in the headlights. *Good start, Teddy.* I miss Liz's familiar smile.

Each class — trig, government, Spanish — same scenario. People who know each other, talking, and laughing while the faceless loners hide behind their books. What did I expect? Someone to include me? Oh, yeah, I forgot. I'm invisible.

Mary

⌒

Baba, in a fresh paisley apron, bustles in the kitchen getting ready for her weekly Canasta group. My mouth waters as I watch her putting spoonfuls of cheese into Phyllo dough, knowing how crispy and delicious it will be. She deftly folds the dough into little triangles as she tells me about, as she calls them, her "lady" friends. From her descriptions, it sounds like I'll have live *Golden Girls* to watch each week.

"June is widow for 10 years and now has boyfriend but she doesn't like him much. He has wooden leg but he likes the dance. She doesn't want to be nursemaid so we say, 'Don't marry, just dance.'

"Opal. She doesn't hear so good, so talk to her right side. Her kids make her little bit crazy. They want money all the time.

"Arlis has husband who sits in the kitchen all day. Does nothing else. Tells her how to do her business. How much soap to put in laundry. How to wash dishes. She tells him, 'I wash clothes and dishes for 50 years without you.'

"They nice ladies. My good friends. They stay with me each day when I get the news of Stan."

She sighs, wrings her hands, pulls out another cookie sheet. She keeps folding the Phyllo dough into triangles. Staying busy must be Baba's therapy. Very industrious.

With Ruby and Teddy in school and Cathy in preschool until noon, I go to the school district office. They tell me I need to take an Indiana history course to validate my teaching certificate and give me a schedule of when and where it is offered.

On the way home, I drive down Main Street, hoping the bookstore

I remember is still there. Baba's talk about her friends makes me miss my book group. As I pull up to the curb, the name on the storefront makes me smile like it did the first time I saw it: A Good Bookstore. Maybe they have a group I can join.

I walk in and immediately there is that exhilarating sense of other worlds to get lost in. For a few hours I might forget my own sad saga. The smell of fresh coffee greets me and I recognize Vivaldi's Spring playing softly in the background. At the checkout counter is a Mrs. Claus look-a-like with wire-rimmed glasses and snow white hair piled in a bun on top of her head.

She says, "Let me know if you need any help. There's fresh coffee in Mystery."

I wander around, sipping coffee, some kind of delicious pumpkin spice concoction. I touch books with interesting covers and a sense of pleasure spreads through me. I don't think I went to a bookstore or library all summer, and I realize now how much it might have helped me. I encouraged Teddy *to try* to live again, but I wasn't setting a very good example just sitting home all day watching silly reruns. Numbing my brain to mask my hurt.

On the bulletin board I see notices for author signings and children's story times. There's a teen book group, reading some sort of zombie romance. No adult book discussions posted, but then I see a flyer. "Part-time help needed. See Dianne."

I go back to the front of the store. "Are you Dianne?"

"Yes." She smiles, not just with her mouth, but with her deep blue eyes.

"Are you still looking for part-time help?"

"Yes, would you like an application?"

"I could fill it out right here." I want to take some action now. To do something positive about my life, even this small step.

She hands me a clipboard and motions to a soft easy chair in the biography corner. "That would be good because I'm making a decision very soon."

It's a simple form. One page. I hand it back to her and continue browsing. The thought of getting an employee book discount excites me until I realize I'll probably spend more money than I earn.

I find a book the grief counselor recommended. At checkout, Dianne doesn't ask if it's for me or someone else, but discreetly says, "I've heard that this is both comforting and inspiring."

As she hands me my change, she says, ""I'll let you know either way in a few days. Want to get someone trained in time for Christmas rush."

When I hear the word *Christmas*, I thank her and leave the store quickly before she can see the tears welling up. I get to the safety of my car and put my head on the steering wheel, wondering how we will get through a Christmas without Stan. I was feeling good for the short time in the store. Two steps forward, one step back.

When I get home, the Golden Girls at the card table are cackling. I see Arlis say loudly to Opal's right ear, "I'm home on Thursday."

Evidently not loud enough because Opal replies, "I'm thirsty too."

Teddy

◦◦◦

After school, I spot Blue Bug in the parking lot and Sophie waves.

"I think I'll walk home, Sophie."

"Are you sure?" she asks.

I wave her off, "I'm good."

The only thing I'm sure of is that I don't belong. As I pass the football field, the band's at one end, the cheerleaders are practicing, and the team is doing jumping jacks at the far end. The bleachers are full of kids just hanging out. I see the coach swat one of the players on the butt with a towel, and it reminds me of Dad. Behind the sunglasses I'm perfecting my blink-blink squeeze routine as I start walking.

"Hey, Teddy, wait up," I hear a voice and turn to see the splash of color — red hair, purple glasses.

She runs to catch up. "It's me, Mindy. Your locker partner."

In the bright daylight yet another color is added to her palate — orange freckles that spread from ear to ear when she smiles.

"Hi, uh," I stammer, as I try to take it all in.

"I was supposed to share lockers with Alicia, but her dad got transferred a week before school started. They left without even selling their house so she could start the year in her new school. Can you imagine starting high school where you don't know a soul?" Mindy covers her mouth, "Whoops, sorry, I guess you can. I know you just moved here. That's how we got paired up." She rolls her eyes but keeps on talking. "So where do you live? I'll walk with you as far as First Street."

Does the rainbow kid ever take a breath? With her corkscrew

red curls bouncing at my elbow, it's like we're a circus side show attraction. Headline: STEP RIGHT UP FOLKS. SEE TALLEST AND SHORTEST TEENS.

"I live on Third Street. I mean my Grandma does. Well, I guess I do now too." I finally put a sentence together, but could I have sounded any dumber?

"Same way I'm going. Where'd you move from? Do you like it here? I've lived here my whole life. I've only been to two other states."

"Arizona. I came from Arizona."

"Wow, so far away! Let's see. Arizona. The 48th state. Came into the Union 1912. On Valentine's Day. Kinda cool. But, oooh, snakes, lizards, Gila monsters. Yuk. I don't care much for animals with scales. I prefer furry things myself. Still kind of the wild west out there, huh?"

"Well, actually it's becoming quite civilized. They have phones, TVs. I think I spotted a car just before I left."

She laughs. "I guess that was pretty stupid, but really, all that desert — sand and rocks and no trees. Do you have trees besides cactus? Or should I say cacti?"

"We had a cocktail tree in our yard that grew oranges, lemons, and limes."

"Really? All on one tree? Wow, that's amazing. How do they do that?"

"Heck if I know."

I'm thinking how dorky it is to be having a conversation about trees of all things with someone my age, when Mindy says, "So are you going to play any sports? You're so tall. I bet you play basketball."

"I did in Phoenix. I need to let the coach know I'm here. Is the team any good?"

"Good? They were in the Sweet Sixteen last year. Lost by one basket! I bawled my eyes out. I think most of the team is back, so we are going *all the way!* You've heard of March Madness. In Indiana we call it Hoosier Hysteria. It's crazy all right."

"The whole team's coming back?" Maybe this won't be as easy as I thought. Gosh, what if Wally was right and I spend the whole season on the bench? Worse yet, what if I don't even make the bench? Why did we ever move here? Why did that drunk jerk get behind the wheel? Why couldn't Mom have given me one more year of varsity ball?

"Yeah, ever since three schools consolidated, our teams have been really good. See you tomorrow. Don't be putting any Gila monsters in our locker. Ha ha," she says and waves good-bye as she turns the corner to First Street.

I walk on alone, thinking I better talk to the coach. I have to see what this Sweet Sixteen team looks like.

Mary

ℭ

Baba has prepared another scrumptious dinner. She calls it *chomlek*. Some kind of beef, onion, and garlic stew that we all dunk our chunks of bread in.

Baba says, "In the old country, *chomlek* means *priest's stew*. We eat on Sundays. You put everything in one pot early in the morning. Cover and put on the fire. By the time church is done, the stew is done too."

"So it takes only an hour?" I ask.

"Oh, no. Church in the old country much longer than in America. In America, the chomlek would not be so tender. Everything in America is fast for Papa and Me. But we love America. We are so lucky to come here."

Ruby and Teddy load the dishwasher which Dan convinced Baba she needed to get with a big family here. It was installed a few days before we arrived but she has never used it. The clear stickers are still on the controls, which I see Teddy peeling off.

"Baba, why haven't you used your new dishwasher?" Teddy asks her.

"What? For my one dish I am going to push all those buttons?"

"That's okay, Baba. I'll push the buttons if you keep cooking all this good stuff," Teddy says.

"Of course, I keep cooking. Now I have someone to feed and my kitchen is busy place again. Happy place."

Teddy

After the kitchen is cleaned up I shoot some baskets and let Ruby chase me around the court. Buster cat watches silently from the corner of the patio like a sentry, reminding us that this is his domain. Winnie runs out, eager to join in. He gets right in Buster's face which causes the usual hissing. Winnie has a short memory and Buster plays good defense.

That night I dream I'm playing basketball with Wally. One-on-one, but there's someone in between us who keeps stealing the ball. Like Monkey in the Middle but I can't see the face. It jumps up and down like someone on a pogo stick and yes, it has red curly hair. Then we're in a big gym. It's packed and the crowd is on its feet. Someone makes a basket, the buzzer sounds, and the crowd goes wild. Middleburg wins! But I'm not on the floor or even on the bench. I'm in the bleachers. I didn't make the Hoosier team. This isn't a dream. It's a nightmare.

Mary

"Mary, it's Dianne from A Good Bookstore," the voice on the phone says. It is as pleasant as one would expect Mrs. Claus to be. "You left your application the other day. I'm impressed with your background. I think you'll be a good fit for my store. And I like your idea of starting a book discussion group. We have one but could use another time slot. Are you still interested?"

"Absolutely," I experience an instant surge of excitement, like seeing three sevens on a slot machine.

"Any questions?"

"Just how soon can I start?" Then I realize how desperate that must sound. "I guess we should talk about hours, pay, and those things." I hope that sounds a bit more professional. Then I level with her. "To be perfectly honest, Dianne, I am so happy to be working, I would probably volunteer."

Dianne laughs. "Come in and we'll talk specifics. The pay, as you can imagine, is not great, being a part-time position, but hopefully some other benefits for you."

My excitement turns to hope. Maybe this job falling into place so soon is a sign that Indiana will become a good home for us.

When I tell Baba, she looks happy for me. "I am good help to you, Mary. With the girls. You get out of the house. Meet nice people."

Teddy's *whatever* attitude brings my hopes down a notch. Is he afraid I will establish roots that keep us from returning to Arizona?

Before I go to sleep I open the book I picked up the other day — M. Scott Peck's *The Road Less Traveled*. I relate immediately to the first line. "Life is difficult."

Teddy

Mr. Beale, my English teacher, has a different Disney necktie every day. I'm wondering if Mondays are always Mickey Mouse and Dumbo is every Tuesday. It reminds me of Ruby's little frilly underpants that say *Sunday, Monday ....* Maybe his mother made him wear boxer shorts with the days of the week and he can't break the habit. Headline: TEACHER UNDERCOVER DISNEY AGENT.

For homework, he asks us to list our goals for the semester. My first reaction is that I can't be totally honest. Probably not a good idea to tell my teacher how much I don't want to be here. I start with an honest list for myself, knowing it won't be the one I turn in.

Goal # 1 Make the basketball team.

Goal # 2 Make some friends.

Goal #3 Stop missing Dad so much.

Goal #4 Stop being so mad at Mom.

Then I realize Goal #1 isn't going to happen unless I let the coach know I'm here, and soon.

The multi-colored elf shows up after school right on schedule as I start to walk home.

"So Mindy, who do you hang out with? How is it you have time to walk the new kid on the block?"

"Well, my best friend, Alicia, just moved. Remember?"

"Oh yeah. Alicia. Chicago. That's how you were sooo lucky to end up with me." My attempt to joke goes over her head, as she seems deep in thought.

"I've got a few other friends, but to be honest, I've never hung around with a whole bunch of kids. I've always had just one best friend, sort of. And to be *really* honest, I know I'm different than most kids. You probably figured that out already."

Now I'm wondering why I brought it up. Although she does remind me of one of the munchkins in *Wizard of Oz,* I don't want to make her feel bad. "Well, just because you don't like Gila monsters, that doesn't make you totally weird. Well, maybe a little." I'm rewarded with the turquoise smile.

"See, here's the problem." Mindy stops walking, looks around, and turns to me as if she's going to reveal a big secret. "I can't help it, but I've always been able to remember weird details that no one really cares about. Like Arizona becoming a state on Valentine's Day. That's not so bad, but then I blurt them out, usually at the worst possible time. "Like today, in science we were talking about atoms and I remembered reading that with each breath we take, we're exchanging about 10 sextillion atoms. Now the interesting part is that on any given day we could be breathing the same air that Plato, Buddha, and Einstein once breathed. Now who would remember that but me? And frankly, who cares? No wonder everyone thinks I'm strange."

I look at Mindy. "So are you saying, that no matter where or when we lived, we all breathe the same air?"

"Well, sort of. It has to do with the inhaling and exhaling and exchange of atoms and there are only so many in the universe. Do you want to see the book?" She looks excited like she's found a science soul mate.

"No, I'll take your word for it. So I could be breathing the same air as my friends in Arizona?"

"Well, not today, but it might be the same air they breathed in and out once upon a time."

"Let me get this straight. Einstein sneezes and hundreds of years later, I can catch his cold."

"Yeah," she says, "I guess you could." She punches my arm the way Wally used to.

Walking with Mindy is more like walking with another guy. Somehow she doesn't seem like a real girl, not like Liz or Pretty Green Eyes.

At home, I check for e-mails from Arizona. Nothing. Before I shut down the computer, I see the scribbles from the *Book of Life* again. *The past cannot be changed; the future is in your hands.* On a clean sheet of paper, I write the quote and put it on the bulletin board above my desk. I better start doing something about my future if I'm going to make the team. Like let someone know I'm even here.

The late refrigerator raids continue and so do the weird dreams. Wally and I are blowing up balloons and then letting the air out of them. I tell him I'm sending my used breath to Bulgaria. He laughs and says the humidity in Indiana is curling not only my hair but my brain too.

Mary

Dianne tells me she got a few calls about the book discussion date she posted. I'm eager to see how many show up tonight. I don't put out too many chairs out for fear they won't all be filled. Small is good for starters, I tell myself. I have name tags ready. I've thought of easy ice-breakers for introductions, like, "What was your favorite book growing up?" I also have a sample of books my group in Phoenix loved.

Dianne brings in a plate of chocolate chip cookies and sets it beside the coffee pot. "I love your enthusiasm for this. I wish I could join you but someone has to work the register. Talk loud so I can hear," she says over her shoulder as she leaves.

I smile to think of a discussion without wine. I thought it was a requirement for all book groups, but chocolate is an acceptable substitute.

By seven o'clock, four ladies and one man have wandered in. We introduce ourselves. I keep it informal with our first names only.

Gladys, probably in her 50s, is dressed smartly from head to toe in grey with a sweeping wrap-around shawl that she removes with a flourish. She speaks loudly and carries a huge book bag which she plops down in front of her chair. I wonder if she thinks she needs to supply all the books or perhaps these are her recommendations.

Lacy, a petite lady I am guessing to be in her 30s, speaks timidly. I'm wondering if her voice will be heard over Gladys'.

Debbie, a cute and perky blonde, literally bounces in her chair as she speaks enthusiastically with a southern accent. "I am so glad to *finally* be in a book group. My sister in Alabama talks about hers all the time. Just last week, she said to me, 'Girl, you need to find a group.' I'm not a fast reader but I just love to talk about the characters. Like Scarlett O'Hara. I could talk about her all night. I brought a list of all my sister's favorites. I think they read mostly romances but I'm not sure."

I see Gladys bristle at the romance comment. I need to reassure her that we'll be more mainstream. I don't want my first drop out before we even begin. "Thank you, Debbie. We'll take a look at them," I say, thinking if she reads only half as fast as she talks she'll have no problem keeping up.

We dub Clint the token man. He's handsome in a bookish yet rugged way with a crew neck sweater, Levis, boots, and tortoise glasses.

"Clint, it will be great to have a male perspective," I say.

"Do I need a permission slip from my wife to stay?" he asks with a wry grin.

The last lady is Rosetta, a tall stunning black lady, with a silken complexion the color of a caramel latte. Her long legs do justice to her designer jeans.

"I'm a surgical nurse and reading is my great escape from the pressures of the O.R.," she says. She looks about my age, mid- 40s?

"I love that our group tonight has a variance in ages," I say. "I've been in several book groups and I've found that the more varied our backgrounds, ages, and experiences, the richer the discussion."

I pull a book out of the bag beside my chair, *Snow Falling on Cedars* by David Guterson, and hold it up. "When our book group read this, a 70-year-old lady from the Northwest remembered that as a young girl, they studied the diagrams of Japanese planes so they could do plane-spotting on the coast. That's the kind of richness different ages and backgrounds can bring." I wanted to say this especially for Gladys who still appears to be in a huff over Deb's romance comment.

We talk about some of our favorite books and before we know it we are having a discussion of sorts that runs close to closing time. Gladys says the book I mentioned about WWII sounds good, and we go with it because there is something there for everyone: a murder trial, history, and for Deb, even romance.

Dianne pokes her head into the room at 9 o'clock and tells the group that even though she is closing, they can browse for a few minutes. I stay at the register to check them out. Rosetta brings up the latest Clive Cussler novel.

"Are you a Cussler fan?" I ask.

"No, it's for my husband. He loves them," she draws out the word *love.*

"My husband does, too," I say and then quickly correct myself, "I mean he did."

"So he got tired of Dirk Pitt's adventures? Seems to me the same character would get tiresome, but my husband says Cussler will never let him die."

Before I can think, the words tumble out. "Actually my husband is the one who died." I put my head down for a second, embarrassed about my outburst.

Rosetta cringes, "I am *so* sorry."

"It's okay. Just takes time, as they say. Whoever *they* are." I hear the grief counselor's words constantly like a running tape in my head, *Talking about Stan eases the grief process.* So I continue, "Stan grew up here and the kids and I came back to ... to be near family."

"Did you say *Stan?*"

"Yes. Stan Kostoff. Did you know him?" I ask eagerly.

Rosetta looks stunned and then says, "Yes, I did know Stan. Again, I'm so sorry." She looks at her watch. "My gosh, it's late. I'm sure you need to close up." She gathers her things and rushes out the door.

I forget that people are uncomfortable talking about death. I shouldn't have mentioned it. I start to close out the register when I notice car keys on the counter. I rush out the door and see Rosetta with her head leaning against the door on the driver's side.

I jingle the keys and she startles.

"I guess you won't get far without these."

Rosetta turns toward me. Even in the dim light of the parking lot, I think she looks frazzled.

"Are you okay?" I ask.

"I'm fine, thanks." She takes the keys and says, "Been a long day."

Rosetta

I put the key in the ignition but don't start the car. I can't believe the emotions running through me just hearing Stan's name spoken out loud. From his wife, no less.

I closed that chapter 30 years ago. And thought I closed it when I read his obituary. And again when I left the cemetery. But the wound is there. It's open and raw. What do I do now? Do I stay in this book club and subject myself to these feelings each week? Of course I can't. That's all in the past and it has to stay there.

As I undress for bed, James says, "Are you alright? Kind of quiet tonight. Was the book club a disappointment?"

"No, it was good." I answer quickly as if my thoughts will give me away. "Actually it was more than I expected." *A lot more.*

"That's good. You need a relaxing diversion from work. You've been putting in way too many hours." James turns off his bedside lamp and turns on his side.

I brush my teeth, put on moisturizer, and come back into the bedroom. From the light of the small lamp on my dresser I look at James who has dozed off. Even in his sleep he looks distinguished, the light blue pajamas a striking contrast against his ebony skin and silver curls. I love everything about him.

Yet, I make sure he is asleep when I reach into the top drawer of my dresser to the far back corner where there is a tiny jewelry box. I open it and pull out a ring that has traveled with my belongings for many years. It's a class ring with a green stone. The initials on either side of the stone are S.K.

Mary

⟨∞⟩

By the time I get home from work, everyone is in bed. I pour myself a glass of wine to unwind. I'm thinking the evening went well and the book discussion group shows promise. I'm surprised to see Baba hobbling down the hallway.

"Hello, Mary," she says.

"Are you feeling okay? Not able to sleep?" I ask.

"This arthritis. It's not letting me sleep. Maybe rain tomorrow. I was going to warm some milk."

"Let me get it," I say as I walk into the kitchen and pull out a small sauce pan. I'm thinking I will invest in a microwave for Baba's kitchen. "Here, I'll sit with you." I motion to the kitchen table, pour the milk, and set it on the burner.

"Did you like your job tonight?" Baba asks. "It is good place?"

"It's very nice. And guess what? I met a lady who knew Stan."

"Oh, that's nice." Baba says. "Stan have so many friends."

I pour the milk into a mug and Baba pulls a bottle of Bufferin out of her housecoat pocket. She sets two pills on the table and takes a sip of her milk. I sip my wine. "Do you know where Stan's yearbooks would be?" I ask, and when she looks puzzled, I realize she may not know what I am referring to. "The books from high school. With all the pictures?"

"Yes, yes, I know what you are talking about now."

I follow her as she walks to the dining room. I am not surprised she would have them, as Stan once told me that Baba is the archival queen and still has every trinket she brought from Bulgaria. "Here,

Mary, right here." Baba goes to a bookshelf with family albums, the old-fashioned kind with black corner stickers holding photos in place. She points to the bottom shelf. "There. I have books for Stan and Dan. I don't know why the boys leave them with me, but it's okay. I don't mind."

I look at the covers and take the one that says, *Middleburg Mavericks 1969* with a white stallion sporting a green saddle. I take it to the sofa and she sits beside me. She takes the book on her lap and immediately opens it to a page with a tattered corner. Stan's senior picture. I can tell she has done this more than a few times.

"There's our Stan. Such a handsome boy. And now we have handsome Teddy who looks like his daddy."

I can't resist hugging her as she hands me the book.

Baba goes back to the kitchen and takes her glass of milk. "I go to bed now with my milk. You look, Mary. You find lots of pictures of Stan here."

I turn to the index to see what pages have Stan's picture. In the sports section there is a team photo with a caption about a Holiday Tourney victory. Stan is in the back row between two black boys, all of them sporting wide grins. Baba was right. In the photo Stan looks just like Teddy does now.

On the opposite page are the cheerleader photos. A pretty black girl is perched on top of the pyramid of four white girls. I read the caption and discover the black girl is Rosetta from our book group. I smile to think of the coincidence. I will have to ask her if she was named after the Egyptian stone or the new language program. Her maiden name was Stone. It gives me a warm feeling to meet someone who knew Stan.

Teddy

 ❧

I get to school early the next day only to be told by the JV coach that Coach Burton is at a district coaches meeting. Shot down on my first goal.

"Can I help you?" The JV coach offers.

"Uh, I'll come back tomorrow. Thanks."

I think I should talk to the main guy but then again maybe it would be rude to refuse the JV coach's offer of help. I turn back.

"I just moved here and wanted to try out for the basketball team."

"Great. What's your name?"

"Teddy. Teddy Kostoff."

"That sounds familiar. You have an older brother who played here?"

"My dad and uncle. Long time ago."

"Oh yeah, I heard of those legends."

I never thought of my dad as a legend, but I say, "Thanks."

He says, "Coach Burton will be here tomorrow. Stop by."

I get through the day with no particular trauma. Mr. Beale, alias *Lion King*, doesn't read my paper in front of the whole class, Blonde Ponytail doesn't pass any notes about me to Pretty Green Eyes. Worse part is lunch. I take my sandwich outside and find a spot on the grass. There's nothing worse than eating alone in a cafeteria.

It's as if I don't exist. I remember the story we read in fourth grade about a kid being invisible. I thought then it would be cool. Now I know it isn't.

 ❧

The next day at Coach Burton's office, I see a stern-looking man behind the desk who looks more like a science teacher than a coach. Kinda scrawny with glasses and a lot older than Coach Mark in Arizona. He even looks older than Dad. He's *probably* lived here forever. He *probably* went to high school here. He's *probably* known this whole team since they were in pre-school. He's *probably* best friends with all their dads. All the good ol' boys. I'm a foreigner, an alien. I walk into the office and stand quietly, waiting for him to look up from his desk. I'm suddenly so nervous. I remember Dad saying, "You only have one chance to make a first impression." *Don't mess up, Teddy.*

He looks up and says, "Yes?"

Immediately, I think it's a bad time. He looks busy. Where's all that confidence I had in myself? In my jump shot? I left it somewhere on Wally's patio or on my goal sheet. For sure it's not with me now.

"Coach Burton, my name is Teddy." My voice comes out high and squeaky like I just inhaled a helium balloon. "I moved here from Arizona and I was wondering. Well, I was on the varsity basketball team there. It's a 5A school. And ... .and I was wondering if I could try out for your team." I realize I'm bumping my closed fists on the side of my thighs and clench them tighter to stop it and stand still. To display some level of confidence.

He looks at me for what seems like forever. It's probably only a few seconds, but it makes me so nervous, I ramble again, now at high speed, "Iknowyouhaveareallygoodteam, butI'dliketotryouttoo."

His eyes get wide, his head jerks back and then he blinks, like he's trying to decipher this foreign tongue I am now babbling. "Sure, Teddy, always looking for a good player, but it might be a tough year to break in. We're pretty much set for this year. We've had the same boys since they were freshmen. Seniors now. Been waiting a long time for this team to come together. But you're welcome to try. What year are you?"

"Junior."

"We have a strong junior varsity team. We'll be posting tryouts soon. Why not come out and we'll see what you've got."

"Thanks, Coach."

He's already looking down at the papers on his desk again. I'm not sure he even heard me say thanks. Even though he said I could try, I am discouraged. Something in his voice told me it would probably be useless. They were *all set.*

I don't want to play junior varsity. I did that my freshman year. Maybe I should just forget about basketball. Even though he didn't say, "Get lost kid," it feels like I have been totally dismissed.

On my way out, I see the JV Coach.

"Hey, I see you got to meet Coach Burton."

"Uh, yeah, I did."

"Everything okay?" he asks, looking at me like he cares.

"He said I could try out, but it sounds like the varsity team is pretty much in place."

"You never know. Come down and give it your best shot," he says and pats me on the shoulder. I wish he were the head coach.

When I get to my locker, I realize I was so nervous I didn't even tell Coach Burton my last name. Maybe he knew Dad and Uncle Dan. And what superstars they were. Maybe he would have thought I had the jump shot DNA in my cells. *I'm such a dork.* I slam my locker door shut and curse under my breath as Mindy walks up.

"Why so mad? "Missing your pet Gila monster?"

"I wish," I say.

We start walking and for a change she's not yakking a mile a minute. Then she says, "I guess it's hard to start all over." I realize she's trying to be kind. I tell her what Coach Burton said. "So you're not going to try out?"

"Sounds pretty hopeless."

"Well, it's a good thing Michael Jordan didn't have your attitude. You know, he never made the final cut his sophomore year."

"No way?"

"You never knew that? Sure, he was only 5'10". But he grew five inches that summer. Didn't make varsity until his junior year. Then there's Bill Russell. He had to share a jersey because 16 kids tried out for 15 spots."

"Bill Russell?"

"NBA, Most Valuable Player, 1946."

"Mindy, how do you know all this?"

"I like to read stuff like *World's Strangest Facts* or *Amazing Trivia.* It just comes back to me when I need it."

"Hey, someday you'll probably be in one of those strange and amazing books."

"You think so?" She looks pleased.

"Well, your memory's amazing ... and you're also very strange." I smile, hoping she will too.

She thinks about it a second and when I say, "Gotcha", she jabs an elbow into my side and turns the corner. Walking on alone, I realize that for a few minutes she gave me some hope. Maybe Coach Burton will think that the *all set* team needs me after all.

That night, lying in bed, looking out the window, I see a sliver of moon between the leafy branches and there's some comfort knowing Wally and Liz could be looking at the same moon. Then I'm sad to think that's all we have in common now — a distant celestial body. I didn't write to either of them tonight. I was so discouraged after school. I didn't want to sound like a whiner again. But I know it's also because neither one of them answered yesterday's e-mail yet.

I hear the sound of the leaves rustling in the cool evening breeze coming through my open window. Although I hate to admit anything good about this move, it is a nice change from windows sealed shut in Arizona, air-conditioner drowning out any outdoor sounds.

Then I hear it again. The music box! I run to the attic door and climb the stairs. Why doesn't anyone else hear it? I hear a noise in the corner and my heart beats faster. My feet are glued to the floor. I'm afraid to move. Then I see Buster's green eyes glowing in the dark. Just like a sneaky cat to follow me. Give me a barking dog any day. I decide to take the box to my room where I can make some sense of this. It might add a nice touch. A haunted music box.

Softly, I tiptoe down the attic stairs. I look like an overgrown Hardy boy. Headline: BOY DETECTIVE SOLVES ATTIC MYSTERY.

But why not? Everything else in my life is a mystery to me right now.

"Teddy, wait for me!" It's the munchkin running to catch up as I walk home from school. "Going to the game tonight?"

"I think my uncle said something about the whole family going."

Mindy confirms, "Oh yeah, Friday night football is a family thing in Middleburg. You don't even have to have a player on the team. Bleachers are packed every game."

We walk in silence for a minute. "Hey, want to do something fun tomorrow?" she asks excitedly.

"Like what?" I ask skeptically, as if there can't possibly be anything fun in Middleburg.

"I don't know. Anything. I could show you the Old Fort from the 1800s. It's kind of neat. We could climb to the top."

"Does this mean I get a history lesson?" I'm trying to be clever but afraid I've hurt her feelings. *Good, shoot down the one person who's nice to me.* If I did, she doesn't show it. I hand her my notebook. "Why don't I call you when I get home? Here, write your number down."

When we get to the corner where she turns off, I say, "The fort sounds good Mindy. I'm sorry if I sound rude sometimes. In Arizona I'd be going to the game with a bunch of friends and here I'm hoping my uncle doesn't try to pass me off on my cousin and her girlfriends."

"It's okay," she says.

We say our good-byes at the corner and I walk the rest of the way wondering how my life could change so much in just a few months.

I follow my nose to the kitchen, which smells like a pizza joint. Baba is very proud of her pizza, so neither Mom nor I have the heart to tell her that we haven't eaten pizza since the fateful night. But somehow it's okay here. This is not take-out pizza. It's Baba's special creation. She's hunched over a big lump of dough.

I bend down and kiss the cheek that has a smudge of flour on it. "Hi, Baba. Smells good."

"Tastes good too. You'll see. When your dad and Uncle Dan were boys, all the time they want to buy the pizza. When I taste, I say I can make better. Every Friday I make the pizza. All their friends, they say my Bulgarian pizza better than store pizza." She gives the dough another punch and I'm thinking she's got a great right hook. "I don't make for long time. Now, I start again. Whole family is coming tonight. Your Uncle Dan, Aunt Joyce, Sophie. Then everyone go football game. Your Mama, she is going too. I stay with girls."

I realize there's no way I'm going to get out of this big family outing. I go to my room to check e-mail.

"You've got mail." Yes! From Wally.

> *Hey man, I miss you too Bud. Tonight's the big game against Red Mountain Shadows. Remember last year? We ruined their Homecoming. I think they're out for revenge now. History with Mr. Wise is as bad as you said it would be, but at least he's letting us sit where we want. Frank, Judy, Liz, and me are a study group and we have our own round table at the back of the room. We're writing own version of history. Class of 2001. Write back.*

Instead of feeling better, there's now an ache spreading through my chest, wishing I were at the round table. I'm not writing back to admit I'm going to a Friday night game on the family plan. Why don't we take a bucket of chicken and lap blankets like all the old geezers do? I know I can't answer Wally's e-mail until things are better here. What century will that be?

Then I hear it. The tinkling sound. I reach under the bed and the music box is playing, softly, slowly. I pull it out, trying to figure out what makes it start.

"Hi Teddy, whatcha doing?" Ruby's standing in the doorway with Cathy hanging on to the bottom of Ruby's t-shirt with one hand and her other thumb in her mouth.

"Oh nothing." I slide the box under my bed and kneel down in front of the girls. "So what are you two doing tonight with Baba?"

"Mommy got us *The Little Mermaid* to watch on TV and we get popcorn too."

"Wow! That sounds like fun." I pick Cathy up and she hugs me tight around the neck. As usual, it makes things better and I take Ruby's little hand in mine.

When we get downstairs we see Uncle Dan in the backyard with huge cardboard boxes. The girls and I walk out. They squeal and jump up and down when they see the picture on the box of a swing set and sliding board.

When Ruby runs to Uncle Dan, he picks her up and hugs her. I feel a catch in my chest and my cheeks get hot with shame of my bad attitude about my family. They are trying so hard to make a home for us here.

"Need some help, Uncle Dan?" I ask him while I blink back the tears.

Rosetta

First I couldn't stop thinking of Stan. Now I can't stop thinking about Mary. I feel the need to go back to book group but don't understand why. Is it to know more about Stan's life? Is it to have a connection with him after all these years? Doesn't make any sense, but then again, what happened between Stan and me never did make sense. Is love ever sensible?

I go back to the bookstore to get my copy of the book we're discussing. Mary recognizes me immediately, smiles, and calls me by name.

"Rosetta, I've got your copy here on the hold shelf. Our order just came in today."

"I'll just browse a bit." I wander through the book aisles still pondering if I should opt out of the group. I could tell Mary my work schedule switched to evenings. But I won't. Is it so wrong to want to know more about Stan's life? Surely, that won't hurt anyone.

As I'm ready to leave, Mary approaches me hesitantly, "Rosetta ...," she begins and pauses. "I'm about to take a short break. Would you ... would you have time to have a cup of coffee with me? I don't mean to make you uncomfortable but my grief counselor said the more I talk about Stan, the better I might heal. I would think the opposite but I would love to talk to someone who knew him in high school. We didn't meet till college." The words spill out of Mary quickly and apologetically. "Do you remember anything about what he was like then? I'd love to know." Her eyes plead.

Once again I want to bolt, but Mary is so earnest. I like her. Her honesty, her openness, putting herself on the line like that. How can I refuse? "I'd love to Mary."

We go to Cup a Cuppa across the street and find a corner table in the back.

The waitress takes our order, and while we wait, Mary asks, "So have you lived in Middleburg all your life?"

"No, I left after high school for Chicago. I have a lot of family there." My mind is racing. *How much to say? Why did I agree to this?*

Our coffees arrive.

"So what brought you back?" Mary asks.

"My father always dreamed of having a little bit of land. Country living with some livestock. I think he watched *Green Acres* too often. So when he retired a few years ago in Chicago — he was a doctor — he convinced my mom to make the move. They're about 12 miles out of town."

I add more cream to my coffee. "We first moved here in '68 ... my senior year... when the auto assembly plant opened. My dad worked at their medical facility for one year but then we went back to Chicago." I don't tell Mary why we left Middleburg.

"When my parents returned here, I wanted to be near them. Mom's in remission with melanoma but it was a wake-up call to me that they aren't going to be here forever. Luckily, I had no trouble getting a job — nursing shortage everywhere it seems." I don't tell Mary the other reason I came back — "the rest of the story," as Paul Harvey used to say. Nor do I say that I made sure Stan no longer lived here before I returned.

Mary sets her cup in the saucer and looks at me. "Stan didn't talk a lot about high school, except of course basketball. The Holy Grail. Oh, by the way, I saw your cheerleader picture in his yearbook. Very nice."

I say, "Wow, that's going way back."

"So, was Stan popular?" Mary asks. Then she adds quickly with a sheepish smile. "I think I know the answer. Guess I just want to hear it. Or tell me anything you remember about him."

My mind is scrambling. *Remember? I remember his hazel eyes, the dimple in his chin I loved to touch. That's what I remember.*

Mary fiddles with the sweetener packets while she waits for an answer.

Think Rosetta. Think of something you can say. "Well, let me think a minute," I say, stalling for time, twisting my wedding band, like it's a magic lamp that might make a story appear. "I remember one thing. Stan was always for the underdog. There was this scrawny kid named Homer." I give a little chuckle. "I ask you, first of all, what chance does a kid named Homer have to begin with? He was pimply, wore thick glasses. You could tell by looking at him he had zero confidence. One day he dropped his tray in the lunch room. Food splattered everywhere. Some of the *cooler* guys, as we called them back then when, really, they weren't cool at all, started laughing and poking fun at him. They have a name for it today — bullying. Several kids walked by and ignored it. But not Stan. He went up to the thugs and said, 'Knock it off.' And then he went to Homer and helped him pick up his food."

Mary puts her hands over her eyes and starts crying.

"I'm sorry. I didn't mean to ...," I say.

"No, no. It's a good cry. That is so like Stan. Thank you, Rosetta. Thank you for that story."

Mary's face is so eager that I continue. "I think everyone liked Stan. He was easy-going, had a great sense of humor. We had a chemistry class together."

"Really? Was he a brain or goof off?"

I laugh. Both I think. He could goof off and get away with it 'cause he knew when to stop clowning and come up with exactly the right answer."

"Oh, a brown nose?" Mary smiles. "I am not surprised."

"You might say that," I say.

Mary stares deep into her coffee cup. When she looks up there are more tears in her eyes. "That's how Teddy used to be, but now ... I don't know, he hardly laughs anymore."

"Teddy?" Rosetta asks.

"Oh, I'm sorry. Our son. My son. He's a junior now." Mary pauses. "It's been hard for him ... 'cause ... well, I know we've barely met but I feel I can trust you. *Please* don't repeat this. It's one reason we moved back here. Where everyone doesn't know how it happened." Mary leans forward and whispers, "Teddy was driving the car when they had the accident."

"Oh no!" I cringe. I instinctively reach across the table and put my hand over Mary's. "How awful for him. For all of you." I remember the obituary saying there were three children. I ask, "You have other children?"

Mary's blue eyes brighten. "Two girls. Ruby is seven and Cathy's four. They're doing better than Teddy. How about you? Children?" She pushes her hair behind her ears. "Hope I'm not too nosy."

"Of course not. Actually, I'm sort of a newlywed," I give her a shy smile.

"James and I have only been married five years. I was a single mom for a long time when I met James. Actually, my son introduced us. James was one of his college professors."

"You don't look old enough to have a son in college," Mary says, then adds, "I guess what I'm saying is you don't look as old as Stan, but you're probably the same age."

I laugh, "Well, thank you. Actually, my son's not in college anymore. Been out several years now."

"No way," Mary says. "You must have been a child bride." Then she looks embarrassed. "I'm sorry. That was tacky. I meant that in the best way. I mean you just look so young."

"No offense taken. I *was* very young. Thank goodness I had a big family to help me raise him."

"Is your son …," Mary starts to ask when I notice a buxom lady approach our table.

"Rosetta, I thought that was you. Nice to see you."

"Hello Martha." I nod toward Mary. "Martha, this is Mary Kostoff. She works at A Good Bookstore."

Martha smiles. "It *is* a good bookstore. I'm a regular there."

"Speaking of work, I better get back." Mary looks at me. "Thank you so much." She picks up the check and says again, "Really. Thanks a lot."

I am grateful for Martha's interruption. It gives me breathing room and time to think about how to answer Mary the next time she asks about my son.

Mary

～

Driving home from work, I think about Rosetta's comment. *Stan was always for the underdog.* Is that how I appeared the day Stan and I met? Was that what attracted me to him? I always did wonder why someone as handsome as Stan became interested in me. A mousy girl with so little confidence.

I relive that day now in my mind's eye, as I have a few times since Stan passed. The memory is in vivid detail, perhaps real or perhaps embellished through the years and especially these past months.

I was walking, actually running, to class with an armful of books that started slipping from my arms. I got caught in a downpour with no umbrella and one of the books splashed into a puddle. As I bent to pick it up, a long arm beat me to it and another hand took my elbow, pulling me toward him.

"Let's get under the gazebo." The gazebo was in the center of the campus square under the clock tower. Several other students had gathered there for shelter from the sudden cloud burst and we were packed in closely.

"Thank you," I said, looking up at the tall handsome boy beside me. The clock chimed three times. "Now I'm really going to be late. Not the best class to be late to. I'm hanging on by a thread as it is."

"I'll vouch for you. I'll say you tried to get there but I held you hostage in the gazebo."

I laughed and then became very self-conscious as I thought of how awful I must look with my hair drenched. His dark wavy hair didn't seem disturbed at all by the rain. More students piled in, pushing me even closer to him. He bent down and put his arms around me in a protective manner. When I looked up into his hazel eyes, I felt a flutter in my heart and let my head press on his chest. I remember hoping the rain would never stop.

When the rain let up, he said, "What will it be? Late to class or coffee with me?"

I had no trouble deciding and we walked to the Student Union. He asked me about my classes and I told him I was trying to catch up in all of them. He was so concerned and kind that I unburdened myself in a way I hadn't to anyone.

"My parents both died recently." I told him.

"I'm sorry. At the same time? Was it an accident," he asked, his warm eyes, now more green than brown, showing genuine concern.

"No, my mother had a long struggle with breast cancer and four months later my dad died of a heart attack. I think he just gave up without her."

"Brothers or sisters?"

"No. Just me. Toward the end my mother made me promise to finish college. They both worked hard to set aside the money for it. They only had high-school educations. So I really need to do it. Not just for me, but for them." I remember gathering up my books. "And that's why I really shouldn't be cutting any more classes. Thanks for the coffee but I really have to go."

Once again he took my books. "Absolutely, you need to go. Let me walk you. Which building is your next class?"

Now in Baba's driveway, I let the tears flow before I go in so Teddy won't see me crying.

Yes, I thought. *You might say I was an underdog of sorts*. Or a damsel in distress. He appeared out of nowhere like a gallant knight in shining armor. Saved me from the rain. Then carried my books like an old-fashioned school boy.

I think in that very moment, I was smitten.

Teddy

It felt good to sit next to Uncle Dan in the bleachers last night. He's the closet thing I have now to Dad. Dad with an extra 20 pounds. When he put his arm around my shoulder, for a minute, I pretended he was Dad. Kinda sick, I know, but I'll take it.

"So what would you like to do today, Teddy?" Mom asks at the breakfast table. She looks more like Mom than she has for months. The dark circles that have been under her pretty blue eyes all summer are gone. Maybe she's not prowling around all night like she did in Arizona.

"I have this friend who wants to show me around town a little."

She can hardly contain her enthusiasm to think I might actually have a friend. "Great! What's his name?"

"*Her* name is Mindy."

"Teddy has a girlfriend, Teddy has a girlfriend." Ruby chants and grins her toothless smile.

"She's not a girlfriend," I pinch Ruby's chubby cheek. "She's just a friend friend."

Ruby dips a piece of her waffle in syrup. "I have a friend, too. Heather. I call her Heather Feather, and she plays mostly with me and we're in charge of the grocery store for the whole class."

"Bet that grocery has lots of junk food, huh?" I tease her.

"No, we have *everything*. All five food groups!"

"Food groups? Vat kind of food is group?" Baba asks.

While Ruby tries to explain the food pyramid to Baba, Mom and I share a smile. It's been a long time since we've done that.

Mary

✑

Even though Baba has never heard of the food pyramid, we're eating better than we have all summer. The kitchen counter has a constant display of what she has picked from her garden that day. Tomatoes, peppers, zucchini. Ruby has adopted a little pumpkin that Baba promises will be just the right size by Halloween.

Uncle Dan, Aunt Joyce, and Sophie stop by to pick up the care package Baba has prepared for Michelle, Sophie's sister, who is a freshman at Indiana University. From the size of it, it will feed the entire dorm. The kitchen smells like a bakery with sheets of cookies and cheese-filled phyllo triangles.

The university is less than an hour's drive and they invite me and the girls to join them but I'm afraid to confront the memories on the campus where Stan and I met.

Baby steps my grief counselor said. *Take baby steps and don't put yourself in situations that are too painful.* Seeing the gazebo where Stan first held me close might definitely fall into the *too painful* category. Baba's kitchen seems a safe refuge today.

Never met a zucchini that made me cry.

Teddy

❧

A few hours later Mindy and I ride our bikes to the edge of town and she points to a grey brick fort on a high hill. "We're headed up there. Can you make it Desert Boy?"

"Yeah, Shorty. I can make it. We do have mountains in Arizona you know. You should see Camelback Mountain. From a distance it looks like the head and hump of a kneeling camel. Kinda the same color too."

"That's cool. Did you know that camels don't really store water in their humps like most people think?"

"So what's in those humps? Wait, don't tell me — I'm not sure I want to know."

"It is kind of gross. I read something about fatty tissue."

"Yuk. But speaking of water, I forgot to bring some," I say.

"Never fear, Mindy's here." She pulls her backpack out of her bike basket as we lock our bikes in the rack in the parking lot.

"Well, let me carry it," I say as I sling it over my shoulders. "What in the world is in here? Are we camping out overnight?"

"Just a few snacks," Mindy grins.

We start climbing, and at one marker she tells me about the 1811 Battle of Tippecanoe which led to the war of 1812. "William Henry Harrison was governor of the Indiana Territories, but I'll spare you the history lesson. Mostly I want you to see the views."

"Spare me? I think I just got a big dose of it. On a Saturday yet."

We climb narrow-notched stairs built into the sides of the fort and are going mostly vertical except for meandering side trails to get a different view. We enter small rooms with openings for lookout points.

Just before we reach the summit, Mindy finds a flat area and says, "How about a snack before we get to the top?"

I sit down beside her and hand her the backpack. She pulls out two water bottles and a sack of sandwiches. She hands me one of each and wastes no time taking a huge bite of her croissant.

"You sure eat a lot for a small person," I say.

"Brain power burns tremendous calories." She takes another bite. "I'm surprised you have any appetite at all." She laughs.

I try to think of a witty comeback but my mouth is full. After I swallow I say, "These taste great, but please don't tell any guys I said so. Aren't croissants like quiche? Like real men don't eat them?"

That warrants a smile from her. "Do you know where the croissant came from?"

"Uh, let me guess. A French bakery? Of course that's going to be the wrong answer because it is way too obvious."

"Actually, it's an Austrian pastry. In the 17th century, the Turks invaded Vienna by trying to tunnel under the city's walls. The invasion was unsuccessful thanks to the vigilance of the only people who were awake during the nighttime raid — the bakers. To celebrate the victory, they created the croissant, shaping it like the crescent moon on the Turkish flag." She holds up an uneaten croissant to illustrate. "I find that so fascinating."

"Oh, me too. I will never feel the same about a croissant."

"Let's go," she says. "We're almost to the top."

Soon I'm looking out over most of Middleburg while Mindy plays tour guide, almost boasting, like she's trying to sell me a new subdivision lot.

She pulls out a pair of binoculars from her backpack. "There's the high school and the Methodist church on the corner. The big white steeple looks like a Playskool toy, doesn't it?" She turns to the other direction. "There's the golf course and look, Teddy, over there. Ooooo, the cemetery. Are you scared?"

I turn to look down and suddenly there's a knot in my stomach and a tightness in my chest. Headline: SATURDAY ADVENTURE TURNS SOUR.

"What's the matter Teddy? You aren't really scared, are you?"

"No, I ...." I look at Mindy's little freckled face. She looks apologetic.

"No, I'm not afraid Mindy. I'm just ... well, see the reason we moved back to Indiana is ... is because my dad." The words don't come out. Mindy appears puzzled and for once is silent. "See, my dad's buried in that cemetery. He died four months ago. And now we're all back here. I'm not really sure why."

I see Mindy's eyes watering behind her goofy purple glasses.

I go on. "My grief counselor said to try and talk about it, that it will help. So, I'm talking about it."

"Oh Teddy, I am so sorry ... I'm such a dork."

"No, you're not. You didn't know."

"So have you been to the cemetery since you got here?"

"No. And if Mom has, she hasn't said anything to me." She said we were moving here because we needed a new start. We needed to be with family. She never said it, but maybe the real reason we're here is she wants to be close to Dad."

We both just stand there, looking down at the view. Standing above Mindy, I see the sun shine through her bright red curls making them almost a transparent orange. The lightness of the day is gone, but it's like that tight feeling in my chest has loosened just a bit. Here I am talking to a girl I barely know about Dad. I never talked about him to Wally or Liz, my best friends. I'm finally talking about something that matters. Not trying to cover it up, or to be cheerful when I'm not. And she just listens and looks like she understands. I never could have understood before it happened to me.

On the other side of the fort I see a man and small boy, climbing, laughing. All of a sudden I feel the ache. Blink, blink, squint under my sunglasses. I look out over the cemetery and know what I need to do.

"Mindy, do you mind if we head back home? I'm glad we came, but there's something I need to do. I need to see my dad's ... my dad's grave." Just saying the word "grave" startles me. I've never said it out loud.

When we head our bikes back into town, Mindy shows me the

shortest route to the cemetery. At the entrance, I say, "Thanks, Mindy. I did like the fort. Really."

"Sure Teddy. See you Monday." She gives me a little wave and starts to pedal.

I watch her leave but she turns around. She hops off her bike and runs to me. I see tears on her cheeks. She gives me a quick hug around the waist and says, "I'm so sorry Teddy." Then before I can respond she hops back on her bike and takes off.

My eyes start to water too. I don't know if it's for Dad or because someone seems to understand. The weirdest thing pops into my mind. A yellow brick road? Maybe because Mindy is such a munchkin. A munchkin who definitely has a brain and now a heart. That leaves courage and I'm the one who needs a big dose of that now.

I take a deep breath before going through the black iron gates, opened wide enough for two cars. My heart is beating fast like before a big game, but game butterflies are good. These feel scary. I wonder if Mom will be upset that I am doing this without her. I don't want to make anyone mad, but I need to do this now. Today.

Once inside, the paths branch off so many ways, I have no idea where to go. I start riding around slowly. All I remember from the day of the funeral is that my shoes got muddy walking back to the car, so the grave must not be too close to the road. I ride back to the entrance and prop my bike near a tall headstone that stands out from the others. *Nelson Family.*

The more I walk through the grassy headstones, the more discouraged I get. It was dumb to come here without Mom. Why hasn't she brought us here? I wander aimlessly, looking at names. Some of the plots have fresh flowers. Others look neglected. Is that how Dad's would have looked if we hadn't moved back here? Baba would come often if she wasn't dependent on someone for a ride. I'm getting frustrated and am close to tears again. I should give this up and come back with Mom.

Then I think I hear the song. The one from the music box. It can't be. I follow the sound and just when I think I'm getting close to it, it stops. I look to my right, my left, and then just ahead of me is a shiny gray stone with the name: Stanley Kostoff. I have goose bumps all over. I walk closer to the stone and touch it.

Under Dad's name it says *1952-1999. Beloved husband, father, son, and brother.* I sit at the foot of the plot, my hands wrapped around my knees. The grass is warm. It's quiet except for a bird chirping and a passing car slowly crunching the gravel on the road. I wonder what people are supposed to do at cemeteries. Do they talk to the person? Do they pray? The only prayer I can think of right now is the blessing before we eat. Somehow, that doesn't seem right.

There were so many things I wanted to say to him these past few months, but now I can't think of a thing. I remember the argument Dad and I had just before the accident. I forgot to set the garbage out on trash day, and Dad said something about my not being responsible. I muttered something under my breath and he said, "If you have something to say, let's hear it."

It's too late now. Because now no matter what I say, Dad can't hear any of it. Or can he? Then I think about the music. Did I really hear it, or did I imagine it? I have to get out of here. My imagination's going wild. I stand up, touch the top of Dad's stone, and say, "I'll be back, Dad. I promise." I look up, spot my landmark, the tall Nelson headstone, and run to it.

Mary

I send an email to Kate.

Subject: Hoosierville update

Dear Kate: I will be brief and hit the highlights.

1. I miss you (not a highlight — that's a very low light).
2. Teddy is trying out for varsity basketball. Pray he makes it so he forgives me for taking him away from Arizona.
3. I'm gaining weight (knew that would make you happy). Baba's delicious meals leave no carbs unturned. Also a Paula Dean disciple — everything is better with butter ... or Crisco.
4. Now sleeping through most nights. Maybe it's the little twin bed I have in the small guest room. Much better than the lonely king-size bed without Stan.
5. Ruby has stopped wandering into my bed at night. Maybe she took one look at my twin bed and decided to go back to her room. Whatever. It's a good thing.
6. The leaves are gorgeous. I forgot how beautiful autumn is in the Midwest.
7. Okay, drum roll — how could I forget this? I got a job! Only part time but at a charming little bookstore-A Good Bookstore — yes, that's really the name. I get to

lead a book discussion group! Met a lady who knew Stan but she's probably sorry she mentioned it — I latched on to her like she's my new best friend.
8. Speaking of friends, did I mention? I miss you.

Love, Mary

Teddy

⌒〰⌒

When I get back to the Nelson headstone to retrieve my bike, I see an old, kinda frail man with a blue Chicago Cubs cap holding one handlebar and looking at my rear tire.

"Is this your bike, son?"

"Yes, I didn't want to ride it through the … the graves. See, I wasn't sure where I was going … and I thought this big headstone would be easy to find again."

"I was keeping an eye on it. Kids will tear through here, you know. Usually at night. They climb over the fence and scare each other to death. Well, not really, or else they wouldn't be leaving. They'd be staying here." He laughs at his little joke, which I don't think is very funny. But to be polite, I give him a weak smile.

"So did you find what you were looking for?" he asks.

"Uh, yes sir." I don't want to talk about Dad, but he just keeps looking at me like I need to explain. "My dad. He's over there." I point 'cause I can't say the word *buried*. "I've only been here one other time."

"I'm sorry. He must have went before his time. Did he pass just recently?"

"In May."

The old man takes off the Cubs hat and runs his hand over a grey crew cut. "May?" He scratches his head and scrunches up his eyes like he's trying to think of who it might be. "Sometimes it's hard to understand why things happen. I've been the caretaker for 12 years — ever since I retired. I've seen a lot of things that don't make sense. You come anytime and as often as you like, but be careful. I just wouldn't want someone to take this nice bike. Although it's a lot easier to replace a bike than a dad."

No kidding. "Isn't it kind of hard to work here? Where everyone's so sad?"

"Well, yes and no. I see a lot of sadness but I figure that's why the good Lord put me here. Whenever I get a chance, I try to say something to remind people that life goes on and it will be better."

"How long does it take — to get better?"

"Well, a lot of that depends on how much people want it to. I mean some things you can't rush. It takes time."

Oh, no! That time word again.

He puts his cap back on and leans on his rake. "People who ignore their feelings find out years later they're crying for no reason at all. It's that grief they kept bottled up all those years. I've seen a grave that's had no visitors or attention for years. Then all of a sudden there are fresh flowers every week. Everybody's gotta deal with it in their own way." I nod 'cause I don't know what else to say. "Are you finding a way to deal with it?" He looks at me like Mom does when she says, "Did you finish your homework?"

"I don't know. We just moved here and I left my friends in Arizona. I'm trying to find my niche here, if you know what I mean."

"Sure, I know. We all gotta belong somewhere. Say son, what's your name?"

"Teddy."

"Had a friend in the Marine Corps named Teddy. Nice chap from Virginia. Or was it West Virginia? Anyway, Teddy, what I wanted to say is someone doesn't have to die for you to grieve for them. You're probably grieving the loss of your friends in Arizona and your life there. Even though it's still going on, you're not a part of it. There's lots of kinds of losses and lots of kinds of grief. So you got a double dose going right now."

Gee, thanks for that reminder. Was this guy a psychologist in disguise? Dressed up like a caretaker and just hanging around tomb-stones to catch people in their time of need? Was I going to get a bill in the mail next week for graveside chat? Maybe psychologists don't really need a couch. *Here, just pull up a patch of this nice green grass and tell me all about it.*

I'm about to get on my bike and escape the lecture when he says, "I'm saying some truths you might not be ready to hear, Teddy. I hope I haven't said too much. If you don't mind my asking, what is your dad's name?"

I grab the handlebars but turn to answer, "Stan. Stan Kostoff."

"Oh son, I knew your dad. For many years. I saw him grow up."

I feel goose bumps on my arms. "You knew my dad?" I ask, feeling a pang of hope, or is it relief, like I found a lost pet. I realize how much I want to talk about him.

"Knew him and his brother too. In a town this size everyone knows everyone. Stan and Dan. They were quite the ball players. I think they called them the Dynamic Duo. Your dad was a fine young man. I was sorry to hear about his passing."

The familiar blink blink is starting the way it often does when people are kind. I don't want to cry now. A car passes slowly. The caretaker waves at them, and while his head is turned I wipe my nose with my sleeve.

"Are you alright, son?"

"No. I mean yes. I was just thinking. I never thought about grief for the living things. There was this lady in the grief seminar Mom and I went to who said she was grieving for her house. She lost it in a tornado a long time ago."

"Sure, it can be things as well as people. Loss is loss. So how are you coping, Teddy?"

"I just go to school every day. That's about all I can do right now. When I make the basketball team, everything will be better."

"And if you don't?"

"I haven't thought about that." I'm thinking this guy has a way of making bad things even worse than they are. *Very uplifting.*

"A fella should have a back-up plan. You're a nice young boy. Coming here to pay your respects and all. I bet you had lots of friends at home." He smiles. "Me and the Misses, we always wanted to take that trip to Arizona. To see that big hole in the ground."

"Yeah, the Grand Canyon is pretty awesome," I say as if I had ownership or anything to do with it.

"I don't pretend to know it all, Teddy, but sometimes you gotta put yourself in a place where the people aren't doing so well. Then you realize things aren't so bad with you after all. What's that saying, 'I cried because I had no shoes till I saw the man with no feet.'?"

"Like there's always someone worse off?"

"Yes, like that."

"Well, to be honest, Mr. ..."

"George, just call me George."

"Well, George, I don't mean to be disrespectful, but sometimes those sayings just ... well, they're kinda far-fetched. A little too exaggerated, you know?"

George laughs and says, "Well, you're an honest boy, Teddy. Sometimes talk is just talk. It's really doing something for someone else that makes a person feel better. My sweet wife, rest her soul, used to visit the nursing home every time she started feeling her aches and pains. She always came home counting her blessings."

"Sounds like my Baba. She's got more energy than me. I better head back home. No one knows I'm here today."

"You run along, Teddy. Come back any time. If you ever need help, just stop in there." He points to the small red brick building near the entrance. He picks up a tray full of clippers and walks away with a little backward wave raising the rake in his right hand. He turns and points the rake to my bike. "Your back tire looks a little low."

Rosetta

On my day off I make my weekly visit to my parents' home in the country. It's a relaxing scenic drive through the back roads surrounded by fields of corn, now tall and ready to tassel. I pass one of my favorite picturesque houses, a sprawling brick ranch home set back from the road with a red barn beside it. I pass the orchard where even from the road I can see branches laden with red apples begging to be picked.

I look forward to seeing what new plants and vegetables my father is experimenting with. I smile at the memory of the year he crossed a plum tree with an apricot tree. When, to his delight, it actually bore fruit, he called it a plumcot. He made a big production of giving it to me, saying, "This fruit, Rosetta, is just like you — one of a kind." Then he went on to elaborate on a recent article he had read in the medical journal that said *like snowflakes, no two humans are alike, not even identical twins.*

To this day, his constant praise of me can trigger feelings of guilt, even after so many years have passed since I disappointed him. His dream, and mine, of following his footsteps to becoming a doctor never materialized. A black girl majoring in pre-med was rare in the '60s. A pregnant black girl was even more unlikely. Through the years, he never once brought it up but always reminded me how important good nurses were. My mother, on the other hand, was not as forgiving of my behavior but through the years she relented and especially with her cancer, she mellowed.

"Rosetta!" She comes out to the porch when she sees my car pull into their circular drive. By the time I park the car, she's in the driveway, arms outstretched for my hug. "You're just in time for lunch. I made your favorite. Chicken pot pie."

"That's what I was hoping. Where's Dad?"

"As they say, somewhere on the south 40."

"That means he's in someone else's field since you only have 10 acres."

"He should be along any minute now. You know your Dad is not about to miss a meal. Especially with you."

"You mean especially with chicken pot pie, don't you?"

She laughs just as I hear his little John Deere tractor coming up the road. He's wearing bib overalls and a big floppy hat that brings a smile to my face, as it does each time I see him that way. Quite a contrast to the crisp white lab coat he wore the last 40 years.

It's a warm and sunny autumn day and Mom has set three places on the patio table.

"So are you keeping those doctors in shape, Rosetta?" Dad says as he takes a second helping of pot pie.

"Of course," I answer. I look at his plate and shake my head. "I don't know how you stay so trim Dad."

"Good clean living. Working hard in the fields." He gives me a boastful smile. "And I might add that all the vegetables in this pie are from my garden."

"You spend so much time in the sun. Are you wearing your sunscreen?"

"Now who's being the doctor?" he asks me. "I've told you many times, black don't crack." One of his favorite lines.

I smile to appease him. "It may not crack but you're not immune, you know." I feel my advice is falling on deaf ears in spite of Mom's melanoma scare.

"So what else is new with you?" my mother asks.

"Joined a book discussion group. I think I'll like it."

I realize I want so much to tell them about meeting Mary and about Stan's passing but that doesn't make any sense. They never met him, and by mutual agreement we never spoke of him after …

"What are you discussing?" Mom's question breaks my thoughts.

"*Snow Falling on Cedars*. It's good so far. And so is this lunch,

Mom. Your crust is so flaky. I never got the knack of that. Thank heaven for Pillsbury."

"I think I read that book last year. Isn't that the one about WWII? The Japanese family that gets sent to an internment camp? And then the girl's husband is on trial for murder?"

"Yes, that's the one." I answer.

We both deftly side-step one of the main themes of the book. Like the elephant in the room, we don't mention the heartache and angst of forbidden teen love.

Teddy

∞

"Teddy, time for school. You overslept." Mom is shaking my shoulder. "What's this?" She looks at the quote on my bulletin board. *The past cannot be changed, but the future is in your hands.*

"Something for English class." Mom can always tell when I'm lying and I don't know why I did, but I'm hoping my sleepy answer fools her.

"Well, it would certainly be a good motto for us all this year." She tucks her chin in the way she does when she thinks something is a good idea. "Baba has breakfast for you. Better scoot."

I think of the quote while I shower. By the time I'm dressed I have given myself a pep talk. *Okay, Teddy, you can't change the past. Start doing something to make your future better. Something besides your jump shot. You haven't tried to talk to anyone in any of your classes.*

Mr. Beale and his Disney companion of the day are late for first hour and everyone's talking when I walk in. Blonde Ponytail and Pretty Green Eyes are leaning across their aisle. So instead of mumbling, "Excuse me," I say, "Hi, my name's Teddy." Their smiles encourage me. "I just moved here from Arizona."

"We know," Ponytail giggles and Green Eyes smiles.

"So, like, do you two have names?"

"I'm Sue," says Pony Tail.

"And I'm Patti," says Green Eyes.

Just then Mr. Beale, alias Pluto, strolls in and everyone gets quiet. *That wasn't so bad.*

Second hour. Trig. I slide into my desk and ask the boy next to me, "Did you think the homework was hard last night?"

"I never did figure out the last problem."

"I'm not sure I did either, but I could show you what I did. If you want. By the way, my name's Teddy. I just moved here."

"Well, uh sure, I'm Jim. Oops, too late, here comes Mr. Lewis."

Third hour. Government. I look around and try to identify the next unsuspecting victim for my *Hey, I'm Teddy* spiel but Miss Wilson beats me to it. "Class, open your books to page 20."

I decide to brave the cafeteria alone. My only companion is the sandwich Baba makes me each morning. So huge it resembles the Subway party platter. Headline: NEW BOY LURES FRIENDS WITH FOOD.

I turn to the last page in my notebook and write the names of the three people I met that morning. I'm not going to stop until the page is full. At the top I write in big bold letters. THE FUTURE IS IN MY HANDS. I put a little star beside Patti's name. That's for people I want to know better.

I'm feeling better when the end-of-lunch bell rings, like I'm doing something positive. But walking down the hall, I see Patti, laughing with a tall, good-looking kid wearing a basketball letter jacket and it looks like they are more than just friends. He's probably one of those "starters" Coach Burton was talking about. From that "we're all set team." Been together a hundred years ... blah, blah, blah. What kind of guy wears a letter jacket on a hot afternoon anyway? What a show off. I try to convince myself he's a real jerk, but it's obvious Patti doesn't think so as she reaches out and squeezes his arm before she turns to go.

So much for my star list. I walk into fifth hour and make no effort to speak to anyone. I wallow in what Mom calls a pity puddle. I'm in so deep that I don't even hear Miss Willis call my name.

"Teddy, hello, are you there?" I look up to see what looks like 40 eyes looking at me. "I'm here Miss Willis. I mean, I'm sorry, I didn't hear the question."

I get through the rest of the hour, but by the end of the day I haven't added any new names to my list, am not feeling good about the ones I have, and want to crawl under a rock.

✑

"*¡Hola class!*"

The next day in Spanish I decide to tackle one obstacle to my goal — getting into open gym with the guys. Pete, who I've seen shooting baskets, sits by the pencil sharpener. I pretend I am in desperate need of a sharp pencil. I lean over and say quietly to Pete, hoping I sound casual instead of desperate. "Hey, did I see you with a bunch of guys shooting baskets after school?"

"Yeah, most of last year's team. Except the guys who play football."

"Think I could join in? I just moved here from Arizona. I was on varsity there." *Please, please don't make sorry I asked.*

"Sure, come on down."

"Thanks. See you there."

I'm so excited that I accidentally drop my pencil and it rolls under his desk. I kneel down to get it from between his shoes. I must look foolish crawling around on the floor, but at the same time I want to kiss his Nikes for making me feel welcome.

I don't remember anything we did that day in Spanish. I see myself jumping, shooting, the guys slapping me on the back, saying, "Wow, are we ever glad you moved here. We can really use you on the team." Life is good. It's a great game. I'm playing.

The rest of the day drags by. Each hour is endless. Finally classes are over. I show up at open gym ready to play. To show them how good I am. To prove they need me.

Nothing goes right. No one passes me the ball. Pete finally does and I dribble it away and lose it. Then I trip over my feet trying to get it back. *What is wrong with me?* I finally get a shot and miss by a mile. It's not even close. This can't be happening. I want to disappear. Or like when we were little kids, I want "do-overs."

Finally, just before we finish, I sink a long one, nothing but net, from the middle of the court, but it looks like one of those lucky shots people make who have never played basketball. The kind where they get a guy with plumber's butt out of the bleachers and if he makes it from half court, he wins a car or something.

Walking off the court, Pete says, "Nice shot," but no one else says anything to me. I am sorry for Pete, who stuck his neck out for me and even sorrier for myself, wondering if I'll have the courage to try again.

The JV coach walks by and says, "Hey, good to see you Teddy." At least someone knows my name.

That night I thumb through the *Book of Life* for some gems of wisdom. I find the perfect one for this awful day. *Every failure is a blessing in disguise.*

Will I have the gumption to go back tomorrow and try again? With an entire season ahead of us, I might be the most blessed player ever.

Mary

❧

I read today that the human population surpassed 6 billion. With 6 billion people in the world you wouldn't think one less person could make so much difference. One less person in the world, but that person was the world to me.

I look at the books on my bedside table. *Why Bad Things Happen to Good People, The Grief Recovery Handbook, You Can Heal Your Life, On Death and Dying.*

I want a reprieve from it all. I don't want to read about death and grief. I want to escape into someone else's beautiful life. I pull out a paperback at the bottom of the stack. Danielle Steel's *Once in a Lifetime.*

Teddy

Mom is at the bookstore, the girls are in bed, and Baba and I are the only ones downstairs. I look at the old family photos in the dining room and go upstairs to get the *Book of Life.*

"Baba, can you tell me something about this book?" I place it on her lap.

"Oh my goodness, Teddy, where you find this old book? I forget all about it." She touches the cover gently like it's something precious.

"When I put those boxes in the attic for you. I was looking in some of the boxes. I hope that was okay."

"Teddy Bear, everything in this house is okay for you to see. This your home too now. We have no secrets here."

"Is this book from Bulgaria?"

"Yes, listen. I tell you the story. How this book come to America. Very important book in our Bulgarian culture. When your Dedo, your father's father, my husband, come to America, he was young boy. I come to America later, but that is story for different night."

She clears her throat like she is about to impart important information. "This story your Dedo tell me many times. How they sail for 21 days in the bottom of the big ship, *The Baltic.* So many people. Stuffed like the sheep herds in their mountain village. People carrying food from homeland. Cheese, sausages, fruit. When it spoils the smell is awful. The ship, it is rocking so much on the rough water, and people are getting sick. More bad smell. But when they see the statue, The Lady of Liberty, they are so happy they forget all the smells, all the suffering. Now they are free."

When Baba says "free" her eyes get wide and her smile is big, like someone has given her a present. I can tell she loves this story.

She goes on, "When they come, they can bring only a few of their belongings. His mother brought her needlework, her rose perfume. The Bulgarian fields are famous for their roses. Your great-grandfather, Variky, Papa's father, he brought his mandolin and this book." She runs her hand over the cover gently again. "This book is one a father reads to his son when he is ready to become a man. It tells him how to be a good person. How to live a good life. It is passed, how you say, from one generation to the next."

Baba wipes a tear from her eye with a hankie she pulls out of her dress sleeve, like some sort of magic trick. "Maybe Uncle Dan, he can read it to you? That would be good, Teddy?"

"Well, if it's alright with you Baba, I would like to keep it in my room and just read it myself. Maybe Uncle Dan and I can talk about it sometime."

"Sure, Teddy Bear. That's good."

"Thanks, Baba." I start to get up but she takes my arm. I remain sitting.

"There is one more part to this story. When they came to America. On Ellis Island, your great-grandfather, Variky, was not able to leave the island."

"What? Why not?"

"The doctors. They check each person for sickness. Your great-grandfather, they write a big "L" on his coat. L for lungs. His were not good. The tuberculosis. He had to stay in the hospital there. When they were separated, that terrible day, Variky said, 'Son, please read the *Book of Life*. Each night. And know that when you read it, I am always with you.' That was the last thing he said to him. He never saw him again."

"That's very sad. And the English? Who wrote the English words?"

"Uncle Dan and your father. They cannot read Bulgarian, so Papa would read it and they would write it in English. So they could read it again sometime without him."

"Do you know anything about a little music box? I found that in the attic too."

Baba looks upward and scrunches her lips like she is thinking hard. "Music box? No, I don't know about any music box from the old country."

"Thanks Baba. I liked your story." I kiss her on the cheek and she puts both hands on my cheeks and squeezes them hard.

I take the book upstairs and open it to another page. The saying is translated. *Life is a gift, but only if we open it.*

I'm not sure what that means. Is it saying to live life? Is that what Dad wants me to do?

Mary

⟨ℰ⟩

Our first book discussion goes even better than I expected. Gladys appears once again in a monochromatic outfit. This time all beige and very smart. Debbie, in spite of it being October, comes in a sundress. Although she is wearing a sweater, she takes it off as soon as she sits down revealing cleavage like a true southern belle. I notice Clint's eyes widening and he shifts in his seat. Is this to avoid her or get a better vantage point?

Debbie, oblivious to Clint, talks non-stop as she sits and pulls out her book, which has several tabs sticking out of the pages. I am impressed if she has marked all these passages.

Quiet Lacy is non-descript in a sweater and jeans and Rosetta once again looks like she stepped out of *Vogue* with designer jeans and strappy silver sandals. She must shop in Indianapolis or Chicago. I haven't seen anything that smart in Middleburg.

The plot of *Snow Falling on Cedars* lends itself to a rich discussion. World War II, Japanese internment camps on the West Coast and the forbidden love between Ishmael and Hatsue. Not to mention the murder trial it opens with.

Lacy surprises me with an astute comment and Gladys still rolls her eyes with every comment Debbie makes.

Debbie, of course being most interested in the romance portion of the story, asks, "What would have happened to Ishmael and Hatsue if there had not been a war with Japan? Would they have married? Would the families have accepted a marriage outside their race?"

Rosetta answers quickly, "I don't think so. I think the war, as awful as it was, spared them great heartache of a different kind. Society would have destroyed their love eventually. Better that it was ended at the height of their love. Forever a sweet memory."

"I don't think anyone ever forgets their first love," Clint says.

"Or the person you lose your virginity to," Debbie says with a mischievous smile.

We all laugh a little, except Rosetta, who just nods her head and looks pensive.

Part Two

Middleburg, Indiana
1968

In the mid '60s a major car manufacturer acquired an expansive tract of land in central Indiana to build a new assembly plant that would employ 700 workers. To ensure that they would have a viable work force they built a model community of 500 homes and advertised to the Negro communities in Chicago and Indianapolis, touting the many benefits of living the American dream in Frontier Village: affordable new housing, good wages, health insurance, and excellent medical facilities.

They offered three housing plans, each one named for one of the car designs they were currently assembling. The smallest model was the Alpine, the medium-sized floor plan was the Berkshire, and the largest, the Sierra, was for the professional families they hoped to attract — doctors, nurses, teachers, clergymen to service the skilled workers' families. Word spread quickly and families came in droves, eager to flee the inner cities with tenement housing and high crime rates. The prospect of a good job and a new home was enticing.

The townspeople seemed to be divided on the new development or as some people called it, *factory town*. When the auto corporation representatives held a town hall meeting to point out the benefits of the assembly plant to the existing residents — the employment opportunities it provided, the boost to the local economy, the development of new businesses — many townspeople were on board. Different rumblings could be heard in the coffee shop as the good ole boys network never failed to point out the civil unrest that was increasing across the country with frequent disturbing headlines.

"I think we're headed for some trouble here in Middleburg. Bringing *those people* in." Some called them colored. Some called them black, some called them Negroes. No one was quite sure what to call *those people*.

The corporation provided funding for a church, a shopping district, and a community center. Medical services were provided at the plant. An elementary school for kindergarten through eighth grade was built in Frontier Village for the many young families. A school bus was provided for students making the five-mile ride to the existing high school in Middleburg.

Some of the people of Middleburg falsely prided themselves on their open-mindedness, which, in fact, had rarely been challenged. Although the television showed riots erupting in the big cities following the Martin Luther King Jr. assassination in April of that year, Middleburg felt somewhat distant and removed from racial tension. The Negroes stayed in their village and socialized amongst themselves. They knew their place and stayed in it.

The times, however, as Bob Dylan warned the American people, they were a-changing.

Rosetta Stone was organizing her school supplies on the dining room table for the first day of her senior year at the new school. She could overhear her parents' conversation in the kitchen, which was stocked with all the latest appliances in avocado green.

Dr. Arthur Stone and his wife Charlotte lingered at the kitchen table after dinner. Dr. Stone pushed his plate aside and leaned toward his wife. "If this position at the clinic goes well, we might buy some acreage, have a big garden, some animals, a horse for Rosetta. What a wonderful retreat for our relatives to escape from the city."

Charlotte sipped the last of her wine and smiled at him. "One step at a time, Arthur."

"Just saying," he said.

She gazed out of the big bay window overlooking tall corn fields. Their house, the largest floor plan of the new homes, was on the north edge of the development, with no homes behind them.

Charlotte agreed. "It is lovely here. So quiet." She sighed. "I just worry that we did the right thing by Rosetta. Having her change schools — an all-white school — for her senior year. A lot has changed in our country since you agreed to take this job."

"I can hear you in there," Rosetta called from the dining room. She walked into the kitchen. "If it puts your mind at ease, Mom, I already decided I'm going to have a great year. When I registered for classes, I saw they were having cheering tryouts this week."

"That's wonderful, darling. Six years of dance and acrobatics. You would be an asset to any cheering squad," her mother answered with a reassuring smile.

"Thanks, Mom." Rosetta started up the stairs. "I'm going up to pick out what I'm wearing tomorrow."

"Those lessons may pay off after all," her father said softly and winked at his wife.

Standing up and making sure Rosetta had gone upstairs, her mother said, "Arthur, I hope she's well accepted. She's never been in an integrated school ... and well ... you know. Anything can happen. Kids can be cruel, especially girls. I know we made a commitment here, but I'm just saying, Arthur, if Rosetta has a bad experience, I'm not sure I can stick it out." She walked to the sink with her plate.

Arthur stood up behind her and rubbed her shoulders. He slipped his arms around her waist and kissed her on the back of her neck. "Baby, I don't think you have a thing to worry about. Rosetta has charmed people since she was a baby. Black and white. That beautiful smile of hers knows no strangers."

Charlotte turned to face him. "I just wish there were more black students her age. Forty in a high school of 300? And they're mostly underclassmen. Five seniors and only one other girl, Leona. Thank goodness they seem to hit it off."

Although Arthur Stone reassured his wife, he couldn't help but think of what transpired near their home up north that year when the Chicago Board of Education voted to bus 573 Negro pupils from the crowded west side ghetto schools into eight all-white schools on the city's northwest side. The residents protested the bussing plan and called for a boycott of the eight schools involved in the decision.

His fears were somewhat laid to rest when, the following day, in September of 1968, less than 200 miles south of Chicago in central rural Indiana, 41 Negro students from Frontier Village walked the halls for the first time in the all-white school of Middleburg without incident.

The basketball coach was happy to get two talented ball players from Chicago on his starting five. The young liberal cheerleading sponsor said she would welcome a Negro girl on the cheering squad. She said it would be a very positive gesture to the people of Frontier Village, showing them that the people of Middleburg were open-mind, not prejudiced like the angry big city mobs in the news.

Following tryouts, had they not chosen Rosetta with her stellar acrobatic performance, it would have been a blatant snub. Mumblings in the bleachers were, "Her skin is so light. Her hair isn't even kinky. How does she get it so straight and shiny?" In the teachers' lounge someone remarked, "She's very pretty ... for a Negro."

Chemistry was the last period of the day for Stan Kostoff and Rosetta Stone who got paired as lab partners their senior year. As Stan slid onto the stool at the last high-top table, Rosetta was turned away from him facing the window. When she turned to look directly at him with her big doe-like black eyes he felt a catch in his chest. Her wide and easy smile revealed straight white teeth with a little gap between the front two. "Hi. I'm Rosetta." Her friendly voice was lyrical.

Stan actually gripped the edge of the table because his stomach felt the way it did when the parachute at the carnival ride dropped suddenly. He knew he was staring but he couldn't get his mouth to speak.

Before he could put two words together, she said, "And your name would be ...."

"Stanley Kostoff." *Oh my gosh*, he thought. *Did he really say his full name like he was reporting to a drill sergeant?* He stuttered, "I mean Stan. My friends call me Stan."

"Well, I guess we should be friends." *That beautiful smile again.* "If we're going to be lab partners."

His brain-to-voice connection still wasn't working, but he managed to mumble, "Yeah, that would be great. Friends."

She was so poised, so assured, and he was acting like a fourth-grader on the playground, praying he wouldn't be the last man standing when they picked dodge ball teams.

Rosetta was about to say something else when Mr. Duncan, in a starched white lab coat, entered the room and tapped his pointer on his desk to get their attention. He cleared his throat as if he had a very important announcement and in a booming voice welcomed them to what he hoped was an "exciting semester of chemistry."

Stan snuck sideways glances at Rosetta, perched on her stool with a straight and eager posture, giving her rapt attention to Mr. Duncan. She had a new notebook open and he watched her write *Chemistry* in lovely cursive on the first page. Her hands with long slender fingers were the color of the coffee his mother drank each morning, a light creamy brown. Stan felt an irresistible urge to touch them.

Mr. Duncan was saying, "Why study chemistry?" He waited for an answer. No one raised a hand. Finally, a redhead girl in the front row said, "Because we need it to graduate?"

Everyone, including Mr. Duncan, laughed, but he continued with a passion in his deep voice. "Chemistry is life. It is the study of matter. You are dealing with chemistry every day of your life because everything you touch, taste or smell is made of matter. This desk, this book." He touched the textbook. "A pencil." He held up a pencil from a desk in the front row. "A person." He gently tapped the top of the redhead's hair with the pencil. "So you might say, chemistry matters. Wouldn't you agree?" He seemed pleased with his play on words and smiled at them benevolently as if he had just given them a blessing.

He went on with more examples. "Please raise your hand if you like to bake chocolate chip cookies." Most of the girls' hands went up. "That is chemistry, as is all baking."

"Will that be our homework?" the redhead asked.

"It could be. And it might help your grade if you bring me some." Mr. Duncan smiled. "How many of you are going out for sports?"

Most of the boys' hands went up.

"The shoes you wear, the ones that keep you from slipping on the basketball floor, the ones that help you run faster around the track. Those special materials are chemistry."

All eyes were on Mr. Duncan who had their total attention, except for Stan. His eyes were on Rosetta. When Mr. Duncan turned to write on the board, Rosetta whispered to Stan. "He's making this so interesting. I am going to love this class, aren't you?"

Stan gazed into her eyes, like liquid pools of chocolate, and said, "Yes, I think I'm really going to love it."

For Stan, the butterflies would start building in his stomach right after lunch when he thought of sitting beside Rosetta again. He had dated a few girls his junior year, mainly for special dances where you needed a date, but none had made his heart race the way it did when he simply looked at Rosetta. It was like his insides turned liquid, squishy but nice. Very nice. By the end of the first week, he realized she was not only beautiful but also smart.

"Have you had this class before? It's like you know everything already," he said to her as they slid onto their stools.

"I made the mistake of telling my dad when I was four that I wanted to be a doctor like him and he didn't miss any opportunity to keep me interested. Kind of overkill with science kits each Christmas, but I do like it. I'll probably go to med school. How about you?" she asked. When she looked directly in his eyes the way she did so openly, so trustingly, he forgot what she asked.

"What ...?" he started to say.

"College. Have you thought about what you want to do? Where you want to go?"

Once again, he felt like a doofus. He hadn't given a career any thought. Just hoped he'd get a basketball scholarship somewhere.

He loved sitting beside her where he inhaled her scent, occasionally getting a waft of it, light and sweet. And something about those long fingers with clear shiny nails and the little half-moons near her cuticles. Mesmerized, he watched her pour liquid from the beaker into a tube. Every movement, so graceful, so assured. He, in turn, felt like a klutz. He could palm a basketball. No problem. But here beside her, no finesse.

The day he dropped a test tube that shattered on the floor, she hopped off the stool and kneeled down to help him pick up the pieces. There under the table, their eyes met as their hands accidentally touched. She pulled away as if it were an electric jolt. Stan touched her hand softly again. And then he couldn't help himself. He wrapped his hand around those long beautiful fingers he had wanted to touch since the first day. He whispered, "Hey, it's okay. We can be friends, can't we?"

She smiled her gap-tooth smile and he saw even through her brown skin that her cheeks had colored slightly. She gave him the slightest nod as if to say, "okay."

❧

That night when Rosetta answered the kitchen phone and heard his familiar voice on the other end, she turned her face away so her parents wouldn't see her blushing.

"Hi. It's Stan. From chemistry."

She said, "Hi, Stan from chemistry."

He laughed.

She wound the long cord around to the hallway and sat on the floor with her legs crossed. She thought for sure her parents would hear her heart beating if she stayed in the same room.

"I hope it's okay that I called you. It's hard to talk in class and I really just wanted to talk to you. About something besides carbon and hydrogen. Is that all right?"

She hesitated and then answered with a breathy, "I suppose it is."

"So where did you live before?" Stan asked.

"Chicago."

"Wow. A city girl. Do you miss it?"

"Some ways. Mostly my girlfriends."

"How about boyfriends? Do you have one there?"

"Not really."

"That's hard to believe. Someone as pretty as you."

Rosetta felt her cheeks grow warm and a little tickle in her chest. "You know we probably shouldn't be doing this."

"What?"

"Talking on the phone."

"We're not hurting anyone. Are we?" he asked.

"No, but we can't really … you know … ever hang out together. Like at school."

"Do you want to *not* talk?" he asked.

"No. I mean yes, I do. But I'm just saying. It can never be more than this."

"It?"

"You and me. Me and you. We can't ever be together." She was almost whispering.

"I know, but can we just take this … for now?" She liked the way his voice almost pleaded.

Rosetta heard her mother from the kitchen. "Rosetta, are you still on the phone? Have your done your homework?"

"I need to go," she said hurriedly into the phone.

"Okay, but can I tell you just one more thing?"

"Just a minute," she said to the mouthpiece before she covered it and called to her mother. "I'll be off the phone in a minute."

"Okay, I'm back," she whispered.

"I just wanted to tell you ...," Stan hesitated. "Okay, here goes. You know those corny sayings like 'love at first sight' or 'I was hit with Cupid's arrow'?"

"Yes."

"Well, I thought those were just sayings for silly love songs, but ...." Rosetta heard an intake of Stan's breath and then a sigh. "Well, now I know they're not silly. The first time I saw you in chemistry ... I loved everything about you — your eyes, your beautiful skin. Even your hands." Rosetta heard him release a big breath. "There, I said it." He gave a little laugh. "When you turned around and looked at me, I thought I was going to fall off my stool. Maybe that's why they say *falling* in love?"

Rosetta pictured Stan's smile. His olive skin. His dark wavy hair. Eyes that some days were green, some days a touch of brown. The cleft in his chin. She felt giddy.

"Are you still there?" Stan asked.

"I'm here. I don't ... I don't know what to say."

"You don't have to say anything, but I had to tell you. I've wanted to tell you every day since we met. Like I was going to burst if I didn't. It feels so good to finally say it. You're not mad, are you? I know I have no right, but how can something that feels so good be bad?"

Rosetta answered, "It feels good to me too, Stan." Then as if she spoke too soon, "but we can't tell anybody how we feel."

"I know, I know, but we can tell each other. And just for the record, I have never used the 'L' word with anyone. I never felt it before and can't believe I'm saying it now. Could you love a paleface like me?"

Rosetta laughed and was about to answer when she realized her mother was standing over her. "Rosetta, that minute was up a long time ago. Who are you talking to that's so important?"

"I gotta go. See you tomorrow." Rosetta walked to the kitchen and put the phone in its cradle on the wall. She said to her mother, "Just trying to figure out a chemistry homework problem."

Homework was the magic word that made allowances for many things.

"I didn't know chemistry was so funny," her mother said with a knowing glance.

Rosetta went to her room, practically running up the stairs. She threw herself face done on her bed and hugged her pillow tightly. She felt like laughing and crying at the same time. The emotions welled up inside her until she could hardly catch her breath. She smiled thinking of how sweet he sounded when he talked about the silly love songs and Cupid.

Then another saying popped into her head. Something about forbidden fruit tasting sweeter. Stan was definitely forbidden. Her parents would be mortified. A white boy? Was it Stan that was making her heart race now or the thought of doing something so forbidden?

Five miles away Stan was stretched out on his bed, hands behind his head, re-living the conversation. He was torn with relief in finally saying what he felt and then feeling stupid for doing so. Did he really use the "L" word? Did he actually ask her if she could love a *paleface* like him, as if he were John Smith talking to Pocahontas? How stupid was that? How was he going to face her the next day?

Then he smiled remembering the sound of her voice on the phone. It was different than in class. Sweet and breathy. So sweet.

The following day, each class seemed endless to Rosetta as her anticipation built toward last hour. When she walked into chemistry Stan was already there and her heart pounded. When she slid onto her stool and he spun around to face her she felt her cheeks burning and had to look away. She couldn't meet his eyes. When she did finally look at him, he was smiling at her. She returned a smile, as if to cement their new secret relationship.

She heard Mr. Duncan expounding the beautiful qualities of mercury. She took a deep breath and opened her notebook. Stan slid his notebook to where she could see it. He had drawn a heart with an arrow through it and the initials SK and RS. She smiled to think that the chemistry going on in this room was not confined to the test tubes.

Her bliss however was shattered as she walked out of the classroom and Otis, one of the Negro students from Frontier Village came up close beside her and whispered, "Looks like you and white boy like being partners. Better be careful, girl."

Rosetta's stomach turned and she felt a tightness in her chest. *What had Otis seen or heard?*

☙

In spite of Rosetta's warning to Stan about Otis, Stan stood as close to her as he could during their experiments, inhaling her sweet scent. It was a welcome respite from the rotten egg sulfur smell in the room.

"What is that perfume you are wearing? It's driving me crazy," he whispered to her one day.

"Heavenly. My aunt said it was just right for a young girl. Not overpowering. She said when you leave a room, your perfume should leave with you."

"Well, it's overpowering me," Stan said. He closed his eyes and took a deep breath, as if to swoon.

When he opened his eyes, Mr. Duncan was standing at their table. "Mr. Kostoff, do you find pleasure in the smells of a chemistry lab? That makes you a true scientist."

Before Stan could answer, he walked away and Rosetta covered her mouth to stifle a giggle.

☙

That night on the phone, Rosetta called Stan, "Mr. Kostoff, a true scientist."

"Yes, lucky you sit next to me so I can smell you instead of the lab. You smell like a beautiful flower. Does anyone call you Rose or Rosey?"

"No. Everyone calls me Rosetta. My mother is enthralled with

Egyptian history. With a last name of Stone, my dad thought Rosetta was the perfect first name. Said I was as precious as the ancient Egyptian stone."

"I think you're precious too, but can I call you Rosey? It will be my special name for you. Rosey, my sweet heavenly flower."

She could hear him taking a deep breath. Then he said, "I love your scent. I wish I could touch and taste you too. Do you think we'll ever ever, ever get to kiss?"

There was a pause and then a sniffle. "We can't Stan. We just can't. What if someone saw us? My parents would be so angry and then I'd be watched every minute. We probably wouldn't even be able to talk to each other. All these phone calls. My mother thinks it's Leona."

"Would your parents understand? About us I mean."

"Not at all. They're very proud of their heritage. It would insult them if I stepped outside my race. Just last month they were talking to friends at dinner about the Supreme Court decision that over-turned laws prohibiting interracial marriages. A black woman and a white man who got married challenged the law. My mother said, "Just because it's legal doesn't mean society is going to accept it. Why would anyone want to make their life so difficult is what I can't understand."

"Have they been in Civil Rights marches?" Stan asked.

"They're not militant or anything like that. But they do get in-volved in their quiet way. They were in Indianapolis last year to hear Robert Kennedy speak. It was the day Martin Luther King was killed."

"Wow," Stan said.

"My parents told me about it so many times, I practically have Kennedy's speech memorized. I wrote a school report on it."

"Really?" Stan asked. "You seem to know a lot about what's going on in the world. Seems all I think of is basketball. And you."

"My parents said Indianapolis was one of the big cities that didn't have rioting following the assassination because of what Kennedy said to the crowd that day."

"What did he say?" Stan asked.

"Mainly, how it would be so tempting for blacks to hate all whites because of what happened but they shouldn't. That he understood how they felt. And he reminded them that his brother was killed by a white man also."

Stan said, "Our country is so messed up, killing the best people."

Rosetta went on, "How about your parents? Could they ever accept you loving a Negro?"

"Not something we've ever talked about. Their first choice would be a nice Bulgarian girl. Preferably just off the boat. No speaka da English. When we visit Bulgarian friends they are pointing out all the ethnic beauties to me. It might have a chance if I discovered one on my own, but who wants your parents picking your date? My parents' marriage was arranged and that seems to be working out after what — 25 years? So I guess they feel it's the way to go."

"I don't think you need anyone arranging dates for you. I hear the girls talking about you. 'Stan's so cute. Stan's so handsome. Stan's so much fun.' Makes me a little jealous," Rosetta admits.

"Oh Rosey, there's nothing to be jealous of. You're all I think about night and day."

Rosetta felt a warmth spreading through her chest and also the familiar ache and longing. "Good night, Stan. And just so you know, I wonder what your lips would taste like too."

The next day in class, while Otis was bent over a microscope, Rosetta slid an envelope to Stan's side of the table. In beautiful cursive it said, "Open later at home."

In the privacy of his room that night, he opened the envelope and the Heavenly scent hit him immediately. He put the piece of blue silk cloth to his nose and breathed in deeply. Then he placed it on his pillowcase where he could breathe her scent in his dreams.

October

In Frontier Village, before Rosetta went to bed, she overhead the conversation her parents were having with their neighbors, the Burns, who came by for their weekly game of Canasta.

"So what is all this fuss about with the Summer Olympics?" Mrs. Burns asked as she shuffled the cards and handed them to Arthur Stone to deal.

Arthur Stone dealt the cards while he described what he had read. "Negro American medalists Tommie Smith and John Carlos won gold and bronze medals for the 200-meter race. When they played the national anthem they bowed their heads but each raised a black-gloved fist. They said later it was a silent demonstration of racial discrimination in the United States. Their protest shocked people and said it damaged the spirit of the Olympics."

"Doesn't seem like such a serious offense to me," Charlotte Stone said.

Mr. Stone replied, "Evidently serious enough for them to be expelled from the U.S. team."

Whenever Rosetta heard her parents talking about racial problems or when white people treated Negroes badly, she felt guilty about her conversations with Stan. Rosetta's last thought as she drifted off to sleep was that by loving Stan she was a traitor to her race.

❧

A few days before Halloween, Stan pleaded with Rosetta on the phone. "Rosey, this is our big chance. If we wear costumes, we can go out together. No one will know if we're black or white. How about it?" His voice was full of excitement and she found herself getting caught up in the possibility.

"Do we dare?" she asked.

They both drove to the school parking lot and left their cars there. Rosetta laughed when Stan stepped out of the car. Stan's face had no mask, just white make-up with a round rubber nose, big red lips and an orange wig.

"Hey, great clown, huh? See, I'm making you laugh already." Stan said.

Rosetta wore black gloves, a full witch's mask and also had the flowing black scarf from her pointed hat to cover her eyes or mouth if needed.

"Let's go," Stan said as he grabbed her hand. Her stomach lurched like it did when she rode the roller coaster ride. They laughed as they ran door to door, holding hands, daring to say "trick or treat" and hold out their bags. For once they were not black or white. Just a clown and a witch. Just a boy and a girl.

After a few houses of trick-or-treating, Stan led her behind a row of bushes. She almost tripped on a fallen branch and he grabbed her around the waist. Holding her closely, he took off his clown nose, wiped the red paint off his lips with his sleeve and lifted her mask. He whispered, "Are you a good witch or a bad witch? You smell like a good witch."

Rosetta started to ask him if he was a funny clown or a sad clown, but as his lips moved closer to hers, she couldn't say a word. They both took a deep breath and closed their eyes. Softly, shyly, their lips touched for the first time. They kissed again greedily, like kids devouring their Halloween candy.

Rosetta finally pushed him away gently and whispered in his ear. "Stan, we have to stop. Someone might come. And I have to get to the Halloween party at the community center before someone starts asking where I am."

Stan put his clown nose back on and when she reached up to

squeeze it, he tried to kiss her one more time. The nose was in the way and they both giggled. Rosetta put her mask and hat back on and they walked back to the parking lot. As they stood outside Rosetta's car, Rosetta put her face in her hands.

"Rosey, please don't cry. What's wrong?" When she didn't answer he said, "Okay, I'll let you have all my candy." He heard a giggle through her sobs. "Oh good," he said. "Clowns are supposed to make people laugh. I thought I'd have to go back to clown school." She laughed and wiped her nose with the scarf of her pointy hat.

"Tell me what's wrong," he asked, pushing her hat off and stroking her cheek.

"I think we're pathetic. That's why I'm crying. Why do we have to wear masks to be seen together? Why do we have to act like criminals or bank robbers? We're not doing anything wrong. It's so unfair."

"Oh Rosey, Rosey." He held her tightly.

They heard another car enter the parking lot and both of them quickly got in their separate cars without a chance to even say good-bye.

He called her that night. "Our first kiss," Stan said. "No trick there. Best treat I ever had. I hope it's not our last."

"Yes," she spoke softly. "Sweeter than all the candy in our bags."

"Sort of like Crackerjacks. It's going to be hard to stop with just one. Kiss that is."

"Do I have to wait for next Halloween to kiss you again?" Rosetta asked.

Stan sighed, "Yeah, not much demand for witches and I don't think the traveling circus comes to town till summer."

She knew he was trying to make her laugh but it wasn't working.

The racial headlines became more frightening. Disturbances and riots flaring up everywhere. The headlines seemed closer to them now, which heightened their fears as well as their excitement when they talked about how they could see each other again.

"We could go for a ride somewhere. Just stay in the car?" Stan offered.

"I don't know. It seems sneaky and I don't want to feel that way about us."

"You'd be the one ostracized more than me it seems if we were caught," Stan replied. "I don't ever want to do something that would cause you to be hurt."

"See, even that word *caught*. It's like we're doing something bad, like stealing something," she said. She twisted the telephone cord in frustration.

"Yeah, all we want to steal is a little time. Time together. It shouldn't be so hard, should it?" Stan replied.

"So I guess until the world goes color blind, we just talk."

"Do you want to stop talking? I don't want you to feel bad."

"Silly boy, talking to you makes me feel good. If that's all we can do, I'll take it."

"Good. Me too. See you in class?"

"I'll be there."

"I like that it's last hour. It's hard to wait, but if it were first hour, the best part of the day would be over too soon. Good night, Rosey."

"TTFN," she said.

"Are you talking chemistry to me? Is that something that's going to be on the test tomorrow?"

"Silly, it's what Tigger always says to Pooh. Ta ta for now."

Stan laughed. "You're so cute Rosey. I believe I love you more than Pooh loves honey."

"Going to Sheldon's party tomorrow night?" Leona, the only other Negro senior girl, asked Rosetta as they rode home on the school bus.

"Sure. I know you are cause you and Sheldon are a thing now, aren't you?" Rosetta smiled at her friend.

Leona smiled back coyly. "You might say that."

"He seems nice. Funny too. I have English with him." Rosetta said.

"How about you? Got somebody nice and funny?" Leona asked.

"No, not really." Rosetta replied.

"Well, you might real soon. Sheldon said Sydney's got his eye on you. I think you might find out about that tomorrow night."

Rosetta panicked. No way she wanted to get involved with Sydney. Or anybody.

"Actually, there is this boy in Chicago," she fibbed. "We were pretty serious when I left this summer and we sort of agreed to ... you know ... stay close. Not get too involved with anyone else."

"What? That's no way to spend your senior year. You got to have some fun, girl."

"I can have fun without dating anybody. Just hanging out with everyone."

"Suit yourself, but ...."

"Could you tell Sheldon that there is a guy in Chicago? Maybe he'll say something to Sydney. You know, to discourage him so I don't have to refuse him?"

"I suppose, but I think you're making a mistake. Letting a good one go. Sending him down to those sophomore and junior girls. They'll snap him up in a minute."

"Yeah, I'm probably crazy." Rosetta said.

When she got home and went to her room to change her clothes, she thought about Leona's remark. Was she wrong to wait each night for a few minutes on the phone with Stan? Right or wrong, she knew it was what she wanted. Or couldn't resist.

November

"Rosey, did you see what happened on *Star Trek*?" Stan's voice was full of excitement.

"No, you know I'm not a Trekkie."

"I forgot. You were probably watching *Green Acres*."

"I can't help it my dad dreams of being a farmer. I think he'd wear bib overalls at the hospital if he could."

Stan said, "You'll never guess what happened. Captain Kirk kissed a black lady. On television."

"Really? On television? Wow. How did that happen?"

"It was on the segment, "Plato's Stepchildren." Captain Kirk's Starship Enterprise becomes enslaved by humanoid Platonians who possess a telekinetic ability to force them to do anything the Platonians wanted them to do ..."

"You lost me."

"Here's the important thing. The censors at the network filmed an alternative *without* the kiss, afraid that their TV stations in the Deep South would refuse to air it."

"Okay ...."

"But William Shatner — he's Captain Kirk — supposedly ruined all the alternative takes so they had to air the one with the kiss!"

"That's cool."

"But here's the best part, Rosey. Kirk's last line in the episode is, "Where I come from size, shape, or color makes no difference.""

"So are you saying we should go to this planet or what?"

"I'm saying I think things are changing in the world. I think some-day we might be able to be together. Color won't make a difference."

"Stan, you are such a dreamer. I think that day is a long way off. Probably further away than the distant planets your Captain Kirk comes from."

⁐

One week later, Rosetta left a note in Stan's chemistry book. *Hey, Captain Kirk. Call me tonight. I think your big Hollywood moment is here.*

"Hollywood? Lay it on me," were the first words Stan spoke into the phone.

"My parents are going to a conference in Indy for the day. All day. Saturday. Why don't you come over?"

"What? To your house?"

"Well, yes, that's what I live in. A house." She laughed.

"Are you sure?"

She interrupted him. "Last time I checked. It had four walls, a door, a roof."

"I mean do we dare? What if your parents come back early? What if a neighbor pops in?"

"They would knock, silly. So we don't answer the door. As for my parents, they'll be with their Chicago doctor friends. They'll talk forever. If anything, they'll be late. Come on, scaredy cat. Be bold. You know, like Captain Kirk. Go where no man has gone before."

"You mean no white man. Okay, but I have to tell you, I'm really nervous. I don't want to get you in any trouble. I'll come over for just a little while."

"Uh huh. Long enough for me to kiss that dimple in your chin I have to look at each day and can't even touch."

Stan felt a lump in his throat and an ache in his chest. There was no way he could resist the promise of a touch and a kiss.

⁐

Saturday he rode his bike the five miles out of town to Frontier Village, afraid to drive his distinctive orange Nova in broad daylight. The thought of seeing Rosetta and the excitement of doing something he shouldn't be doing caused his heart to beat as fast as the pedals he was pumping. Rosetta's home was on the edge of the development and he parked his bike behind the house facing the cornfield.

As soon as her parents left that morning, Rosetta closed all the blinds in the house except for the kitchen bay window, which faced the open fields. She kept watching out her bedroom window. She had told Stan to go to the back of the house. When she saw him coming up the drive, she ran down and opened the door before he even got to the back porch. She whisked him in and locked the door behind him. They just stood looking at each other, suddenly both shy and hesitant to make a move. Big smiles spread across their faces and each one finally let go of the breaths they had been holding.

"I've got butterflies really bad. More than before a basketball game," Stan said.

"Me, too," Rosetta said with a giggle.

"Oh, you play basketball?" Stan asked and they both started laughing. Each one took a step closer and then they were holding each other tightly. Stan took a step back and touched her shiny black hair.

"I can't believe I'm here. So close to you."

"Me neither," she said in a whisper. She reached up and put her finger on the dimple in his chin. He took her finger and kissed the tip. The next thing they were holding each other so close, so tightly, it made his knees weak. He looked at her lips, so full, so inviting. When he put his mouth on hers, he couldn't believe how soft they were.

"You taste like Doublemint gum," she said.

"Is that good?" he asked. "I think I put a whole pack in my mouth on the way here."

She laughed. "It's really good. Yum."

They kept kissing, both saying more than once, "I can't believe you're really here."

They were still in the foyer.

"I guess we don't have to stand *here* all day," Rosetta said, leading him into the living room.

Stan looked around the elegantly furnished room. "So, do I get a little concert?" he asked, pointing to the piano in the corner.

"Sure," Rosetta slid the bench out and patted the place beside her.

He slid in. "Am I too close? Don't want to cramp your style."

"I'm not sure I even have a style. You want something classical? Or boogie-woogie?" She spread her fingers on the keyboard and titled her head toward him.

He slipped one arm around her waist and kissed her just below her ear lobe. "Can you play and kiss at the same time?"

"Uh, don't know. Never tried it. My piano teacher usually doesn't kiss me while I'm playing."

"He better not," Stan said.

"It's a she," Rosetta said and began playing "Beautiful Dreamer." "First piece I learned."

When she finished, he clapped and said, "I can play 'Heart and Soul.'" He began banging the keys with one finger like a four-year old.

Rosetta laughed. "Wow. What talent. I think you're ready to cut an album."

When she placed her hands on the keys next to his he took her long brown fingers and kissed them over and over. "I've been wanting to do this since the first day I met you. Watching you handle those test tubes so gently and carefully. Never thought I'd want to be a test tube."

Rosetta felt her cheeks grow warm at the thought of caressing him. "You mean the ones you're usually dropping and spilling? They say opposites attract."

"We're not as opposite as you would think. Look." Sitting so close together, Stan put his arm next to hers, his plaid shirt sleeve rolled up. "Our skin's almost the same color. In the summer my skin is probably darker than yours." They looked at their arms and then at each other. "It would be funny if it weren't so sad," Stan said.

"It's stupid, isn't it?" Rosetta agreed. "Why does color make such a difference?"

"Makes no difference to me," Stan said. "You're the prettiest girl I know. Every time I see you at the school dances, I just want to hold you."

He hugged her again. "Hey, wanna dance?"

"Sure, my parents have a great record collection." Rosetta led him to the hi-fi console in the other corner of the living room. They thumbed through the wide range of LP's stacked in the left side of the console. Billie Holiday, Nat King Cole, Ella Fitzgerald, Johnny Mathis.

"Pick your favorite," Rosetta said as she began to roll up a corner of the rug on the wood floor. When Stan gave her a puzzled look, she said, "What? My parents do this all the time when their friends come over. Dance party."

"Really? That's cool. Let's start with a slow dance. I want to hold you really close."

They danced slow to Nat King Cole's "When I Fall in Love."

When the song was over, Stan pulled Rosetta even closer. He pressed her against him as hard as he could. "Rosey, this song is exactly how I feel. No matter what happens to us, the way I love you now … it will be forever."

When Frankie Valli's "My Eyes Adored You" played, Stan said, "This is our song too. My eyes adored you for so long before I could touch you." He ran his hands up and down the back of her soft white angora sweater.

"Do you have 'Hey Jude'?"

"I do. Now don't tell me that can be our song too," she looked at him skeptically.

"No, but that way we get to dance close for seven whole minutes," he said.

"We don't have to dance to stand close," she smiled at him. "How about something groovy? Let's see if you can dance as good as you move on the basketball court," she teased.

She went to the right side of the counsel where the 45 rpms were stacked and picked "Happy Together" by the Turtles. *I can't see me loving nobody but you. Me and you. No matter how they tossed the dice. It had to be ....*

"Oh, this is our song too," he said as he grabbed her and twirled her around.

Rosetta laughed. "Stan, *every* song can't be our song."

"Why not? Every love song is exactly how I feel."

When Johnny Mathis sang "The Twelfth of Never," Rosetta said,

"This is really our song Stan. Talk about never ... there's *never* going to be an *us*."

"Don't talk about it now, Rosey. Just let me hold you."

They kept dancing, swaying, kissing, laughing.

When Stan felt like the buttons on his Levis were going to burst open, he said, "Let's take a little break."

"Thirsty? How about a Coke?" Rosetta led him to the kitchen. The kitchen counters were spotless, gleaming with the sun coming through the bay window with the only blinds she hadn't closed.

Rosetta reached for a high cupboard. "Here's where all the good stuff is stashed," she said as she pulled out a bag of Frito-Lay chips, Cheetos, and Oreos. "As if its being on a high shelf is going to keep me out of it." She laughed. "My mom is sort of a health nut. Doesn't like me to eat junk food, but luckily Dad likes it too much too."

"Well, you sure could use a few extra pounds," Stan said.

"What?" she asked him in mock surprise.

"No, no, I mean I love the way you look. But you are really thin. Like Diana Ross thin. I can feel your ribs when we hug."

"Better to do those handsprings and cartwheels at the games," she said.

"Yeah, I don't mind when Coach benches me like I used to. Get to watch you and get a peek of those green satin tights."

Rosetta took an Oreo and pulled it apart. "I like to eat the middle first," she said.

Stan was mesmerized watching her tongue lick the white crème. "I wish I was an Oreo cookie."

"In a way, we are." She held a cookie apart, one side in each hand and tilted her head as she said, "See, black and white."

"And delicious, just like you." Stan placed an edge of a cookie in his mouth and asked her to take a bite of it. They both took little bites until their lips met. They burst out laughing when they saw the chocolate all around their mouths.

Then Stan stuffed a whole handful of chips in his mouth. "Hey, we're like normal teenagers. Dancing, eating junk food.

"We're perfectly normal, "she agreed as she delicately picked up a chip and took a bite out of it.

"Oh, I can see I'm going to have to teach you how to eat like a teenager. You have to put a whole handful of chips in your mouth at one time to get the full flavor effect." He reached into the bowl again but his hand froze when the doorbell rang. It was like when they played Statue as kids and stopped in action. They looked at each other, eyes wide in panic.

"Now what?" Stan mouthed to her.

Rosetta put a finger to her lips, took him by the hand through the living room and tiptoed up the staircase. From the little window in the hallway at the top of the stairs, Rosetta peered out carefully, lifting a corner of the lace curtain. She saw a mail delivery truck as it was backing out of the driveway.

She breathed a big sigh. "The driver always rings the bell when he leaves a package."

"Whew, that was scary." Stan said."

They started down the hallway when Stan said, "As long as we're up here, uh, I don't mean to be nosy, but could I see your room?"

"Sure," she took his hand and led him to the room at the end of the hall.

He took one step into the room and sighed. "Rosey, it's so pretty, so perfect. It looks just like you." He took a deep breath. "It even smells like you."

The canopy twin bed had a puffy pink bedspread with a pyramid of stuffed animals on it. "This one's my favorite," she said. She picked up a tattered Winnie the Pooh that obviously had seen better days and held him close to her breast. "I sleep with him every night."

"Lucky bear," Stan said wistfully. He looked at her bed, cupped her face in his hands and kissed her gently. "We better go back down." Rosetta hesitated, pulling him toward her bed. He took her hand and led her to the door. "I just don't trust myself with that bear." Rosetta laughed and put her arms around his neck and he held her tightly.

Then he heard her whimper. He whispered in her ear, "Are you laughing or crying?" She just burrowed deeper into his chest. He knew why was crying and he felt like crying too. "I won't hurt your bear. Honest," he said trying to make light of their situation.

She laughed and stepped back, wiping her eyes with the back of her hand. "But really, Stan, why does it have to be this way?"

"I don't know, Rosey. I wish it were different. No one wishes it more than me."

At the bottom of the stairs, Stan took both her hands in his. "Rosey, this has been the best day, but that doorbell was scary. I think I should leave. You know, quit while we're ahead."

"You're right. I don't want anything to spoil this. It's been perfect."

Their kiss at the back door was just like their goodbyes on the phone. Neither ever wanted to be the first to hang up and now neither wanted to be the first to let go.

"Okay, I'm really leaving now. Watch me go." Stan said as he kissed her again.

"Go already," she said as she gave him a playful shove.

"Wait, there's one thing I have to do. Been wanting to do since the first time you smiled at me."

"What?"

"I love that little gap in your front teeth. Can I touch it?" He raised his finger to her mouth.

"You are so weird. Now you *really* have to go." She laughed, but took his finger and placed it across her front teeth. "There, you sicko. Feel better? Maybe you should be a dentist. Such a great bedside manner."

"Maybe you should be a comedian."

They both laughed and hugged one more time. "Rosey, Rosey, I don't want to leave." Finally he opened the door slightly and looked around to make sure no one was in sight.

"I hate this. It seems so sneaky," Rosetta said.

"That's cause it is. But remember, our best day ever. Okay?"

"Okay," she smiled wistfully.

Riding his bike home, Stan felt like he was flying. Rosetta put the rug back in place and stretched out on the living room sofa, listening to the music they danced to over and over.

In spite of their precautions, Stan did not see the black boy coming around the corner on his bike as Rosetta waved goodbye to him from her doorway.

⌒

The following Monday night, the varsity basketball team emptied out into the parking lot after practice. Darkness has settled in.

"See you tomorrow," Stan called out to the group of boys getting into another car as he zipped up his letter jacket. The evening air felt cold on his hair, still wet from the shower. He walked to his Chevy Nova when he heard someone call his name.

"Hey, Kostoff."

Stan turned but didn't see anyone.

"Over here," the voice said and he turned the other direction. He saw three boys come out from behind a parked car and swagger toward him. They were wearing ski masks and he couldn't recognize them. He took a quick look around the parking lot but they were the only ones left.

Before he knew it, they were on him. One on each side grabbed his arms leaving him defenseless while the other one punched him hard in the stomach. He doubled over and then took another punch to the face. He tasted blood. Another punch to the side of his head, just above his eye.

"This is just a warning, white boy. We see you with Rosetta again, you'll get a lot more than this." The attackers started to walk away, then turned around and said, "If a black boy went to a white girl's house, he'd probably be lynched. So what make you think you can help yourself to our girls? Stay on your side of town, white boy."

The encounter took less than three minutes. Stan was still reeling from the shock of the blows when he saw them running off into the darkness. He picked up the satchel he had dropped, staggered to his car, climbed into the driver's seat, and sat there stunned.

When he got home he went straight to the upstairs bathroom before his parents could see his face. His first stop was usually the kitchen to see what they were having for dinner.

"Be right down, Mama," he called out as he passed the kitchen. He was thankful his older brother Dan was at college. He might be able to fool his parents but not his brother. He washed his face and looked in the mirror. His upper lip was swollen twice the size and there was a cut beside his eye. He knew it would be black and blue by morning. He took two aspirin.

When he walked into the kitchen, his mother took one look at him and dropped the big spoon she used to dish out the stuffed cabbage rolls. "Stanley, what happened?"

"It's okay, Mama, a couple of us guys ran into each other on the basketball floor. It's nothing."

"Nothing? You call this nothing?" She touched the cut beside his eye.

He winced but tried to joke about it. "But I got the ball, Mama, and I made the basket too."

"You put medicine on it?" she asked.

"I did, Mama. It's fine."

When his father came into the kitchen his mother said, "Look, look at your son. I don't like this kind of game where boys play so rough."

Stan's father looked at his face. He registered surprise, but calmly said, "Dora, you should not worry so much. Boys need to be tough today. It will make your son a strong man."

Although Stan was hungry, his stomach was in knots. He couldn't let his mother see him not eating, especially since cabbage rolls were his favorite. In spite of his cut lip he managed to eat several of them and then quickly ran to the bathroom upstairs and leaned over the porcelain bowl where all the cabbage rolls came up. He flushed them and took two more aspirin.

He knew he had to call Rosey. To prepare her somehow for the face she would see in chemistry. It wasn't the cuts and bruises that were upsetting him. It was wondering what he was going to say to her. He didn't want her to know what happened. She would be expecting him to call as he always did after 9 o'clock.

When she answered "Hello" in her sweet breathy voice, Stan found himself fighting back hot tears for the first time that night. He could not give up talking to her. He would not. But what if he were jeopardizing her too? He couldn't be responsible for her getting hurt.

"Hi Rosey. How are you tonight?" His chest swelled with love for her, like the first time he told her.

"I'm good," she answered in a perky voice. "But you sound funny. Is everything all right?"

"Oh yeah, everything's good, but I just wanted to tell you we had a little skirmish on the basketball floor tonight at practice. I got in the way of a couple of fists, so don't be surprised when you see me tomorrow. I look pretty beat up."

"Stan, what happened? Fighting with your own teammates? That's not like you."

"Not really. A couple of guys lost their tempers and well, it just happened. Not a big deal. I'm just telling you so you don't fall off your stool when you see my shiner or whatever it's going to be in the morning."

"Oh, I wish I could kiss your boo-boo," she said sweetly.

Her words stung him deeply, knowing he might never kiss her again. "Please don't say that Rosey. It hurts too much."

"Don't say I want to kiss you? Since when?"

"I mean, it would really hurt if you touched it. You'll see." Stan tried to recover. "We better say goodnight. I'll talk to you tomorrow, okay?"

"Okay," she answered in a bewildered voice. "I hope you feel better Stan. I'm so sorry."

"Not your fault, Rosey. Not your fault at all. Goodnight."

After he hung up he thought, *It's all* my *fault. I started this and now she's going to be hurt.*

He lay in bed, his head still throbbing when his father came into his room and sat on the edge of his bed. "Stanley, I do not want to make your mother worry more than she does so I don't act upset about your face. I treat it like boy's adventure. But I ask you now. Is everything all right or is there some kind of trouble for you?"

"Papa, everything is okay. Just a little roughhouse on the basketball floor. A couple of guys have a bad temper. I just got in their way."

Papa looked at him and said, "I want my boys to be strong, but you know if there is trouble of any kind, you can tell Papa."

"I know that. I'm fine. Really. Everything is good."

"Goodnight, my son." Papa took Stan's face gently in both hands and kissed him softly on each cheek, as was his custom.

ॐ

The next day Rosetta got to chemistry class before Stan. Otis walked by her stool and said, "I think your white boy got a talkin' to last night." He went on to his seat before she could respond.

Stan walked in. She gasped when she saw his face. Swollen, black, and blue. The cut above his eye was covered with a bandage.

Shawn, another varsity basketball player, came up to Stan. "Man, what happened to you?" Just then Mr. Duncan came in and everyone got quiet as his booming voice started expounding the wonderful qualities of lithium.

All during class Rosetta kept stealing glances at Stan's face. Stan, aware of Otis and Sheldon, the other black boys in the class, never responded to Rosetta's glances and never once looked at her. When the bell rang, he gathered up his book and papers and left the room quickly without so much as a glance toward her.

At basketball practice, the guys were asking him about his shiner. He tried to joke about it saying, "Yeah, you should see the other guy." Then he looked at Sydney and Cornelius, the two black boys on the team. Did they know what happened? Were they involved? He couldn't believe they would have been. They were teammates, friends. They didn't act any differently. During practice Stan tried to pass them the ball more than usual to show them that he didn't have any bad feelings toward them.

That night Rosetta called him shortly after dinner well before their normal designated time. "Stan, what is going on? If you got those bruises at basketball practice why didn't Shawn know about it?"

"Maybe he left early. I don't know." Stan hated lying to her, but he couldn't bring himself to tell her what happened. If she knew she had put him in harm's way she would probably never speak to him again. He couldn't stand not to hear her voice each night.

"Stan, I don't think you're being honest with me and that hurts me more than your bruises do. Please talk to me. Tell me what happened. Otis said something about you got a talking to last night."

Stan took a deep breath and said, "Okay, Rosey, I promise I'll tell you about it tonight. Our usual time. I can't talk long now. Dinner's ready."

Again the knots in his stomach kept him from enjoying one of his mother's delicious dinners. Mama kept looking at him and shaking her head. He tried to act normal so his parents wouldn't suspect that he was hurting in so many ways. Inside and out.

After dinner during their phone time, Stan told Rosey of the parking lot encounter. "I'm only telling you this because I don't want anything to happen to you. We have to be careful."

"To me? You're the one in danger. No one has said anything to me. But I won't risk it again Stan. We can't be seen together. Ever. There is no safe place. We just can't meet again."

"Can we keep talking?" Stan's voice broke. He was afraid of her answer. He couldn't give her up. Her sweet voice, her giggle, the way she said his name when they said goodbye.

"I don't know Stan what we should do. The whole country is crazy right now. Riots everywhere — in every city."

"But we're not in the city. We're just two kids who love each other. We aren't hurting anyone by talking. Are we?" Stan pleaded.

"Just ourselves. At some point we are going to have to say goodbye forever. Will it hurt any less then? Probably more. Soon we'll both be in college. In different colleges and —"

Stan interrupted, "Rosie, please let's just take these few moments we have each night. Every day when things happen to me, I can't wait to tell you about them. It's like things don't matter until I tell you."

Rosetta said, "I feel the same way. And before I fall asleep I remember the things you said that night. I say them over and laugh in my pillow."

"So you're saying we can still talk?

"We can talk, but not at school any more. I think we should stop sitting together in chemistry. It's hard not to look at you. I'm sure it shows in my eyes, my expressions. How much I care for you." Rosetta sighed.

"What will we tell Mr. Duncan? We need a reason to not be lab partners."

Rosetta said, "There's that new boy in the class. What's his name? Brian or Byron ... something like that. Why don't you ask Mr. Duncan if you can pair up with him?" You know, make him feel welcome or something like that."

"I guess that would work. I'll ask him tomorrow. You know of course I'm probably going to fail chemistry now without your brain beside me."

"Your brain is fine. And I want to make sure it stays that way. Nobody punching the daylights out of it."

"Goodnight Rosie. Please let's be friends. Don't let anyone, or anything, especially narrow-minded people, take that away from us." Stan was almost begging now.

"It is narrow thinking, Stan, but don't fool yourself into thinking two love-sick kids in rural Indiana are going to change the country."

They rarely spoke in chemistry anymore. At basketball games they flashed each other smiles across the gym floor, which could have been for anyone on the opposite side, but they knew who they were meant for.

One night at a game, Stan, easy-going Stan, committed a personal foul that evicted him from the game. He flagrantly elbowed an opponent in the ribs and then shoved him off the floor. His teammates, as well as Rosetta, were surprised by his unusual behavior.

In their phone conversation, he confessed what provoked the attack. During warm-ups he heard the boy he fouled say something about the pretty black cheerleader. He said he had heard dark meat was pretty tasty. Stan looked across the floor at Rosetta who was doing cartwheels, her green satin panties showing. The other boy was watching her. The whistle blew to end warm-ups but the remark kept eating at Stan, the anger building. First chance he had, he gave him the elbow.

"Stan, you're not going to survive your senior year at this rate. I'm not good for you."

"No, Rosie, you are very good for me. And I'll be good too. I promise."

December

On the last day of school before Christmas break, Stan surveyed the activity in the chemistry lab before he slipped an index card in Rosetta's chemistry book, the top of the card sticking out so she would see it. It said, *Rosey, look under the chair in the first row of the auditorium on the left side facing the stage.*

She got a hall pass from Mr. Duncan to use the restroom and ran to the auditorium. Luckily there was not a class meeting that hour. Under the first chair, just as promised, was another note. *Go to the far west corner table in the cafeteria. Look under the table.* Rosetta, now caught up in the spirit of it, ran to the cafeteria. It was virtually empty except for one custodian mopping the floor. *West? What direction was west?* She ran her hand under one table. Nothing. She ran to the opposite corner and found the index card. *Go to the Christmas tree in the foyer at the school entrance. Santa left something there for you.* Now almost giddy in the scavenger pursuit she found the shortest route to the foyer and to the Christmas tree the art class had decorated with handmade ornaments. There were several wrapped packages beneath it. She picked them up, one at a time, shook them and realized they were empty. No name tags. She peered behind them and moved a few when she saw a little box with her name on it. She grabbed it and ran to her locker where she put it in a zippered pocket of her backpack.

When she got back into the room and returned the pass, Mr.

Duncan looked up and said, "Why so happy? Did Santa come to your house early?"

Rosetta, not realizing she was smiling from ear to ear replied, "I think he did."

Later that night in the privacy of her room, she placed the box in the back of her sock drawer and couldn't wait to talk to Stan. Was she supposed to open it now or wait till Christmas day?

That night on the phone, clutching the box in one hand, she asked Stan, "Do I open my present now or Christmas morning?"

"Now!" His voice was full of excitement.

She unwrapped the little box and he heard her gasp when she saw a class ring, a bold green stone with a gold Maverick insignia and initials SK on either side.

"Oh, Stan. I can't keep this. It's too special. You should keep your class ring."

"I want you to have it. Please keep it forever. No matter what happens to us, I'll never love anyone the way I love you. I know it. This way a part of me will always be with you."

"If I had a class ring I would give you mine," she said. I guess you had to order them your junior year. I'll think of something special though."

She took the ring to bed that night and in the morning her hand was still clutched around it. She returned it to the little velvet box and put it in the back of her sock drawer. Then she changed her mind and put it in the drawer with her panties. She knew that was as close as Stan would ever get to her most intimate and private self.

Christmas Eve, most families in the country gathered around their televisions to hear the words of astronaut Frank Borman as Apollo 8 circled the moon, saying good night and giving blessings "to all on the good earth."

Rosetta's home was filled with Chicago relatives. She and Stan had no chance to talk until late on Christmas night. After all the presents were opened, the turkey and trimmings eaten, the kitchen cleaned and opened again for turkey sandwiches, all the family games played, including the traditional charades that allowed even little cousins to join in, Rosetta crept downstairs to the kitchen phone. Making sure everyone was asleep she called Stan as they planned.

Stan's first words were, "Rosey, did you hear the broadcast from Apollo 8 last night?"

"Yes, it was so beautiful. When Frank Borman said something about the good earth, I thought of you Stan. Of us. I wish it were a good earth. One where we could be together."

"Maybe someday it will be Rosey. I mean who ever thought we would circle the moon? I just want to circle my arms around you. Maybe someday our love will be as normal as a rocket to the moon."

Stan's brother Dan was home from college for Christmas break and Stan wanted so much to tell him about Rosey. He wanted to tell someone. No, not tell, he wanted to shout it. Then he thought about the beating in the parking lot. What if Dan advised him to leave Rosey alone? No, he couldn't risk Dan's disapproval. It would taint what he and Rosey had. It was special and he was going to keep it that way.

April

In the months after the holidays, they gave each other secret smiles in chemistry when no one was looking. On their phone calls, they told each other everything they were feeling about anything. They were best friends in every sense of the word. Their yearning and passion grew but they knew they couldn't risk being together. They caressed each other with their voices, their laughter, and sometimes their tears. In lieu of real kisses they talked about how good it would feel to kiss again, for their lips to touch. One night they both confided to one another that neither of them had ever "done it."

"I want you to be the first with me," she said.

"Oh, Rosey, Rosey. I wish I could be the first. And the second and the third."

The next day in class Rosetta looked away when she saw Stan. She blushed recalling the intimacy of their conversation of the night before as if he were seeing her without her clothes on.

May

The entire school was buzzing with prom talk.

"Rosey, I wish we could go to the prom together. I really don't even want to go with someone else."

"I don't either, but we have to, Stan. This is our senior year. We should be enjoying this time in our lives. My parents would never understand if I didn't want to go."

"I know, I know. We have to. Bad enough not being together but watching you dance with some other guy. So who is this guy from Chicago? I'm jealous. Should I be jealous?"

"Silly, of course not. I've known him since third grade. Our families are good friends and I'm sure he has a *real* girlfriend in Chicago. He's being very nice to come down so I have a prom date. After all, I've told everyone all year that I have boyfriend in Chicago. I better produce someone. And our parents are in cahoots — planning a big weekend."

"So his whole family is coming? They're staying with your family? He's going to be with you all weekend? This is getting worse by the minute."

"How about you? You're going with Julie, one of the prettiest girls in the senior class. And on top of that, she's nice too."

"Rosey, Julie is nice and she is pretty. But she doesn't make me feel like mush inside when I see her."

"Mush? Ewww. I'd hate to dance at the prom with a mushy guy.

So glad you're not my date." Rosetta tried to make the moment light and when Stan laughed she felt better.

The Friday before prom, Rosetta waited until Otis left the room in chemistry and spoke to Stan. "Okay, let's make a pact. We're each going to have a good time at the prom tomorrow. Agreed?"

"Agreed," Stan replied. They smiled bravely at each other, like two kids trying to say goodbye without crying after a week at overnight camp.

❧

Prom night the gymnasium was transformed, thanks to the hard work of the decorating committee, into an *Evening in Paris*. As couples entered one at a time under the fake Arc de Triumph they saw the makeshift Eiffel Tower in the center of the room, reaching to the ceiling under a dark blue starry night and a crescent moon. Stan and Julie had just passed thru the Arc and turned to watch other couples arriving.

When Rosetta and Mr. Chicago walked through, Stan was not prepared for the strong ache and longing that filled every pore of his body. The sight of Rosetta in a dress the color of ripe peaches, layers and layers of peach petals against her beautiful brown skin took his breath away. It was all he could do to not walk up to her and wrap her in his arms. Like a star-struck kid, he continued to watch her and when her eyes met his across the way, she flashed her big smile and his heart did a flip-flop like the first time he saw her.

"It's just not fair," he thought. He looked at Julie beside him, smiling up at him in her pretty blue gown. He thought, *It's not fair to Julie either.* He recalled the pact he and Rosetta had made.

"Julie, would you like to dance?"

❧

"Talk time" as they called it, was running out for Stan and Rosetta. Their senior year would soon be over. Rosetta's father wanted her to spend the summer in a Chicago enrichment program for pre-med students. In September, both of them would be leaving for separate colleges. Rosetta to Purdue and Stan to Indiana.

On graduation night, in their dark green gowns and caps with gold tassels, all the seniors were lined up outside Middleburg's Civic Center auditorium, the only building in town big enough to house the families of the graduates. Boys were in one line, girls in the other, and as they heard the first strains of *Pomp and Circumstance*, they began marching to the main entrance where the two lines met and they formed a two-person entry.

Neither Stan nor Rosetta could contain their excitement that afternoon at rehearsal when they discovered that when the two lines joined, they were marching in side by side. It was all Stan could do to not reach for her hand. To hold the beautiful fingers.

After rehearsal they found each other and in all the commotion no one seemed to notice them. "Isn't this a wonderful end to our year, Stan? You and me together." Rosetta flashed her big wide smile.

"It's a perfect finish," he said.

When they walked away from each other, Rosetta's temporary joy was replaced with a tinge of sadness as she thought, *Yes, this will soon be the finish of* us.

After graduation there was a big party in the gymnasium with a band until midnight. Most of the seniors were then going to house parties and celebrations the parents were happy to host to keep them from driving to Indianapolis. It was customary to stay out all night and return to the school in the morning where parents had volunteered to cook breakfast.

When the band announced the last dance, as couples poured onto the dance floor, Stan saw Rosetta walk out of the side door of the gymnasium.

He followed her out. They were the only two there. "Rosey," he called. "Where are you going?"

She turned, surprised to see him. "It got so hot in there. Thought I'd wait outside for my ride."

"Are you going to any parties tonight?" he asked.

"Frontier Village is having a big party at the community center. Wanna come?" she asked jokingly. They both knew he would be the only white person there. "How about you?" she looked up at him, wishing she could touch his face.

"There's a couple of them I'm going to pop in on. Then come back here for breakfast."

She looked around to make sure they were still alone. "Would anyone miss you if you didn't go to the parties?"

He wasn't sure what she meant. "No, I don't think so. Everyone's going every which way tonight."

She said, "I need to show up at Frontier Village for a while, but no one would know if I left a little early. My parents are meeting me back here for the breakfast. They're cooking."

"Are you saying we should try and meet up?" he couldn't believe what she was suggesting.

"Why not? It's our last chance. I'm leaving for Chicago tomorrow."

"Oh, Rosey," was all he could say.

They heard the music stop and a few kids were walking out of the gym. Quickly, she said, "Let's meet back here at 2 a.m.?"

"I'll be here," he said as he walked back into the gym.

At promptly two in the morning, Stan's orange Chevy Nova pulled into the school student parking lot where he saw Rosetta's parents' car, the largest model, the Sierra.

"How did you get the car?" he asked when she slipped into the front seat of the Nova.

"I had my ride drop me off at home before the party. I told my parents I wanted a car in case I wanted to leave the party early."

"Where shall we go?" he asked.

"Don't ask me," she giggled nervously. "I've lived here less than a year. You're the native son. Don't you know any romantic secluded spots?"

"Anywhere with you would be romantic," he said. "But I guess we should get off of Main Street." Some cars were cruising up and down Main Street, horns blowing and kids screaming out of the windows.

Neither one spoke as he drove out of town and turned off on a dirt road surrounded by tall trees. It was a balmy spring night and after an unseasonably cold winter, the warm air, fragrant with lilacs made the evening full of promise. A mile down the dirt road, Stan turned left and they were in a clearing with a small lake. The water glistened under an almost full moon.

"Wow, how did you know about this?" she asked, obviously impressed.

"My dad took me fishing here a few times."

"Did you catch anything?" she asked, trying to keep the conversation light while her heart was beating furiously.

Stan turned off the ignition and looked at her. "Never anything as beautiful as you."

"So, Mr. Smooth Talker, do you bring all your girls here?" she teased.

"No, I take most of them to the make out spot up on the hill behind the school."

"Really?"

"Rosey, you know there's been no other girls for me. You've been my only girl all year. But there is a make-out spot where everyone goes. Probably lots of cars there tonight."

"So ...," she said.

"So ... what?" he answered.

"So, do you want to make out?"

"I thought you'd never ask." He leaned over and she met him halfway. He kissed her lips, her neck, her eyes, her ears. Then back to her lips again and again.

Finally, Rosetta said, "It's too beautiful a night to stay in the car. Can we sit outside?"

"I think I have an old blanket in the trunk," Stan said as he got out of the car. Rosetta stepped out of her side as he pulled a blanket out.

"Well, aren't you the good 'be prepared' boy scout?"

"Do you think they give badges for making out?" Stan asked. "I'm going for one of those!"

Rosetta felt the tears starting. "I'm going to miss your corny jokes."

Stan wiped the tear on her cheek with his finger. "Sure, I make you laugh. That's why you're crying now."

They had spread the blanket and were both on their knees facing each other. When he hugged her they collapsed side by side.

"Don't cry, Rosey. We can write and talk once a week. I'll have lots of money with my summer job. We'll use pay phones and no one will ever know."

"Stan?" she said his name as she ran her fingers through his curly hair.

"Yes?" he responded in a throaty voice.

"You know how we talked about how neither one of us has ever done it?"

"Yes."

"And how we wish we could be the first for each other?"

"Yes."

"Well, I think we should. Here. Tonight."

"Oh, Rosey," was all he could say. "Are you sure?" I don't have anything with me ... like to keep you from getting pregnant. I mean I did not expect this at all. Not to mention I don't even own one."

Rosetta gave a little giggle. "So you really aren't the prepared scout after all." Then she said in a serious tone. "I didn't plan on it either, Stan. If you hadn't seen me leave the dance we wouldn't even be here and certainly not talking about ... about *it*." Rosey touched the dimple in Stan's chin and her beautiful full lips were so close to his. Although there was not another person in sight, she spoke in a whisper. "I was thinking while we were driving here that we've been denied so much. All we wanted to do was be able to see each other, to walk home from school together, to dance. We wanted so little and it would have been so harmless. *They,* whoever *they* are, have robbed us of so much, but they can't take this moment from us." She kissed him with an urgency. "I don't want to spend a lifetime regretting that we didn't. We may never have this chance again," she whispered.

"But —" Stan started to protest again.

"It's okay. We can be careful. Can't we?" she asked.

"I guess we can. I don't know. I've never done this."

The warm spring night scented with lilacs, the moon, the love they felt for so many months. The sadness of the possibility that they might not see each other for months. It was too much to resist.

There were a few clumsy moments as they began to undress.

"Your graduation dress is so pretty. I don't want you to mess it up,"

Stan said. "Let me help you." He reached for the back zipper, pulled it down and the dress fell off her shoulders to her waist. Then he got his arm caught in one of her bra straps and they both giggled with embarrassment. Then it came easily, step by step, all the things they had talked about for so many months. They were like kids who had never tasted sugar, now in a candy store.

Afterwards, he stroked her shiny black hair. "Are you okay? Not sorry?"

She smiled and twisted his curly hair with one finger. "I'll never be sorry that you were my first. When you gave me your class ring you said it was for me to remember that you'll always be with me, wherever we go. I wanted to give you something special too. All year I've been thinking what I could give you that could only be from me. You know, like a lock of hair? But this ... my virginity. The most precious thing I have ... had ... is now yours ... forever."

Stan kept touching her face and asked her again, "You sure you're not sorry?"

"Not for a minute. Are you?" she asked.

"Well, I am sorry that I don't think I was as careful as I should have been." Stan lowered his head. "I just couldn't stop myself."

"Hush, hush," she said softly. "It'll be fine."

"What if you get pregnant?"

She felt invincible. She knew kids that did it all the time and got away with it. She brushed off his comment glibly, "What if I do? I'll have a baby that is probably lighter skin than you are. Remember the arm test. Your skin was darker than mine."

"We could get married," Stan said. "We could move to Chicago where color doesn't matter."

"Stan, color matters everywhere today. The country's gone crazy."

"But, Rosey, we could make it work."

"No Stan, we'd be in no-man land shunned by both our families ... our friends. I won't let you ruin your future."

"I can't imagine any future without you."

At the graduation breakfast Stan sat with his friends and Rosetta with hers. Evidently no one missed them at the parties. Each time they stole glances at each other his chest filled with a love so strong, there seemed to be no room for food. He could hardly eat.

There were two black sets of parents along with four white couples serving the food. Stan recognized her parents as her mother looked like an older version of Rosetta. Tall, graceful, thin. Her father looked distinguished, even with an apron, in a white shirt and tie. He felt a tenderness for them rising in him because they belonged to her. He wanted so much to tell them how much he loved their beautiful daughter, to thank them somehow for bringing her to Middleburg. Instead, he thanked them for the hash browns, bacon, and cinnamon rolls.

June

After Rosetta arrived at her grandmother's house in Chicago where she would be spending the summer, Rosetta sent Stan a letter, signing it, "I'm so blue without you."

Three days later a bouquet of a dozen red roses and one pink rose arrived at her grandmother's house with a message, "Red Roses for a Blue Lady. The pink is for how sweetly you blushed at the graduation breakfast. Love always, S"

Her grandmother smiled and said, "Well, well, young lady, looks like *you* have a secret admirer."

Rosetta blushed. *If Grandma only knew how secret it was.* "Just a special boy, Grandma. Nothing serious."

The next week she received a package from Stan with a 45 rpm record. She ran to the turntable and played it. The words made her ache. Andy Williams crooning, *Though we gotta say good-bye for the summer. Baby I promise you this. I'll send you all my love every day in a letter. Sealed with a kiss.* She played it constantly.

July

The next six weeks Rosetta and Stan wrote to each other and talked once a week. For the first time ever Rosetta was not totally honest with Stan. She told him Chicago was fun, especially to be with her childhood girlfriends again. She told him the summer enrichment program was challenging. She told him she loved him and missed him. What she didn't tell him was that she had missed her period.

The suspicion had starting growing in her when she was a week late, but she tried to ignore it. Then she told herself it was her fear that was messing up her body rhythms. When her small breasts started to plump up and feel tender, her anxiety grew and it was the first nagging thought when she woke up. Her second thought was how to get to the bathroom in time to throw up and to do it quietly so her grandmother would not hear.

Finally, on July 20, 1969, Rosetta took a city bus to the free clinic on the far south side of Chicago alone. The waiting room was crowded with pregnant women, many with babies on their laps or toddlers with runny noses playing at their feet. What was she doing here? The reality of her situation was a stark and grim contrast to a moonlit graduation night when she so foolishly had a romantic notion. *How could she have been so naive, so stupid?*

Although she was prepared for the worst news, when they confirmed her pregnancy, it was like someone had punched her in the stomach. She couldn't get her breath. The doctor was asking her something but his voice sounded far away.

"Do your parents know?"

She shook her head. She had to get out of the office. It was suffocating. She needed some air. "I'll tell them tonight," she assured the doctor and walked out quickly. She made it to the curb before she threw up.

On the way home from the clinic, as if she were not sad enough, someone on the bus had a boom box playing Jefferson Airplanes new hit, "We Can Be Together." The tears rolled down her cheeks as she knew this would never be true for her and Stan.

The evening news that night showed footage of Neil Armstrong and Buzz Aldrin landing on the moon. She heard the words over and over, something about a small step for man and a giant leap for mankind. Another painful reminder that it was not a giant step for her and Stan. Not their kind.

The following week Rosetta's parents were coming to Chicago for her summer program graduation. She knew she had to tell them of her situation before it was too late. Although abortions were illegal, she was sure her father would find a way to terminate the pregnancy. She had overheard her parents talking once of how her father arranged a safe abortion for a friend's daughter with a colleague.

Rosetta struggled with her decision. She wanted so much to keep a piece of Stan. The very thought of his baby growing inside her made her weak with desire for him, but after much soul searching she knew there was no way she and Stan could have a life together. She could never tell Stan. He was such a foolish idealist. He would insist on being with her, on marrying her and trying to raise this baby in a world that would never accept them. She wasn't going to allow him to do something so crazy and stupid. Her parents would never approve of a mixed marriage either. Although she berated herself daily for her foolish act, insisting on giving him her virginity, fulfilling their love, a part of her stubbornly had no regrets. There were still moments when she cherished the memory of that night with Stan.

Rosetta's parents arrived the last day of the enrichment program. Graduation was that evening with a big party at her Grandmother's house, partly her celebration and partly family reunion. Not wanting to tarnish a special evening, Rosetta vowed to tell her parents the following morning.

Fate, however, intervened.

Early the next morning, everyone was gathered around the breakfast table, basking in the celebration of the night before.

"Rosetta, we are so proud of you." Her father pinched her cheek as he had often done since she was a toddler.

Grandma said, "Yes 'um. Soon we'll have two doctors in the family." She beamed at her granddaughter. "Your granddaddy would have been so proud of you."

Rosetta smiled and hoped the wave of morning sickness she was feeling did not show in her face. The smell and sight of the scrambled eggs made her want to throw up again. She already had once earlier that morning. She was about to respond to Grandma when the doorbell rang. "I'll get it," her father said as he went to the front door.

Two men in Army dress uniforms stood there, one holding an American flag folded into a triangle. Dr. Stone had a sinking feeling in the pit of his stomach. He couldn't catch his breath.

"Is this the home of Luther Johnson?" they asked.

Dr. Stone nodded and answered in a barely audible voice, "Yes."

"Is Mrs. Johnson available?"

"She is. I'm her son-in-law. Luther's brother-in-law. If this is the bad news I fear, would you please let me tell her? I'm afraid seeing you would be a terrible shock — she has a heart condition."

They offered him the flag, the official documents, and their condolences and confirmed his worst fear. His wife's younger brother, Luther had been killed in Vietnam. Dr. Stone stood in the foyer holding the flag. How could he tell his wife and her mother? There was no easy way to do it. He was still standing there when his wife came out of the kitchen.

"Arthur, who ...?" She spotted the flag and ran to him. "No, no, not Luther. It can't be Luther."

Dr. Stone held her, the flag crushed between them. "Go back to the kitchen and make sure your Mama is sitting down. I'll get my black bag. She'll need something."

Mrs. Stone left the flag on the table in the foyer, not wanting her mother to see it till they could prepare her. She wiped her face of tears although she knew there would be many more.

"Mama, please seat down a minute." She said when she returned to the kitchen.

Her mother, who was standing by the kitchen sink, scrubbing a pot, asked, "Sit down? Girl, I got work to do. No time for sitting."

"Please Mama. Just sit."

When Dr. Stone returned with his bag, Mama looked from her daughter to her son-in-law. Her face froze in terror. She knew something was wrong. Charlotte Stone went to her mother's chair.

Dr. Stone started, "Mama, it's Luther ..."

Even though she was sitting, she fell to her knees, crying, "My boy, my baby boy. They killed my boy."

Rosetta and her mother both rushed to lift Grandma. All three held each other and cried while Dr. Stone prepared a sedative injection.

Rosetta couldn't believe it. Her favorite, Uncle Luther, so handsome, so young, so strong. The life of every family gathering. He couldn't be gone. She knew she could not tell her parents her own tragedy in light of this one. Later, she would tell them. Later.

The funeral was delayed for several weeks, awaiting the return of Luther's body to the States. In the meantime, the household was in a state of mourning. People coming every day, food on the doorstep each morning. Friends they hadn't seen forever showing up to offer sympathy. There never seemed to be a right time for Rosetta to tell her parents, especially since her father had to return to the clinic in Middleburg until the funeral.

"Rosetta, do you want to come home with me. To see your friends before you go to college?"

"No, Daddy, I want to stay here with Mommy. I think she needs me now." Rosetta longed to see Stan, but she did not want him to see her. There was no way she could keep her secret if they talked each night again, and especially if he saw her. He would see it in her eyes. She could never lie to him face to face. No, Middleburg was not an option.

The night she told Stan on the phone of losing Uncle Luther, she added, "Stan, I've been thinking. We're both going off to college and we shouldn't try to hang onto each other. We need to live our lives fully on campus. We had our wonderful senior year and our last night together and ...," she didn't know how to continue. But she knew she had to let him go.

"But, Rosey, I would miss you so much. Can't we write to each other? And when we're home for holidays maybe we could see each other. No one would be paying any attention to us like they did in high school."

"Stan, please, don't make this harder than it is. I'm so sad now about Luther and I might as well be sad about us too and get it all over with at the same time. I don't want us to sneak around anymore. Please, Stan, try to understand. I'll love you always, but it just isn't our time."

"Rosey, I'll always love you too and to prove it I'll do whatever you ask, even though it hurts so much. I won't call you or write, but promise me if you change your mind, maybe later, if you ever want to talk, you'll call me? Promise?"

"I promise, Stan."

❧

After the funeral, when the house had cleared of all the guests and Grandmother was asleep, Rosetta knew she could not delay the talk with her parents any longer. She joined them in the kitchen where they were sitting quietly. To Rosetta they looked so forlorn, and she knew in a few minutes they would be even sadder.

"Mom, Dad, I have to tell you something. I know you're going to be disappointed in me, and I'm so sorry. So sorry." She put her face in her hands and cried.

"What is ...," her mother started to say.

She blurted it out, "I'm pregnant."

Her parents looked stunned. Her mother said, "Are you sure?"

"Yes, I saw a doctor at a clinic. Here on the south side."

"You went to a clinic?" Her father seemed more disappointed in that then the fact that she was pregnant. "Why didn't you come to me?" he asked. His voice was kind and sympathetic, yet hurt.

"I guess I was hoping it wasn't true."

Her mother, however, made no effort to hide her anger and disappointment. "Rosetta, you have thrown away the wonderful future your father and I had planned for you. I can't believe you were so foolish. We talked about this. How important education is for a black girl."

"I'm so sorry." Rosetta put her face in her hands and continued sobbing.

Her father put his arms around her but her mother kept her distance, shaking her head in disbelief. She walked around the kitchen in circles, her arms crossed tightly against her chest.

"It's going to be alright, baby," her father said gently. "Everything's going to be all right. We'll take care of this. Don't you worry."

Rosetta cried harder and kept saying, "I'm so sorry to disappoint you. I was going to tell you sooner and then Uncle Luther ...."

Then her mother started crying too and her voice softened a bit. "Do you want to tell us who the father is? I didn't know you even had a boyfriend."

She looked at them and knew she would not deceive them anymore. "You didn't know because you never met him. You never met him because ... because he's white."

Her mother put both hands to her forehead and shook her head in disbelief. She shrieked the next words to her, "Why Rosetta, why? Why would you dishonor your family like this?" Her father's chin dropped while he looked at Rosetta and his mouth seemed frozen open.

When neither of her parents said anything else, she went on, "And I don't want to tell him because he'd want to get married. That's how he would be. He would want to do the right thing. He's too idealistic. He has no idea how hard it would be for us. Not now with the whole country in an uproar. How could a black and white marriage ever work? You said so yourself one night at dinner."

"Did you consent to this? Did he force himself on you?" Her mother asked.

"Of course not. I love him. He's a good person. Nice ... and decent ... and kind. All we ever did is talk on the phone. We never saw each other."

"Well, you must have seen each other once," her mother said sarcastically.

"I mean we didn't see each other on a regular basis. We just talked and we were good friends. One time, when you were in Indianapolis, I did invite him to the house. We just talked and danced. That's all. It was all so innocent. The next Monday, three black boys who saw him leaving the house beat him up and we agreed to never see each other again. He was afraid mostly for what might happen to me. He never wanted to hurt me."

"So how did ...?" her father started to ask.

"Graduation night, we ran into each other after the dance and agreed to meet later instead of going to all the parties. It was spontaneous. We never planned to be together so we really weren't prepared for what happened. Please don't blame him. It was my fault. I insisted 'cause I felt the world owed us one night. Crazy prejudiced people who think skin color matters. They robbed us of so much and I wanted our say one time."

"Graduation night." Her father said. Rosetta could see him doing the math in his head. "We may be too late, Rosetta, to terminate this pregnancy safely. I'm not going to put you in any danger. We'll take good care of you and if the pregnancy goes full term, there is always adoption."

"Are you in touch with him at all?" her mother asked, still in an angry tone.

"No, I told him we each needed to go on with our lives — alone. He's going to IU. He thinks I'm going to Purdue but obviously that's not going to happen." Her voice quivered when she saw the disappointment in her father's face.

Dr. Stone looked at his wife, "I think it's time we all came back to Chicago. Home where we belong. With our people."

Rosetta took a deep breath and looked both her parents in their eyes, "I've decided though. If I have this baby I'm going to keep it. And if it's a boy, I'm going to name him Luther."

All three of them cried.

＜＞

Two days before Stan left for college he took a ride through Frontier Village. When he saw the *For Sale* sign in front of her house, he couldn't remember ever hurting so much. The saddest day of his young uneventful life was the day his dog died five years ago and this was 10 times worse. He drove home and shot baskets until he was too tired to think anymore.

The next day he started packing boxes for his dorm at Indiana. As he sorted through his belongings, he saw the music box he had stumbled on at the neighbor's yard sale, the one he planned to give Rosetta to take to college.

He turned the key at the bottom and listened one last time to the song she loved from *Doctor Zhivago*, "Somewhere My Love." Its sad and haunting melody reminded him that Rosetta was right. This chapter of their life was closed. He put the music box in the stack of things going to the attic.

Part Three

Teddy

Indiana
October 1999

"Hey, can you use one more guy?" I spot a game of basketball in the park. They look like junior high kids, but I'm desperate for a game. It's a decent scrimmage even if it's with the playground set. Before I know it, it's almost dark. I pedal home as fast as I can. I know Mom will be worried. She worries more about things now than she used to. Like she knows bad things can happen for no reason.

Out of nowhere, a dog runs in front of me. I swerve and miss the dog, but then a little boy darts in front of my bike. I hit my brakes and try to swerve but my back wheel clips him. I hear his cry. He's on the ground. I jump off my bike and run back to him. A lady's bending over him, crying, "Mikey, Mikey, are you okay?" She's holding his head in her arm.

I'm terrified. "I'm so sorry, I didn't see him."

The lady looks up at me and pleads, "Call someone, quick. Get help."

I run to the closest house and bang on the door. "Help, please, someone. Call 9-1-1. There's a little boy hurt. In the street."

I run back to the boy. "They're calling 9-1-1. Is he okay? Please say he's okay. I didn't see him — honest."

The mother's still trying to revive him, holding his head in her arms. "Not your fault. He chased that dog between the cars. He's too quick. I know better than to let go of his hand even for a second."

Although she's trying to make me feel better, I hear "not your fault" and wonder how many times I'll be in accidents that are "not my fault." *Please, please let the boy be okay.*

We hear a siren. As the sound gets louder and then stops, people come out on their porches. Soon there's a crowd on the sidewalk. The paramedic runs to Mikey who isn't moving or making a sound. I stand back and watch everything like it's a scene in a movie. A horror movie. There's no blood and I hope that's a good sign.

"Is this your bike?" someone asks. It's on the side of the road. I pick it up while people stare at me like I'm the villain. *Not my fault, not my fault. Wish I could believe it.* I overhear the paramedics, "His vitals are good. Let's get him in." They pull out a stretcher.

"What hospital?" I ask. "I need to know he's going to be okay."

"There's only one in town. Middleburg Memorial."

I'm left standing by the curb. I walk back to the house that called 9-1-1 and ask if I can use their phone.

Mom must hear the panic in my voice, "Teddy, where are you? What's wrong?"

"A little boy ran in front of my bike. I have to know he's okay. Can you take me to the emergency room?"

"Oh, Teddy." I can tell by Mom's voice she's about to cry. Hasn't she cried enough? And now I do this? "Just tell me where you are."

I'm on the curb when Mom pulls up and runs to me. I try the blink, blink, squeeze trick but it doesn't work. I start crying while she holds me bent over her shoulders. "It's okay, Teddy. It's okay." She keeps rubbing her hands up and down my back.

I want the little boy to be fine, but now I'm crying for all of it. For Dad, for the friends I miss, for the basketball team I probably won't make, and for all the rotten changes in our lives. It's months of tears gushing out. I'm glad no one is in the street but us. I wipe my face with my sleeve and throw my bike in the back of the Explorer.

When we get to the emergency room, Mom and I rush to the mother.

"I'm Teddy's Mom. Mary Kostoff. How is he?"

"I think he's just got a few bruises. He came to and started crying in the ambulance and that was a relief to us all. It wasn't your son's fault. It's nice of you to come."

"If you don't mind, we'd like to wait here with you."

"I'd appreciate the company. I'm Joan Keck by the way."

Mom and Mrs. Keck talk and I wander off to find a bathroom. When I come out I make a wrong turn and find myself in a different visitors' waiting room. There's a boy in a wheelchair who's wrapped almost entirely in white gauze with two teens talking to him. Even from where I'm standing I see his dark blue eyes are a stark contrast to the white bandages. They all laugh, including bandage boy.

"We better go," one of the boys says. "Do you want us to take you back to your room?"

"No, I think I'll stay here awhile. I need a change of scenery — even if it is just different wallpaper." He turns his head in mock admiration of the wall. The boys leave and bandage boy and I are left in the room. He looks at me and says, "Hi. Welcome to Pharaoh's tomb." Before I can respond, he says, "A joke — bandages, mummy, tomb, get it? You visiting someone tonight?"

"No, I was on my bike. A little boy ran out in front of me. He's in the emergency room now."

"That's too bad, man. Hope he's okay."

"You and me both."

"My name's Joe. I'm sort of a regular here at the Halfway House. That's what I call it. Half way between the Burn Center in Indy and the time I get to go home." Here's this kid with bandages head to toe and he's trying to make *me* comfortable like it's his hospital and he's the host.

"I'm Teddy." I'm not sure what the etiquette is for questions, but my curiosity is high. *What happened to him?* Like a mind reader, he answers, "Burns. Got a little carried away. I saw that new movie *October Sky* and got all inspired by the rocket boys. Things got out of control. It's my own fault. I wasn't exactly following the directions. I almost went farther than the rocket."

I wonder how he can joke about all this, "So how long will you be here?"

"When the new skin is safe from infection," he says. "Great movie though. Did you see it?"

"Yeah, it was good. Made me want to build a rocket, too, but science isn't exactly my strong suit. Lincoln Logs are more my speed." Although his face is covered with bandages, I think I detect a smile.

Just then Mom comes in. "Teddy, there you are. They're going to let Mikey go home. I think it will be good for you to see him talking." I breathe a sigh of relief.

"That's good news, man," Joe says.

"Joe, this is my Mom."

"Hi Mom."

There's an awkward pause, like I should say something else, but I'm not sure what. "Hope you get home soon, Joe," I say as I turn to follow Mom down the corridor.

In the emergency room, Mikey's sitting up holding a little stuffed bear. There's a big white gauze wrapped around his knee. One cheek has a dark red bruise and is almost twice the size of the other one. He shows me the bear close up, like right in my face. "Look what they gave me. His name is Teddy."

"Well, my name is Teddy too." Everyone laughs like I'm the world's greatest comedian.

The burly dad asks Mom is she's related to Dan Kostoff. "My brother-in-law," she says.

"Tell him Bruce Keck said hello. We were in the same class." I could sense that Mom wanted to ask him about Dad too, but figured it wasn't the time for it.

At home, Mom tells the whole story to Baba, who sits on the edge of her chair, hanging on to every word, like it's one of her soap operas. Headline: TUNE IN TOMORROW. WILL TEDDY LOSE HIS BIKE PRIVILEGES?

Before I turn off my bedside light, I glance at the latest quote in the *Book of Life*. *Without hope, there is no life.* That's it. That's what I saw. Hope in that mess of gauze. He seemed happy, positive. How could he be that way when he's probably been in pain for what — weeks? Months? Then I remember George, the caretaker's words. *Find someone worse off than you.* Joe's worse off than me physically, but that spark in his eyes tells me he isn't worse off inside. I already know I want to go back. I want to see what hopeful looks like again.

So am I doing something nice for him like George said, or is it something for me? Somehow it doesn't matter. It's something I have to do. The last thing I remember before I fall asleep are Joe's bright blue eyes.

⁂

Thursday night is Middleburg's Homecoming bonfire in the big empty lot next to the football field. From the way people are talking, the whole town shows up — parents, grandparents, little brothers, and sisters. That's one thing about this small town. I don't know if there isn't anything else for people to do, but everyone's wrapped up in what the high school is doing. It's corny, and even though I don't want to admit it, I do like it.

It's a warm October evening. I'm hearing things all week about Indian Summer. Knowing who will have the exact definition, I turn to Mindy, the walking encyclopedia. She doesn't disappoint me.

"According to Webster, 'a period of warm, dry weather usually accompanied by a hazy atmosphere, occurring in the United States and Canada in the late autumn or early winter.' Once you live here awhile, you'll like it even more because what we all know that you don't is that it's some of the nicest weather we're going to have for a long, long time."

"In Arizona we have only two seasons — hot and hotter." She laughs, so I don't tell her we do have seasons in the desert. I don't tell her how the beautiful spring evenings smell like someone cut open a whole crate of oranges. Or how, in the late summer, the dramatic monsoon storms build in a just a few minutes. They move across the sky faster than you can drive out of the blinding dust and pouring rain that follows. Or how the spectacular heat lightning puts on a dazzling show in the night sky. Who ever thought you could grieve weather?

⁂

When I get home I find out that even Baba's coming to the bonfire. "Your Dedo and me. We like the big fire. We go every year with Stan and Dan. Dedo, he likes so much, he keeps going after boys go to college. I never go for a long time."

We have Baba's special pizza with a Bulgarian twist. The kitchen smells good and when Uncle Dan, Aunt Joyce, and Sophie arrive, we fill our plates like starving refugees.

After dinner we all pile into Uncle Dan's SUV. Ruby sits on Sophie's lap and giggles when they put one seat belt around both of them. Sophie's teaching her the school fight song to sing at the bonfire. Cathy bangs the bumper of her car seat in rhythm. It's times like this when we're having fun that I miss Dad the most. My chest is tight and it's hard to breathe. I avoid Mom's eyes.

The bonfire is lit, the flames flare high and the crowd cheers when they throw the opponent dummy into the flames. Even from where we are standing, the flames give off a scorching heat. I think of Joe and all the bandages. I can't help but wonder if he'll ever get near a fire again.

Mary

Aunt Joyce takes Baba, the girls, and me to the annual Covered Bridge Festival in a neighboring community about 10 miles away. It's a scenic ride with brilliant foliage of red and orange leaves. As Aunt Joyce drives, she also keeps us entertained with stories of the latest antics of her junior high students. "They should all be theatre majors. So much drama every day."

We take the girls to the face-painting painting booth, the petting zoo, and the kiddie rides. We indulge their food fair requests, including big sticky cones of cotton candy. We explore all the craft booths and discover a display of a beautiful memory quilt made of little girls' dress fabrics.

As we admire it, the owner says, "This one's not for sale. It's a wedding gift for my daughter who hasn't even seen it yet." She runs her hand over the fabric with a gentle touch. "I don't know why I saved so many of her dresses growing up. I passed most of them on to her cousins but some of them I couldn't part with. I guess I had a premonition that someday I would do this."

Baba looks at me and Joyce, "I save many clothes from when Dan and Stan were little boys. I think they are in boxes in the attic."

"I've always wanted to learn to quilt," I say.

"I can teach you, Mary. Let's do quilt together. A memory quilt of Stan. That would be a good thing, no?"

"I think it would be a very good thing," I say and like the expert quilter in her booth, I know now what possessed me to bring some of Stan's favorite shirts with me.

Driving back home on this beautiful autumn day with Cathy asleep in her car seat and Ruby working hard to create a pot holder from the kit Aunt Joyce bought her, I feel contentment and a sense of belonging. Today, I think we did the right thing to move here, especially grateful that the girls can experience the love of an aunt and grandmother. My thoughts are never far from Teddy however. Someday will he be glad we came?

Teddy

Tonight is the Homecoming dance. I'm lonely, missing my friends in Phoenix. I wonder what Liz is doing. Feeling sorry for myself, I think of Joe who is also not going to the dance.

"Mom, would you give me a ride to the hospital? I'd like to visit Joe — the boy with the burns."

She jumps on that like a sale at Macy's. "I'll come back in about an hour?" she says.

I realize I don't even know his last name, but I ask the receptionist if she knows what room Joe, the boy with the burns, is in. "Oh sure, everyone knows Joe," she says and points to the elevator. "Room 304."

His door is partially closed. I knock softly. "Hello, anybody home?"

"Come in." Joe's in bed watching a TV on the wall. He mutes the sound with a remote.

"Hi, I'm Teddy. Remember?" I say the headline running through my head out loud. "RECKLESS BIKER REDUCES TODDLER POPULATION."

"Is the kid okay?" Joe asks.

"He's fine. They sent him home. I just … well, I was just thinking about you and thought you might like some company."

"Why aren't you at the Homecoming dance?"

"I just moved here from Arizona. I know now what that expression, *lonely in a crowd*, means."

"So, is this your good deed for the day? Cheer up the burned boy? Or is it that misery loves company?"

His words shock me. "Hey, if you don't want any company ...." I start to back up.

"I'm sorry. I guess I'm a little low myself tonight," he says.

"The last time I saw you I couldn't believe how upbeat you were. Maybe I was hoping some of that would rub off on me." I'm still standing in the doorway, not sure if he wants me to come in. We both look at each other for a minute and then the spark comes back in his eyes.

"You want *me* to cheer *you* up? That's a good one. How's this for starters? You may not have any friends yet, but you've got two good legs and arms and can walk out of here and go to school every day. And I bet people don't stare at you like you escaped from Pharaoh's tomb."

"Actually, they don't even look at me. No one knows I exist."

"So whose fault is that? Did you ever go up to new kids at your old school to include them?"

"Well, no, not really." I was beginning to be *very* sorry I came. Here, I thought I was being a good guy and now I'm getting a lecture. My opinion of caretaker George's free advice is going down by the minute.

Joe seems to realize he came on too strong. He says, "Hey, let's start over. Come on. Sit down." He points to the chair beside his bed. "Let's pretend we're best friends and you came by to tell me how everyone at school misses me and that cute girl in the last row has a crush on you."

"There *is* a cute girl. How'd you know?"

"Isn't there always? What's her name?"

"Patti, but she's dating some guy on the varsity basketball team, which by the way, I probably won't make. They have some great team that's been together since first grade or something."

"As for me, I don't think I'll be going out for any sports this year. These bandages are kind of a pain to take on and off." It takes me a second to realize he's joking. Then we both laugh.

I tell him about Wally, Liz, and even Dad. I get through it with no blink, blink, squint until I see *his* eyes tearing up. He says, "Yeah, I learned how life can change in just a minute. Too much time to think in here. I want to get out, but not sure I'm ready to face the real world. Not with this face. Hey, that's a good one — face the world."

Once again I'm amazed at his good attitude and wonder what's under all the gauze. I'll be one of the few people who won't ever know what he looked like before.

"Hey, boys, visiting hours have been over for a long time." A nurse peeks her head around the door.

I say, "I'll see you around." Then I realize how stupid that sounds.

Joe laughs, "Oh sure, I'll see you around ... around what? The x-ray room, the hospital cafeteria? Just your normal teen hangouts."

"I mean, is it okay to come back? Can I bring you something?" I ask, as if that's the most unique idea in the world. "Baba, my Grandma, makes the best pizza in the world. Do you like pizza?"

"Hey, I'm a teenager. Of course, I love pizza. I'm supposed to load up on fat grams. Guess it takes a lot of calories to make new skin."

"Great. I'll be back with deep dish sausage."

"Go easy on the garlic. The nurses hate it when I kiss them with bad breath."

As I start to leave, I spot a familiar book on his bedside table, *A Tale of Two Cities.*

"My class is reading that too," I tell him.

"I'm trying to," he says, "but my eyes start to water and sting after a few pages."

"I could read it to you. I have to read it anyway."

"Really?" he says. "That would be great."

I leave Joe feeling much better than when I walked in. Old George might be on to something.

Rosetta

❧

On my next visit to the bookstore, I buy a new book on quilting. At the register, Mary says, "Oh my gosh, are you a quilter too?"

"Yes, it's so relaxing. A nice change from the OR which is so precise. Not much chance for creativity there." I hand Mary my credit card. "Do you quilt?" I ask.

"No, my mother-in-law does and I've always wanted to learn. This is a perfect time for me with an in-house trainer."

"If you need any help, I'm available," I offer. *What am I doing? Rosetta, let it go.*

Mary's face lights up. "We talked about starting one this weekend. Would you like to stop over Sunday? If you have time, that is." She looks apologetic. "Maybe you'd probably rather work on your own project."

"I could stop in for a little while to see what you're doing. I have lots of quilting books. I'll bring some."

Driving home, I wonder why Mary is such a magnet I can't resist. If I'm honest, I know it's because now the window of opportunity is open to know about Stan's life and if I'm really honest, I guess I have wondered all these years. Was he happy? What kind of life did he have? Mary can fill in the blanks. All of them except the one that matters most to me.

Was a little piece of me still in his heart all these years?

Teddy

Mom and Baba are digging through a big box of clothes and spreading shirts all over the dining room table. Buster's fat head and two pointy ears are peeking out of an empty box. As I look closer, I realize they're Dad's clothes. Golf shirts, plaid shirts, old t-shirts with crazy slogans he used to wear when he was washing the car. I recognize the one we got him last year for Christmas that say *Still Plays with Cars.* Why has Mom brought them all the way to Indiana? Why did we have room for *these* when we had to leave other things behind?

"Mom, what's going on?" I ask.

"Oh, Mary, look here." Baba digs in a different box that looks like it's been in the attic a hundred years. She holds up a little red and green plaid shirt that would fit a five-year old. "Christmas. Stan and Dan have two shirts the same. They look like little men. So cute those boys."

"Baba, look!" Ruby pulls out a red t-shirt that says INDIANA in big white letters. "This is where we live now." Then she picks up a gold and maroon t-shirt, ARIZONA STATE. She wrinkles her nose. "Yuk, this one smells funny."

"What are you guys doing?" I ask again. I think they've all lost their minds.

Baba looks up from another box. "Oh Teddy Bear, you're home. Your Mama and I, we take your Daddy's old shirts and we make memory quilt. That's a nice idea, no?"

Mom says, "We saw these beautiful quilts at the Covered Bridge Festival. Teddy, you should have come. Next year, we're taking you for sure. They had all kinds of fun things to do there."

"I got my face painted," Ruby says. "And we saw the biggest pumpkin. It weighed over a hundred pounds! But it's not the biggest in the world. The biggest is 1,092 pounds." Ruby shows me with arms outspread.

"Now how do you know that?" I ask, thinking surely she's been talking to Mindy.

"It said so. There was a picture of it. It's in Canada."

"Teddy, do you want to help with the quilt? You could make your own square. Just pick out your favorite shirt that Dad wore," Mom says enthusiastically.

"Maybe later, Mom, I've got to check e-mail." I escape to my room.

TO: Desertwall@aol.com
SUBJECT: IT'S ALL WEIRD

Hey Wally, I think everyone is losing their marbles here. They're making quilts out of Dad's old shirts and they think I'm going to help. Oh sure, I probably won't make the basketball team, I don't have any friends, and now I'm supposed to take up quilting. My life is a mess.

Delete. Another email I won't send. Maybe I should surf the 'net for a quilt chat room. We could exchange patterns. Whatever. *You know, Dearie, I found the cutest little stripes.* Headline: FIRST TIME BOY WINS QUILTING BLUE RIBBON AT STATE FAIR.

Rosetta

～

As I drive to the Kostoff home, I notice my hands that are so calm in surgery are now perspiring as I grip the wheel. *Why did I agree to this?* I wonder, but I already know the answer. All the days I was in love with Stan, I never went into his home and now for whatever pervert reasoning, I am longing to see it. To see where he grew up, the kitchen where he ate, where the phone was that he called me on every night. I want to see the bottom step where he said he sat, stretching the long cord from the kitchen. He teased me about being the rich kid who had two phones. It embarrassed me and I tried to down play it, saying doctors were often called in the middle of the night. I even remember Stan's reply, "I wish *I* could call you in the middle of the night. Sometimes I can't sleep just thinking of you, wishing you could lay down beside me someday." Things I haven't thought of for years and now his very words are returning. They cause an ache in me.

I sit in my car a few minutes after I turn the ignition off. *Why am I doing this?* I consider leaving when I see Mary open the front door and wave. *Too late now.*

I reach into the back seat for the quilting books while Mary walks to my car. She reaches for some of the books, "Wow, you do have a lot of quilting books. Here, let me help. This is so nice of you to come."

She leads me into the parlor where I am greeted with a delicious aroma. "Something smells wonderful," I say.

"Baba's making bread. I think I've gained 10 pounds since we moved here." Mary leads me to the dining room table where an array of clothing is spread from end to end.

"Well, I can certainly understand why if it tastes as good as it smells." I say.

There are boxes of clothing on the floor. Two little girls are bent over digging through them.

"Rosetta, meet the family. This is Cathy and Ruby. Teddy's upstairs."

Cathy and Ruby look up. I see two little clones of Mary. Blonde hair, blue eyes, and petite features. The older one gives me a smile with front teeth missing and the little one continues digging into a box.

"Mary, your girls are adorable," I say.

An older lady walks out of the kitchen, drying her hands on the corner of her apron. Mary says, "And this is Baba ... I mean Mrs. Kostoff, Stan's mother." Mary tells Baba, "Rosetta went to school with Stan."

"Oh, that's nice. You know our Stan. You call me Baba, too. I don't like to be Mrs. I am not so important."

I give a little laugh, but inside I feel such a tenderness toward this woman. "Oh, I bet you are very important to this family." In a face of olive skin creased with wrinkles I recognize familiar hazel eyes. I have to look away. "What's all this?" I ask pointing to the clothes on the table.

Mary seems energized. "When we were at the Covered Bridge Festival yesterday, there was a memory quilt that was so beautiful we thought we could make a quilt out of Stan's old shirts. Baba saved some of the clothes the boys wore growing up." Mary leans into my ear and says quietly, "Her attic is a firetrap, I'm not kidding," but I'm transfixed on the table and clothes. I knew I shouldn't have come. The first thing that practically jumps off the table is the plaid shirt.

"It's a wonderful idea. Really," I stammer, hoping my false enthusiasm covers my nervousness. Before I know it, I am touching the plaid shirt and a memory floods me. Stan, sitting beside me on the piano bench, rolling up his shirt sleeve to show me that his skin was almost as dark as mine. "I love this shirt, always loved it," I mumble. When Mary looks my way with a quizzical expression, I realize my slip of tongue. "I mean this pattern. So colorful." I try to recover. "I think my dad had the same shirt."

"Could you suggest the best design for what we're attempting to do?" Mary asks.

I start leafing through some of the books I brought, relieved to have something else to look at. I turn several pages and then lay it open. "This might work," I say, taking the book to Mary's side of the table.

Mary has her nose in a denim shirt. She is breathing it in. "Stan wore this around the house all the time. He even retrieved it from the bag I had set out for Goodwill once. I couldn't part with it when we left Arizona." She pulls it to her nose again and takes another deep breath. "I can smell his shaving lotion."

I see the deep grief on Mary's face. *I'm intruding on private moments.* The room is suddenly too warm. I slip off my cardigan. "I'm just a little warm," I say as if to justify my hot cheeks which I'm sure are turning red.

"Can we offer you some iced tea or water? Coffee?"

"Water would be good."

I follow Baba into the kitchen and take it all in. A chrome red and grey table with red vinyl chairs. Probably from Stan's day. I caress the top of one of the chairs by running my hand over it.

I return to the dining room sipping the water and pause to look at the framed family photos on the dining room hutch. Photos of Stan and his brother at all ages. Two wedding photos. Stan looks handsome. And happy. On a side buffet table are photos of, I assume, ancestors. A sepia photo of a man with a handlebar mustache in a vest and baggy wool pants, wearing a Doctor Zhivago hat.

Baba comes to my side. "That is Stan's grandfather, Variky." She points to another photo, a man in a tight-fitting suit. "Milan, my husband, God rest his soul."

"You have a wonderful heritage," I say wistfully.

"Yes, we very proud to be Bulgarian, but we love America too. So much. Such a wonderful country."

I stand there regretting that Luther might never know this part of his heritage. Mixed emotions cursing through me. Regret, sadness, a little anger, and then a sudden flood of love for Luther. *Perhaps it's time he did know.*

Teddy

⌒

They're posting the basketball tryout results after school. The day drags on forever. I'm all psyched up while telling myself it doesn't really matter. Who am I kidding? When I come down to the locker room, there's a bunch of guys looking at the white sheets posted on the board. I can't make my feet walk toward them. Can't trust my emotions these days. The least little thing can set me off. Where are those sunglasses when I need them?

In a few minutes, everyone leaves and I walk to the bulletin board. My heart's beating so loudly it feels like a basketball dribbling down the court. I look up. "VARSITY TEAM." I recognize first names from the scrimmages we've been having. Pete, John, Brett. I keep going. I read all the way to the bottom of the list and my name's not on it. The names become a blur but I go to the top again. Maybe I missed it. I didn't expect it but the rejection hurts even more than I expected. I am sick to my stomach. I want to barf.

"JUNIOR VARSITY." A few names I don't recognize and then I see it. "Teddy Kostoff." Junior Varsity? Who wants to play Junior Varsity? I did that my freshman year. Who even wants to play basketball? Not me. Forget it. I'll take up chess or something smart kids do. Not a stupid game like basketball.

I walk away angry, my eyes blurry with tears when I almost bump into the JV coach.

"Teddy, I'm so glad to have you on the JV squad," he says, putting his hand on my shoulder. His smile is so genuine I try to hide my disappointment. I switch into my new MO, *Fake it till you make it.*

"I'm ready Coach. When's our first practice?"

"Tomorrow. I've been watching you practice and you have some great moves. Our JV can use some new blood. What would you think about being captain?"

"Me? Why Coach? Won't the other guys sort of resent that? A new kid coming in and taking over?"

"I don't think you're the "take-over" kind from what I've seen. There's some rivalry between a couple of the guys and rather than choose between them, I think it will be good for the team and you, too. I imagine it's hard to start over." The anger I felt a few minutes ago is subsiding. Like someone understands. "I heard about your dad. I'm really sorry." He adds. "I hope you don't mind my saying."

Is this a sympathy ploy? My suspicious feeling brings the anger back. He senses my apprehension.

"That's not why I'd like you to be captain. I see leadership and teamwork in you. I saw you passing shots you could have made."

Funny what pops into your head at weird times. I think of the Willy Wonka movie. That old guy telling Willy, "No good deed goes unnoticed." The thought of that movie makes me smile and I say, "Thanks, Coach. I'd love to be captain."

Mary

I take Baba and the girls to the cemetery to show them the new granite stone. Baba wants to plant mums so we stop at a roadside stand. Baba cries when she sees the stone. I keep my arm tightly around her waist, holding her closer to me. Ruby keeps our visit light by dancing and chasing Cathy around a tree. Then she sings one of her silly make-up songs, "We're putting mums on Dad." At first I want to scold her. Seems disrespectful and then realize I want this to be a place she wants to come often. If she wants to sing and dance, what could be a better way to visit her dad?

I send the girls to the water pump with a little pail that they fill till it runs over. Then they spill most of it walking back. They pour what's left in the bucket on the new plants and then go back for more. We wipe our hands on the old towels we have brought with us.

I want a moment alone with Stan. "Girls, please walk back to the car with Baba." Baba walks between them holding their hands. I watch them and feel glad that we are here for her.

"Hey, Stan, I thought you'd like to know that your son will be playing basketball at your alma mater. He didn't make varsity but the JV coach seems to have taken him under his wing. Asked him to be captain. Maybe things will work out here after all."

Teddy

❦

Halloween's on a Friday this year and all the buzz at school is about parties — none of which I've been invited to. At home, Ruby's already in the costume Baba made, twirling and posing. She's Little Bo Peep and Cathy is her little wooly lamb with a furry white sweater and cap with pink lamb ears. Mom asks me if I want to walk the girls or stay home and pass out candy. I opt to fill the little monsters' bags.

After running to the door 10 times in 10 minutes, I just sit on the front porch. I scare one little guy by talking to him before he sees me. He runs crying to his dad who's waiting on the sidewalk. Feeling like an ogre, I walk over to him while he hangs onto his dad's pant leg, and put extra candy in his bag. "Sorry 'bout that," I say, mostly to the dad. The little Dracula peeks in his bag and gives me a big toothy monster grin. I go back to the porch swing and the ache in my gut returns remembering the haunted house Dad made in our garage one year. He was a bigger kid than my friends sometimes. Grief is uglier than any mask I've seen tonight.

When the girls get back, Mom gives me a ride to the hospital to see Joe. He's sitting in his wheelchair with an obnoxious Miss Piggy mask pushed up on his head. He pulls it down when he sees me.

"Oink, oink, did you bring me some food? I love pies with whipped cream — I could eat the *whole* pie."

"Looks like you already did — maybe more than one!" I'm laughing, but I'm ashamed of myself. Why didn't I think of wearing something funny? Having a pity party for myself as usual. I'm supposed to be cheering him up and instead, *he's* making *me* laugh.

"I couldn't decide between Miss Piggy or just trick-or-treat as I am. Mummy Boy. Nothing like wearing your costume all day — all week, all year. Better yet, why don't I peel off all the bandages. Bet that would be the scariest sight in town." This doesn't sound like the Joe I met the first night. He sounds scared. I try to think of something clever to say, but know there's nothing funny about the scars Joe will have.

"How much longer?"

"The doctor says soon. I've been waiting for this for so long, but now I'm not so sure I want it to happen. It's a lot safer under these bandages."

Joe's blue eyes look anxious and I want to look away but I can't. It's what he fears the most — that people will look away. I can't be one of them. I keep looking him right in the eye and say, "Hey, did you hear the Rodney Dangerfield joke about how ugly he was as a kid?"

"No."

"Yeah, he was sooooo ugly, his mother had to tie a pork chop around his neck so the dog would play with him." Joe laughs and I assume superhero status. I think of the quote, *Life is a gift, but only if we open it.*

All of a sudden I start spouting philosophy, "You know, Joe, if my dad had lived, it wouldn't matter to me if he had scars. At least he'd still be here. I know the people who care about you won't see the scars. They'll just see *you*. And what do you care about anyone who would ridicule you? They're shallow, insecure, not worthy of your friendship." I'm surprised these words have come out of me.

"Oh Worthy One, thank you for your wisdom."

I grab the handles of his wheelchair. "Come on, let's go down the hall and see if any of the nurses dressed up like ... uh ... Brittany Spears?"

"Here, take a mask. Mom brought a bunch." I look in the sack and pull out a Bill Clinton, a Batman, and Kermit the Frog. I opt for the frog and tip Joe's chair like a wheelie.

"Here we go!" We pass the nurses station, where someone says, "Look. It's Sesame Street on wheels!"

"It's not easy being green!" I shout. We get a few chuckles from the weary faces in the waiting rooms. We see an entourage of visitors arriving in costume and then realize it's all Joe's family. A mafia hit man, a gypsy complete with crystal ball, a clown, a hobo. We stay in the waiting room, entertaining the people coming and going and then head back to Joe's room where we take off our masks.

"I get to keep most of my costume on," Joe says. "Mummy Boy!"

Joe's little brother, Vince, says, "I know a Mummy joke."

"Okay, let's hear it."

"Why don't mummies take vacations?"

"I don't know. Why don't they?"

"They're afraid they'll relax and unwind." We all laugh, mostly at Vince, who laughs the hardest at his own joke.

"Come here you little monster." Joe reaches for Vince who climbs in the bed beside him and tries to hug him around all the bandages. All of a sudden I want to get home to Ruby and Cathy.

It's getting late and Mom's probably waiting out front. I wish I had made her come up to meet Joe's family. She might have laughed at Vince's little joke too. I want more than anything to hear her laugh like she used to.

I say goodbye to everyone and shout to Joe, "Bye Miss Piggy — hope you have a little bedtime snack. Maybe a 10-pound box of chocolates." As I walk out of Joe's room, I'm wondering how people can have fun in such a sad place. Maybe his family has figured it out. *The Book of Life* is right. *Life is a gift.*

When I get home Ruby and Cathy have their candy spread out over the kitchen table and Baba's checking for things that aren't wrapped. I spot a few of my favorites, Snickers and Butterfingers. Cathy has chocolate all around her mouth, still wearing her lamb costume. She looks so cuddly I have to squeeze her. I put my face in her furry tummy and realize that's just what Dad would have done. I can see him doing it. When my tears start, I hide my face deeper in her wooly costume, thinking Dad will never see another cute Halloween costume. I squeeze Cathy so tight she squeals, "Tedddddy." I hold her up high in the air and she giggles, chocolate oozing down her chin.

I'll tell Dad all about it tomorrow on my Saturday visit.

Rosetta

I love Halloween. At dusk, I put candles in all the jack-o-lanterns lining our walk and display extra candles all across the porch so there is no mistaking that we are welcoming all ghosts, goblins, and princesses. I'm glad it's a warm night and they don't have to wear their winter coats over their precious costumes as I did so many years in Chicago.

But it isn't the Chicago Halloweens I'm remembering so much this year. Now with Stan back in my thoughts I'm reminded of my first Halloween in Middleburg, 30-some years ago, when a clown and a witch had the courage to risk appearing together in public. Although we were in disguise, there was no disguising the joy we felt as we ran door to door together, sharing a simple innocent experience.

James knows how much I enjoy the spirit of the holiday so he doesn't question me at all when I say, "I decided to give the trick-or-treaters a thrill this year and dress up too."

In memory of Stan, I appear in a billowy black witch dress, pointy hat, and flowing black silk scarf. There are many ways to honor the dead.

Teddy

November

When I get to the cemetery the morning after Halloween, I see toilet paper hanging from the branches, draped over the gravestones. Eggshells are laying everywhere, yellow splotches of raw egg on the grass. I run to Dad's stone as fast as I can. There's a gooey yellow gob on the *S* and splatters of yellow on the *K*. It's starting to dry already. There's a puddle of raw egg at the base of the stone with ants crawling through it.

I want to hit something, but instead I run to find George. I need to get a brush. Something. I have to clean it off. I can't let Mom or Baba see this. I hop on my bike and start around the circular road till I spot George ahead.

"George — what happened? This is awful!"

George shakes his head as he snaps open a large black garbage bag. "Oh, these kids. They think it's so funny. This is the worst we've seen in years. They used to have police patrol the cemetery on Halloween but we hadn't had any problems for years, so they stopped. Budget cuts or something." George looks so discouraged. "I have a lot of clean up to do here."

"I'll help you. Where should I start?" I tear off a bag from the roll beside him.

"Once that egg dries, it's almost impossible to get off. We must have had a little rain last night or it would be dry by now. We've got to work fast. But here's the worst." He points to a small headstone that's been cracked in two places. The flowers beside it are trampled. *Baby Sarah March 1996.* There's a little angel on the headstone and a big muddy footprint on it. I think of Sarah's parents and how sad they would be to think their little baby was trampled in the night.

Then he points to the veteran's section. "I don't think those men gave up their lives so kids could have this kind of freedom. Freedom to destroy. Kids have got it too easy today, Teddy."

I want George to know that I'm not one of those kids. "Whoever did this should be punished. They need to come here and clean this. Shouldn't they go to jail or something?"

"I reported it to the police already. But it's a once-a-year thing. Not like they're going to do it somewhere else next weekend."

"Someone at school will say something. I'm going to find out who did this."

"You be careful now. This is a job for the police. If you really want to help, there's some buckets and brushes in the tool shed. We should start on the eggs before they get too dry."

"Is there a phone there?" I ask.

George points to the office. "Door's open."

I call Mindy who shows up and helps scrub the stones. George follows behind us with a long hose, rinsing them off.

While we're working, a reporter named John Marshall, wearing a rumpled brown trench coat like Columbo, shows up. He walks through the cemetery writing things in his little notebook. Then he starts taking pictures of the toilet paper and the eggs on the stones. "I won't take any pictures showing the names. It would upset the families to see that," he tells us.

Yeah, tell me about it.

We keep at it for a couple hours. George disappears but returns with a sack of burgers and soft drinks. Mindy almost tackles him and his sacks as she runs to him.

"Here, kids, take a break," he points to a bench under a grove of trees. We step around shattered pumpkins which have been smashed in the night.

"Did you know that the first jack-o-lanterns were made in Ireland out of hollowed-out turnips?" Mindy says between bites.

"I do now," I say. Then I laugh. "That would be weird to carry a turnip."

"Yeah, good thing the Irish thought pumpkins would be easier to carry when they brought the tradition to America."

George says, "That's a bit of interesting information young lady."

Mindy smiles smugly at me as if to say, "See, someone appreciates my knowledge." I roll my eyes and keep eating.

George says, "I was looking forward to putting American flags out for Veterans Day." He starts laughing. "I just remembered a big cemetery mystery they blamed kids for, but it wasn't them. No one could figure out why the American flags from the vets' graves were disappearing. Finally one of the landscapers saw the crime in action. One of the little flags was *running* across the cemetery. As he got closer, he saw a squirrel with a flag in his mouth, scampering as fast as he could to a big tree stump with a hole in it. When he looked in, it was chock full of little American flags! A 10-year mystery finally solved."

"Well, they were patriotic little weasels, weren't they?" Mindy said. "Actually, a squirrel, bushy tailed rodent, is part of the genus, *sciurus*."

"Oh, no, George, get ready. You're about to have a biology lecture."

Ignoring me completely, Mindy goes on, "Squirrels are a social animal. You see them often in pairs and —"

George laughs and says, "Young lady, you have a bright future ahead of you."

"Yeah, her braces glow in the dark," I say.

Mindy glares at me. "You better look out. If there's any raw eggs left around here, they're headed your way." She swipes a couple of my fries.

George says, "Since you like facts so much, young lady, here's some for you. Do you know about the coin tradition in cemeteries?"

Mindy's eyes light up. "No, tell me."

"You'll see this often at military cemeteries. A coin left on a headstone is a message to the deceased soldier's family that someone else paid respect. A penny means you visited. A nickel means you and the deceased trained at boot camp together. A dime means you served with him in some way. A quarter means you were with the soldier when he was killed."

"That is awesome, George. Do the coins stay there?" Mindy soaks up this trivia.

"I heard that it's collected and put toward maintaining the cemetery. I think it became common during the Vietnam War. It was such a controversial war that it was easier to leave a coin than to talk about the men who served.

As we gather up our lunch wrappers and throw them in the garbage bag, I sense that George has risen a few notches in Mindy's opinion. We keep working and find some broken beer bottles when we're picking up the toilet paper. I wonder about the kids who did this and suddenly I feel so old. Like I'm not a kid anymore. Would I have thought this was funny a year ago? Nothing about drinking appeals to me since the drunk hit our car.

Just as I'm leaving the cemetery, I see something shiny on the edge of the road. I pick it up. It's a watch with a prancing horse on the face. I've seen it before but I can't remember where. I put it in my pocket to show George.

The headline next morning in the paper reads VANDALS RAVAGE CEMETERY. The article goes on, "There is a reward for finding the persons responsible. This has gone beyond an innocent Halloween prank and could result in criminal charges."

&

In school on Monday morning, an announcement is made that anyone involved in vandalism faces school suspension.

After Spanish class, I wait for Pete outside the door. "Pete, wait up. I just wanted to say thanks for encouraging me to try out for varsity. I didn't really think I would make it this year, but there's always next year."

He acts distracted but says, "That's not right man. You should be varsity." He turns and walks toward the long-haired, black-leather-jacket guys down the hall.

After school, I'm reading the practice schedule posted on Coach Burton's window. He waves me in.

"Teddy, I wanted to talk to you. I can see why you made varsity at your other school. Even if I could have suited you up, I was afraid you'd spend most of the season on the bench. What with seven good seniors we have from last year."

"Thanks Coach." I'm surprised. I didn't think he even remembered who I was.

"Like I told your buddy Pete … he came in here all upset that I didn't put you on varsity."

"He did?"

"I told him you were a good player, but most boys want to *play*. They don't want to spend the season on the bench. With JV you're sure to start each game. What would you rather do?"

"I'd rather play every game Coach, even if it is JV." I can't believe I said that.

"I thought so. That's what I told Pete."

I leave his office, nine feet tall. He knows who I am. And Pete — what a guy. Looking out for me. All of a sudden, it's good. So what if it's JV? I'll suit up. I'll play every game. Somehow this isn't so bad. The *Book of Life* says, *If a man cannot do great things, he can do small things in a great way.* Okay, okay, I'll play JV in a great way.

After scrimmage, I see Pete. "Hey, Coach told me you're my secret agent."

"Why not?" Pete says. "You're good. We could use you on that bench. Johnson fouls out all the time."

"I guess I'll be the big pebble in the little pond instead of the little pebble in the big pond." I had heard Dad say that once.

"Whatever, man."

"Hey, Pete," Brett walks up to us. "Can I grab a ride with you?" I'm supposed to be home by 5 o'clock. What time is it anyway?"

"Don't ask me. I lost my watch somewhere. Come on. I'll drop you off."

And then I remember. The watch. I saw it on Pete, the first day I walked over to the pencil sharpener to ask him about open gym. I remember the horse. Just like the horse on the watch in the cemetery. I have this sinking in the pit of my stomach. Worse than when I was searching the varsity list that I didn't make. Worse because I can believe I didn't make varsity, but I can't believe that Pete is a vandal. It can't be. He's too nice a guy. The person who did that in the cemetery can't possibly be a nice guy. Or my role model. I'm glad I forgot to give the watch to George. But now what do I do with it?

All the way home, I ask myself questions. What'll happen to Pete if I turn in the watch? Should I ask him if it's his? Maybe it's not. But I know it is.

I want to talk to Joe about this but Baba has dinner ready. "Teddy, come eat. I make city chicken, mashed potatoes, gravy. Please to the table."

Coming in from the cold, the kitchen smells delicious. We sit around the table with steaming plates of food piled high. I know I'm expected to make a huge dent in that mountain of potatoes Mom passes me, but my stomach is like a giant knotted pretzel thinking about the watch. I take a big spoonful so as not to disappoint anyone.

Luckily, Ruby diverts attention away from me by trying to solve the mystery of the city chicken. She is turning her stick with chunks of meat on it over and over. "Baba, how do you know where that chicken lived?" she asks.

Mom laughs. "No honey, it has nothing to do with where he lived. Chickens live on the farm. It's called city chicken because of the way Baba fixed it. It's a fancy name for meat on a stick." She turns to Baba, "It's veal and pork, isn't it?" To Ruby she says, "It's not even really chicken."

"It's not?" Ruby stops chewing on her stick and looks at it in disgust.

"TMI, Mom," I say.

Baba says, "Vat is this, TMI?"

"Too much information — for a seven-year old," I tell Baba.

Mom picks up her chicken stick as if to prove it's okay, "Honey, it's like a corn dog. Meat on a stick."

I can't stop thinking about the watch. "Mom, do you think I could go see Joe tonight. Just a few minutes."

"Teddy, it's a school night. Don't you have homework?"

"I did it in study hall." Not exactly the truth but I just have to tell someone about the watch. "Please Mom, I want to talk to Joe about not making varsity."

Mom knows how much varsity meant to me and I play on her sympathy tonight. She relents easily on the Joe visit. She starts to console me about not making the team, although we've already had this discussion.

"It's okay Mom. I'll make it next year. A lot of seniors graduating."

Mom looks astonished and relieved all at the same time. "Teddy, I am so proud of you. That's a wonderful attitude."

"Your dad and Uncle Dan — they play basketball night and day — every day." Baba pipes in. Now she's holding her stick of city chicken in front of her, turning it slowly and examining it. "Next time not too much veal, little more pork." Baba's always improving on her recipes.

"Baba, this is good just the way it is," I tell her. She beams and pats my shoulder.

Mom says, "We better go so you're not out too late. I'll wait in the lobby — 20 minutes max."

Mary

❧

In the hospital lobby I take out the book I brought along but can't focus. Did Teddy really say *next year*? Does that mean he likes it here? That he wants to stay? That I did the right thing in coming here?

I do some people watching in the lobby. Coming and going, but mostly going at this late hour. Not as happy a place as airport waiting areas. A lot of raw emotion on faces here.

"Mary, is that you?" I turn and see Rosetta in her nurse's scrubs. "Are you visiting someone? Hope everything is okay."

"Hi Rosetta. Just waiting for Teddy, seeing a friend. You're working late, aren't you?"

"We had an emergency appendectomy. I was on call."

"Here, sit with me," I say to her. "Oh, you're probably tired and would like to get home to relax."

"No, not at all. James has a meeting tonight with some clients. I don't even have to cook dinner. I think there's some leftover casserole waiting for me. And a glass of wine. Want to join me — for the wine at least? Can't guarantee the casserole's any good or even there."

She smiles warmly and I realize this is the first invite to anyone's home I've had. *Why not? God knows I could use a girlfriend.* "I'd love to. I'll drop Teddy off and come by. What's your address?"

Teddy

⁜

"Teddy, what're you doing here on a school night? This is cool." Then Joe sees my face. "Uh oh, this is not cool?"

"I need to ask you something."

"Sure, man what is it?"

"I don't know where to begin."

"How about at the beginning?"

"Well, the beginning is sort of complicated." I don't want to use Pete's name. "What would you do if you found out a good friend of yours had done something wrong? Would you snitch on him?"

"I didn't do it man, honest. I didn't steal the bedpans."

"Joe, this is for real. It's serious."

"I guess it would depend on how wrong it was, but I doubt I would tell on a friend. What's that saying, *with friends like these who needs enemies*?"

"That's what I think. But then I think of Dad's headstone and the baby angel stone."

"What *are* you talking about?" I realize Joe can't help me if he doesn't know the whole story. I tell about the vandalism and how mad it made me to see the egg on Dad's name. How I found the watch. How I think it belongs to the guy I admire most in school and also my one link to the varsity team.

"I've seen him with these other guys that look like thugs. They look very capable of it, but not him."

"Why don't you ask him? Give him the watch back and tell him where you found it. Just ask him if he was there."

"That sounds easy enough, doesn't it? Part of me wants to do that and just forget it ever happened, but part of me wants him or whoever to be punished. They shouldn't be able to get away with it. It's just not right. But they're making such a big deal of it at school. He would be suspended and that would be the end of his varsity basketball this year, for sure."

"That would open a spot on the varsity team, wouldn't it? From what you told me, you might be the next logical one. You might even get to play."

"Oh no, I never thought of that. This is getting worse by the minute."

"This might be the chance you're waiting for. You know, things happen."

"Not this way. I can't be responsible for him getting kicked off the team."

"Teddy, you wouldn't be responsible. Everyone's responsible for their own actions. Do you think I'm sitting in this hospital bed because of someone else? No, *I'm* the one who ignored the rules. *I* lit the match. *I* thought I was smarter than the instructions." I just look at Joe and know the burns have left scars inside as well as outside. He goes on, "Well, I think you shouldn't do anything for a day or two. My mom always says, 'just sleep on it'. One more day won't make much difference, will it?"

"I guess not. I better get going. Mom's in the lobby. Thanks Joe."

"I don't think I've helped you much, man. I wish I knew what to tell you. Can you come back tomorrow?"

"I'll try. And yes, you did help."

On the ride home, Mom asks about basketball again, trying to make a big deal about junior varsity. "When are the practices? When's the first game?"

I try to be upbeat, but I'm so tired of it all. I wish I was back in Arizona. Life was much simpler there.

Before bed, I page through the *Book of Life* to see what pearls of wisdom are speaking to me. Sure enough. There's always one that fits. *Doing what's right is its own reward.* I have to do something about the watch. Either give it back to Pete or give it to George who would probably turn it over to the police. Then they'd be coming around the school asking questions. Someone would know it's Pete's. I bet there's not another one like it in the school. Joe said to sleep on it, but it's hard to sleep on something that keeps you from falling asleep in the first place. Tomorrow I will do something, right or wrong. No reward required.

I think I hear the music box as I am falling asleep but I'm not sure.

Winnie is snoring so loud, he could drown out a marching band. Buster must have given him a tough day.

Rosetta

By the time Mary arrives, I have changed from my scrubs to lounging clothes, purple velour pants and top.

"Wow, you look great," she says when I open the door. "I knew you had style the first time you came to book group."

"Get out," I say. "What's your preference? Red or white?"

"Whatever you have open," Mary answers as she looks around the room. "Your home is lovely,"

"Thank you. Let's sit in here." I take her into the den with soft lamps glowing and a log in the fireplace just starting to burn and crackle. "There's a chill in the air tonight. Winter isn't far behind, I'm afraid. That will be a new experience for you, won't it?" I say.

"Yes and no. I grew up in Indiana but we've been in Arizona so long. I think it might be a rude reminder. The kids are excited about seeing snow. We did have a ski resort just a few hours north that Stan took Teddy to."

I am always surprised at how much I love hearing Stan's name. "Just two hours away? Wow, who would have guessed that?" I say as I set down glasses and pour the wine.

"Arizona's a big state. Lots of diversity in elevation and climate."

"What made you move there?" I ask as I place the platter of cheese and grapes on the coffee table in Mary's reach. "I'm guessing Stan's work, but I don't think I ever asked you what he did."

"In sales and marketing. He was good at it too. Not pushy. Had a great relationship with people. He always said, 'People buy from people they like.' And he was easy to like," Mary says wistfully. She takes a sip of her wine.

"I could see that. I don't remember who got voted "Most Likely to Succeed," but it wouldn't surprise me if it were him. Did you ever come back for any class reunions? You know with family still here and all."

Mary shrugs her shoulders. "No, he never wanted to. I thought that was a little strange. I thought he loved high school, but he always found some excuse not to go. I didn't mind 'cause I don't think those are much fun for the spouses anyway. How about you? Did you go?"

"No, it seems there was always a conflict." I remember being torn each time a reunion invitation arrived. *Would Stan be there?* My fear that he might be kept me from going. My greater fear was how *I* would feel seeing him again. I could not trust my feelings.

Mary pops a grape in her mouth and points to the easel set up in the corner of the room. "Do you paint," she asks.

"Not really. That was one of my projects before quilting. Didn't go so well." I laugh. "To give you some idea of *how* not well, I've seen kids' drawings posted on the refrigerator that show greater promise. I don't know why I leave the easel there. Fills the corner. I did manage to do one watercolor worth hanging." I point to a small-framed watercolor beside the easel. A bouquet of red roses with a pink rose in the middle.

"I've seen that painting somewhere. Can't place it now," she says.

I suddenly remember the bouquet I left at the gravestone. Did Mary see it? I turn to her, "Now let's talk about you. How are you settling in? Making friends? Probably meeting some nice people through the bookstore."

"I am getting to know the customers. What they like to read, so I can recommend other titles to them. But as for friends? Not really. My sister-in-law, Joyce, is really nice but she's so busy. Teaches middle school. That would wipe out anyone. And with two daughters, she has her hands full. To be honest, you're probably someone I've talked to more than anyone. You're easy to talk to — maybe it's the Stan connection. Sadly, I'm trying to hold on to any piece of him I can."

Me too, I thought. *And that's even sadder.*

Mary

The night of Teddy's first JV game the gym is packed. The pep band is playing, the cheering section is going strong and the smell of buttered popcorn fills the air. Cathy and Ruby want to sit near the cheerleaders and wave the green and white pom-poms Sophie helped them make.

I see the JV coach Teddy has talked about so much. He's younger than I expected, a good looking, fair-skinned African-American. As I watch him talking to the boys, there's a familiar mannerism about him. I can't quite put my finger on it, but each time I see him jump off the bench, it tugs at me. Like someone you've seen before although you can't remember where. After the game I work my way through the crowd to meet him.

"Coach, I'm so happy to meet you. I'm Teddy's mom." He's much taller than me and I'm shouting over the sounds of the pep band and the cheerleaders. "I want to thank you for the special interest you've taken in him. He talks about you all the time."

Coach leans down to talk to me so I can hear him. "He's a fine boy. I really enjoy his love of the game."

Up close I see that resemblance again. Like I know him. Is it the eyes or the smile? "This may sound crazy but you look so familiar to me. Did you ever spend time in Phoenix? Go to school there perhaps?"

"No, I was raised in Chicago, got a basketball scholarship to Indiana. Then this job in Middleburg. It's a great little community."

"It is nice. Good to meet you Coach."

He flashes that familiar smile again. "Just call me Luther."

Rosetta

I love watching Luther coach. Even though it's the first game, James and I take our usual seats, the ones we sat in all season last year. I spot Luther on the floor, his clipboard in one hand as he goes over plays with some of the team and feel a sense of pride.

A few of the boys are shooting baskets on the floor, and when I see Teddy, it takes my breath away for just a second. There's a yearning. I cannot believe the visceral reaction to seeing the striking image of Stan at that age. As the longing floods through me, I wonder how that can happen after so many years.

James voice, "I'll get the popcorn and drinks," sounds distant although he's right next to me. It brings me back to the present moment. I watch James as he walks through the crowd, stopping to talk to several people on the way. I'm always proud to be with him. His genteel manner with me and others. His acceptance of my past situation was one of the reasons I knew I could spend the rest of her life with him. When I told him Luther's dad was a white boy in high school who never knew of the pregnancy, James just held me and said, "I understand and I'm sorry." He never asked for more.

But now, seeing this young boy on the court, so much like the boy I first loved, I wonder if I ever loved anyone with the passion and tenderness I felt for Stan. Did all people cherish their first loves or was it just me?

Mary

❦

After the basketball game, I'm sitting alone on the sofa. Everyone's gone to bed but something is nagging at me. Like when you have a tooth pulled and your tongue keeps going to that spot.

Stan's yearbooks are still on the coffee table. I thumb through his senior book again. I look again at Stan's basketball photo and his senior photo. The wide young smile. And then it clicks. Why Coach Luther looked so familiar. Something about the mouth. Yes, it's the smile. And the cleft in his chin. It's just like Stan's. I'm glad to have solved that nagging little feeling and as I close the yearbook, I chalk it up to a weird kind of coincidence.

I remember the grief counselor saying it was common to see people who would remind me of Stan. Or I might even think it *is* Stan. In a crowd, from behind, walking down the street, or a head bent over a cup of coffee. She called it *transference*. I'll have to ask Teddy if Coach Luther reminds him of his dad. On second thought, better to leave it alone.

Teddy

୧

I wait for Pete before Spanish class. He's walking down the hall with the black leather jackets and he looks angry. They stop a few feet from me and I hear the taller jacket say to Pete, "Don't flake out man. We'll be looking for you."

Pete's jaw is set tight. He sees me and relaxes it. "Teddy, how's it going?"

"Just wanted to ask you something."

"Sure, go ahead."

The bell rings. "Maybe after practice we could meet by Coach's office."

"Yeah, sure."

After practice, I shower quickly. I'm waiting for Pete, hoping no one will be with him. I see him and breathe a sigh of relief that he's alone, but the hard part is still to come. I hope I don't chicken out.

"So, Teddy, what's up? Are you changing your mind about junior varsity?"

"No, this isn't about basketball. Well, in a way, maybe it is." I know I'm stumbling and sounding stupid. "See, Pete, I heard you say you lost your watch and I found one. And I was just wondering. Well, I was wondering if this might be yours." I pull out the watch.

Pete takes it, looks at the face of it, turns it over, and gives me a big grin. "Teddy, this is great. It *is* my watch. I've been looking everywhere. My brother got it for me when I made varsity. See on the back, it's engraved, H O R S E. We used to play HORSE almost every night in the driveway. He says it's the only reason I made the team. Pete laughs, "So where'd you find it?"

I look at Pete and then down at my feet. I stall while two guys walk by with their duffel bags. "Well, that's the reason I had to talk to you. And it's the reason I haven't given it to you sooner. I've had it for a while, but I just didn't know what to do about it. I kind of thought it was yours 'cause I saw it the first time I talked to you. So unique and all."

"Yeah," Pete says and just keeps looking at me. "Go on."

"Well, I found it in the cemetery. The morning after Halloween. You know, after all the vandalism."

Pete's face turns red. He scowls. Finally he says, "Uh, so what were *you* doing in the cemetery the morning *after* Halloween?"

The way Pete says it, he acts like *I* was doing something wrong by going there in the daytime. "I go almost every Saturday." Pete looks puzzled. I blurt it out, "My dad's buried there."

"Oh man." Pete just looks down at the floor and shakes his head. "Oh, man, I'm sorry."

I'm not real sure what Pete's sorry about. Dad or the vandalism. "I guess I was hoping somehow that you weren't involved." I wait to see if he says anything, but he doesn't.

Pete shakes his head, looks down and rubs the back of his neck. He mumbles something that sounds like, "Oh, fuck."

"And if you were, Pete, I'm not going to say anything. That's why I'm giving the watch back to you instead of the police."

"So why wouldn't you turn me in? I heard there was a reward."

"You think I want a reward for turning in someone who's been a good friend to me? I don't think Coach Burton would even know who I am if it wasn't for you. Do you think I want to be the one who gets you kicked off the team? You know if you're suspended that's what would happen, don't you?"

"Even if I wasn't, it would be hard to play once my dad got through with me, not to mention my brother."

"Pete, are you saying you were there? In the cemetery? It just doesn't figure."

"Yeah, Teddy, I was there. And you're right. It doesn't figure. I don't know when I'm going to have the guts to break away from those guys. Shit, we've been friends since grade school. Through junior high.

Then in high school, they went one direction and I went the other, but they still wanted me to do dumb things with them. They're a bunch of losers. And I'm not very good at saying 'no.'

"They say things like, 'Man, you think you're better than us now. Big jock. Honor student.' I knew I shouldn't have gone with them on Halloween, but we've done pranks almost every year since we were in junior high. Nothing really bad, but this time they brought a case of beer. It just got out of control. You know how sometimes you just do stuff for no good reason? And now I'm no better than them. Instead of pulling them up, I let them drag me down."

Hearing about the beer makes me mad again. "You know, Pete, maybe I *should* turn in the watch. It was a drunk driver who killed my dad. Maybe someone should have turned that jerk in when he was a teen."

"Well, go ahead man, there's the phone." He points to the pay phone at the end of the hall. "I don't know why you even bothered to talk to me. You can give the police the watch with an unsigned note to protect your little butt."

I can't believe the way this is going. He's turning on *me.* The tightness starts in my chest and worse yet, familiar tears starting to burn my eyes. I can't let Pete see me be a crybaby now.

Before I can even think of what to say next, Pete starts apologizing. "I'm sorry, Teddy. I'm just scared. I know what I did was wrong. I've been worrying about it since that night and I'm too chicken-shit to come forward. I know I'd get kicked off the team." He runs his hand through his hair. "You know I envy you. I wish sometimes I could go to a new school and start all over. I used to run with those guys, but things are different now and I can't shake them."

I can't believe that my anger for Pete turns to sympathy for him. Or that he would envy *me.* Pete, who in my opinion, has everything a guy could want in school. "Well, I'm not saying a word to anyone," I say. "I was pretty mad when I first saw the damage. I wanted whoever did it to see it in the daytime. To see how ugly it was and not funny at all. I guess the worse one was Baby Sarah."

"Who's Baby Sarah?"

"Oh, it's a little baby's headstone. Probably be upsetting to her parents to see it broken."

"Oh man." Pete looks down again. "Do you know their name?"

"No, but I could probably find out."

"Maybe I could send them some money. Like pay for the stone to be fixed? Or buy a new one? Do you think so?"

"Probably. But how about your friends. Shouldn't they pay too?"

"Are you kidding? They would never admit to it. But this is it. This is absolutely the last time I'm doing anything with them. I guess what I should do is turn us all in. They'd be so mad at me, they'd never ask me to do anything with them again. But who knows what crazy thing they might do to get even."

"Are they dangerous?"

"I don't know, Teddy. I just don't know. They're a bunch of misfits. That's why they all stick together. They just want to belong to something, even if it's a loser's club. Come on. Let's go. Need a ride home?"

When we get to my house, I start to open the car door, then turn to Pete. "Like I said earlier Pete. I'm not saying anything about the watch or what we talked about. I think that's something you need to decide for yourself. Thanks for the ride. And thanks for all your help with the team."

"I don't know what I'm going to do about all this, Teddy, but I do know one thing. You're a good guy. Oh yeah, one other thing. Your left jump shot really needs some work." He gives me a half-hearted grin, but I can tell he's still worried.

I go up to my room and of course, I hear it. The music. I pull out the box and it stops. I glance at *the Book of Life. A good life is not measured by what you have, but what you are.* Maybe I don't have a spot on the varsity team, but I are, well, *am* a good friend. It's a good decision. No knots in my stomach now. I'm ready for one of Baba's good dinners. Bring on the food.

Rosetta

The next time I'm in the bookstore store I find Mary shelving books at the back of the store. I smile at her and say, "I saw Teddy play in the JV game. He did great."

"You were at the game?"

"Sure, we go to all the games. I probably forgot to mention that my son is the JV coach."

"Coach Luther is your son? Oh, my gosh, I had no idea. He's been so good to Teddy. A life saver actually. I was devastated when Teddy didn't make varsity. I was praying he would. Not just for his sake but that then he might finally forgive me for taking him away from his Phoenix team. When your son asked him to be captain I think it was just the boost he needed."

"He wouldn't have asked him if he didn't deserve it. I can guarantee you that. Luther takes his basketball pretty seriously. He got some offers at bigger schools in Chicago but he said there's nothing like Hoosier basketball. He's hoping to get the varsity position when Coach Burton retires."

"So you're living near your parents and your son. How nice is that?" Mary says.

"Yes, it was fortunate that both James and I could find work in a small community. Well, James could work out of a popsicle stand. He became a financial planner when he left the university. Have computer, will work. But I do feel quite lucky how it's all turned out."

Mary takes a few more books out of box. "My luck's a little down right now," she says and then quickly apologizes. "I'm sorry. I usually wait until I'm alone to have my pity party." She places a book on the shelf and turns another one face out.

I want so much to give her a hug, but instead I say, "Please don't apologize. You have every right to be sad. And I think what you're doing is so admirable."

"You do?" she asks as if surprised.

"Moving across the country, starting all over ...." Before I can go on she starts to cry and then I do hug her. I realize in that moment how much I have come to care for this fragile lady. In my arms she feels like a little bird — one with a broken wing.

"Thanks, Rosetta." She sniffs and pulls a tissue out of her bookstore apron pocket. "Some days I feel like I'm making great progress and then it's back to square one. I have to be strong for the children, but often it all seems so meaningless without Stan. I miss him so much."

"Of course you do. Of course." I say. I know that my loss of Stan no way compares to hers, but I do know how much it hurts to realize someone will never be a part of your life again.

Teddy

❧

It's a crisp fall Saturday morning unlike anything in Arizona. Most of the leaves have fallen off the trees but a few red and orange ones hang on. Lawns are covered with dried brown leaves and some of them crunch under our footsteps in the path.

I ask Mindy, "So where are we headed?"

Mindy ignores my question and keeps walking. It's another Mindy adventure. She leads. I follow. With the sack of food I promised to bring. For a small person, she eats like a sumo wrestler.

"It's a surprise," she says.

We walk past houses, churches, parks, and gas stations. Just when we've reached the end of town, we see a weathered red and white faded sign. "Enchanted Island Amusement Park — Est. 1956". Not a sign of life.

I say, "This place looks ancient — do they still use it?"

"All summer long. Didn't you ever come here when you visited?"

"You know, I think we did. I think it was my first roller coaster ride."

Mindy leads me around the back way and then slips through a decorated panel door that looks like a fence going all around the park. Then she runs to a big merry-go-round in the middle of the park. All the horses are covered with clear plastic tarps.

"Don't tell me you know how to make this thing start, too." I ask.

"No, I haven't figured that out yet. I think they take the motor out for the winter. I just like to walk around and look at the different horses. One year I even named them all."

"You know you're weird, don't you?"

"Yes, I tried to warn you, but, no, you had to tag along. Which one do you want?"

"What do you mean, which one? What am I going to do with it? Ride off into the sunset?"

"No stupid, just pretend. If one was yours, which one would it be? My favorite is this light brown one with the red saddle. His eyes look so real. I call him Sandy." Mindy peels the plastic off and puts her foot in the stirrup. Jumping on the horse, she lays her head down close to its shiny wooden mane. "Hi Sandy, did you miss me?"

"Hi Mindy," I say in my best Mr. Ed voice. "I thought you had grown up and were never coming back. Say, who is that handsome boy with you?"

"Oh him. He keeps following me home from school. I only brought him because his Baba makes good pizza. He bribed me with food."

Still in a deep Mr. Ed voice, "Did you say food? I haven't had an apple for months."

"Here's a lump of sugar, ole boy. Did you think I would forget you?"

I throw my head back and neigh as good as I can. Then I jump on the black horse next to her and say, "Come on Sandy, I'll race you. No one beats Midnight!" I don't even bother to take the plastic off.

Next thing I know we're laughing and running through the carousel, jumping on and off horses, hiding behind them, having a great shoot out with make believe pistols. We finally get winded and end up where we started.

"I'm thirsty," Mindy says. "Is there anything to drink in that back pack of yours?"

I pull out a soda and a water. "Name your poison, pard'ner."

"Soda for me," she says reaching for the can.

We sit on the edge of the merry-go-round catching our breath and quenching our thirst.

"Kind of stupid, isn't it?" she says.

"Yeah, but kind of fun too. I haven't played cowboys and indians for at least 10 years. I knew something was missing from my life. I just couldn't put my finger on it."

"Oh yes, you've been playing real serious things. Like basketball.

Now that's a really grown up game. Bounce, bounce, shoot. Run and do it the other way. See Teddy bounce the ball. See Teddy make the basket."

"Teddy wasn't making any baskets the other night. It was like I never played before in my life. They must have thought I was a real dreamer. To think I could play on the Sweet 16 team."

"Well, take a lesson from Michael Jordan."

"So which lesson is that?"

"Well, you know he was a high scorer but not a good defensive player."

"So ...."

"So he ends up winning Best Defensive Player of the year in 1988 as an all-time leader in steals and set records for a guard with blocked shots."

"Your point is?"

"My point is he must have had to work hard to get good at something that didn't come to him naturally like scoring did."

"I get it, Coach. I'll keep trying to be the best player Middleburg ever had." I look at Mindy and suddenly all her goofy eccentric colors — purple glasses, turquoise braces, red hair, orange freckles — don't seem weird to me. They look adorable.

"Let's go to the Ferris wheel," she says and I take it my pep talk is over. We walk to the back of the Ferris wheel into a little opening in the fence. Mindy raises the bar for us to sit in the first seat. "The seats are actually called paddles, but don't ask me why."

"What, something you don't know? Call Channel Five now. Breaking news." She grins. "What if it starts moving?" I say, hoping to scare her. What if the carnival is haunted with ghosts? The fortune teller? The sword swallower?"

"All I want to swallow is some pizza. I'm starving."

We squeeze under the bar of the seat which I now know is a paddle. I wedge my backpack between us and we sit there rocking the seat a little and eating. No one's talking, but it's okay. There's a little breeze and we can see some trees that still have color. I see the top of the roller coaster rails and I think of what the grief counselor said: "Your emotions will be like a roller coaster ride for the next year.

Some days you'll be so up you'll think you're past the sadness. Then, whoosh, you'll hit bottom again and have to start that long, slow climb back to the top."

I'm wondering how many times Dad came here as a little boy. Did he ever sit with a girl eating pizza on the Ferris wheel? I'll have to ask Uncle Dan for some Dad stories.

After lunch, we walk around the park some more. It looks dingy, old and faded. Mindy, as if she can read my mind, which scares me more than the thought of a haunted amusement park, says, "Next summer this place will smell like a giant ball of cotton candy."

Summer seems a long way off. Will we still be here? Will it ever feel like home to me? All I know now is that it feels good to be with Mindy. I look at her little red head bobbing at my elbow with her jaunty walk and realize I am developing a special fondness for an elf with a turquoise smile. In spite of her steel-trap mind, she seems more like a girl to me each time we meet.

Back home, I grab my bike and head for the cemetery. The afternoon sun is making golden rays through the thick branches of colored leaves and the grass is warm when I sit down beside Dad. I look around to see if anyone is in listening distance but I am alone.

"Dad," I whisper, "If somehow you're looking down from above you know I didn't make the varsity team. I don't want to be a quitter, but maybe I'm not as good as I thought. Maybe I should just accept that. There must be some other things I can do. You told me once I was a pretty good golfer. Maybe that should be my new sport. I wish you were here to tell me what to do." Then I realize if Dad were here, I wouldn't have this dilemma or be talking to a tombstone. At first, it's strange, but once I start, the words seemed to roll out. It's natural. Easy. "Well, Dad, I guess I'll just figure it out. I'll be back next week."

And then I remember that one piece of pizza in my backpack that escaped Mindy. I leave it at the foot of the headstone. "Here, Dad, I bet Baba would like you to have this. It's probably as tasty as you remember."

I weave my way back when I see George. I wave to him and he

walks toward me. "Say, I took your advice — you know, finding some-one worse off."

"Oh?"

"Well, not really on purpose. Sort of by accident. I mean really an accident." I tell him about Mikey and Joe. "In fact, I'm on my way to see him now."

"Well, that sounds good, Son. I won't keep you." George walks away, waving a shovel high in the air behind him as a good-bye.

I pedal as fast as I can to the hospital, anxious to see Joe.

⟡

"'It was the best of times, it was the worst of times.' Don't you love the way this book starts?" I'm reading out loud to Joe. Even though we're further into the book, I always start out with the first sentence. He's sitting up with his head against the headboard, eyes closed. I'm sitting in his wheelchair beside him. It's just the two of us. I think that although in some ways it's the worst time for both of us, this might also be the beginning of something that could be the best time.

⟡

The following week, I'm finally making good on my promise to take Mindy to *my* choice of a Saturday adventure. When we get to Joe's room, he's sitting up in the chair, having lunch.

"Hey Joe, what's up?" I say.

"I'm trying to figure out what sadistic person is cooking in the kitchen. Tell me you brought me something good to eat. Anything."

"No, I brought you something better. Joe, this is Mindy. Mindy, Joe."

For a minute, no one says anything as they stare at one another. One all in white, one in blinding colors. Mindy's the first to break the silence. "Hi Joe. I don't have a clue why I'm here, but I'm sure Teddy will reveal his master plan. Or maybe you can tell me?"

"Me? I know nothing. I lived a thousand years ago in Pharaoh's tomb. I am on loan to this century. I have had many past lives. My penance is to be an eternal teenager in America."

Mindy blurts out, "Pharaoh's tomb is actually about 3,500 years ago and —"

I interrupt. "That is precisely why you are here, oh Wise One." I bow to Mindy. Your knowledge is needed. Joe, meet Middleburg's brainchild. You said you needed a tutor to catch up and she's the smartest person I know." I turn to Mindy. "Joe has been informed by his teachers that if he doesn't get help soon, he may revert back to his sophomore year. An evil downward spiral."

Now I've really got Mindy's attention. "Well, why didn't you say so, Teddy? I would have brought —"

"Mindy, everything you need is in your little red head. You've got more stuff stored up there than the entire Internet."

Although she tries to deny it with, "I don't know about that," I can tell she's flattered. And in all honesty, she probably agrees.

"Joe's a junior," I say to Mindy.

"Hey, aren't you the boy who was making the rocket? I remember reading about it. Wow!" Mindy seems awed. Anyone who would attempt such a science project obviously earns her admiration.

"That's me — from rocket boy to scar boy in one easy lesson."

Mindy says, "Did you know that the movie title *October Sky* is an anagram for Rocket Boys?"

Joe seems impressed. "No kidding?"

"See what I'm saying, Joe. It's all up here." I pat the top of Mindy's head while I try to get us back on track. "He's got all his books right here." I point to his bedside table, which looks like the inside of a locker, less smelly lunch bags and scruffy shoes. "A couple of weeks with Mindy and you probably won't have to finish your junior year. You'll probably get to skip it altogether. There will be a slight fee, however, for arranging this service."

"Just put it on my bill. Dad says they'll be naming a wing of the hospital for us by the time I'm out. My white gauze supply alone equals the national debt."

"Which is about a trillion dollars today. That's before compound interest," Mindy pipes in.

"See what I mean? A fountain of knowledge. Well, I'm going to leave you two alone." I decide *I* don't need to be tutored. It's a good time to pay Dad a visit and see if George is around. "I'll be back in about an hour. I might even pick up some milkshakes. Flavors?"

"Chocolate for me," Joe says.

"Strawberry for me," Mindy says, her eyes already devouring Joe's books.

Why did I know Mindy's could never be a plain vanilla? Way too bland a color for her.

I take a quick spin to the cemetery. I tell Dad about hooking up Mindy and Joe. Doing something nice for my two new best friends. No sign of George. I swing through Burger King for the milkshakes.

As I approach Joe's room, I can hear them talking like they've known each other forever. Joe's in the wheelchair, Mindy's in the big chair across from him and three books are open on the cart between them.

"I hate to interrupt this great brain power, but I bring great nourishment."

While we're drinking our shakes Mindy tries to bring me up to date on their long-range tutoring program, which she already has in place. "Spare me the details" I say. "I trust the mission will be accomplished. Way ahead of schedule."

Joe doesn't say a word as he slurps his milkshake as fast as he can, hardly surfacing for air, but I can tell from the way his eyes are sparkling that he likes Mindy. I'm not sure if it's for the homework or just to have a new face in the room. She definitely adds a lot of color to the sterile all-white environment. What he doesn't realize, however, is how he'll either have to share or guard his food. As Mindy always reminds me, brain power burns calories.

Before Mindy leaves, they set a day and time for her to return. I'm going to stay and read to Joe for a while, but I walk Mindy to the front door.

Mindy says, "Teddy, this is the best! This is really the best! Better than the fort, the amusement park. You win hands-down. I can't wait to come back."

Back in Joe's room, we are transported to Paris as I read, "A large cask of wine had been dropped and broken, in the street. The wine was red wine and had stained the ground of the narrow street in St

Antoine in Paris. It had stained many hands and many naked feet. One tall joker scrawled upon a wall with his finger dipped in muddy wine —BLOOD. The time was to come when that wine too would be spilled on the street — stones and the stain of it would be red on many there.'"

⌒

The following Monday at our locker Mindy says with a dreamy smile. "Joe … Joe is so cool. I mean look at him. He could be such a sorry soul, but he's so upbeat, so funny. I think he's great. Smart too."

Something about the way Mindy says Joe's name, makes me uneasy. What is it? Can I be jealous of Mindy and Joe? *No way. I'm the one who wanted them to be friends.* I felt so good about it, but now, for a second, I think she likes him more than just as a tutor. More than she likes me. She walks away and I feel deserted. I slam my locker door shut. I hate it when I have all these mixed emotions and I have them a lot. I love Mom but I still get mad at her sometimes for bringing us here. I like Pete, but see red when I think about the cemetery. And I hate it when Wally and Liz say they miss me. Like what am I supposed to do about it? Like I'll ever see them again. Isn't anything ever easy?

Mary

⌒

I look at the pieces we have chosen for the memory quilt spread out on the dining room table. It makes me both sad and happy. Then I have that nagging feeling again. Something Rosetta said about Stan's shirt. She always liked it. I think of Coach Luther. I think of Rosetta. I think of how much Luther looks like Stan.

These thoughts are jumbled in my mind. I have to stop and think of what I know for sure. I know now that her son is Coach Luther. I know she was a single mom. I know she graduated the same year as Stan. She told me she had her baby right after high school. That's all I really know.

I think then of her comment at the book discussion. How quickly she responded to the question about the interracial love between Ishmael and Hatsue. Something about how the relationship would have never worked. Society was too prejudiced. Better to have ended it while they were still in love.

I think of Luther, the hazel eyes, the chin dimple. Coincidences? I open the yearbook again. What I'm thinking is ridiculous. But I need to satisfy my curiosity. I see that Rosetta has signed her name by her senior photo but I can't find a blurb on either inside cover where most of the signatures are. I see other stereotype messages. *Good Luck Stan in college. Sitting next to you in English was a blast. I'll never forget that three-pointer that took us to overtime. Too bad we blew it. Ha. Take it easy on the girls this summer.* Why wouldn't she have said something? Anything? Like *Good luck* or whatever. Was it because what she wanted to say was too personal?

Did he and Rosetta ...? So what if they did? I struggle with this possibility and finally realize I am not so much jealous at the thought of a relationship, but if it is true, that Stan never told me about it. I thought Stan and I told each other everything about our lives before we met. I told him about the time my friends and I were caught trying to shoplift some cheap costume jewelry. So cheap it would have hardly been worth getting a juvie record. He told me about the pranks they played in high school and about a bunch of them trying marijuana. We had no secrets. Or at least I didn't think we did.

I walk to Baba's liquor supply on the dining room buffet. I uncork a bottle of merlot and pour myself a glass. My brain is fuzzy with so many unanswered questions. With weird possibilities. Is Luther Stan's son? Can there be that many coincidences? If he is, did Stan know? Would he not take responsibility? What does Baba know?

And if it *is* true? Oh jeez, that means Teddy has an older brother. Coach Luther, the man he likes so much, could be his half-brother? It's preposterous. I fill my wine glass again and drink it too quickly. My head is throbbing now and I climb the stairs to bed. I look in at Teddy, sleeping so peacefully. My heart aches for him. For all of us. Perhaps we should have stayed in Phoenix. Is that why in my dreams, Stan told me to come home? To find his son?

I fall into my little twin bed and the room spins.

Rosetta

Mary calls to cancel the lunch we had planned. She gives no reason but sounds abrupt and cool. Have I done something to offend her? Does she suspect anything? Have I carelessly said something incriminating? I go to the store late one evening. I linger and browse. The few remaining customers are now checking out. Looking at my watch, I know the store will be closing soon. When the last customer leaves I approach the counter. Mary continues typing on the computer, not even acknowledging me.

"Mary, I just wanted to let you know that I probably won't be coming to book group anymore."

She finally looks at me, but shows no concern that I might not return. She simply says, "Oh?"

"They've changed my work schedule," I say the first thing that pops into my mind even though it's not true.

"They do surgery at night now?" she asks skeptically.

I was not prepared for that remark. I rebound with "I'm going on the floor. Ready for a change."

"I see," is all she says.

I decide to confront her. "Mary, could we talk for a few minutes after you close?" When Mary hesitates to answer, I'm a bit offended. I think, *How many times has Mary asked me to talk and I've always complied.* But I wait politely for her answer.

"I suppose. Give me a few minutes while I close up. I'll meet you back in the children's section."

I'm sitting when Mary approaches but she remains standing.

"Mary, please sit a moment," I put my hand on the chair next to mine. The chairs are in a semi- circle and although Mary sits, she leaves an empty space between us. "Mary, have I offended you in any way? You seem upset with me. Or is there something else bothering you? If I'm a sad reminder of Stan, I won't come around anymore."

"There's no new night shift, is there?"

"No. To be honest with —," I start to say.

Mary puts her head down and rubs the back of her neck with both hands. "If you really want to be honest ...," she interrupts me.

"What? Please tell me," I move to the chair next to Mary. She inches away as if I have something contagious.

"I don't know what to say. It sounds so ridiculous. So far-fetched."

"So it is something. Tell me."

Mary takes a deep sigh and looks at me. "It's Stan. I just don't know how to say this. If I'm way off base, I'll be so embarrassed. But did you and Stan ... were you more than friends?

I reach for Mary's hand as a gesture of friendship, then hesitate and pull away. I look around the room to avoid her eyes. Picture books are facing out. I look at *Goodnight Moon* and *The Very Hungry Caterpillar* crawling on the cover. I wish I could crawl away some- where. I'm stalling. Should I say anything? The truth? Deny it? How would she ever know, now that Stan is gone? I look into her pleading eyes and know it is time for the truth.

"Mary, I'll spare you the anguish. Yes, Stan and I thought we were in love in high school. I should have told you, but it was nothing, really. A teenage crush. You know, in the '60s, we couldn't let anyone know how we felt. The tension all over the country, the riots, the killings. Why, inter-racial marriages only became legal in '67. I guess I was so used to keeping it a secret. Maybe I thought it should stay that way."

Mary covers both eyes. A little sob escapes and she sniffles. "I guess what hurts me is that Stan didn't confide in me. I thought we told each other everything. Maybe it's not you I'm upset with. It's him. I'd like to ask him why he never told me about something so important to him but I can't. That makes me angry and the anger makes me feel guilty. A vicious cycle."

I nod. When Mary looks at me, I avoid her eyes again, looking up, noticing one of the fluorescent lights is flickering. Like me. Wavering. This would have been so much simpler if I had just said from the first day. 'Of course I knew Stan. In fact I had a little crush on him. I think a lot of girls did. He was so handsome.' Could have avoided this awful confrontation.

Mary goes on, "You mentioned marriage. If you could have, would you two have married? Was I a second choice? Because he couldn't have his first choice?"

"Oh Mary, how can you even think that? Look at the life you've built together. Look at your beautiful family. Of course he loved you far more than me. We hardly knew each other." It hurts me to say this, but I need to assure her somehow. I stand up, as if this conversation is over. "It's late. We're both tired, but I am glad you told me what you were thinking. I hope we can still be friends. And that you'll forgive me for not mentioning this."

Mary stands as well. "You're right Rosetta. Grief does funny things to your mind. I imagine to your heart as well."

As we walk to the front of the store, I say. "You've been through a lot. And it's only what, six months? Don't be so hard on yourself."

Mary turns the key in the now-locked door to let me out. Before I go, I pause, "Mary, I'm just curious. What made you think Stan and I were more than friends?"

Mary covers her eyes with her hands and then starts rubbing her forehead with both hands. When she finally looks up, she pushes her hair behind her ears, takes a deep breath and says, "It's so preposterous I can't even say it. If I'm wrong, and I'm sure I am, you'll think I'm really nuts. I'm letting my imagination run wild."

"After all you've been through Mary, I would never judge you harshly. What is it you're imagining?" I hold my breath.

Mary looks at me. "Okay, I'm going to say it and be done with it. If I say it out loud I'll realize how ridiculous it is."

"Yes?" I ask nervously.

Again Mary says, "Okay." She takes a deep breath. "It's Luther. He reminds me so much of Stan. And when I went to talk to him about Teddy, to thank him for being so nice to him … up close. His eyes. The cleft in his chin. It's Stan all over again. And even his mannerisms.

That half-smile. I know it's crazy. My counselor said I would keep seeing Stan in so many people. Tell me it's all coincidence. Tell me I've lost my marbles."

I look at Mary but don't say anything. I don't know how begin, "Mary, I —"

My faltering causes an alarmed look on Mary's face. "What?" She interrupts me. "Why aren't you saying I'm way off base? Why are you hesitating? Is it true? Rosetta, talk to me."

I close my eyes and run my hands through my hair. I can hardly face her. When I open my eyes there are tears in them and I say, "You're not imagining things, Mary. Luther is Stan's son."

Mary

C⌒⌐

Although I suspected, knowing it for a fact cuts into me deeply. I can't look at Rosetta. I look everywhere but at her. The best-seller shelf with the new hardbacks facing out. The sale table with paperbacks piled high. "Buy two, get one free." The greeting card rack by the front door. I see a sympathy card and recall how comforting the cards were after Stan's death, especially those with a note, saying something they loved about Stan. I don't imagine there's a specific card for what I'm feeling now. Betrayal. Betrayed by Stan and Rosetta both.

I push my hair behind my ears. Over and over. I look at her. "And *you* want to be friends? I thought you cared about me, but you just wanted to know more about Stan. I feel so used. How could you?"

Rosetta's eyes fill with tears. "Mary, please don't say that. I do care about you. Honestly, I would never have had any conversations with you if I didn't. Of course, I was curious about Stan, but you, our friendship, became important to me. You have to believe that."

How can I convey to Rosetta how inferior I feel at this moment, like the mousy self-conscious waif caught in the rain the day I met Stan. How I felt this way most of my life growing up, until Stan came along and to my wonderment, chose me. "You want to know what I believe? I'll tell you what I believe. I look at you and see a beautiful, sexy, confident woman, one Stan would have chosen to marry if he could have. You said Stan was always for the underdog. I guess that's why he chose me and that's how I feel now."

"Mary, Mary, please don't say that. Stan fell in love with the sweet, tender person I am getting to know. And you want to talk about looks?

C⌒⌐ 225 ⌐⌐

A petite blond with beautiful blue eyes and a terrific figure who looks 30 instead of 45. And confidence? Moving across the country with three children, starting over? Don't you know what a strong woman you are?"

Rosetta's words make me cry. I don't want her to be kind. I don't want to like her.

She goes on. "You are right, Mary. I had no right to intrude into your life and risk revealing the past. I admit at first I did want to know about Stan's life, but the more we talked the more I wanted to know you." Rosetta shakes her head. "Now, I've done nothing but cause you further heartache, as if you didn't have enough. I am truly sorry. I understand if we can't be friends, but please, please find it in your heart to forgive me. I never meant to hurt you."

"So this love child of yours and Stan's … did you send photos? Stay in touch?"

"Oh, my gosh, Mary, Stan never knew. I never told him. You have to believe that."

I want to believe her, but it seems impossible she wouldn't have told him. "I don't know what to believe anymore, Rosetta."

I start turning off lights in the store and get my purse from under the counter. I walk to the front door. She follows. I gesture for her to leave and I lock the front door. We walk to our cars without saying another word.

Everyone's in bed but me. I'm sitting in the living room trying to make sense of all this. It's been six months since Stan died. The grief counselor said don't make any big changes in your life the first year. I should have listened to her. Why was I in such a rush to get out of there? If we had stayed, I might never have known about Rosetta, about Luther. Should I tell Teddy he has an older brother? It's too much to absorb. I start crying and rub my eyes with the palms of my hands. I don't even hear Baba until she is beside me. I startle when she puts her arms around me.

"Mary, Mary, I know how much you miss Stan. My heart too, it is breaking. For you. For the children."

"Oh, Baba, I didn't hear you. I'm sorry for you to see me this way."

"Mary, what way should I see you? Happy? Of course not. You don't have to be such strong person. I wonder some days how you be so strong. That you don't cry more."

"Oh Baba, I am crying inside. I don't want Teddy to see me unhappy because he blames himself."

"I know," Baba says. "You are good mother, Mary."

Her kind words make me cry harder. I want so much to talk about Stan. About Rosetta and Luther. But I can't risk upsetting Baba. I walk to the kitchen for a box of tissues.

When I return to the sofa I say, "Tell me more about Stan when he was in high school. Did he have lots of friends? Did he have a girlfriend?"

Baba fiddles with a button on her yellow quilted robe while she thinks a moment. "Stan have so many friends. Dan, he was more quiet, more serious. But not Stan. All the time, the phone ringing. Boys in the house, laughing. The boys come all the time to play the basketball in our backyard. Then they are hungry. I loved to watch those boys eat. When Stan went to college I miss the noise. The house, it was too quiet."

"Did he have a special girlfriend?"

"Girlfriend? No, not so special. He went to the dance with a pretty girl. What they call it? Prom?"

Baba goes to the hutch in the dining room and brings a scrapbook to the sofa. She sets it on her lap, wrings her hands and opens and close them. She licks her index finger and turns to a page where Stan is wearing a white sport coat with a blue boutonnière and matching cummerbund. Beside him is a pretty blonde girl in a blue gown with an orchid corsage on her wrist. The backdrop is the Eiffel Tower. I touch the photo and there is a catch in my chest looking at Stan's young and vibrant smile. Baba goes on, "You, Mary, are the first girl he brought home to meet us. From college. Papa and I like you very much from the first time."

I look at the lined face of my mother-in-law. In my own grief I often forget Baba's sadness. "Baba, sometimes I'm thinking so much of myself and Teddy, I forget that you have lost a son. How is it that you are not more angry? Or bitter. *You* are the strong woman, not me."

"Of course I am very sad Mary, but let me tell you story. Something you do not know. It was long time ago. Dan and Stan were little boys. Maybe five years and three years. That was our family, Papa, me, two little boys. We live in Indianapolis, where there was work for Papa and close to my parents, but when they died, he said, 'Let us move where we can have a big yard, a garden. Fruit trees and rose bushes like Bulgaria.'

"We came here. It was open country, not so much like today. First he worked for the butcher in town. Then he was able to get a job at the new car factory. There is a Bulgarian saying, *new house, new baby,* and I did become pregnant. I was hoping so much for a little girl." She sighs. "The baby was a girl but she come too soon. Her lungs. They did not grow yet. She lived one day."

"Oh, Baba, I didn't know this. I am so sorry."

"It is long time ago. But to tell the rest of the story. I was so sad. I cry every day for this little girl. I was busy with the little boys, but my heart was heavy. Papa didn't know what to do to make it better. Then one night, just like I find you tonight, Papa found me crying alone in the kitchen. I was holding little pink booties I knitted. I make pink with hopes for girl. Papa was kind. You know how he was. You had a chance to know him little bit."

"Yes, he was a gentle man."

"That night, he took me in his arms. He said, 'Dora, we can try again? We can have our little girl someday. We are still young.' This made me cry more, but here is the part I want to tell you Mary. What he said next, I never forget. He said, 'Dora, I am sad for us too. But when I think of our parents, what they did for us by coming to America. You know what is going on in our homeland now? Still communism, ethnic wars. Still the people fighting like they did centuries ago. My father had such courage to come here, to leave his beautiful country. To leave his brothers. To look for a better life. Because he was brave, we have this wonderful opportunity in America. We have freedom. We can say what we want, go to church where we want. We don't have to be looking over our shoulders to see if someone is going to hurt us. Dora, if we are not happy here in America, then everything my father gave up in his homeland, it was for nothing. You see what I am saying? To honor our parents, we must be thankful each day. We must enjoy life. It is our ....' what is the word?"

"Duty ... obligation?" I ask.

"Yes, that is the word. Then he tell me funny story that his father passed to him. When they were coming through Ellis Island, there were many health inspections and the officials, they ask many questions. Do you have $25? Do you have someone expecting you? There were questions to see if a person was intelligent. They asked a young girl 'If you were washing the steps would you start on the top step or the bottom step?' The young girl answered, 'I did not come to America to wash steps.'"

I laugh with Baba. "She was spunky."

Baba says, "What is this spunky?"

"Spunky means lots of courage. Strong, confident," I told her.

Baba nods her head in agreement. "Yes, she was. Many times in our marriage Papa would remind me when things were not so good. 'Our ancestors did not come to America to wash steps. They came to enjoy life.' Those dirty steps, Mary, they have helped me many times."

I go to bed but I am restless. Too many thoughts running through my head. I draw a hot bath, the hottest water I can stand with bubbles up to my neck. As I soak in the old tub with claw legs, I think of Stan having a bath in this old tub as a toddler, with a young Baba kneeling beside the tub, shampooing his dark curly hair. When I picture him as the adorable little boy in Baba's photo albums, the toddler, the gawky adolescent, and then the handsome teen, the anger I felt earlier because he did not share his Rosetta story with me begins to subside like the bubbles diminishing in the tub. I imagine how frustrated he must have been to have loved Rosetta and not been able to show it. Before I fall asleep that night, I ponder over Baba's remarks.

I think, "How ironic. Stan's grandfather came here for freedom, yet his grandson was not free to love the girl of his choice."

Rosetta

When I get home, James is watching the late evening news. I would normally sit down beside him. Give him a kiss on the cheek. Instead I walk directly into the kitchen, take a big drink of water, pour another glass, and sit down at the kitchen table, sipping it. I feel an unquenchable thirst for some reason. Dehydrated and drained. I also feel like a louse, a low-life.

Should I have denied it? Assured her a chin dimple and hazel eyes were a coincidence? I know in my heart that was not the answer. The true answer was I should have avoided her the day I knew she was Stan's wife. I should have left the past where it belonged.

"Hi baby, how was your book discussion?" James comes into the kitchen and strokes the top of my head. I look up at him and wonder how much to say. "Hey, what's wrong?" he asks when he looks into my eyes.

"I've done an awful thing."

"You? I can't believe that. You left the scissors in a patient-again?" We often joke, but when he sees tears well up, he apologizes. "I'm sorry. You're really serious."

"It's a long story." I look at him like it can't possibly be something he wants to hear.

"It's not like I'm going anywhere," he says, as he goes to the fridge and pulls out a beer. He sits across from me, takes a drink, and covers my hand with one of his. "So tell me this long story."

"Where to start?" I mumble.

"How about at the beginning?" James says.

"I told you when you asked me to marry you that Luther's dad was my high school crush, a white boy I couldn't marry. Never told him about it."

James nods his head to indicate he remembers. "And I said, I totally understood why you never told him. Don't forget, I lived through the 60s too."

I look up at him with a wry smile. I'm reminded again of how lucky I am to have him in my life. "The first night of book discussion I met his wife, Mary. The lady he eventually married. She moved back to Middleburg because Stan … her husband, Luther's father, was killed in a car accident. In Phoenix. Where they lived."

"Oh, baby, I'm so sorry."

I acknowledge his comment with a nod. "When she told me who she was, I casually mentioned that I went to school with Stan. She wanted to have coffee and talk about him, what he was like at school. She was grieving and hungry for any connection with him. I agreed."

"Nothing wrong with that, baby. That was a kind thing to do."

"Perhaps, but my motives were not so innocent. I don't mean to hurt you but I don't want to keep anything from you anymore. I wanted to know about Stan, too. More than I should have wanted to know after all these years."

"Baby, baby. That seems perfectly normal to me. He was the father of your child. Of course you would want to know."

I look at James and wonder why I would ever doubt his understanding.

"But it gets worse. When I saw her son, Teddy, on the basketball court … he's on Luther's team, if you can believe it."

He shakes his head. "Truth is stranger, they say …."

"When I saw Teddy, he looked exactly like Stan did his senior year and … and James, such strong feelings rushed back into me. Feelings of passion like I was a teenager again."

James smiles. "Was Stan your first?"

"My first love?"

"Well, that too, but was he the one you lost your virginity to?"

"Yes," I say with a bowed head, as if confessing to a priest. *Forgive me father for I have sinned.*

"Baby, baby, that is so normal. I still have a warm spot in my heart for Juanita. A part of me will always love her."

I snap out of my pity party. "Juanita?"

"She was my first. I was a junior. She was a sophomore. Want more details?" he smiles.

"No," I answer quickly. Perhaps too quickly.

"Is that what's bothering you? Teen angst returning?"

"No. What's bothering me is I've spent time with Mary, slipping up on things in my past with Stan, and then the nail in my coffin was when she met Luther. He's been extra nice to her son, Teddy. She went to thank him and thought she was seeing Stan again. Tonight she confronted me and I admitted it."

"Ah," says James. He takes a drink of his beer and says, "The plot thickens. So what happened next?" He seems to be inching his chair closer to the table to get the next installment of this soap opera.

"She was angry. Said I had betrayed her by pretending to be her friend when all I wanted was to know more about Stan."

"Was she right?" James asks, non-judgmentally.

I avoid James' eyes as I run my hands through my hair. When I look up, I say, "Yes, there was some truth to that. I told her I did want to know about his life, but as I came to know her, the more I wanted to be her friend." I shake my head. "That's never going to happen now."

"I'm sure she needs a little time to digest all this. Had to be quite a shock."

"I told her Stan never knew. She can't blame him at all for not telling her. She thinks he should have told her about me, about us, at least the romance part."

"I see," was all James says. He looks down at the table and has the look I recognize when he's trying to solve a problem.

We sit there quietly for a few minutes. He finishes his beer, tosses it in the recycle bin, and I finish my water. Some of the anxiety I had earlier is dissipating. My breathing doesn't seem so labored. Talking to James has helped.

"Now that I've had a whole 30 minutes to think about this," I say shaking my head, "I think what's bothering me most is how I handled this situation. I mean from the very beginning, 30 years ago, I was so mature. But now, after all that time, I blow it."

"You didn't blow anything, baby. You were just honest. Something good might come of this after all. Let's go to bed and talk again in the morning if you want to. Sleep is a wonderful balm." He walks around the table, takes my hand and pulls me out of my chair, close to him. "Rosetta, you are an amazing lady. Don't lose sight of all you have accomplished. As a person, as a single mother. I knew the day I met you how special you were. And don't forget, if you hadn't had Luther, we would have never met."

"Oh, I'll never regret having Luther," I say adamantly. Then softly, "Or you." I put my arms around him and hang on like he's a life jacket on the *Titanic.*

"You're really okay with what I said. About feelings for Stan resurfacing?"

"Of course I am. Besides I can't be jealous of a dead man. But you, on the other hand."

"Me what?" I ask.

"Juanita is still very much alive," he says with a wink at me.

"You are terrible," I say, as I swat him on the chest and hide my smile, not wanting to give him the satisfaction.

One of my last thoughts before drifting off to sleep were James' words. The very things I was trying to tell Mary. *You are a beautiful and strong lady.* I want so much for Mary to believe that of herself.

Teddy

Uncle Dan picks me up early Saturday morning. Baba's bustling around the kitchen, happy to have one more person to feed. She stands at her stove, flipping thin fried crepes she calls *pee-tool-its-see*, straight from her hot griddle to our plates.

"She has that wrist action down good," I mention to Uncle Dan.

"Years of practice," he says with his mouth already full. I follow his lead, spreading cream cheese and jelly over the *peetoolitsee* and then rolling it up like a burrito. We barely finish one and Baba's flipping the next one on our plate. Good insulation for what looks like a cold day outside. The sky is overcast.

"Probably snow headed our way," Uncle Dan says as he drives toward the high school. He pulls into the vacant school parking lot, turns off the ignition, and turns to look directly at me.

"Teddy, your Mom says you're nervous about driving again and I get that. But I think your dad would want you to keep driving. So I'm going to fill in for him. Are you alright with that?"

"Sure," I answer, although I'm not sure at all. I do know Uncle Dan wants to help somehow and I should let him. Give it a try. Guess I don't want to get snow tires for my bike.

He gets out of the truck and we trade places. When I'm behind the wheel, he has me adjust the mirrors and says, "I'm starting you here. It'll give you a feel before we get in traffic. And I brought the old truck because I want you to learn on a stick shift. That way you can drive anything. Anybody can do automatic. Real drivers can do both," he says, like that's something I should want to be. A real driver. I'm silently relieved he told me about the clutch. My first thought was he was afraid I would wreck his late-model SUV.

Uncle Dan is going on. "I never learned to drive until I had driver's ed my senior year. We never had a family car. Papa took the bus to work each day. He was one for American slogans and took to heart the one that said, 'If you drink, don't drive.' He wasn't about to give up his homemade wine."

"So when'd you get your first car?"

"I worked every summer. Finally between my junior and senior year in high school — that would have been about '66 — I had saved enough money. It was a pretty big day for the family. A 1957 black and white Chevy convertible. A classic. Your dad and I polished that beauty for hours. We couldn't wait to cruise Main Street. I'll never forget it. We were backing out of the driveway ... thought we were so cool. Then Baba stands on the front porch and yells loud enough for the whole neighborhood to hear, 'Boys, don't go in the street!' Like we were still on our bikes with training wheels. Your dad and I started laughing so hard, I could hardly back the car out. Finally, we cruised Main Street, with the radio blaring. Whenever I hear 'Good Morning, Starshine,' I think of that day."

I try to picture Dad as a cool teen and the thought of it makes me smile. *Happy Days* in action.

Uncle Dan says, "Okay, put your left foot on the clutch and turn the key to start the engine. You have to step on the gas and let the clutch up slowly at the same time."

The car lurches ahead and then dies. *What?* I feel totally stupid but Uncle Dan calmly says, "That's why we're in the parking lot and not on the street. It takes a while to get a feel for a clutch. If that hadn't happened, you would have been the first kid in America who skipped the bunny hop ritual."

We do it over and over and soon I'm making smooth starts, stops, and turns. The truck makes only one more gigantic leap when I'm talking to Uncle Dan instead of paying attention.

"You're doing great. You're a natural," he says. "Even better than your dad. It took him a lot longer."

"You taught my dad to drive?"

"I taught him a lot of things. Not that he would ever give me credit for any of it. Always wanted to do things his way. I never saw anyone so hard-headed!"

"Really? Like what?"

"Where to begin? Like the time we went sledding. I told him to go down the bunny hill, but he insisted on the steep hill with trees. Said he could dodge them. I never should have let him go, but he was so cocky, I said, 'Go ahead and don't cry to me when you go bouncing off the first tree.' Sure enough, he was building speed and couldn't control that sled. He clipped a tree with the edge of the sled and went flying. I was so scared. I ran down the hill as fast as I could. He was laying face-down in the snow. I kept calling him but he didn't move. Baba always told me, 'Look out for your little brother.' I was sure he was dead and it was all my fault.

"I kept saying, 'Stan, Stan, please get up. Please be all right.' Then he jumped up and said, 'Fooled you!' I was so relieved, but then I punched him out for scaring me. I think that hurt him more than the tree would have. Then, of course, he was always wanting to tag along with me and my friends. A regular pest."

It was hard to imagine Dad as a pesty little kid.

We've circled the parking lot so many times, I think Uncle Dan is getting dizzy. As if to confirm it he says, "This is a good start. Had enough for today? Next week, we'll head for some quiet country roads, but real roads where you can go a long stretch. How's that sound?"

"Great. But I think I'm ready for the real roads now."

Uncle Dan laughs and pats the back of my head, "Okay, let's try the back road around the school up to the edge of the park."

I'm doing fine and then we come to a four-way stop at the same time two other cars pull up. "Remember, person to your right goes first." I wait my turn. Another car has pulled up and is waiting for me. "Your turn," Uncle Dan says.

I slowly let the clutch out and step on the gas. The truck doesn't die but hops across the intersection like a kangaroo. I feel my face turning red. Wish I was Gumby so I could slink down in my seat out of sight.

Uncle Dan waves at the car waiting and the driver gives the two finger salute acknowledging us with a knowing smile, like it's the most normal thing in the world to see a car jerking through the intersection. Somehow I think that friendly exchange wouldn't have happened in Phoenix, where the evening news was filled with road rage incidents.

When I get to the other side, my palms are sweaty, but Uncle Dan says, "You're doing fine, Teddy, just fine. Just keep going. When we get to town, pull up in front of the drugstore and we'll trade places."

Okay, I have my composure back. Speedometer says I'm doing 40 miles per hour in a 50 mile-per-hour zone. I step on the gas thinking I can at least get it up to 45 when I see an intersection approaching. I start to back off when Uncle Dan says, "You're fine Teddy. You have the right of way. Keep going. There's a stop sign for the cross traffic."

My palms get slippery again. As I approach the intersection I see another car approaching from the right. I can't catch my breath. "I can't do this, Uncle Dan." I'm trembling. "I need to get out of the car. I have to stop."

Uncle Dan leans over and lightly puts his hand on the steering wheel. "Okay, Teddy, I've got it. We're fine." We pass the intersection where the other car has stopped at the stop sign. "Just take your foot off the gas pedal, slow it down, put the clutch in second and start to brake slowly. We'll pull off on the shoulder." Dan looks behind us. "We're good. There's nothing coming. That's good. Slow it down. Easy."

Someone I manage to slow the car and pull onto the shoulder and stop. "I'm so sorry Uncle Dan. I thought I could do this, but it all came back. I'm not ready." I put my head on the steering wheel and the sobs come loud and heavy. I open the truck door and step out just before I throw up near the left front tire. Now I'm both sorry and embarrassed. Uncle Dan comes around to the front of the car. From somewhere he's grabbed a towel which he hands me to wipe my face and he keeps rubbing my back while I'm still bent over.

"Teddy, Teddy, not your fault, son. My fault. It's too soon. I shouldn't have rushed you."

"Is it ever going to be right for me Uncle Dan?" I look at him. His eyes are so kind. "I'm sorry to disappoint you."

"Teddy, Teddy, I'm not disappointed in you at all. I just want to help you move on. There's no rush. Heck, if you start driving, you'll be asking me for my car keys all the time. What was I thinking?" That makes me smile. I wipe my nose with my sleeve. "Jump in and I'll drive us into town. And by the way, what happened here, it's just between us guys. As far as anyone's concerned, we did really good today. And actually, Teddy, you did. Got that clutch down good."

I start to walk to the passenger side and then I turn to Uncle Dan. "I want to try again."

"We will Teddy, whenever you want to."

"I mean now. I don't want the day to end like this. What do they say about when you fall off a horse?"

"Are you sure?"

"Yes. I can't ride my bike all my life." My turn to make Dan laugh.

I get behind the wheel. There's not a car in sight. I take a deep breath and pull out slowly. I get it back up to 40 miles an hour. My heart's beating pretty fast but I'm taking deep breaths and it feels better. As we approach town, the speed limit drops to 25. I slow down and stop at the first stop light. There are cars crossing the intersection and I'm not freaking out. Another deep breath and a sigh.

When the light turns green, Uncle Dan says, "Pull over in front of the drugstore. I think there's a spot open." Parking is at an angle which is good because I have no clue how to parallel park. I turn off the ignition and Uncle Dan rubs the top of my head. "I'm really proud of you, Teddy. Facing your fear. Getting back on that horse. We'll stay at it until as long as we need to."

He points to the drugstore. "Your dad and I spent a lot of time in there. Had my first cherry coke at the counter. Your dad liked those awful lime phosphates. Lot of teen romances started — and ended — in those red vinyl booths. Come on, I'll show you something."

We get out of the car and he walks me to the end of the sidewalk. "Yep, still here." I look down and see carved in the sidewalk in crooked letters, *Dan loves Janice.*

"Who's Janice?"

"Nobody I wanted to know, but your dad thought he was a comedian. We were walking home from school the day they poured this new sidewalk, the same day Janice Dombrowsky put a mushy love note in my locker. She was uglier than a mud fence in a hail storm. Of course she got the last laugh. She went to New York modeling after high school and when I saw her at our first high school reunion, she was a knock-out. I called your Dad and told him he was a real prophet. His sidewalk prediction finally came true."

"So, did you ask her out?"

"Oh, gosh no. By then I was engaged to your Aunt Joyce. I learned some stores are just better left in the past. Know what I mean?"

"I think so."

"Want to see another favorite place of ours when we were growing up?"

"Sure."

He heads back toward Baba's house. On a corner there's an American Legion building with two big cannons in each corner of the field.

"This used to be an empty lot before they built the Legion. Every Christmas, the fire department would flood it for ice-skating and put up a huge Christmas tree. We found out it was about 100 little trees in a pyramid. They had it wired to play Christmas carols and rigged up lights. It was like a Currier and Ives Christmas card with everyone skating around it while the music played."

Uncle Dan is smiling. "But the best times were on Saturday mornings, after they took down the tree. All winter long your dad and I would get up real early, even before Baba, and you know how early that is. We'd be the first ones here and skate till our toes were numb. And we were starving. Then we'd go home, eat some of Baba's *peetoolitsee* while our wet socks dried on the hot radiators. Now there's an unforgettable smell. Then we'd start off again. By the time we got back there'd be a hockey game going or a bunch of kids playing Crack the Whip. We spent hours here, but the best times were those early morning hours with just the two of us, making up all sorts of crazy games." Uncle Dan looks straight ahead out the windshield with a faraway look in his eyes. Then he hits the top of the steering wheel like a jolt back to reality. "We sure had some fun times."

I think of Dad's old brown hockey skates in the attic and maybe that's why Baba can't throw them out. She doesn't see old skates no one will ever use. She sees two little boys with cold, rosy cheeks and Saturday mornings with smelly socks on the radiators.

Uncle Dan says, "Say, I've got to run out to the mall. Want to come along? I know a back road where you might be able to drive a little stretch if you want to." I'm thinking all the roads here look like back roads but I don't say it.

"Let's go." I do want to drive some more to test myself, but I think we both want this morning with Dad stories to last a little longer.

We're near the edge of town when he pulls over and says, "Let's trade places. Turn left here and head out of town. Should be a quiet two-lane road with not too much traffic. We can build up some speed and you can practice slowing the car by downshifting and not using your brake."

All right. Now we're talking some real driving. These two lane roads are so different than the roads in Phoenix, sometimes with four lanes of traffic each way. It's a free feeling and I'm glad Dan insisted on this lesson.

Uncle Dan fiddles with the radio. "I'll find Sophie's favorite station for you, but just remember, when the music gets faster and louder, you still stay at the same speed. This isn't like dancing where you have to keep up with the music."

I'm cruising along with Brittany Spears, thinking I could drive forever. Maybe Mom will let me drive back to Arizona. *Sure. Fat chance. First of all, even getting to go back and secondly to drive.*

As we get near the mall, Uncle Dan says, "You better pull over. You don't have your Indiana permit yet and I don't want you to spend the night in jail."

I think to myself, *Why not?* I already have a roommate picked, thinking of what might happen to Pete. "Uncle Dan, when you and Dad were growing up, did you ever do anything that got you in real trouble?"

Uncle Dan laughs. "Sure. Probably mild by today's standards, but we were in trouble a lot. Like the time we got caught smoking. It was your dad's fault because he kept inhaling and got sick. We had to drag him home and Baba smelled the tobacco on his breath. We kept telling him not to inhale."

"How about Halloween? Did you do any pranks?"

"Oh, yeah, the time we tried to egg old Boozy's house." Uncle Dan's laughing now.

"Who's Boozey?"

"This crabby old man. I can show you the house. It still looks creepy to me. I think his real name was Mr. Bowser. Sometimes we'd cut across his yard on the way home from school and he'd come out, ranting and raving. We figured he was tipping a few in the afternoon. Halloween was a good time to get even with him.

"There were a bunch of us. We each brought a dozen eggs and had this great strategic plan to egg his house. But your dad tripped over a little bush in the yard and fell with his face landing in his open egg carton. Eggs broke all over his face. The rest of us laughed so hard we couldn't run. Then the lights came on in the house and we all tried to get out of the yard before Boozey saw us.

"We started saying stupid things to your dad, like 'Hey, give us your best smile. Sunny side up.' Your dad got so mad, he started throwing his eggs at *us*. It ended up to be a great egg fight in the middle of the street. Boozey never got one raw egg but we were covered."

I laugh again and decide I need to go see Dad and have one of our little chats. Maybe he didn't mind the egging the other night as much as I did. Maybe he liked being part of a boy's Halloween prank again. I think of the quote. *Life is a gift but only if we open it.* "Thanks Uncle Dan. I can't wait to go again."

"How about next Saturday? Same time same place?"

I'm about to answer yes when I hear it. The song from the music box. It's playing on the radio.

Quickly, before the song ends I say, "Uncle Dan, what's the name of that song?"

He turns the radio a little louder, looks real puzzled, then gets this weird look on his face. "I can't believe they're playing a Broadway piece on Sophie's station."

"What is it Uncle Dan? What's the name of it?"

"It's from *Doctor Zhivago*. "Somewhere My Love." His voice quivers a little and I see his eyes start to water.

"Is it a special song for you?" I ask.

He leans over and tussles my hair. "Yes, Teddy, it is. But it was even more special for your Dad. For some reason, he loved that song."

I can't help but wonder if an angel isn't perched on the radio tower and Dad is having a little fun with us earthlings.

Mary

When I see in the local paper that *Toy Story 2* is coming out this weekend, I am excited for Teddy. I know he's been anxiously awaiting the sequel.

"Teddy, I'm taking the girls to see *Toy Story 2*. Want to come with us?" His reaction surprises me. Instead of excitement, I see his lips start to quiver and he turns to walk away.

"I don't think so Mom."

I follow him to the other room. "You'd probably rather see it with a friend. I understand."

He turns and glares at me. "No, you *don't* understand Mom. You don't get it. I'd rather not see it at all. Watching it without Dad? Every funny line would make me cry instead of laugh if he weren't beside me. Don't you remember? *Toy Story* was *our* thing."

He walks away and this time I don't follow but let him go. Then I recall how many times I'd hear them repeating lines from the first *Toy Story* to each other and bursting into peals of laughter when I rarely understood what was so funny. Stan in a big cowboy voice: "This town ain't big enough for the both of us." Teddy in a panicky potato head voice: "Where's my ear? Who's seen my ear? Did you see my ear?" Stan in a squeaky alien voice: "We are eternally grateful."

Now I get it. If I couldn't risk seeing the gazebo on the Indiana campus again after 30 years, how can I expect Teddy to face *Toy Story* friends without Stan? To put salt in a wound that is still open?

Teddy

⟨∾⟩

I go to my room, lie on my bed and wish the ache in my chest would go away. Just when I'm getting a grip on things, out of the blue, a silly movie throws me down a dark hole. What would Dad want me to do?

I thumb through the *Book of Life*. Nothing fits but then I see one: *Sorrow prepares you for joy.* Okay, I got the sorrow part down. When will the joy arrive?

Maybe I should go to the movie. Alone. If I cry no one will see me in the dark. Then I can go to the cemetery and tell Dad all about it. Yes, I'll do it. I'll watch it over and over until I know the best new lines from Woody, Mr. Potato Head, Rex, Buzz Lightyear — all his favorites. If Dad can't go to the movie, I can bring it to him. To us. With a big bag of buttered popcorn.

Mary

The memory quilt is still laid out on the dining room table, far from finished. I have lost my enthusiasm for the project since it involved Rosetta. I find myself wondering what shirt he wore with Rosetta. If we're going to make a *true* tapestry of his life, it would of course include that, I think sarcastically.

Teddy breaks my train of thought when he comes in and switches on the television. "There's a documentary I have to watch as homework. About significant events of the century." He plops down on the sofa and puts his long legs on the coffee table. He's looking and acting more like Stan each day. A pang of sadness pierces me.

The news media is full of millennium stories. As the countdown approaches to the year 2000 there are fears of Y2K. Fatalists are predicting the world will end with a huge computer crash. I think my world ended with a crash in May and just when I was starting to rebound Rosetta hurls me back into outer space. I'm free falling. I'm half listening to the show as I fiddle aimlessly with the quilt squares on the table, but soon find myself drawn into it when they talk about the '60s. "This looks good Teddy," I say as I sit down next to him on the sofa. "For you this is history. For me, it's memories."

"It was 1968", the announcer says. "Green Bay Packers win Super Bowl II, Rowan and Martin debut *Laugh-In*. The first Big Mac is introduced at 49 cents." Teddy and I both chuckle at this. "The Beatles hit the charts with *Hey Jude* and *Rosemary's Baby* by Ira Levin is made into a thriller movie."

"Did you see that movie, Mom?"

"Yes, it creeped me out."

"Can we rent it? I like creepy."

The announcer continues, "Historically, 1968 was the tumultuous year when history was being made every day. On April 4, Martin Luther King Jr. is shot and killed." They show footage of the balcony at Lorraine Motel in Memphis, Tennessee, and the door of room 306. The voice-over says, "The last words he allegedly spoke were to the musician Ben Branch, who would be performing that evening at a local club. 'Ben, make sure you play 'Take My Hand Precious Lord.' Play it real good.' Martin Luther King Jr. died at 8:19 p.m. and by 9:25 riots had broken out in Detroit, Chicago, and Washington, DC."

Then more grainy black and white footage shows a young Robert Kennedy at a podium on a flatbed truck and a voice-over says "New York Senator Robert F. Kennedy, campaigning for the 1968 Democratic Presidential nomination, spoke at Notre Dame and Ball State University in Indiana earlier that day. Just prior to his last speech in a predominately black neighborhood in Indianapolis, he learned of King's assassination and aides feared a riot would follow if he delivered the news. But deliver he did. Once the crowd quieted down, Kennedy acknowledged that many in the audience would be filled with anger." Now Mary and Teddy hear Kennedy's actual voice, in his clipped Boston accent, in the background. The announcer's voice is heard again. "In conclusion, Kennedy said that the country needed and wanted unity between blacks and whites, asked the audience members to pray for the King family and quoted the ancient Greeks on the theme of wisdom that comes from pain. The speech was credited in part with preventing post-assassination rioting in Indianapolis though there were riots in other parts of the country. It is widely considered one of the greatest speeches in American history. In Washington, LBJ signs the Civil Rights Act in April, days after MLK is shot." They switch to a commercial break.

Teddy says, "What difference did it make what color someone's skin was? I don't get it. I know some people still think that way. Back home, Doug's dad was what you might call a racist. I heard him say some things that were pretty awful. I know Doug was embarrassed, but later I heard him repeat some of the same things his dad said. I'm glad Dad was never like that. Lots of times I saw him try to include people when they didn't feel they belonged." I look at Teddy and a sense of pride fills me both for Teddy and Stan. I think of Rosetta, one of the few black students at her school in the '60s. Was she ostracized, excluded?

The documentary continues. They show a clip of *Sesame Street*'s first show and then Woodstock. "So Mom, were you and Dad at Woodstock?" Teddy asks.

"Not hardly. Two innocent kids from the cornbelt? We were still in high school. Didn't even know each other yet."

The announcer goes on: "The revolution was no longer just in the city streets but had made its way to the suburbs. It was in Iowa and Indiana. It was even in Zap, North Dakota. Kids who had gathered there over spring break destroyed much of the town."

Teddy looks at me as he points to the screen. "But it says that this revolution made its way to small towns. Like places you and Dad lived."

"Probably true, but I don't remember it happening in my town."

"We're studying the French Revolution. Reading *A Tale of Two Cities*. Boy, talk about angry mobs. Heads rolling, blood everywhere. Makes Woodstock seem tame. Wars are bad enough with other countries, but to hate people in your own country? Why?" Teddy asks. He appears wise beyond his years. He goes on, "I guess if it weren't for revolutions, we wouldn't even be here. I mean you and me. The girls."

"What do you mean, Teddy?"

"I was asking Baba about this book I found in the attic. She said it came from Bulgaria with Papa's father. Something a father is supposed to read to his son. Anyway, Papa's father came to America to flee all the tyranny in his country at that time. She said villages were being ransacked, people were being killed. Countries fighting for the land. If our ancestors hadn't escaped, I guess we wouldn't be here in America."

"Yes, they were brave to leave their homeland," I say, recalling Baba's story to me the other night. I think of where I was in '69. Like Stan, a senior in high school in a small Indiana town, so sheltered from was happening in many of the cities. I think of Rosetta again. The year she was pregnant with Luther. With all the civil unrest, of course they couldn't get married. I think of how unselfish it was of Rosetta to spare Stan. To go through what she did alone. My resentment is waning and somehow it is turning to sympathy. Even admiration and respect. Perhaps I have judged too harshly. Before I change my mind, I find the book discussion notebook with names and numbers. My hands are shaking while I dial. I hit three numbers and hang up. Do I really need a friend whose presence reminds me that Stan loved her?

Teddy walks by. "Goodnight, Mom. I'm glad Dad wasn't prejudiced. And glad you aren't either." His words fill me with shame. I pick up the receiver and dial again.

When she answers, I say, "Rosetta, I've been thinking ... and well, I think I'd like to talk again. In person. Would you meet me? At *Cup a Cuppa*. Say five tomorrow?"

Rosetta is there when I arrive. She smiles timidly, almost apologetically. Perhaps bracing herself for another verbal lashing on my part. We both sit quietly. I wait until our coffee arrives before I speak. Finally, I say, "Rosetta, it must have been awful for you. To go through it alone."

She looks surprised and relieved. "I wasn't really alone. I mean Stan wasn't with me, but my extended family was great. Of course, we returned to Chicago. My Dad kept blaming himself for bringing us to Middleburg that didn't have a big enough black population, especially my age. Most of the black families who came had younger children. He said it put me at a disadvantage socially."

"And your pregnancy. I guess in 1969, a pregnant girl didn't have many choices."

"I told you my father was a doctor. I'm sure he could have found someone to end the pregnancy. He told me once doctors performed abortions more than anyone knew, but I waited too long to tell them. The morning I was going to tell them, we got word of my Uncle Luther dying in Vietnam. It was such an awful time. I procrastinated and then it was too late."

We just look at each other, pondering the irony of fate. I shake my head and say, "I am so sorry, Rosetta. For what you went through, and I guess most of all, for my not understanding how hard it must have been for you to not tell Stan. That was an unselfish and loving thing to do."

Rosetta's face registers surprise at my comment. Then a look of relief. She says, "Once Luther was born he brought us so much joy we couldn't imagine life without him. It was like the son my dad always wanted. And my extended family. They just took that little baby and loved him to pieces. Sometimes it does take a village."

"Oh, like Hilary Clinton's new book?"

"Actually, that is an old African proverb that's been around a long time. I thought of it many times fondly while raising Luther. Or watching my family love and raise him. I'm surprised he's not spoiled rotten."

"He seems pretty grounded to me," I said. "I guess once the baby was born people suspected the father was white? Luther being so fair-skinned."

"I suppose, but I'm sure it wasn't the first instance in our blood line. As you can see, I'm not very dark myself. My family didn't criticize me for that or at least not to my face. I think they knew I was hurting enough." Her eyes get a faraway look as if she is remembering something. Then she grimaces, "Well, there was Aunt Beatrice. Always throwing a punch or sneaking in a degrading remark, but she did that to her own kids all the time. The whole family called her Bitchy Bea."

"I guess every family has one, huh? I envy you your large family, even with Bitchy Bea. I was an only child, too. Born to older parents who died within a year of each other. That's one of the reasons I came back. I needed Stan's family."

"I understand about needing to be with family after a death. That's another reason we moved to Chicago after Uncle Luther died. My mother needed her family." We both take a sip of coffee and let our thoughts sink in.

"So, then you became a nurse?" I ask.

"I never did get to college or med school as I planned, but when Luther started school, I went to nurses' training. In Chicago."

"You sacrificed a lot."

"I could have gone to medical school. I had enough help at home. But I knew how many hours med students put in for so many years. I just didn't want to be away from Luther that much."

"And you never married till Luther was grown? Someone as attractive as you, I imagine you had many opportunities."

Rosetta looks away. Out at the other tables. Then back at me. "I did marry again when Luther was 10. I'm so ashamed of it I don't talk about it much. He became abusive and I finally left. Took me years to admit I had made a bad choice. I didn't want to fail. I kept trying to make it work."

Rosetta shakes her head with a wry smile. "Why do women blame themselves for everything that goes wrong? I volunteer at a woman's shelter now hoping my story might help another woman get out of a bad relationship sooner than later."

I look at Rosetta and realize her road was much tougher than mine is even now. I lost Stan, but at least I had good years with him. I want to make it up to her somehow. I want her to know that I realize her sacrifice could not have been easy. "I know you must be so proud of Luther. The boys really like him."

"Thank you, and, yes, I am proud of him."

"I guess what I really wanted to say to you today, Rosetta, is that I have so much respect for you. Hopefully we can be friends. Luther too. We are, after all, connected in a very special way. I came here to be with family. I guess I found a little more than I expected." I smile through the tears. She smiles back at me but her eyes too are brimming. "I was thinking," I said. Maybe we could visit Stan's grave together. Perhaps that would help us both heal."

Rosetta looks surprised but says, "That might be a very good thing to do. I thought I had closed that chapter of my life but seeing Teddy who looks so much like Stan, I realize I still have some wounds open."

I cover Rosetta's hand with my own. "Maybe we can close some wounds together."

Rosetta

I think of a few things I didn't tell Mary. How when I was in that abusive marriage I often thought of how I might have been better off with a white Stan who respected me than a black man who didn't. Or how as the country's views began changing about inter-racial marriages, I would look in envy at a couple who dared to go against the norm, making a courageous statement that their love was stronger than the prejudice in the world.

Mary

‿∞‿

It's a Saturday morning and the weather has changed from cold brilliant sunshine the day before to a dreary overcast sky of winter. The wind chill is biting. As Rosetta and I walk from my car to the headstone, the dried fallen leaves are slippery under our footsteps. My previous visits had been on sunny days and now I'm wondering if this is a good idea. I zip up my vest and wrap my scarf tighter around my neck.

When we reach the gravesite, we both stop talking and just look at it in silence. The mums we planted are now faded. Like the day, they too are somber colors of rust and brown. There is no lightness to this day.

Rosetta says, "I've been here before. I had to come."

"I know," I say.

"How?" she asks, looking surprised.

"I saw the bouquet someone left. Then at your house, that night, I saw the painting. It didn't register then, but it was one of those, sit-up-in-bed-in-the-middle-of-the-night moments when I remembered where I saw it. It was another piece of the puzzle that made me wonder."

"I'm so sorry, Mary. I never intended to deceive you."

I keep looking down at the ground, but ask Rosetta, "Do you believe in God?

Rosetta does not hesitate. "I do. Luther was a blessing. Are you a believer?"

"Yes, but I'm not religious if that's what you mean. Stan and I had the children baptized because his mother asked us to. The family is Greek Orthodox and Baba observes all the saints days on the church calendar she has thumb-tacked on her kitchen wall. She prays and crosses herself before all meals. She has a little shelf in the dining room with votive candles and icons. That kind of religious. I believe there is a God but the last six months has made me question why bad things happen to good people." Again, a silence except for the wind blowing the dried fallen leaves. The temperature drops as we stand there. We can see our breath when we speak.

Rosetta says, "I wasn't sure this was a good idea, but I'm glad you asked me, Mary, and I'm glad I came. My marriage to James is good and it gives me comfort to know Stan had a good marriage. You must have had some wonderful years together."

"We did. And yes, Stan was good. In so many ways." I hesitate. "I think he would approve of us being together here. Don't you?" Rosetta smiles and nods her head in agreement. I put my arm through Rosetta's. "It's cold. Let's head for our coffee spot. Maybe we can share some favorite Stan memories." Rosetta looks surprised. "I know, I know," I say. "Now I sound like my grief counselor."

Teddy

Who's the black lady with Mom? They don't see me and I just stay behind the tree from where I first saw them. Once they get in Mom's car, I walk to Dad's stone and as usual, start to sit down but the ground is damp and cold. I crouch instead by the headstone. I tell him about my driving lessons with Uncle Dan and then a little smile inside me when I think of the pranks they pulled as kids.

"So, Uncle Dan tells me you were sort of a rascal. Eggs on Halloween, girlfriend's initials in fresh cement. Speaking of girls, there's one here I like a lot, but I think she's falling for my new best friend, Joe. Now what am I supposed to do?" I pick up a large brown maple leaf and twirl it around.

"I've been reading the *Book of Life. I* got some good stuff in there but I don't think any advice for your love life. I never asked you if you had a girlfriend before Mom. I'm sure you did in high school. Basketball star and all. Maybe I'll take a peek in your yearbooks and see if I can find some mushy stuff." The cold air is biting and my nose starts to run. I wipe it with my sleeve.

"I'll see you next time, Dad. I miss you. And, Dad ...." I unexpectedly start crying and can't stop. I don't know if it was the driving lesson or what, but the sorrow seems to well up and fill every pore in my body. "Dad, I'm so sorry. So sorry." I run to my bike and head home, the tears running down my cheeks and cold snot running onto my lips.

Mary

⌒

Rosetta and I meet again at *Cup a Cuppa* where the buzz of conversation is competing with the whir of the expresso machines. The smell of coffee and something baking with cinnamon permeates the air. The warmth and aromas are comforting on this damp chilly morning. Rosetta and I sit at our usual corner table, huddled over our cups.

"Are you and I the only ones who know that Teddy and Luther are half-brothers? Should we leave it that way?" I ask, almost in a whisper, although no one could possibly hear me over the background noise.

"James knows. I felt so bad the night I told you I couldn't keep it from him. I told him I had no right to stay in the book discussion group or try to be your friend. I should have kept my distance and spared you all this. This … heartache. I think you've had your share without my adding to it."

I look at Rosetta and realize her genuine kindness. "Your path wasn't easy either, yet you're thinking of *me*." I reach across the table and put my hand on hers.

She covers my hand with one of hers. "The question now, is what do we do?"

"If we tell the boys, I think we should tell both of them or neither. I'm not sure. I'm just thinking out loud here," I say. And what about Baba and Uncle Dan and his family?"

"There's a lot to consider. I'd love for Luther to know he has such a wonderful heritage. Now that I've met Baba and seen the photos of the ancestors."

"And Teddy thinks the world of Luther. He's taken such an interest in him from day one." I sigh, weighing the options and consequences.

"I guess we don't have to decide this minute, do we?" Rosetta gives a little laugh. After 30 years, what's another few days?"

This makes me smile too. "You're right. Let's sleep on this and keep talking." I start to get up, but sit back down. "Wait. One thing I can't understand is why no one sees the resemblance. I mean between Luther and Stan and Teddy. It's so obvious."

"To us perhaps. But no one is looking for it, Mary. If we pointed it out, they might agree, but to discover it on their own. Not likely."

"I guess you're right."

When we get to our cars, Rosetta starts to give me a hug, then backs off. "I hope it's okay."

"What?" I ask.

"To hug you?"

"Isn't that what friends do?" I hug her back. "I ask myself each day if moving here was the right thing to do. Like I'm keeping a tally sheet. *Yes, no, yes.* Today it's a definite *yes.*" I look straight into her beautiful brown eyes and say, "I think not only has Teddy gained a brother, I've found ….," I start to say *sister,* but settle for "… I've found a friend. Someone I'd really like to know better."

As I drive away I feel the warmth of Rosetta's hug, yet I'm nervous to think of possibly having that conversation with Teddy. A brother? He's not the *only* son? What if it blows up?

Teddy

We wake up Sunday morning to a quiet, snow-covered world. Inside it's not so quiet. Ruby and Cathy are screaming about snowmen. Winnie's picked up on their excitement and is yapping frantically to go out. Baba bought a little sweater for him, but the sight of an Arizona desert dog wearing a sweater sets us all off in hysterics. Buster doesn't find any of this amusing. He observes smugly from a window ledge where the sun is reflecting off the snow.

By early afternoon, Mindy's voice is squealing through the phone. "Isn't it beautiful? Isn't it the best thing you've ever seen? Can you come out? I want to be there when you make your first Indiana snowman."

"Too late. I already made one for Ruby and Cathy this morning in the park. And he's quite a handsome specimen, I might add. Well, his head's a little cockeyed, but it gives him character. Like he's listening to you. Know what I mean?"

"Well, how about snow angels? Did you do any of those?"

"Nope. No angels."

"Let's meet and head for the park."

I'm out the door with my new winter parka and wait for Mindy on the corner.

I cover my eyes, "Oh my gosh. I need sunglasses. The glare."

"From the snow?"

"No, from your snowsuit. Help, it's blinding me!" Her snowsuit is bright orange, the color highway construction workers wear. It's also one-piece like little kids wear. I always suspected she shopped in the children's' department.

Next thing I know a snowball lands in the middle of my chest. The fight is on. We're running and racing behind tress and throwing snowballs as fast as we can make them. I'm looking back at her to dodge one when I run smack into the snowman."

"Oh, no!" Mindy laughs so hard she falls over. "You knocked his head off. How could you? Poor innocent Frosty."

His head is now lying beside him, cracked in three places. Carefully, I pick it up, feeling like the ax murderer, and pack it together, then place it gently, but firmly, back on his body. "There, buddy, nothing personal. Just didn't see you." I yell to Mindy, "It must be a <u>snow*girl*</u>. They all lose their heads when they see me."

"Oh sure, Mr. Arizona. One look from you would melt anyone." She walks up to me, steps up on her toes and rubs a snowball she had hidden behind her back into my face.

"Hey, you get me out here talking about angels and then act like a little devil. Your snowsuit should be red. Oh yeah. I think I see little horns sticking out." I pat the top of her head.

"Okay, let's do angels. First we have to find a big clear spot with no tracks."

We walk farther into the park and I discover where the phrase *winter wonderland* came from. Every branch is covered with snow and there's not one footprint before us. The only sound is that of our boots crunching the snow that sparkles like a box of sugar crystals. That is until Mindy goes into science mode. "Were you awake when it started to snow last night?"

"No, I guess not. Why?"

"The flakes were so big. You know the warmer the temperature, the bigger the flakes."

"Oh sure, I knew that," I fib.

"Right. I suppose you also know how long it takes a flake to hit the ground."

"About a half-second," I say and tackle her into a snowdrift. "You're the biggest flake I know. See, that didn't take long."

Mindy starts giggling. "Okay, okay. Remember, we're *angels*." She rattles on, "You've probably heard how no two snowflakes are the same."

"Well, we didn't have many snowstorms in the desert. Now I know that's a news flash for you, but just thought I'd remind you."

"Yes, birdbrain, I know it doesn't snow in Phoenix, but I thought maybe you had seen a snowflake? Like maybe a Christmas in Indiana? Anyway, even if we tested five billion snowflakes we still wouldn't find two the same. Isn't that amazing? The reason, just in case you wanted to know, is because the number of ways molecules can be arranged into six-sided crystals is vastly larger than the number of snowflakes that have fallen on the earth." She stops babbling and looks around. 'Here's a good spot. Now just lay down with your arms at your sides," she points to the ground.

"Oh sure, like I can trust you now. You first."

Mindy lays down, her little orange arms at her sides flapping like jumping jacks over and over again, still talking. "For the record, it can take up to two hours."

"Two hours to make an angel? I thought it took a lifetime of good deeds."

"No stupid, it can take two hours for a snowflake to hit the ground."

"I'll file that away for the next game of Trivial Pursuit."

Carefully she gets up and there in the snow is the perfect little angel. "Your turn," she says as she admires her work. I lay down and do the same thing and when I stand up I see an angel beside Mindy's. Just taller.

I practically see the light bulb go on over Mindy's head when her face lights up and she says, "Let's make a whole family of angels. In a circle."

We take turns laying in the snow and waving our arms. When the circle's done, we stand back to admire our work. A loopy chain of angels, short, tall, short.

"Perfection. A work of art!" Mindy looks pleased. I look at her with the snow on her goofy purple glasses and rosy cheeks. I'm thinking that maybe angels don't always come in white. Maybe she's my own angel, sent in living color to make me be a carefree kid again.

"Mindy, do you believe in angels?"

"You mean as in a celestial being?"

"I don't know what I mean. Since my dad died, I wonder about those kinds of things. Can people come back as angels? Or are they watching over us, maybe from some puffy cloud?" I look up at the sky which is a cloudless blue. "At the grief seminar this man said a little hummingbird kept coming to his kitchen window after his wife died. That was her favorite bird and he just knew it was his wife saying 'good morning' to him every day."

"Well, if it made it easier for him to face the day, then I guess you could say it's *his* angel. My Grandma says there's an angel on my shoulder." She pats her shoulder smugly. "So who would you come back as?"

"Probably my dog, Winnie. He's got it made. Everybody spoils him. What about you?"

"I would never be anything so ordinary as a dog. No offense to your buddy, the Weiner, but I'd come back as some exotic bird."

"That's it! That explains everything!"

"What?"

"In your former life, you were a parrot. It's why you can't resist dressing in the entire color wheel. It's in your DNA."

Mindy tries to act mad, but starts laughing. "You're going to eat more snow. Furthermore, I'm reporting you to the Snowman Patrol: Destroyed. One snowman in Patriot Park. Now headless. Talk about vandals."

The word reminds me of Pete, but I don't want to think about that on this beautiful afternoon. "Mindy, I've got an idea. Follow me." The park is near the cemetery and Mindy follows alongside me quietly, not talking. Very unusual.

At the cemetery gates, Mindy gives me a knowing look and a sweet smile, turquoise braces sparkling in the sunlight. We walk to dad's stone and I start rolling a snowball. "I'll do the bottom. You do the middle." Her whole face lights up when she realizes what we're doing and soon we have a body, a middle, and a head. We look for twigs for arms and find some little stones for the face.

"Gotta have a hat," I say. "No respectable snowman would be without one. Especially on Sunday."

"Should we put a necktie on him?"

"No, Dad hated ties. Took them off in the car on the way home from work." We walk around, looking, looking. "There it is. The perfect touch!" I spot an empty clay flowerpot sitting beside a stone. We go back and set it upside down on the snowman and stand back to look. "It's stunning!"

"Yes, but …." Mindy looks around. She sees an old plastic bouquet peeking through the snow a few feet away. She breaks off one little flower and puts it in the hole at the top of the flower pot. We look at the snowman, then at each other, shrug our shoulders and smile. It is the perfect touch.

I touch the corner of Dad's stone the way I always do when I leave. "Bye Dad, I won't tell Mom there's another woman in your life. Especially a pothead!"

Mindy rolls her eyes. Then she takes my hand. "Come on Teddy. Maybe celestial beings don't need nourishment, but I'm starving." Even with our gloves, her little hand fits perfectly in mine. Although it's cold enough to see my breath, I feel a warmth spreading through me. Then she pulls away and starts running. "Let's step it up. I can't wait to see Joe and tell him about our romp in the park. And *Jeopardy* is on in 30 minutes. Joe and I try to watch it together every day."

Mindy and Joe? Together every day? Suddenly the day has turned cold again.

Teddy

◯

Tonight's the big game against Middleburg's toughest rival, Collinsville. We skip practice but meet with Coach Luther after school for a pep talk. He says, "They beat us last year by one point in overtime. Let's get revenge tonight."

When I get home there's an email from Wally, talking about Southwest Canyon's game. *They'll miss you on starting line-up*, it says. That comment doesn't make me as sorry as it would have a few weeks ago. I'm too excited to be finally playing in a real game, an important game. Anywhere.

Mom picks up on that at the dinner table. "You're really pumped up, aren't you Teddy?"

"Yeah, Coach Luther said it's a big game. He said we're the best JV team he's ever had. After the meeting he pulled me aside and said making me captain of the team was a good thing. We're clicking. Working together. You know, he makes you believe you can win so you start to believe it too. And you don't want to let *him* down."

"I got green and white pom-poms," Ruby says proudly, as if that will cinch the win.

"That's great, Ruby." I rub the top of her blonde curls. "I better go," I say, grabbing another piece of pizza as I leave the table.

As Mom drives me to the gym, we pass the hospital and I think of Joe alone in his room. Maybe Mindy will be with him. I want her to see me play but I don't want Joe to be alone either, especially now. His mother told me he's struggling. It's time for his release and he's worried about reactions to his face without the bandages. I'll visit him first thing in the morning.

Mary

⌒

Driving back home, I'm thinking about Teddy and Luther. When I get home, I call Rosetta. "Rosetta, I'm thinking I'd like to tell Teddy. He's really high on Luther right now. The timing might be right."

"Funny you should say that. I've been thinking Luther needs to know. He deserves to know. But I think we stick to our agreement. Tell them both or not at all."

"Tonight after the game might work for us. Teddy and I are usually up later than everyone."

"I'll invite Luther over after the game. I made a German chocolate cake the other day, one of his favorites, so he'll hardly refuse. He's always starving after a game."

Teddy

❦

The whole family is at the game. Baba, Mom, the girls, Uncle Dan and Aunt Joyce. I'm one of the JV starters. The whistle blows. Kovich makes the first basket for us and the place goes wild! You would think it was the winning basket for a state championship, not the first basket in a piddley junior varsity game. I see now what Mindy means about Hoosier hysteria. It definitely gets your adrenalin going and my heart is pumping as loud as the crowds' cheers.

I'm doing okay. Nothing spectacular, but our team is working well together. At the half, the score is tied 24-24. When we return to the gym from the locker room, the crowd goes wild again.

The second half starts. I'm in again, but we're not clicking like the first half and before we know it, we're down 24-30. It's all happening too fast. We miss some shots, we miss a couple rebounds, and all of a sudden, we're scrambling to catch up. We are falling all over ourselves. I get the ball, start down the court, and then hear the whistle. *Oh no. What a stupid time to double dribble.* Coach calls a time out and we huddle around expecting to get our you-know-whats chewed, but he's real calm and says we should settle down and play our game. I'm ready to go back in and do something right, but he pulls me out and puts Warsocki in. I head for the bench and hang my head low. I hear the crowd roar again and we're now only down 28-30. Looks like taking me out was a good move. I'll probably spend the rest of the game right here on my sorry butt. They shoot. We block it and Warsocki passes it to Martin who's under our basket. Yes. We're tied 30-30.

At the next break, I jump off the bench to join the guys coming in, hoping I'll get another chance, when out of the corner of my eye I see it. Bright red hair. Only one person has hair that color. It's Mindy at the corner of the bleachers and ... what? She's holding on to a wheelchair and Joe's in it. They see me and both wave frantically. Well, Joe tries to wave but with his big bulky sweater covering up his bandages, he almost hits Mindy in the face. She just laughs and gives me her big turquoise grin. Meanwhile, she's pointing to the top of Joe's head behind him. He can't see her. It's as if she's saying, "Look who's here. Look who came out — in public — for you!" He's wearing a knitted cap which covers most of his face. Kinda like a ski mask but it's in school colors so it's not so weird. I grin back and a surge of adrenalin curses through me, like I'm 10 feet tall.

I've got to get back in the game! How do I let Coach know that all of a sudden I think I can whip those guys single-handedly? Coach is drawing a play on his clipboard. The game starts again, but I'm still on the bench. It's back and forth. When the third quarter buzzer rings, we're ahead by two. I'm trying to think of what I can say to Coach to get back in the game, when I hear him say, "Kostoff, go in. Warsocki needs a break."

I run onto the court with one quick look at Mindy and Joe. Suddenly, like instant replay in my head, I can see every corny sports movie I have ever seen. I see *Air Bud*. I see the kid who had springs in his shoes. I see *Angels in the Outfield*, and in a flash, I picture Dad's face. I know he's watching. I don't see him, but I feel him and I play like it's the best chance I'll ever have to make him proud. Right here where he grew up. Right here where it really counts.

With all that positive energy surging through me, I play like a Harlem Globetrotter. I'm definitely in the zone. Any time I touch the ball, it's magic. I pass, I shoot, I block. The crowd is going wild, and when the final buzzer blows, the score is 44-38. Everyone on the team is hugging me like I made all 44 points.

I look into the crowd and see Mom laughing and crying and punching Uncle Dan's arm. Next to her, I see only the top of Baba's head bobbing up and down. When I look at Mindy, she's tipping Joe's chair back and spinning him around. Even above the noise of the crowd, I imagine I hear Joe's laugh. It's a beautiful sound.

I shower as fast as I can and run out to find Mindy and Joe when I almost trip over the wheelchair. They're waiting right by the locker room door.

"Joe, this is the best surprise. You're out! You're here! I can't believe it!"

Mindy is grinning from ear to ear and the spark in Joe's eyes reminds me of the first night I met him. His bright blue eyes jump out of the ski mask he's wearing. "I had to come and see you play. You were so awesome, man."

"You're the awesome one. Look at you. School colors and all." I tap the top of his green and white cap. "World's greatest fan. And you," I turn to Mindy. "You have a license to drive this thing? I saw you doing those wheelies."

Mindy has a glow that starts in her eyes and radiates right through her clothes, which as usual are glowing anyway. "We can't stay for the varsity game. We're on a special pass tonight. So *hi* and *bye*. Joe's dad is picking us up out front in a few minutes."

The only downer of the evening is seeing Pete on the sidelines. He's sitting on the varsity bench in street clothes. Couldn't even suit up because he's been suspended from play for the five games. This is all as a result of telling the coach and the principal what he did Halloween night. He also turned in his friends and told them in so many words that he wouldn't be involved in any more of their pranks. Pete even asked Coach to put me in his place on varsity but I told Pete I would never do it, even if Coach asked me, which he didn't.

Coach Luther has been so good to me. I would never bail on him. Watching the varsity team now I realize how good they are. They have a 15-point lead at the half. Even with Pete out, they make it look easy. I see what Coach Burton meant when he said he waited a long time for this team to come together. I wonder again how such a little school can have so many good players. Then I remember. This is Indiana. Basketball country. Hoosier hysteria. Even in a small way, I'm part of something big.

Mary

၁

Back in Baba's kitchen after the game, I'm glad Teddy and I are alone so we can have our "talk."

"Teddy, you played like a superstar tonight. I'm so proud of you."

"Yeah, seeing Mindy and Joe there gave me extra energy or adrenalin, whatever." Teddy takes a huge bite of the Baba's leftover Friday night pizza. I watch him eat with the vigor he used to have before. Before the accident. "Coach Luther makes me want to play well too. He's so encouraging. It's like he expects me to be good so I want to live up to it."

"Actually, that's something I wanted to talk about …."

"And Mom," Teddy interrupts, "I know it sounds crazy but I felt like Dad was there tonight. Like he saw it all." This comment throws me for a loop. Not what he says so much but that he is talking about his dad without tears, without guilt, and with a smile on his face. He takes a big bite and keeps talking, "You know, Mom, I miss Arizona, but lately I think maybe this move was a good thing. Like everyone who knew Dad tells me what a great guy he was. I know it, but to hear it from all these people he grew up with. Well, it makes me proud. To be his son. I mean it's great that we have Cathy and Ruby, but you know, being his only son, I need to follow in his steps. And as someone said, those are big steps to fill."

I know in that moment that I cannot risk shattering Teddy's image of his dad. Not tonight. Teddy, thinking he's the only son. I rustle his dark curls and say, "Keep eating. I'll be right back."

I step into the living room out of Teddy's earshot and quickly dial Rosetta. It keeps ringing. *Pick up. Pick up.* Finally she answers. I blurt it out as quickly as I can. "Rosetta, I can't tell Teddy tonight. I'll explain later."

"Oh, Mary, I just told Luther."

Teddy

⌒

The next morning I'm lying in bed reliving the game and my great last quarter when Mindy calls.

"Teddy, Alicia's in town. I want her to meet you and Joe."

"Who's Alicia?"

"You know. My friend who moved to Chicago. They sold their house here and came back to sign some papers. She says it sold fast because they buried the Saint Joesph statue on the front lawn."

"So who's he — like the patron saint of real estate?" *For quick sale, pray with Joe at Re-Max.*

"I don't know."

"You're admitting you don't know something? Channel 5 Newsflash."

"Would you shush and get over to Joe's? His mom's really excited that we would be with him on his first night home from the hospital. She says you and I are the best thing that ever happened to him."

"Sure, I'll be there." I'm kind of excited myself. It's a Saturday night and I actually have someplace to go ... with kids my age ... with kids I want to be with. *A life at last?*

Mom and Baba are in the kitchen helping Ruby stick feathers in an orange. I think the finished product is supposed to resemble a turkey.

"Gobble, gobble," I greet everyone.

"Hey, it's Middleburg's superstar." Mom tussles my hair and Baba jumps into action to do her favorite thing ... feed me.

"Teddy Bear, you make so many baskets. I so proud of you. What you like to eat?"

"Is there any pizza leftover? That's the best breakfast!"

"Sure, Teddy Bear. You know Baba makes big pan. Too much."

"Never too much pizza — how come yours tastes better than anyone else's?"

"My father was baker. He make the best Bulgarian bread. Everyone, all the neighbors come. Bulgarians, Italians, Polish, Germans. They all want his bread. So from this bread, I make the pizza." She turns away and then adds, "And I always put extra sausage."

I tell Mom it's the first Saturday night I won't need a ride to the hospital. I can just walk to Joe's house a few blocks away. "So you're off the hook Mom. In case you have a wild Saturday night planned." I'm only joking, but as soon as I say it, I feel like a schmuck. I overheard her say just last week that the world's designed for couples, not singles, and most of the women she's met are married. I want to say something to make it better, but I'm afraid I'll make it worse. Lately I've been thinking about what a jerk I was when we first moved here. As much as I hated going to a new school, at least I've had a chance to make friends.

Back in my room, I'm ready to send Wally an e-mail about last night's game when I see the next quote in the *Book of Life. Fragrance always clings to the hand that gives roses.* The e-mail can wait.

I ride my bike to the drugstore on Main Street. The cold air whips around me but it's invigorating. I'm not sure what I'm looking for, but I'll know it when I see it. I go to the card rack. Next stop, the flower shop. When I get back home, I sneak in the back door and up to my room. I open the card and apply a few creative touches.

On the front of the card, there's a drawing of a big group of people — including kids, cats, dogs, grandparents. They're posing for a picture. In the background someone is sneaking out the door. The message says: *It was easy to spot you in the family photo — you were the one running away.* Inside: *Happy Birthday from all of us.* I cross out the "Birthday" and leave *Happy Day.*

Then I write: *Dear Mom, I hope you don't want to run away, but I wouldn't blame you if you did. I haven't been easy to live with since you decided to move us here. And I was a real jerk on the long ride out. I know now you were trying to do what was best for us and I hope you make new friends here too. Since you are both Mom and Dad now, I guess I love you twice as much. Teddy.*

Then I put a silly face next to my name so it won't be too mushy. I put the note and lay a single red rose on the kitchen table just before I leave for Joe's. I don't know if the fragrance stayed on my hands. Gosh, I hope not, but I do know I feel a little better about going off to have fun with my friends.

I start wondering what Alicia will be like. Will she also have Mindy's bizarre color schemes or some other eccentric trait? I can't imagine a friend of Mindy's being normal. Then I realize *I'm* Mindy's friend. What does that say about me?

When Joe's mom opens the door, I follow the sound of his laugh to a room that has a banner across the wall, "Welcome Home Joe." It looks like a mega media store. There's a huge TV screen, a complete sound system, a computer station, and an old jukebox in one corner. In the other corner is a treadmill and weights with a floor mat. That's futuristic since Joe still walks with a walker.

The only bandages left on Joe are the ones on his face. Mindy told me he didn't need to wear them once they released him from the hospital, but he's still too self-conscious to have anyone see his scars. Sitting at his feet like an adoring audience are Mindy and a cute girl with short puffy blond hair. Mindy jumps up, grabs my arm, and drags me to the inner circle, as if I were going to turn around and leave.

"Teddy, this is Alicia — Alicia, Teddy. You two can compare your moving experiences. Is it better to go from a big city school to a small town school or vice-versa?"

"Oh no, is there a questionnaire we have to fill out too?" I ask.

Alicia just laughs and rolls big brown eyes as if to say, "Oh, here she goes again." Instantly we have a common bond — both Mindy victims.

Before I can say another word, Joe's mom comes in with a big plate of sloppy joes. Baba would approve. Food and plenty of it. Mindy jumps up as if she's never eaten, helps her set it on the table, and yells to Joe, "Do you want some of everything?"

Alicia's still looking at me in a way that causes a little flutter in my chest, but the last thing I need is a crush on someone 200 miles away. I smile back, trying to think of something clever to say when Mindy suddenly trips over my foot on the way to Joe's chair and the sloppy joes go flying. Alicia makes a leap for it in the air, misses the plate, but miraculously catches some sloppy joes before they hit the ground. She lands on top of me with them, the gooey sandwiches now smashed between us. Although this has happened in a split second, it's like it was in silent slow motion. Then everyone starts laughing and we can't stop. Joe starts yelling, "Food fight, food fight!" I think he wants to throw more food on us, but thank goodness he doesn't have any in his reach. His mother runs back into the room with a look of horror.

Mindy tries to explain, "I'm so sorry ... I tripped ... I'll clean it up." Alicia jumps up and looks at her clothes and mine. We start laughing again.

"I've heard of ice-breakers at parties Mindy, but I think this takes the cake," I say.

"More like it takes the bun," Joe says, and we all break out in peals of laughter again, including his mom. She's so happy to see Joe laughing, I think she's ready to throw another sandwich at the wall herself to keep it going.

She runs to get paper towels and then decides we need to get our shirts off. She comes back with two identical white long sleeve button down shirts of Joe's and drags Alicia off to another room to change. I change mine right there. Mindy decides she needs one of Joe's shirts too and now it's an official Joe look-alike party. "Now if you really want to look like me, you need about a mile of gauze bandage," he says.

"Sorry, mummy boy," I say, "you get the starring role ... we're just the supporting cast here."

While we're finally eating, I spot a whole stack of books next to Joe's chair.

"Mindy, we're not doing homework tonight and we're not playing any brain games. Well, maybe the three of us against you, we might have a chance, but probably still lose our shirts."

"Looks like we already did," Alicia pipes in.

"Funny, funny," Mindy says.

We're sitting in a circle at Joe's feet. "I love having this adoring audience at my feet, but I'd give anything to be sitting on the floor with you guys — you know just like a normal person."

"You're too strange to ever be normal," I tell him. I've learned the way to keep Joe from going into a funk is just insult him. It works. He tries to kick me with his foot, which I grab. "Careful man, we could tickle you to death and that's not a funny way to go."

Mindy takes on the role of a talk show host and starts asking questions, like, "What's the best thing about your new school? Alicia, you go first."

Alicia thinks a minute. "I guess it would be this group called OSHNO."

"OSHNO? Isn't that something we talked about in civics class?" I ask.

"That's OSHA, stupid," Mindy pipes in.

"Well, *excuse me* for making a connection."

Alicia saves me from Mindy's brutal look. "It stands for Old Students Helping New Ones." They have so many new kids moving in all the time, they decided to do something to make them feel welcome and included.

"Like what do they do?" I ask.

"About once a week there's a group that calls you out of class and just answers questions you have about the school and plays some name games so you get to know them. Then they match a new student with an old one and take you to lunch or something like that. The group thing was fun but the one-on-one was sort of strange. I felt like part of someone's homework assignment."

"How about you Teddy?" Mindy asks.

"I guess it would be that we don't have OSHNO or OSHA or whatever it is." Alicia looks hurt. "Just kidding," I say.

"Come on Teddy, be serious. Think of the ratings if you don't say something good. They'll cancel my show," Mindy pleads dramatically.

"I guess it would be ... I'm not sure what to call it. It's like school spirit. Everyone's got it. But it's even more than that. The whole town revolves around us kids and what we're doing. Like we're the most important thing here. It's neat."

"Yeah, I miss that part," Alicia says. "Chicago's so big. Even though our suburb has its own Main Street, there's just too many things to do in the city. I miss being able to walk anywhere and see people I know. People who know me and my mom and dad. Never thought I would say I miss my parents' friends." She rolls her eyes.

"Joe, you're not getting out of this. What's the best thing that happened to you in the hospital?" Mindy asks.

"Having that cute nurse give me a bath." He starts to swoon and leans over like he's going to fall out of his chair.

"Joe!" Mindy says, "Come on, for real."

"Okay, it really was the nurses. They were great. Always joking about serious stuff so it wouldn't be so morbid. I knew they really cared about me. Me, the person, not just treating my burns. I'll never forget them — ever. In fact, I think I want to do something like that. Work in a hospital. I don't know if I'm smart enough to be a doctor, but maybe a —"

Mindy looks appalled. "Joseph Mazarus, *you* are smart enough to be anything you want to be."

"Oh Mindy, you're just trying to beef up your tutoring brochure. 'You too can go from simpleton to Ph.D. in 20 weeks. Just send $39.95 plus shipping and handling,'" I say.

"Everyone except you, birdbrain. It would take 20 years," she throws a pillow at me, which misses but almost hits Joe's little brother, Vince, who just walked into the room. He's wearing his costume for the Christmas play, a tall gold foil hat with five points.

"This is a stupid part," he says. We all try not to laugh as one of his points bumps into a lamp.

"But Vince, you're a star! Everyone wants to be a star," Joe tries to console him.

"Real stars have good parts. They get to say something. I'm just a star in the sky. I don't get to say anything."

"So what *do* you do?" I ask.

"Mom says I have an important job. To stand there and shine."

"Well, shining is good. And very important. Without you, no one would find their way," Mindy joins the pep talk. Vince looks at her to see if he can really believe this.

"And if they shine a spotlight on you, you can sort of turn your points. You can be a twinkling star," Alicia adds. Vince turns his head a few times very slowly to see if his role could possibly be an action part. Then he walks out not saying a word, still turning his head left to right.

"I sympathize with him," I say. "I think one year I was a lamp post. Something about Christmas carolers going down the street. They told me to be sure not to sing."

We spend the rest of the night talking about stupid things we did in grade school and watch *Back to the Future Part III.* Joe's mom comes in with a camera and says she has to capture this special night — Joe, back home, with friends. Joe says, "Mom, that's pretty risky. This face might break your camera."

I say, "Lame joke and very old. You'll have to do better than that." But Joe's remark stings. I think he believes it and I don't know how to make it better. We gather around him, Alicia and I on either side and Mindy sitting at his feet. We take one smiling shot and then a goofy one where we're all making weird faces. As we laugh, I feel a pressure in my chest and have to fight back the tears. It catches me unawares, this warm feeling of having fun with friends. It's been so long.

Joe's mom gives us a ride home. She drops the girls off first and I say goodbye to my new-found friend Alicia, who's leaving tomorrow. She gives me her e-mail address and says we should keep the new kid chat line open. She's nice but I doubt I will initiate anything. I already have long-distance virtual friends. I want to focus on the friends I can see and touch.

When Joe's Mom pulls up to my house, I jump out and then I turn around and poke my head back in the car. "Mrs. Mazarus, would you mind taking me back to your house? There's something really important I forgot to tell Joe."

"Well, sure, if it's okay with your mom."

Mom's in the living room reading. "Teddy …." Her face lights up and then I remember the greeting card.

"Mom, can I go back to Joe's, just for a few minutes. I forgot to tell him something really important. His mom will bring me back home — she's waiting outside."

"Well, sure, I suppose …."

"I'll be back real quick … promise."

When I get back to Joe's house he's still in the wheelchair, fiddling with the TV remote. He sees me and his blue eyes light up. "Hey, you miss me already. Oh, I know, you want to have a sleepover."

"Actually, I want to have a very serious talk with you."

"Oh, man. I'm scared. Now what?" I wheel him over to the edge of the chair where I sit down so we're close together, eyes on same level.

I'm not sure how to start. "I did something really scary the other day."

"What?"

"I had a driving lesson. With my Uncle Dan."

"That's cool, man. How did it go?"

"Uh, not so good. What's that called that some soldiers have after they've been in battle? Seen terrible things. Post traumatic something?"

"Yeah, PTSD — post traumatic stress disorder. The doctor said I might experience it when I get around fire."

"Well, I had it alright. I was doing fine and then when I saw another car approaching from the right — even though he had a stop sign — I freaked out."

"Oh, man, I'm sorry. What happened?"

"I barfed."

"I heard barfing can be a good thing. That's probably what you'll do when you see my face without these bandages."

"I'm glad you mentioned that. It's exactly what I wanted to talk to you about. Your remark about breaking the camera. It made me sad 'cause most people say it as a joke, but I think you believe it."

"Of course, I don't believe it. Just an expression."

"But you think people are going to freak out."

"A little, yes."

"I think that's *their* problem. They might flinch at first but what the heck? I do that when I see the girls who go Gothic. What I'm trying to say, Joe, is, I know it's scary for you. But I gotta tell you the rest. Uncle Dan said we would wait to try again, but I got back in the truck. I was scared — no, terrified is more like it, but I did it. I got behind the wheel again. And if I can do that, you can take off your bandages. I know you can. Please Joe, do it for me."

He doesn't say anything. Just looks at me. I keep going. "I think there's a reason we met that night in the hospital. Remember how we said, you got the scars outside. I got 'em inside. We can help each other. We understand. Wouldn't you give anything to make me not hate myself for what I did?"

"Of course. Anything, man. And, for the record, you didn't *do* anything. It happened."

"Well, I'd do anything to give you confidence to face the world. Please Joe, take off the bandages. Take them off right now. For me."

Joe looks at me. Neither one of us says a word. I don't know what else I can say. He looks away, down at his feet. I have a sinking feeling he won't do it. Then he lifts his arm around the back of his neck and starts to peel. He's watching me watch him. I give him an encouraging smile. Yes! As the bandages unwind I see red and white scar tissue. I steel myself to not flinch or show any sign of repulsion. It looks painful to touch. I ask, "Does it hurt when you touch it?"

"Not really. It's sensitive, but not anything like what I felt at first."

When all the bandages are in a heap in his lap, I raise my hand for a high-five and he slaps it. "Good job, Joe. Promise me you won't put them back on—ever. Unless the doctor says you have to.

"And I'll tell you what Joe, as soon as I get that driver's license … and I'm going to get it. You and I are going to cruise Main Street. Me driving and you riding shotgun with no bandages. Like we own this town. What do you say?"

"Great plan, Teddy. I'd ride anywhere with you."

"And I'll stand beside you … anywhere."

I turn to go find Mrs. Mazarus in the kitchen. "Guess I'm ready." I want to leave before she sees Joe with the bandages off. I want to keep it just between Joe and me.

She pulls up to my front door. "Thanks Mrs. Mazarus." I realize she's going to wait until I go in. I open the front door and she drives off. As soon as she is out of sight, I go back and sit on the front porch step. It's been snowing again and I'm still in awe of this miracle of nature which I've seen only on a few Arizona ski trips. The houses across the street have little mounds of snow on their roofs and some icicles hanging low. Like a perfect Christmas card. When I look up at the streetlight, I can see big flakes swirling down and crossways. It reminds me of the old snowglobe in Baba's house that Ruby shakes constantly, making the snow swirl on the little ice skaters inside.

I think of the old brown hockey skates in the attic and of Dad. I wonder if he missed the snow when he moved to Arizona. I doubt it, remembering each time the weather channel showed a storm in the Midwest, he'd say, "That's why we live here, Son. Summers are hot, but you know, you never have to shovel sunshine." I guess what I'm learning is that each place you live has its own beauty. But I'll never tell Mindy. She'll turn it into an hour-long talk show or send me to Jerry Springer, "How Weather Affects Teen Behavior."

I remember that Mom was waiting for me so I go in. She's fallen asleep on the couch with the book open beside her. I shake her gently. "Mom, let's go up to bed."

"Teddy, I was waiting for you …."

"Let's talk in the morning. I'm really tired."

"Me, too," she answers groggily. I'm relieved. Enough emotion for one night.

That night I dream of a basketball game where Alicia and Mindy are the cheerleaders. They're doing pyramids that keep tumbling down. The scoreboard reads: Chicago 32, Phoenix 100. I keep trying to tell someone that it's the temperature, not the score, but the crowd ignores me and keeps cheering for Phoenix.

Teddy

⌒

Uncle Dan and I are doing our Saturday drive the week before Thanksgiving. Each week I drive a little farther and today was the first time I drove in snow. I haven't had stress disorder since that first day. I'm starting to trust myself. As usual, we end up at the mall, which is decked out for Christmas. Walking through the mall, even this early in the morning, the shoppers are out in full force. I see a few kids I know from school and then out of nowhere there are shrieks and giggles at my elbow.

"Teddy, don't you think this would be perfect for Mr. Beale?" Patti and Sue from English class pull a necktie out of their bag, showing Mickey Mouse with a Santa cap.

"So that's how you two have been getting those As?"

"We're going to get the whole class to pitch in. Should we give it to him early and beg for no homework over Thanksgiving break?"

"Sounds like a plan to me — count me in."

Uncle Dan just laughs and puts his arm around my shoulder as we walk away. "You're making a lot of new friends, aren't you Teddy? You're so much like your dad. I only had one or two good buddies, but the house was always full of your dad's friends. And girls calling the house all the time. Baba would always say, 'Nice girls no call boys.' Then she'd shake her head as if her son would be ruined for life.

"I remember the first time your dad brought your mom home from college. Baba got him off in the corner and said, 'Is she good girl, Stan?' Your dad said something like, 'She looks good to me!' Somehow I don't think that's what Baba meant."

In spite of the snow, the holiday music, and decorations, or maybe because of them, a sadness starts to creep into me as we walk through the mall. It's going to be the first Thanksgiving without Dad. Who's going to pull the other half of the wishbone or watch football with me the rest of the day while we keep on eating? No sooner would we finish the pumpkin pie than Dad would say, "Time for a turkey sandwich?" Mom bet him he couldn't go 30 minutes without eating and snooze time on the couch didn't count. It had to be waking hours. Living now with Baba, I can see he spent years training for days like Thanksgiving.

Uncle Dan's getting his usual coffee to go at Café Court when I spot George, sitting by himself at a table watching the shoppers go by.

"Oops, excuse me. Sorry." I say to two little ladies, almost knocking them and their packages over, as I rush to George. "George, I've been looking for you each week. At the cemetery. Where have you been?"

"Teddy, my boy. How are you? You know, there's not much to do until spring. Did you come down to talk to Santa?" he says with a wink. "I can vouch that you've been a really good boy this year. Did you see they got those vandals?"

"Yeah, I did." I don't want to go into the Pete thing. "So George, what are you doing these days?"

"Oh, mostly just relaxing at home. Got a few little indoor projects. Thought I might buy myself one of those fancy computers and join the 21st century. Don't want those brain cells to die, you know. How about you? Playing basketball?"

"Yes, would you like to come to a game?"

"Well, sure. I'd like to see you make those baskets."

"Let me have your phone number and I'll call you with a schedule."

George pulls his wallet out, fiddles with some papers in it, looks at some business cards, which he examines carefully as if he's never seen them before. Finally, he takes a stubby pencil from his shirt pocket and wets the end of it like I've seen Baba do so many times. He slowly and carefully writes a number. "I don't suppose I need his card anymore." He crosses the printed name off the card as if I would call that person instead of him. "Wanted to sell me some insurance."

Just then Uncle Dan spots us and I introduce him to George. We say goodbye, but as we walk away I realize something isn't quite right. "Just a minute, Uncle Dan."

I walk back to George who still has a little smile on his face. "I forgot to tell you something, George."

"Oh?"

"You know our little talks?"

"Yes."

"Well, I've been missing them. I want you to come to my games, but mostly I'd like to find a way to keep having our talks each week. Maybe I could help you with your new computer."

George just blinks his eyes and swallows. I know what that blink routine is all about. "Well," he answers, "I'm certainly available. Not going anywhere, except maybe to Florida for a little fishing this winter. You call me, Teddy, and we'll set a time to meet. Maybe I can buy you a hamburger or something. I'd cook something for you but my cooking is not the best." He laughs. "You can bring your little friend too if you want. The one who helped us clean up that day. Looks like Raggedy Ann. All that red hair. Talks a lot."

"That would be Mindy. Eats a lot too." I resist the sudden urge to hug the old man, knowing that would embarrass us both. Then I'd have to explain it all to Uncle Dan. Instead, I just put out my hand and George shakes it and winks, like we've closed a big business deal. I don't think any big mergers ever happened with a wink and a shake.

Somehow the emptiness I felt a few minutes earlier thinking of the holidays isn't such a big aching gap. It's still there, but I think seeing George let a tiny bit of holiday cheer creep in to crowd out the sadness.

When we step out of the mall, it's still snowing and Uncle Dan drives. It gives me time to think of a way to get George to sample some of Baba's home cooking.

⤺

We have Thanksgiving dinner at Uncle Dan's house. I don't know if Mom told him how Dad and I always did the wishbone pull, but Uncle Dan does it with a big production of his winning strategy. In spite of his big plan, I win. Then I wonder if I really won or was it compensation for Dad not being there. Sometimes I'm still suspicious when people are really nice to me. Is it really for me or is it a sympathy ploy? I never questioned peoples' motives before Dad died. It's funny how a death plays with your head.

Mary

‿

December

Rosetta and I meet at our usual table in the coffee shop. The buzz of conversation is loud as people try to talk over the whirring of the espresso machines. I lean in close. "Rosetta, I know we agreed to tell both boys after the game, but Teddy was so proud to be Stan's son. He even said his *only* son. I just couldn't risk spoiling that moment for him."

"Of course not," Rosetta agrees.

"And Luther? How did he take it?" I ask anxiously.

"Mary," Rosetta speaks in her usual calm voice. "There's no right or wrong to this situation. Let's face it. There's no Dr. Spock chapter on what to do here."

"Oh, you too?" I smile as I think of the dog-eared Dr. Spock book that was my Bible.

"I told Luther years ago that his father was white and that he never knew of the pregnancy. Back then he said, 'You should have told him, Mom. You shouldn't have gone through that alone.'" Rosetta fiddles with the napkin she has placed between her coffee cup and saucer. She goes on, "Of course all black families have told their kids what the '60s were like. I tried to explain to Luther how impossible our situation was. I told him, 'I'll never know, but I believe your father would have tried very hard to keep us together as a family with no real concept of how difficult that would have been for us.'" Her brown eyes, as they begin to fill with tears, look like pools of melted chocolate. "Luther accepted the explanation and so this wasn't a total shock to him. But to finally know who it was and in the next breath realize he would *never* know him. That was a double shock, I'm afraid." Rosetta continues. "I did give him something that I think helped. I had kept the few letters Stan wrote me when I first moved to Chicago. So many times I was going to throw them out, but could never do it. When I handed Luther the letters, I told him the most important thing he needed to know was that he was conceived in love. Call it what you will — a teenage crush, puppy love. It was a culmination of nine months of a beautiful friendship."

I nod my head and blink back the tears.

"Oh, Mary, I'm saying too much. I don't mean to hurt you."

"Honestly, I am feeling a pang of jealousy. But an even stronger feeling is a sadness for you and Stan. So young, running scared. And I've learned something about myself through all this, Rosetta. I've never told anyone this but ... as long as we're sharing secrets. I've never been a confident person when it comes to looks. Beautiful girls, or those who I thought were, always made me feel inferior. I could never believe Stan chose me. I think I was that underdog you said he always rescued." I push my hair behind my ears. "I thought you were beautiful the first night of book group. Stunning in fact, before I ever knew of you and Stan. So then when I knew, of course I assumed he would have preferred you over me. It's my own inferiority I didn't want to face more than the thought of you and Stan. It's not a quality I admire in myself."

"Mary, Mary," Rosetta says. "I must remind you. As handsome as Stan was in college, I'm sure he could have had his choice of girls. He chose *you*. That should tell you something."

"You would think so, wouldn't you?" Now, I'm laughing as I cry. The tears are those of relief for unburdening something I've carried so long. To bring it out in the open and face it.

Rosetta says, "My mother once told me something Eleanor Roosevelt said, 'No one can make you feel inferior without your consent.' Don't give that consent to anyone Mary. Least of all yourself." I look at Rosetta skeptically, like how did she come up with that saying exactly at the right time. As if she can read my mind, she says,

"Growing up black, my parents bombarded me with positive sayings to keep my confidence high. I used to give my mother a hard time, like, 'Yeah, Mom, sure.' But it's funny how often something she said popped into my head when I needed it."

"Like now?" I smile.

"Like now," she smiles back.

"You were so lucky," I say. "Your parents sound wonderful."

"They are. I hope someday you can meet them. And I'd love them to meet Teddy. They never met Stan."

The waitress swings by with a coffee pot for refills. When she leaves, I say, "Luther can know Stan a little through Teddy. He's like him in many ways. And you know how he feels about Teddy."

Rosetta perks up, "Can you believe Luther said the same thing? Once he realized he had a brother and it was someone he liked, he got excited. After your call, when I told him you hadn't told Teddy, Luther said, 'Maybe someday we can tell Teddy too. He's probably had enough changes in his life for one year.'"

"Sounds like Luther is wiser than both of us," I say. "You raised a fine young man."

"Maybe it's partly that good stock he comes from." Rosetta pats my hand and then we both sip our coffees pondering the wonder of life's turns and events.

Teddy

⟋

Going down Main Street on the way home from the mall, riding shotgun, I spot Pete shoveling the walk in front of the drugstore. Across the street are the thugs, as I call them, shoveling the other side.

"Uncle Dan, could you let me out? I'll walk from here." I go over to Pete. "Hey, Pete, got another shovel?"

"Teddy, what're you doing here?"

"I was driving by and saw you slaving away. Let me help. We can beat the chain gang across the street."

"No way, man. You're not doing my community service."

"Oh yeah, well what if I want to do *friend* service? Can't stop me you know."

I run into the drugstore to find another shovel and soon I'm scraping it beside Pete's shovel. I get to the end of the block and turn back to clear the other half. By the time we get to the drugstore again, the whole sidewalk is clear.

"So now what?" I ask Pete.

"Now we go in and I get you some hot chocolate."

We sit down at the counter with the red vinyl stools that look like they've been there since Dad's day. While we wait for our hot chocolate, I ask Pete, "So how's this community service thing work?"

"I just show up every Saturday morning and they tell me what I have to do that day. Let's see, 100 divided by four. I should be done in about 24 Saturdays. What's that? Half a year for one night of fun. That really wasn't that much fun now that I think about it. " Pete shakes his head like he can't believe it himself.

"Is it 100 hours each or between the three of you?"

"I think each of us. I'm not really sure. They're not exactly speaking to me, but I like it better that way."

"So how bad was it at home? Was your dad really mad?"

"Not as bad as I thought it would be. First he was really mad, then said he was disappointed. You know when they lay that *disappointment* thing on you. It's worse than if they're screaming at you. Finally he said he was proud of me for coming forward the way I did. Said he hoped I learned my lesson. I know it's tough for him to see me sitting on the bench. He's nuts about basketball."

"So who isn't in this town? I never saw so many people at a game in my life. They sure like seeing a win."

"Funny thing, though. Like it isn't the only thing that matters. A few years ago we had a team that lost almost every game and you would've thought they were state champs the way the crowd cheered each time they came out."

"Yeah, I noticed."

"Hey, thanks for the help. See you around. I'm on duty at the cemetery next Saturday. If raking dead leaves is your thing, come on down," He gives a little laugh like saying *fat chance that will happen*.

As I walk home, an idea's beginning to form. I wonder if I can pull it off. Headline: TOWN VILLIAN BECOMES TOWN HERO. I talk myself out of it, thinking of all the reasons it won't work, but then again, why not? I need to make a few calls. See what George thinks. At home, I run up to my room and find his card next to my computer. I dial. No answer. He's probably still sitting at the Café Court, watching the world go by. Maybe he's moonlighting as Santa and doesn't want me to know. Probably thinks I still believe.

He finally answers his phone Sunday night.

"George, it's me Teddy. I need your help. Remember the first day we met you said something about not just seeing somebody worse off but doing something about it?"

"Well, yes, Teddy, that sounds like something I might have said."

"I have an idea that might help a lot of people." Then I tell him about Pete and the thugs and how I think Pete's not such a bad guy after all — and maybe something good can come of all this. I lay out my plan. "Do you remember the name of the man from the newspaper who came to the cemetery after Halloween?"

"No, can't say that I do. But if you call the paper, they can probably tell you. Middleburg's not such a big place, you know, like that city you came from."

"I'll call them tomorrow. See you Saturday?"

"I'll be there."

"Thanks, George." I knew I could count on a Marine. Just a few good men and all that.

I know I have to work fast if this scheme is going to work. Just a few days left before Christmas break at school. The next day in English class, I lay out the plan to Patti and Sue. They like it and agree to help. I tell them to keep it a secret for now, so I'm sure the whole school will know within 24 hours, which is just what I'm hoping. Everyone except Pete that is. I leave a note on our locker for Mindy. *Meet me in the lunchroom 11:45. Important mission.*

Mindy shows up right on time and starts drooling over my lunch. Baba as usual, has packed a bit extra in the event a few friends join me — like the entire junior class. While Mindy devours half my sandwich, I talk. "I need to find the guy who wrote the last article in the *Middleburg Monitor*. The one who implied that kids today are irresponsible, self-centered."

"That's easy." Mindy says between bites. "Is this spicy mustard? It's really good!"

"Hey, this is not the Martha Stewart lunch club."

"The library keeps all back issues."

"I knew you would know. Here, have a brownie too. Be right back."

I leave her with the rest of my lunch and run to the library. I'm back in a few minutes with a name I copied off the article.

"Here it is. John Marshall. Should I call him now?"

"To come here right now? Well, I'm not sure there's enough." Mindy pulls the rest of the sandwich in closer as if I'm going to give it to Mr. Marshall.

"No, your sandwich is safe. But I think I should see him in person, don't you? I just don't know when I could go. I bet their office closes before I finish practice."

"Maybe he would come here and meet you at school. Like tomorrow at lunch?"

"Great idea!"

"Of course, what did you expect?"

"Do you really think it will work? Will anyone show up?"

"For sure they won't show up if you don't try it. What do you have to lose?"

"Oh, nothing. Just look like a clueless dodo bird out there Saturday morning all by myself with the news reporter. He'll probably put my picture in the paper — with a caption: Loser."

"Did you know the dodo bird is about the size of a turkey but actually related to the pigeon? Quite extinct."

"Dodo, turkey, loser. Guess it's all the same, huh?"

"Teddy, you should have more confidence in yourself. It's a great idea. Really." She looks me right in the eye, gives me one of her turquoise smiles, and for a minute I forget about turkeys. Instead there's a flutter in my chest, not turkey-sized, maybe dodo-bird-sized. Then I think of Joe's chest fluttering too. Does he need Mindy more than I do?

At practice I ask the guys in JV and varsity to stay a few minutes after and tell the story again. A few hem-haw around and say they're kind of busy. Some of them think it's a good idea and agree to be there early Saturday.

The next day in the lunchroom I recognize Mr. Marshall from the ratty Columbo raincoat he's still wearing.

"Hi Mr. Marshall. I'm Teddy Kostoff. Thanks for coming. I have an idea for a story."

"Always looking for a good story Teddy. What's it about?"

I tell him, but I can't tell what he's thinking. No expression. No response. *Do they teach them that in reporter school?* "So what do you think?"

"I think you just might have something here, Teddy. The holidays coming and all. Maybe a jump start on Christmas spirit. Yes, I think this might be good. What time did you say?"

"Nine. At the cemetery."

"I'll be there. Here, take my card and call me if anything changes." He pulls a business card out of the notebook he brought but never opened.

"I don't have a business card," I say. As soon as it's out of my mouth I realize how stupid that must sound. *Of course, a high school junior doesn't have a business card. What would it say? Student? Senior wannabe?*

I start to laugh and he does too. "It's okay, Teddy. There's plenty of time for that. What's your phone number? "He writes it in his little notebook which looks as tattered as his trench coat. "What did you say your last name was?"

"Kostoff."

"Any relation to Dan?"

"My uncle."

"Good guy. I went to school with him. Say 'hello' for me."

"Sure," I say, thinking I ought to be on Uncle Dan's reunion committee. So far I've rounded up two of his classmates. I keep forgetting this is small town, USA.

I can hardly get to sleep Friday night. What if no one shows up? That will give the reporter a real story. Kids are flakes after all, just like he made it sound in his first story. I twist and turn and envy Winnie who is snoring, as usual. He's like a 20-pound sack of potatoes on my foot.

The light from my clock radio shines on one of the quotes. *Great things are achieved through cooperation. Look what happens when a wagon loses one wheel.* I sure hope all the wheels show up Saturday, or Mr. Marshall is going to think I've lost not only my wheels but my marbles.

The music box is still under my bed but I haven't heard it play for some time. Maybe I'll go to the cemetery early and have a little chat with Dad. It's been a while since I've done that too.

Mary

I call Rosetta and tell her what Teddy has planned. Maybe Coach Luther has heard what's going on from the kids at school, but if not, I'm thinking maybe Teddy would like him there.

But I know it's more than that. I want Rosetta there for me. A way to let her know I do want *her* in our lives.

Teddy

⌇

I wake up to a room full of sunlight. I panic. Did I oversleep? Mom wouldn't let me do that. She knows all about my plan. I smell coffee and bacon. It's only 7 a.m. I'm okay. I have lots of time. In the shower, I realize I forgot to tell Uncle Dan I won't be able to do our driving lesson today.

I run downstairs and overhear Mom and Uncle Dan talking in the kitchen. About me and my idea. Like an undercover agent, I stand where I can hear them but they can't see me. I can't resist because what if my idea is stupid but no one will tell me. Mom's saying, "It's so good to see Teddy excited about something again. That's the kind of kid he was before. Always organizing something. Half his brainstorms fell through but his enthusiasm and confidence were so much fun to watch. I was afraid he'd lost that quality when he lost his dad."

Uncle Dan takes a bite of the Phyllo dough cheese triangle from a plate Baba has set out. "Been a lot of changes in his young life. He won't ever be the same, but hopefully his strengths will come through. From our Saturday drives, I can tell he's got Stan's sense of humor."

I'm thinking I can snoop around all day listening to these praises, but decide to jump in before all this good stuff I'm hearing has a chance to go any other direction. "Uncle Dan. I forgot to call you."

"No problem. Your Mom told me. I think you have a great idea. Want a ride to the cemetery?"

"Sure. I was going to go a little early. I ... there's something I need to do before everyone gets there."

"Whenever you're ready. Dress warm though. It's cold out and you might be there awhile from the sound of things."

"I hope so. If anyone shows up."

"Well, I know eight you'll have for sure."

"You do?"

"Sophie rounded up two carloads of seniors."

"She did? Cool."

Mom rides along and they drop me off at the gatehouse. "Good luck, Teddy. I'm really proud of you. Your dad would be too." She jumps out of the car to give me a big hug and hangs on like I'm going on a long trip. She feels smaller and shorter than I remember. In spite of Baba's good meals, she seems fragile. I'm really glad no one's here yet because holding her makes me want to cry.

I wave to Uncle Dan who gives me the thumbs up sign. As soon as they're out of the driveway, I run to Dad's stone. The cold ground and bare trees make me sad. Dad in the cold ground. For a minute I wish I were back in the warm car with Mom and Uncle Dan. Then I start talking. "Well, Dad, I know you probably know everything that's going on. You probably know more than I do, but I'll tell you my version anyway." I run in place to stay warm. Then I tell him how it felt to play in the gym where he played, how this little town is growing on me, starting to feel like home. I hear a car crunching the gravel and touch Dad's stone. "Gotta go. Gotta see a man about a wheel."

I run back to the gatehouse and see George getting out of his truck. He unlocks the little maintenance shed and we start pulling out all the rakes and plastic bags we can find. The next car is Mr. Marshall from the paper. It's 8:50 and we're the only ones here.

Then a car drops off Pete. "Teddy, what are you doing here?"

"I just came by to help George with some things."

"Oh, I see. I'm supposed to report to George too. He looks at Mr. Marshall. "Are you George?"

"No, Pete, I'm John Marshall from the *Middleburg Monitor*. I've been following your story."

Pete looks angry for a minute. "Checking up on me? To see if I'm doing my community service?"

"Well, not exactly. Working on another story. Different angle."

"I see," Pete says, although I can tell he doesn't see anything. He looks confused. "So you must be George."

"Yup, that's me. Guess we'll do some raking today. Hope you wore your gloves."

Pete pulls a pair out of his pocket. "Right here. Ready to go."

I look at my watch. 8:55. Where is everybody? I take a deep breath to ease the tightness in my chest and there's a sinking in the pit of my stomach. How stupid I was to think I could pull this off. The plan was for George to get Pete started on the other side of the cemetery so he wouldn't see everyone coming in. No worry. Nothing to see. George puts the plan into action. "Hop in my truck, Pete. Let's start on the other end." WWII training kicking in.

Mr. Marshall and I are left standing there. I kick some of the dead leaves at my feet and say, "Maybe kids today would rather sleep in or play Nintendo or watch Saturday cartoons. I'm sorry I got you out here so early."

"Let's give it a little more time, Teddy. It's a Saturday. And a cold one, at that. Did you tell them 9 a.m.?" By now I'm so panicky, I can't remember what I said.

Then I spot Sophie's Blue Bug. It's followed by another car. And another. It's a steady stream of traffic. Oh, my gosh, they're coming! They're really, really coming! I run out in front of Blue Bug. She almost hits me. I always suspected Sophie couldn't drive. Now I'm directing traffic, keeping them moving so there's enough room for everyone to get in and park.

Most of them are just getting dropped off, but some of the parents are hanging around. Some brought their little brothers and sisters. There's dogs on leashes. Mr. Marshall is grinning. He's going to have his story after all. He starts taking pictures and talking to the kids.

We gather around and then I see Uncle Dan's car. Grandma and Mom and Mindy get out and they're carrying white sacks. What in the world? Ruby and Cathy run to me. Ruby screams, "Teddy, we got donuts. Lots of donuts." Everyone surrounds the sacks at the word donut. Mindy has one hanging out of her mouth as she helps pass out the others. I'm certain she also has a secret stash hidden somewhere. I ask Uncle Dan if he'll drive to the other end and bring George and

Pete back. There's a little tractor parked on the side of the road. I jump on and look over the entire scene. I'm still amazed. They're here. They're totally here.

George's truck returns. Pete opens his door, looks around and steps out cautiously. "What's going on here?"

"Have a donut." Mindy runs up to him and hands him a chocolate covered.

"I can explain it all, Pete," I say from my tractor perch.

Someone in the crowd whistles and they get real quiet. Everyone's eyes are on me. I hear Mr. Marshall's camera clicking rapidly. For a minute, I panic and my lips are frozen shut. Then I see Mom and Uncle Dan and know I can do it. I start to talk but my voice sounds shaky. I need to be louder. Not just for the kids, but my voice needs to carry around the bend, across the granite stones to one in particular.

"I guess the first thing I should say is thanks for coming here so early on a Saturday morning. Most of you don't know me. You probably came because you like Pete." I spot Mindy. "Or maybe you heard about the free donuts." A couple of snickers rise from the crowd. "Most of you know I'm new here. Pete was one of the first people to make me feel welcome. So this is about Pete, but it's also about Middleburg. Maybe it takes an outsider to show you all how lucky you are. See, where I came from, we had a good school and a good community and I'm sure people there loved their kids too. But we were so big and there were so many other things to do. The world didn't revolve around us kids the way it does here. To have the whole town in the gymnasium to watch a basketball game. People who care about you no matter if you win or lose the game. They want you to know they support whatever you do. I don't think that happens in all schools … or all towns.

"I asked Mr. Marshall from the newspaper to come here because I wanted him to see that what his story implied about the Halloween pranks really isn't true. Kids today aren't irresponsible. So there were a few pranks and some damage. It shouldn't have happened. It's not right to destroy property and whoever did it should pay the price. They will. But kids have run through cemeteries on Halloween for years. So it got a little out of control, but I thought we should support

Pete for being honest enough to come forward and say he did it, even though he knew the price he would pay. So, Pete, we're all here today to show you that you're *not* alone. It isn't right that community service should be a punishment. It should be a privilege, something we should all want to do. To give back to the people who care about us. The ones who want to make sure we grow up with good values. Today, we're going to help you serve your 100 hours. Let's see, there's about 30 kids here today. Times two hours. We can do 60 hours of service today."

I notice a man who looks like Pete off alone under a leafless tree, dabbing his eyes with a handkerchief and blowing his nose real loud. I stop. I've rambled on too much. In the crowd I spot Coach Luther. He's smiling and gives me two thumbs up. It gives me encouragement to continue.

"But I don't think we should stop here. I think we should find a way to keep on doing things for our community. There's old people who need hot meals and can't get out in bad weather. Some who need their driveways shoveled or groceries brought in. Maybe it's been years since they've had the energy to put up a Christmas tree. People in the hospital who don't have family close by, so no visitors. Maybe they'd like someone to read to them or just someone to listen to their stories. I think we can take what happened here on Halloween and turn it into a positive. Don't you? We can turn that trick into treats for a lot of people."

I take a deep breath and stop. I don't hear a sound. Was I too corny up here on my John Deere soapbox? I haven't lived here long enough to tell these kids what to do and how they should act. And who am I to tell people how to be good? Then someone starts clapping. Just one person, then two, and soon the whole crowd is clapping hard and saying, "Yes, we can!"

"Okay grab a rake and let's get started. We'll meet back here at 11. Maybe Mindy can track down some more food!"

Mindy's eyes light up. Yes! A food mission. I see her running to Uncle Dan, talking a mile a minute. He starts laughing and they drive off. My sympathy for whoever she approaches. I have a feeling they're about to part with some free food and lots of it.

Soon the rakes are scraping, people are holding garbage bags open while others fill them up. By 11 there's over 40 bags of leaves stacked at the gate. Mr. Marshall is taking pictures of it all. The last picture is the whole gang gathered around the sacks with Ruby and Cathy and somebody's beagle sitting on top of the pile.

Right on cue, Uncle Dan pulls up and Mindy jumps out with sacks of food from four different fast-food chains. "Free food! Come and get it!"

"How did you manage that?" I'm almost afraid to ask.

"Easy. I told each one the other one was doing it and Mr. Marshall would give them lots of free publicity in his article. I said, 'You don't want to be the only one who doesn't contribute, do you?' Oh, there's someone in the car who wants to say Hi."

Joe's sitting in the back seat, all bundled up. "Wish I could help, man."

I jump in the backseat where Mindy has stashed away Joe's personal bag of food. "You did help, Joe. Way back when I first told you about Pete. You said a friend doesn't tell on his friends. You told me to go to him and give him a chance to do the right thing. You stay warm and I'll come see you later. We'll get to the end of that revolution."

By noon everyone's gone. The rakes have been put away and Mr. Marshall has left with his camera and his story.

Pete and his dad come by to say thanks. I'm kind of embarrassed and glad that Pete doesn't make a big deal of it. He only punches me in the arm and says, "See you at practice."

Funny how four little words can make you feel you belong.

Mary

⌒

I walk over to Rosetta standing with Luther and an older gentleman I assume to be her husband. I was happy when I spotted them in the crowd this morning. "Thank you so much for coming," I say as I take Rosetta's hand.

"Mary, I don't think you've met my husband, James."

He smiles and says in a deep baritone voice, "You should be proud of your son. Brave thing he did here."

"On his soapbox you mean?" We all laugh.

"Really, it was quite remarkable," Luther says.

I say to Rosetta. "And you should be proud of your son too." I nod to Luther. Teddy says the team thinks you are the coolest. Those are his very words."

This is the first time I have had a close look at Luther since the night of the JV game. I look into the familiar hazel eyes, warm and full of life. Beyond Luther I see rows of headstones and something wells up inside my chest. It's good to see life here in this place where so much life is gone. I feel tears starting. I say quickly, "I better go. The girls are waiting in the car." I turn and walk quickly through the headstones.

Teddy

After dinner I walk to Joe's. Mindy said they'd be hanging out there. Mindy and Joe are in rockers next to the fireplace with lap blankets like two old folks. The only sound is Mindy's voice, reading, "Along the Paris streets, the death-carts rumble, hollow and harsh. Six tumbrels carry the day's wine to La Guillotine." Then she says, "Hi Teddy. You're just in time for the end."

I'm surprised that she's reading my book. She's supposed to be the tutor and I do the pleasure reading. *A Tale of Two Cities* was my thing with Joe. I don't say a word, but sit at their feet and let myself be carried back to the year 1775. Sydney Carlton is at the guillotine. *They said of him, about the city that night, that it was the peacefullest man's face ever beheld there. It is a far, far better thing that I do, than I have ever done.* In just that instant, the touch of jealousy that nagged me about Mindy and Joe liking each other dissolves. In its place is a warm feeling. *I* want to do a "far, far better thing" for Joe. And the good news? I don't have to put my head in a guillotine to do it. He's looking at Mindy like she's a chocolate sundae with the cherry on top. I realize that he needs her love more than I do. I'll settle for her quirky friendship.

"What in the world are you smiling about Teddy? This is the saddest ending in the world! How can you be so insensitive?" Mindy is sniffing and wiping her eyes. "Who said this book was about history? It's the greatest love story in the world!"

"Oh, I was just thinking of another love story. One that's about to unfold right here in Middleburg."

"Really? Who is it?" Mindy asks, totally clueless for once in her life. "Teddy Kostoff, do you have a girlfriend?" she looks at me wide-eyed.

"No, I'm dedicating my life to basketball." And while Mindy's blowing her nose and wiping her glasses, I look at Joe who gets my gist and even through the scars I detect his blush. I wink at him which is my way of saying his secret is safe with me.

"I'm starving. All this emotion burns up tons of calories. Can we order in a pizza?" Mindy jumps up to find Joe's mom.

So much for love.

Mary

I send an e-mail to my grief counselor asking her advice on how we get through Christmas. As it approaches I feel an impending sense of doom. Her reply, "Try not to avoid the sadness. Embrace it, take it in, and let it pass through you. To shut down your feelings could keep you from experiencing joy either." Her advice gives me some comfort knowing I have permission to not act happy every moment or keep up the false bravado. But we can't appear sad for Cathy and Ruby. If they believe in Santa and all that entails, we must too.

"Teddy, before you go up, can we talk about the holidays?" I approach him as he starts to go to his bedroom. Baba and the girls are in bed. I pat the space beside me on the sofa and he plops down.

"Sure. I suppose you want my Christmas list. I can tell you now that my own phone would be great. He smiles and wiggles his eyebrows like Groucho Marx, even though he has no clue who Groucho is. This was something Stan used to do and a fleeting touch of joy lifts me, to think Teddy is starting to be his funny self again. I realize he has just given me an early Christmas gift. No wrapping paper required.

"I know it's going to be hard. We're going to be missing Dad, but I wanted to keep it happy for the girls. I did bring a box of our special ornaments from Arizona and I think we should have a big tree like we always do ... and decorate it together. Are you okay with that?"

"I guess I'll have to put the star on top now," he says, blinking rapidly. I had forgotten that was what Stan always did when we had put the last ornament on the tree.

"You've grown so much this year you shouldn't have any trouble reaching the top," I say as if that were the bigger issue.

I stand beside him and give the tall kid a hug around his middle.

Rosetta

I kept it all through the years, rarely looking at it, but the few times I would stumble onto it, I heard his words, just as he asked me to. "Just remember, a part of me will always be with you."

I never thought I could part with the ring, but now, this Christmas, I knows it's time to let it go. I wrap it once again in Christmas paper as it was wrapped 30 years ago and place it under the tree. The gift tag says "Luther."

Teddy

Mom talking about Christmas gets me thinking about gifts I should buy and that gets me thinking about what a weird assortment of friends I have now. At home my friends were pretty much just like me and I acted the same with all of them. Just plain Teddy. Here I seem to play a different role with each one.

With George: I don't have to hide my sadness about Dad. He's a good listener and a good storyteller. I learned what a turret gunner is on a Marine torpedo plane. What it's like to have a plane shot down and sink in 90 seconds and to wait on a rubber raft in the middle of the Pacific to be rescued. How he held one of his buddies on his lap till he died, promising he'd call his family when he got home. I never thought one of my best friends would be 74 years old.

With Joe: Boost his spirits. Tell him how rotten school is so he doesn't miss it. We both know what's going on but we play the game well. I like reading to him and the way his eyes light up when I come into the room. It's the next best thing to Winnie wagging his tail when he sees me.

With Mindy: Strangest little person I ever knew, but she makes me laugh … like the self I used to be. Can't believe I'm starting to think of her as a real girl. Sometimes now when I look at her I wonder what it would be like to kiss that cute freckled face. Then I think of how Joe's face lights up when Mindy comes in the room. I'll settle for her quirky friendship.

With Pete: I try to be Mr. Jock. All-around American high school athlete. So pumped I could do Nike commercials. Like anyone would buy shoes from some kid who didn't even make varsity. Headline: NIKES LAST HIM FOUR SEASONS … ON THE BENCH.

At home: Give Baba lots of hugs. Make Ruby and Cathy laugh. Don't let Mom see me cry.

With Dad: Definitely a one-sided conversation but I like it. Sometimes I don't even know what I'm thinking until I'm sitting on the grass at his stone, spilling my guts to the little flowers Mom planted.

Alone in my room: Reading quotes out of some ancient book like the original *How to Win Friends and Influence People.* A bizarre music box under my bed that spooks me half the time and comforts me the other half. When I was little, my imaginary friend was Jiminy Cricket. Maybe this box has replaced him as my conscience. I seem to hear the music mostly when I'm sad. How does it know?

Mary

⌒⌒

I'm checking Teddy's room for dirty clothes as I do laundry and pull on a sock that's peeking out from under the bed. I kneel down to see what other specimens might be rotting there when I see a little globe. I pull it out. *What in the world?*

It's a charming little music box. I turn the key and recognize the haunting melody — "Somewhere My Love" from *Doctor Zhivago*. Does Teddy have a girlfriend?

That night when I peek in to say goodnight to him, I sit on the edge of his bed. "I have to ask you something. And I don't want you to think I'm nosing around in your stuff. I was looking for dirty socks and instead I find this adorable little music box." I reach down and pull it out from under his bed where I left it near the edge. Teddy blushes and I think, *he* does *have a girlfriend.*

He says, "I found it in the attic. In a box with a bunch of Dad's old stuff. I thought Ruby might like it but thought I should ask Baba first." He looks like he was caught with his hand in the cookie jar. "Then I sort of forgot about it." He seems to be groping for words and I suspect there is more to the story but I don't ask.

I say, "I think Ruby would love it and I'm sure Baba wouldn't mind. Why don't you wrap it up for Christmas?"

"Good idea, Mom."

I leave his room but return in a minute. "On second thought, do you mind if I keep it for myself awhile?"

"Sure, Mom. But, uh, there's a couple things you should know about it."

"What's that?"

"Maybe you already know but Uncle Dan said that was a favorite song of Dad's."

"Really?" *News to me.*

"And the other thing. "Sometimes it starts playing on its own. So don't get spooked."

"Well, that is a little strange, isn't it?"

"I thought so too. Kinda freaked me out, but then I was in the mall one day and there was a kiosk that sold music boxes. The guy there was so old he reminded me of an ancient wizard or something. Figured he might know. So I asked him if music boxes could start playing on their own."

"And ..."

"He said it was possible. That some music boxes have a start/stop lever that's held in place by a wooden screw. Over the years, the tension could loosen and something as simple as a creaky floor or a jolt could make it start. The attic floor is creaky for sure."

"Well, thanks for the warning," I say as I pack my little treasure out.

Teddy

Uncle Dan says its time I got my driver's license. He goes with me to the DMV, but is not able to be in the car with me, which makes me really nervous. My big security blanket. To my relief, I pass both the written and the driving portion. To my greater relief, I didn't even barf.

On the way home I ask, "Can I drive?"

"Sure thing. I'd be proud to ride with a licensed driver."

"Thanks Uncle Dan. And thanks for getting me behind the wheel again."

Dan pats my knee. "I think it's what your dad would have wanted me to do. Hey, where are you headed?"

As I pull into the cemetery gates, I say, "I think you're right about Dad." I drive slowly through the gates that I first rode my bicycle through four months ago, but now seems like another lifetime. I didn't know where to go then, but I'm finding my way now.

It's the last day of the year and everyone's talking about the millennium, the Y2K fears and how the world will crash. I watch some of the TV celebrations around the world in each time zone. It reminds me of our last trip to Disneyland as a family and the little car rocking through It's a Small World. I think Mr. Disney had it figured out before anyone else, as I have already watched the fireworks in New Zealand, Japan, Russia, and Paris. They don't seem so far away after all.

Coincidentally I'm on the last page of the *Book of Life* on this last day of the year. The quote: *Life is a song — find your melody and play it.* I think of the music box I gave Mom. Even though the old wizard in the mall had a logical explanation, I like what the *Book of Life* says better: *We don't have to understand all of life's mysteries to enjoy it.*

I don't suppose I'll ever solve the music box mystery. I do know I'll always miss my dad. For the rest of my life. But I am doing the *blink, blink, squint* thing a little less. And I haven't thought in headlines for weeks.

And now, more than not, when I think of Dad, it's like a warm and tender spot inside me instead of that big gaping hole. We always did have our little secrets — like popcorn for dinner when Mom was out, or winking at me when I gave Winnie my broccoli. And these things — the music box, the *Book of Life* messages I think he wanted me to have--those will be our secrets forever. Maybe Dad's way of telling me it's okay to enjoy my life even if he's not here. I think it's what he would want me to do.

To bring in the 21st century, we decide to have a party. Baba's bustling in high gear. "We no have party for long time in this house. Today I bake the New Year's cake."

There is a Bulgarian tradition to bake a New Year cake in a big round pan and cut it into pieces for each member of the family. One piece has a silver dollar baked into it. Whoever gets the silver dollar will have good luck all year. I wouldn't think of tampering in Baba's kitchen but, I'm also thinking it's time a little good fortune shined down on Mom.

Mom and Mrs. Stone have become good friends and she invited their family to our party. That means Coach Luther will be here too. They show up first, walking through the streamers Sophie and Ruby have strung throughout the living room. There's a pretty lady with Coach, who he introduces as his fiancé, Marletta.

"This looks interesting," Coach says, pointing to the *Book of Life* on the coffee table.

"It's from Bulgaria. Came with my great-grandfather. Someone translated parts into English. Has a bunch of corny sayings, but I like them."

"Can I see it?" he asks.

"Sure." I hand him the tattered book. "See, what Baba explained to me is that each father passes it onto his son. Like rules to live by. To be a good person, or I should say a good man. I guess it worked cause my dad was. Um, a good person, I mean."

"I'm sure he was Teddy. I wish I could have known him."

"Oh, you would have liked each other, basketball and all. He had a great jump shot." Coach Luther has a funny look on his face but before I can say anything, Winnie, who is usually cautious of strangers, starts sniffing Coach like he's his favorite doggy treat. He starts whining and giving little jumps like he wants to be picked up. Coach bends down and pats his head. I say, "I guess dogs know a good guy when they see one. I've heard they have a sixth sense or something."

Mindy bursts in with an explosion of hot pink. Once she got wind of the party, she decided we needed to have a theme and agenda. She laid the ground rules last week. "Everyone should pick their favorite decade and dress accordingly. You didn't have to live in that decade," she clarifies so as not to thwart our creativity in any way. Mindy's hot pink is a poodle skirt complete with black and white saddle shoes and a black ribbon trying to contain her massive head of red curls into a ponytail.

Joe follows behind Mindy. It's his first outing without a wheelchair and he is sporting a tee shirt that says Microsoft that looks like a freebee promo item. "I chose the '90s for my decade. All the new technology helped me in the burn unit more than anything else."

"More than my tutoring?" Mindy asks in seeming disbelief.

Uncle Dan and Aunt Joyce enter the scene as '60s hippies flower children. "Do you like my daisies?" she asks, pointing to her painted cheeks.

"How about these bell bottoms?" Uncle Dan says, but it's hard to take my eyes off his fake tattoo arms and his hairy chest that the leather vest barely covers. He's a brave soul to go bare on a frigid December night.

"Wow, look at you!" Mindy says to Mom who wiggles in with a short red dress with shiny beads and long fringe. She even has a couple of feathers in her glitzy red headband over her blonde hair.

"I always wanted to be a flapper," Mom says and does a little Charleston step.

Mindy found a CD called *Music of the Millennium*, so we have dance music from the Charleston to the Macarena. From Benny Goodman to the Beatles. Soon Elvis is belting out, "Don't Be Cruel." Mom's teaching Ruby to jitterbug when all of a sudden George, in his 1942 Marine uniform, which he can still proudly button, grabs Baba, in her 1942 apron, and starts twirling her around.

Baba giggles and blushes. "Oh George, you go too fast. My pizza … it is burning." She quickly dashes to the kitchen in spite of her arthritic hip.

I notice one of her Canasta friends, June, steps right up to George. "I love this song, don't you?" His dance card might be full tonight.

Arlis is shouting into Opal's right ear. "June loves to dance."

Opal answers, "June has new pants?"

Next thing we know Chubby Checkers is belting out the Twist, and Uncle Dan and Aunt Joyce take the center spotlight. I didn't know old people could move that way. The music changes and Sophie and her friends line up to teach us all the Electric Slide. Then the Electric Slide line becomes a Conga line, everyone holding on to the person in front of them, and next thing we know, it's the Bunny Hop with Uncle Dan at the head of it and me whipping around the tail. He leads us all through the house and then right out the front door. Everyone but Joe, who's not quite up to these gymnastics. Baba picks up on that and is consoling him with the universal symbol of comfort — food. We can see our breath in the air, but who cares? We keep going around the wrap-around porch and then back in the side door.

When the music finally stops, we all collapse on the living room floor and sofas while Winnie runs in circles barking. Then he snuggles up to Buster, near the fireplace, who puts one big furry paw on Winnie's low, shiny back. The planets must be aligned perfectly for this rare millennium merger. Cathy's sleeping through all this, curled up on the corner of the sofa, covered with Dad's memory quilt. Her little bottom is pooched up somewhere between Arizona State University and the Hoosiers logo.

It's a few minutes before midnight and Uncle Dan has poured

bubbly champagne for all of us. Even Mindy, Joe, and I get a sip. Ruby has sparkling apple cider, but she thinks it's champagne. "Look at all the bubbles in my glass." She looks at it as if it's a magic potion.

Uncle Dan raises his glass. "I propose a toast to the person we are all thinking of tonight, wishing he were here. But as long as we keep him alive in our hearts, Stan will always be with us." Dan begins in his deep voice, "Should old acquaintance be forgot ..."

If *the Book of Life* is right and life is a song, I think the best way to keep the melody alive is to sing with all your heart. I join in, "For auld lang syne, my friend, for auld lang syne."

Mary

As things wind down, I sip my champagne and watch everyone in the room through a happy little buzz. James and Uncle Dan are having a conversation, probably about investing. Maybe a get-rich scheme. Marletta is helping Baba with yet another food tray. Sophie, Mindy, and Joe are playing Chutes and Ladders with Ruby who's eyelids are drooping. I doubt she will make it up one more ladder. I see Teddy and Luther in one corner laughing about something and Teddy's laugh warms me more than the champagne cursing through me. Across the room, I notice that Rosetta sees them too. Our eyes meet and we both smile. We walk toward each other.

"Come with me." I put my arm through Rosetta's as I lead her into the dining room. I pull a package out of the bottom drawer of the hutch.

"Mary, what is this? You shouldn't have. I didn't bring you anything."

"It's not a Christmas gift. And it's not really from me. From an old friend of yours, I think." Rosetta looks puzzled. "It's something Teddy found in the attic. I might be wrong, but I think it was meant for you."

Rosetta begins unwrapping. When she sees the globe, she says, "Oh, it's so charming. Is it a ...?"

"Yes, a music box." I reach under the globe and turn the key. The refrain from "Somewhere my Love" plays and her eyes fill with tears. She hugs the music box to her heart.

"Mary, I'm speechless. I will treasure this always." She looks at me earnestly and shakes her head as if in disbelief as she sets the globe on the hutch. She takes my face in both of her hands. "But more than that, I treasure *you*. Your kindness. Your goodness."

Now my eyes water. "I looked around that room tonight, Rosetta, and I wished so such Stan could have been here. To see us all. His whole family, together. I think it would have made him very happy." Rosetta nods as she sniffles. I go on. "Maybe by this time next year the whole family will be celebrating what you and I and Luther know. Baba deserves to know her other grandson and Teddy his brother. If anything good can come of Stan's death …."

Teddy bursts into the room, "Mom, Coach Luther has two tickets to the Pacers' game in Indianapolis tomorrow night. Wants to take me. Can I go?"

"Of course." I smile at Rosetta and together we walk back in the living room to join the rest of *our* family.

Epilogue

Teddy
June, 2000

Mom and I had the talk about our "deal." That I could possibly go back to Phoenix after a year. I did go back for a week on spring break to stay with Wally. It was great to see him, but I realized if I lived there again how much I would miss all the good things happening in Middleburg my senior year.

Mindy's going to be a contestant on *Jeopardy* Teen Tournament in August. They did auditions in Indianapolis last week and, of course, she was one step ahead of Alex Trebek. And I have to be around to hear about Joe's trip this summer to a special camp for kids who've been burned. All the counselors are burn victims themselves. He'll be able to put on swim trunks without everyone gawking at his scars. Middleburg Fire Department has been doing fundraisers each month to sponsor him. At the last bake sale, Baba's Bulgarian pizza sold out the first hour. Mindy and Joe are still a thing. Joe is in awe of her brains and she is in awe of his courage. I guess I'm in awe of my matchmaking. It's good to have two best friends.

George and I have some special plans for the summer. He says there are some good fishing holes he needs to show me that no one else knows about. I've never fished before but if it means sitting for hours hearing more of George's stories, I'm in.

Sophie will be a freshman at Indiana and says she's going to major in community service. She started a local chapter for teens through the high school after my soapbox pitch.

Coach Burton is retiring this year and Coach Luther will be the varsity basketball coach. With so many seniors graduated, I'm sure I'll be a varsity starter. What I like about Coach Luther is that even though he says I've *got game*, I'll have to try out like everyone else. I want to earn it and feel that I can. He and Marletta are getting married in August. We're invited to the wedding, which I hear is going to be a big fancy bash at a swanky hotel in Indianapolis. Mom says we'll spend the weekend in the city and do some sightseeing. From there we'll take a little road trip around the state checking out the campuses. Indiana, Purdue, Ball State, Indiana State — home of Larry Bird — and even Notre Dame. Mom says I can do most of the driving.

Then back home to start my senior year. I once said that Middleburg was the *middle of nowhere* but now I know there's *no where* I'd rather be.

THE END

BABA'S RECIPES

Author's Note: *Most of these recipes were not written down anywhere, but recreated from memories of watching my mother cook ... also lots of trial and error. I rarely used exact measurements (a pinch of this, a little of that) but I have tried to give you some idea of accurate amounts. If you have any questions, feel free to contact me at vyarmour@gmail.com. I hope they bring you as much pleasure as they have our family through the years.*

STUFFED CABBAGE

This is a three-step process: (1) preparing the cabbage leaves, (2) preparing the meat mixture, and (3) stuffing the leaves. It can be done on stove-top or in oven. This makes approximately 18 to 20 cabbage rolls depending on the size of the cabbage heads you use. Normally it would serve 8 to 10 people, but the cabbage rolls also freeze very well if you have leftovers.

1 large head of cabbage or two smaller ones.

4 pounds of ground meat, a mixture of ground beef and ground pork

¾ cup long-grain white rice (not instant)

1 onion

1 large can diced tomatoes

1 can or jar of plain sauerkraut (not sweetened and not with caraway seeds), drained

Salt and pepper to taste

Prepare cabbage:
You will need a very large pot to boil the cabbage. Fill about half or three-quarters full of water. Before placing the cabbage in the boiling water, make deep cuts with a sharp knife around the core so you can remove the cabbage leaves easily one at a time as they boil. This is best done with a fork stuck in the core and tongs to gently pull away the leaves without tearing them.

After you remove the first few leaves, you might have to score the core again. This is best done if you remove the entire cabbage to a plate as the boiling water can scald you. Score and return to boiling water. Repeat as often as necessary.

As you remove the leaves, place them on a platter to cool. When they are cooled, with a paring knife, carefully slice off the thick membrane on the outer side of the leave so it will fold easily. Now they are ready for the filling.

Filling:
Dice the onion and stir fry in a little bit of the oil. Add the raw rice just to coat with the onions and oil. Place in a large bowl and add the raw ground meat. Pour some of the diced tomatoes in the mixture for moisture. Add salt and pepper to taste.

When the cabbage leaves are cored, place a few of the outer leaves in the bottom of a large Dutch oven to cook on top of stove. If you use a speckled roasting pan to bake in oven you can omit this step as there is no direct heat on bottom of pan.

Put some filling in the cabbage leaves and roll up, tucking in the sides. Place them side by side in the bottom of the pan in a single layer. Layer a little bit of the sauerkraut and some of the meat loosely on top of the sauerkraut and then prepare another layer row of cabbage leaves. Top this row with sauerkraut and a little loose meat. Continue this process until all the meat is used up. It's often hard to get the meat and cabbage leaves to come out exactly the same — you might have some leaves left over. You can chop these finely and add to the pan if desired. Leftover meat can be placed loosely on top of the cabbage rolls.

Add remaining diced tomatoes on top of the entire mixture and add some water to the pan. The liquid of tomatoes and water should come almost to the top of the pan.

Cook on stovetop in covered Dutch oven at medium heat for about 40 minutes, or roast in oven with lid on at 350 degrees for about 40 minutes. I prefer the oven method. You can check it halfway through to make sure there is enough liquid in the pan. Add some if needed.

CITY CHICKEN

I've been told that this recipe originated in the Midwest in the '50s when pork and veal were easier to obtain and less expensive than chicken. Hard to believe. Because veal today is very expensive, this recipe can be made with just the pork and it is just as delicious. Serving size portions discussed below.

Preheat oven to 300 degrees.

Ingredients:

3 pounds cubed meat (either 2 pounds cubed pork tenderloin and 1 pound cubed veal or 3 pounds cubed pork only)

2 eggs (can add a tablespoon of water) to egg wash

About ¾ cup flour seasoned with salt and pepper or some type of prepared seasoning coating mix (such as Safeway Kitchens Pork Seasoning)

A few tablespoons oil to brown the meat

Salt to taste

2 cans cream of mushroom soup

2 foil packets beef bullion cubes

Wooden skewers — ideal length is about 6 to 8 inches but these are hard to find. Most of the wooden skewers available in the stores today are much longer. You can cut them in half but be careful that they don't splinter. Shorter is better because they need to be browned and the longer ones often don't fit lengthwise in a frying pan. Check with a butcher to see if they have the shorter wooden skewers.

Salt meat lightly and spear meat cubes onto skewers. If using both meats, alternate pork and veal. You will fit about 6 pieces of meat per stick. Three pounds of meat should make about 10 to 12 sticks or you can put 8 pieces of meat on the longer sticks and have fewer sticks.

Dip meat skewers in egg wash.

Dip meat in seasoned flour.

Put breaded skewers in refrigerator for about 30 minutes to secure coating.

Place skewers in frying pan of hot oil, but do not crowd the pan. Brown on all sides. Remove to roasting pan. It's nice to have a large enough pan to make just one layer but you can put them on top of each other. I prefer the blue speckled pan but any pan you can seal tightly will work.

Heat 2 cans of cream of mushroom soup and add 1 cup water to thin it out a bit. Pour soup mixture over the meat in the roasting pan.

Crumble and place the bullion cubes over the meat and soup. They will dissolve in the baking.

Cover the roasting pan with aluminum foil to create a tight seal. Then cover with lid. If using a pan with no lid, put the foil on tightly.

Bake at 300 degrees for 2 or 2.5 hours depending on how much gravy you want remaining. This dish is usually served with mashed potatoes and the extra gravy.

BABA'S PIZZA

I have tried to recreate the delicious deep dish pizza my mother made. I don't think I quite mastered it but here's what I came up with. I think the key is getting Italian sausage that is well-seasoned and not being so health conscious as we are today — in other words, leaving some of the grease in the meat for full flavor.

Ingredients:

Pillsbury Hot Roll Mix in box. (Recipe on back of box is for both sweet rolls and pizza mix. Refer to the pizza mix recipe.)

1¼ cups hot water

1 ½ pounds of loosely ground Italian sausage (can use hot or mild)

A few tablespoons fennel seasoning unless the sausage already has enough — it's a personal taste.

Pizza sauce (sold in jars)

¾ cup grated Parmesan cheese

6 tablespoons olive oil

Non-stick cooking spray

Preheat oven to 425 degrees.

Prepare the dough according to the package mix recipe for making pizza. It tells you to mix the yeast included in package with 1 ¼ cups water and 3 tablespoons oil. Mix by hand until dough pulls away from sides of the bowl. Knead dough on floured surface for 3 minutes or until dough is smooth.

Spray 11 x 14 jelly roll pan with non-stick spray. Using your hands that are oiled with the remaining 3 tablespoons oil and spread dough on pan to the edges. Cover and let dough rise 15 minutes while preparing sausage.

Brown sausage. Add fennel seasoning if needed. Add ½ cup pizza sauce to the sausage or enough to coat all the sausage. Do not drain grease.

Spread sausage mixture over dough and top with Parmesan cheese.

I tried two variations. You can experiment for your personal taste:

(1)   A thin layer of pizza sauce on the bottom of the crust. Add the sausage with no pizza sauce in it. Add the Parmesan cheese. Add more pizza sauce on top and bake.

(2)   No sauce on the bottom crust. Mix sauce in the meat and place that mixture on the dough. Add Parmesan cheese and bake.

I think one of the key factors is not draining the grease from the sausage (not as healthy, I know) but that grease seeps into the bread giving the crust a good flavor.

Bake 10 to 12 minutes or until crust is a deep golden brown.

PEETOULEE (CREPES)

Ingredients:

1 cup flour	Crisco (my brother, the excellent
¼ teaspoon salt	crepe maker, insists Crisco is
1¼ cup milk	the key)
2 eggs	Yield: 12 to 16 crepes depending
2 tablespoons butter, melted	on size of skillet.

Combine flour, salt, and milk. Beat until smooth. Add eggs and beat. Stir in melted butter. Refrigerate batter for at least thirty minutes.

Prepare pan: In a 6- or 8-inch skillet, melt a small amount of Crisco. Heat on medium until hot, but not smoking.

Pour 2 or 3 tablespoons batter into pan. Quickly tilt pan in all directions so batter covers pan with a thin film. Cook about 1 minute. Flip crepe and cook about 30 seconds on the other side.

Place crepe on serving dish and spread with cream cheese and roll up like a burrito. Can add jelly if sweeter crepe is desired.

If you are making a batch to be served later, stack crepes between layers of waxed paper to prevent sticking.

STUFFED PEPPERS

Ingredients:

6 to 8 green peppers (small ones work best for more pepper flavor)

4 pounds ground meat mixture (a mixture of ground beef and ground pork)

¾ cup long-grain rice (do not use instant)

1 onion

1 teaspoon minced garlic from jar or 3 or 4 cloves chopped fine

2 cans of diced tomatoes (14.5 ounce-sized can) Use plain or seasoned — if you like your food spicy you can use the fire-roasted diced tomatoes.

Salt and pepper to taste

1 tablespoon paprika

Small can diced green chilies (optional if you like spicy)

Small amount of oil

Large roasting pan (I prefer to use the speckled pan with lid, it gives the peppers a darker color when roasted)

In a sauce pan large enough to eventually brown all the meat, sauté diced onion and garlic in small amount of oil, until translucent. Add rice to onion mixture and mix well so rice gets coated with the oil and onion flavor. Add paprika to onion mixture and green chilies if you are using them. Add one can of the diced tomatoes to this mixture. Continue sautéing for a few minutes and then remove to a side dish.

In same pan, brown the beef and pork. You want it to be ground loosely in small pieces. Can use a potato masher as it browns to achieve this. Spoon out meat to side dish and drain excess grease. Return meat and onion mixture to pan. Salt and pepper to taste. Add paprika. Continue to break up meat if there are still large chunks.

While the meat is browning on the stove, prepare the green peppers. Wash, slice off tops and scoop out seeds and inner membranes. (Some recipes say parboil the peppers to remove the thin layer of outer skin, but I have never done this. The skin browns nicely and can be easily removed when eating, but the skin contains many vitamins).

Dice the tops into small pieces which you can add to the meat mixture for more flavor and color. Put a thin layer of meat mixture in bottom of roasting pan. Stuff each pepper with meat mixture and lay each pepper on its side in pan. Put excess meat in between peppers or on top. Pour other can of diced tomatoes on top of the peppers. Add water to pan, about one-quarter of the way up.

Bake covered at 350 degrees for 30 minutes. Then turn peppers carefully so as not to spill filling but so other side of pepper is facing up. If all the water has been absorbed, you might want to add a little more. Bake another 30 minutes with lid.

Remove lid and continue baking for about 20 minutes to darken the skin of the pepper. Peppers can be rotated once again during this time.

Serving at table. Spoon out a pepper and add some of the loose meat beside it. A nice garnish is crumbled Feta cheese sprinkled over it or red pepper flakes for extra seasoning.

PHYLLO DOUGH CHEESE TRIANGLES

Ingredients:

1 package phyllo dough from freezer section; have it thawed out when ready to start. Keep in the box until ready to use. Exposure to air will dry it out.

16-ounce carton of small curd cottage cheese

1 pound feta cheese crumbled

2 eggs

1 stick butter, melted

Non-stick spray

Optional: 1 package of frozen spinach, thawed and well drained, can be added to the cheese mixture.

Makes approximately 24 triangles.

Preheat oven to 325 degrees.

In a mixing bowl, mix cottage cheese, feta cheese, and eggs (and well-drained spinach if using).

Remove dough from box but keep it covered with a damp paper towel as you work.

Separate three sheets and spread melted butter over top sheet with a pastry brush. Working with the sheet in a horizontal direction, with a sharp knife slice into six even sections.

Place 2 tablespoons of the filling in the bottom of the vertical section a little bit away from the edge and then fold up one bottom corner to the opposite side forming a triangle. Then fold again in the other direction until you have reached the top of the dough in repetitive triangles.

Place the triangles on baking sheet which has been sprayed with non-stick spray and repeat the process until all the phyllo dough and filling is used up. If you have extra filling, it freezes well until your next batch. This filling is also good mixed into scrambled eggs.

Brush melted butter on top of each triangle. Sometimes, a little more melted butter is needed but be sure to brush each triangle.

Bake for 30 to 40 minutes at 325 degrees or until the dough is brown on top and edges. These are good served hot or at room temperature. Refrigerate extra portions. Freezes well also.

MAR 2 3 2016

CPSIA information can be obtained at www.ICGtesting.com
Printed in the USA
LVOW08s2244120116

470290LV00003BA/567/P